Matthew Lovett
Capital Punishment

A Novel

Copyright © 2023 Matthew Lovett

All rights reserved.

ISBN: 9798865747048

CONTENTS

PART ONE	Winter	1
PART TWO	Spring	116
PART THREE	Summer	244
PART FOUR	Autumn	351

Winter

1
CHAPTER 1

London: Steven and dating: Annabel shopping: London at dog level

The City. A picnic of glass tumours, spreading across a skyline topped by cranes and their red aviation warning lights, winking at foreign investors; city of the unused balcony, the lost cat, the roadside mattress.

A night flight home on approach over London described a place of quiet and order, trails of white and red lights snaking the arterial roads, shuttling workers home to their families. The difference was stark at ground level. The relentless pursuit to *get what was necessary done*. To hold the office at bay, to acquire and consume to tick over the household. To keep a partner, children and more, interested, safe and progressing. In pursuit, aspirational colleagues, a partner's suitors, problem family members, health issues and any number of situations children must confront on their own. Compounded beyond with current affairs, government edicts, societal evolution and planetary difficulties.

For the highest flyers down to the lowest, there was ever more to go after and to cope with, to stand still. Increasing complexity, morphing procedures, stricter terms and conditions. It was unceasing. For many in middle age, however that was defined, a city of too many exes, where any path cornered may turn up someone you misled, rejected or who was too cool *for you*. Or their friends who knew what had happened. City of neighbourhoods: Islington, Kensal Rise, Wapping, Leyton, Chelsea, each with their demographic and cultural profiles, and their unique local attitudes and prejudices.

It was uncontroversial to say that London delivered. Abuzz with vans of consumer goods, moped chefs, pedalling pedlars – those push bike pushers, plus any number of *services* which were a text or a phone call away. When it came to the residents themselves, discovering someone's name, their locale, their profession and a favourite restaurant and brand, would reveal a great deal.

Steven Axford *(Ladbroke Grove, Sales Director, The Barbary, Panerai)* left his flat on a Friday morning in early December, to get lunch alone on Portobello. His thin, angular, pale face was topped with chestnut hair, swept backward, and straightforward blue eyes. He owed his appealing looks to his straight nose, his easy voice and warm laugh. Five-ten, seventy-five kilos, a middleweight. And attractive to women in a way that other men couldn't quite pinpoint or fathom. Approaching the 'v' of thirty-seven and *still* dating. Whereas his long-term married friends would give *anything* to have sex with someone new, this whole situation was becoming tiresome. At work he had fifteen years' experience; in love: one year's experience, fifteen times.

The weather was such that getting dressed didn't require too much deliberation – it was cold and it would stay cold. He wore a lightweight, comfortable black T-shirt and plum pullover, with a trusted navy overcoat, a check scarf, and casual white trainers. Leaving home, he passed a nearby string of shops he knew well, yet he still scanned over the brand names, confirming nothing had changed, and managed a cursory glance beyond the window displays. He decided to drop in, but not that weekend.

Displaying a mix of architectural styles, the street was built a couple of storeys high, and despite its proximity to the main thoroughfare was low on traffic, giving it a roomy feel. Dotted between the kind of buildings one might expect in the area, some mid-twentieth century brick constructions verging on brutalism, and a white, flat-topped building with stained glass windows, reminiscent of something one might find in Central America.

He turned corners and pushed on toward the ever-present homeless man, in situ with the same corrugated cardboard sign declaring unwavering, constant feelings of hunger and despair. The regular payment he had in place with a charity assuaged him of any guilt. Even the tramps re-branded in the noughties, he thought. Not an original thought but a recurring joke he kept to himself. Steven flicked his eyes to meet for a moment as he whispered, "Sorry mate" and continued to his warm destination.

He rounded the corner pub, forever the place where his ex dropped a tray of drinks, back when one could smoke. And as he replayed the gasping topple, central characters from the time and the drinking and struggles of his twenties fleeted by in his mind. Now in the grip of nostalgia, he rubbernecked next into the local tapas bar, recalling a handful of different dates he had taken there when he lacked imagination. Some more successful than others. It was the one that got away that rankled.

Walking toward him, a girl who lived in the neighbourhood and with whom he had once been on speaking terms via a work event, and had shared flirtations at drinks. Someone with whom he had on occasion stopped in the street to talk. Over time, as it became established it would go nowhere, it had degraded to a hello, then to the nod and smile, and then to nothing, as if complete strangers.

The established diner was under-capacity so that he was able to grab the spot he took any time he could - the tall stool next to the wood panelled wall, by the front window. He would swerve this place on a Saturday, packed with lay brunchers, prams and humid noise.

Steven folded his scarf and placed it on his overcoat laid across the next stool, and re-checked it remained flat, un-creased and stable. He then reorganised the counter top items in the same way he did every time. Water glass to the right, salt and pepper, napkin to the left. The waitress anticipated that he would order the burger and he obliged. There was now community consensus that a burger with a salad offered everything and covered the bases. Single cheeseburger, pickle, sweet potato fries. Medium well. *English* mustard and ketchup on the side. Bloody Mary, spicy. It was a day off, after all.

This safe space may have meant no surprises, yet he would be untroubled here by the myriad of issues he could experience at an untested or inconsistent restaurant, while catching up on his digital correspondence. Work had piled up overnight from the US: contracts *at red lines*, signatures to be chased, *warm leads* to be followed-up on with *year-end approaching*. *Key* KPIs to be agreed to measure the ROI *returns*. NDAs to be signed. The CFO required forecasts for SMBs, YTD vs SPYA. New RFPs for the PPC SMEs. And a JD to agree with HR. Sorry, *Talent*. It was *Personnel* when he started, and there were now rumours of *Employee Success*. Triple re-brand. His head hurt, long overdue some PTO.

While the deals that would make the quarter, and indeed the year, could go either way, automated reminders ordered him to complete mandatory online training, to prevent an AI-snitch to his manager. On completion of a *fun* quiz, a contributing token would allow him to *level up* from a *Newbie*. Achieving *Rock Star* status, for the clicking clique, would furnish him with a branded gilet. This infantilisation of the workplace. Swimming and scouting badges. Thirty-seven years old.

There were boxing gym classes to be booked, home admin long overdue, friends and family to keep spinning, and the dating pipeline to be funnelled. Real dates to be organised, screening calls to be slotted, chats to be continued and new connections to be established. A dating army advanced on him.

His food and drink arrived together within ten minutes and he put his digital tasks to one side. He wrapped his napkin around the burger, nappy style, and tucked in. The Bloody cut through and the vodka bit and refreshed. The soft food required minimal mastication and without a companion, was dispatched without fanfare. He took some time to finish his drink and cut down his burgeoning tasks. The waitress brought the technology with her and with the multi-stage payment process compressed, he was in and out in twenty-five minutes.

Steven arrived at home and after removing his coat and shoes, and emptying his pockets into the tray in the kitchen, put some reggae on at a low volume and flopped on the sofa. He returned to his dating pipeline, an automated human task fulfilled many times, double-digits per day. Before dealing with those already *in conversation,* he went to review his feed for new options. An open-minded fellow, his age preference was set from 22 to 55 years old – a range which offered a mix of merits and concerns. His profile contained a list of implicit signals – a favourite gallery, city and cooking style. An arthouse movie, TV character, book. Those who were a good fit would cotton on. A handful of decent photos in different settings, conveying style. He had learned much on how to navigate this scene. To ensure no nasty surprises, a swift 'no' to those solely providing head shots or wearing sunglasses throughout. Must see their eyes, must see their teeth. Beware clever dressing. The worst photo was reality. A 'no' to: amusing perspective shots, world citizens, Dubai and Vegas trippers, MBA bores, lovers of banter or vino, diners at The Shard. Love to travel – you mean holidays, no shit. Men happy to pick up the tab for everything, all the time, might choose a partner seeking a *gentleman with traditional values*. One should fast-track potentials through a range of hurdles with minimal bespoke effort to identify those where there was mutual attraction and a degree of seriousness and application. Establish three trusted questions and recycle, over and over and over again, thousands of times. Keep running the code. On culture, they would love the V&A or Southbank. Move on if questions weren't asked in return. Shed the chatters by asking: *'What questions do you have for me?'* – the interested would respond with effort. Twenty-four hours without a response at any point, gone. Steven checked for children, after a date where the two *wonderful boys* came up on the real life date. Italian lady too, so those boys were her gods. Beware only sons. Someone else's children – not happening. No mums, sorry mums. Don't chat for an age. If it felt like there might be a connection, and unless they were exceptional or close to home, set up a quick screening call – better a bland five minutes on the phone than hours of prep, travel and *live awks*. In London most people were an hour away. Five minutes to save four hours. It concerned him how few callers he wanted to meet in person. A good phone call should be a joint enterprise, a coordinated dance, not an opportunity for the man to entertain. From his own experiences and what he had learned from his datees themselves, Steven came to the view that most women were decent enough and a not insignificant cohort of men were dicks. Endless tales of men who turned up drunk, brought a business contact with them, spilled their guts about ex-wives or confessed bad habits. Dining on a first date became expensive and was to be avoided. Gird your loins, strap in, this could take a while. *Do* try for first-date coffee; a quick meeting of the eyes and thirty seconds of chat should be sufficient to assess suitability. Three seconds could be sufficient. Do recognise that if one wished to play at the upper echelons, this could require substantial sunk costs - high risk/low conversion/high reward. On occasion, do just go for dinner, don't over-complicate everything. This may become a facet of one's social life. Relax, take the opportunity to try a new restaurant with an attractive new face. And should the bill come and they do *the slow reach* to their low slung handbag, it's OK, I'll get this. Unless they were a terrible person. Don't take too many different dates to the same venue, or the staff will become familiar for the wrong reason. On a dull first date, throw out question after question – better that they exhaust *them*selves while the clock was run down. Some surprising additional exclusions might start to emerge. For Steven, these included: small hooped earrings (creepy, however big hoops were appreciated), buttons on one shoulder, visible zips, a love of sailing or watching rugby, bad sunglasses. Baseball caps in any setting. Earlsfield and West Hampstead residents. One shouldn't feel bad about any filters and lists; they had these too. One could be surprised – they may be well read or learned in history, not revealed on a light profile. Part of a well-connected circle. Aficionados of New York, art, the club scene. Acknowledge and raise a glass. Contrary to what he had read in lifestyle magazines, this was dating and not hook-ups. It nagged away at Steven that he had missed something. Maybe a generational thing, or it was just better lookers than him enjoying all the ONSs. Though he smiled at a declaration of 'no FWB, no ONS', which should be followed by '(these days)' for clarity. It was OK for anyone to date a range of people concurrently; a cycle of dates could take weeks and disappearing acts happened all the time. Options should be kept open. A positive mutual connection could leave one feeling exposed, but let them meet other people. To meet one special person is a rarity, a second implausible. Good luck, and one shouldn't take things to heart.

On the Saturday night approaching, Steven had a first date dinner planned with Russian Marina. Date three was often the first night a western couple would spend together, all going well. Second date a possible with a strong connection. Having passed preliminary checks, one's probity probed, stay on the right side of drunk and don't be too much of an arsehole. And hope for no *force majeure* that could not be mitigated against. Still, one never knew, so on this optimistic basis and thinking ahead, he would go for eggs, smoked salmon, chives, crème fraiche and bread, for Sunday morning, should they end up at his with hangovers.

Leaving home for the second time after sifting through some work, he was despondent that his Friday off had ended up so task led. First stop the organic store for Sunday supplies and something for that evening. He had to pick up dry cleaning and a missed postal delivery. His odd-job man needed contacting to set up repairs to the bathroom fan. He had to visit the shabby chic bric-a-brac interiors place where they sneered if one didn't buy anything; it was expensive but there was always something he *needed*. He ran through a lengthy list of purchases he had on his mind: sunglasses (go to Ferragamo), a luxury watch (Harrods), scarves (two-hour round trip to the centre), cooking pans (showroom it in a department store, order online to swerve lugging). He calculated how the following Saturday he could tick these off in one tour, starting mid-morning and be back by lunchtime. And still have the rest of the day free. These items would haunt him midweek. He would have to be lucky to get a massage this late in the day, but he decided to try. Further dating correspondence interspersed his afternoon.

As long as he'd known Ladbroke Grove, it was the choice of rich Europeans, to which any Saturday afternoon stroll down Westbourne Grove would attest. At best he could say he enjoyed a few years when the nightlife had some edge to it, before, for the young at least, the action became all about East London. As with Soho, now sanitised, all the best local options were known by all with a wifi connection. Sixties, seventies, sure; twenty-twenties, nowhere. The area now offered access to quality bakeries, rangy delicatessens, and bars and restaurants giving comfort without risk. At his age, he had settled in even further to the armchair it supplied, and the springboard it gave him to central London and elsewhere.

For a *best practice* third date, Steven would offer to cook dinner. This would follow date one coffee or a drink (cheap, if he could get away with it) and date two dinner out or an activity (mix it up). Dinner at his place would allow them into his world, imply some skill in the kitchen and signal general competence. All going well, the arc of the three dates would create an illusion of progression, variety, thoughtfulness and investment, in money and time, on his part.

A well-made risotto was a regular on the date three menu. It didn't take an age to make, and the forty-five minutes in prep and cooking time would demonstrate some smarts, while allowing him to remain in the moment. It was low risk and allowed for *active listening* and flirting at the counter top with a chilled Gavi. Keeping focused during prep would allow the guest some time to nose around. Careful – bookshelves, décor, keepsakes and photographs were a window into the soul for any visitor, able to poke about inside one's mind.

For the date, he had booked a restaurant bisecting their two neighbourhoods, so they could go their separate ways, or go her way or his, depending on how it went and what her Sunday entailed. It also avoided the sheer stress and decibels of a central London restaurant on a Saturday night, with its sea of dispirited faces, impressed by little any longer.

He reminded himself of the mantra. He excelled at his job and was enthusiastic about the upward trajectory his career was on, and for his future. Bathrooms plural, cast iron radiators throughout, and a second home awaited. His friends were successful, and his friendship groups got up to all sorts. He was family oriented, and had a close relationship with his mother. He would retain some key facts, so that after a first date, he could mirror some of the views she aired last time, and call back to some humorous moments already shared. To create an air of familiarity, compatibility and connection. He would complement her on a detail, not the big picture, and initiate footsie if things went well.

Steven had drinks planned with a friend that Friday night, which required a journey for both, so he expected a cancellation on his part would be well received. One of those meet-ups which were a good idea three weeks ahead of time, but a drag when the day itself had arrived. It was fair to expect this was a mutual feeling. Who wouldn't mind getting a free night back at this age? There was plenty of wine at home, some coke left from midweek and a myriad of digital subscriptions to provide content. Surf's up.

It was early afternoon on Saturday and one of those classic English winter days that materialised each year. A clear blue sky, a bright yet soft sun, the air still and cold. Steven's cousin, Annabel Oakes (*London*

Fields, Charity Fundraiser, The Mash Inn, Joseph), was pained to have to pick up a couple of things in central London on such a day. Saturdays at her age were best spent close to home, away from the tangle of town.

Annabel was five foot four, slight and light, in her late thirties, and moved in an easy and gentle way. She had to wrap up in such weather, to warm her greyhound torso and cold hands. Her dark brown hair was fresh from being cut short, by someone who knew what they were doing. She wore a light grey double-breasted wool blend coat, with a cream cashmere knit and black trousers. White trainers and a navy beret completed *weekend chic*. In that American tradition of wearing shades in winter, she wore a pair of Givenchy sunglasses. This made her self-conscious as the British wore sunglasses when it was hot, not when it was bright, but she wouldn't defy logic to fit in. On this matter, at least.

When it came to fashion, Annabel chose quality over quantity, and evergreen pieces to avoid the fast fashion lane. However, despite her acceptance that to be human was to be a hypocrite, she remained conflicted by her consumerist desires, and their impact on global warming. Another re-brand, *climate change*. Climate *emergency* next. Almost like the elites kept changing their mind.

It all became landfill. As she surveyed the half million square feet of prime department store retail space, every last, shiny item was on the fast-track to a hillside in Durham or Leicestershire – it was a question of: months or years? Some lucky items might be hoarded for decades in a warm semi, but for the rest – the journey from the child labours of creation in Asia, to resting in Western peace was complete in a short timeframe. The answer to any question relating to the economy and individual wealth was increased production, diversification into new and emerging categories or products, or more of the same.

Once the last necessary task in Selfridges was complete, she decided to walk to Soho, despite the centre ground she would have to cover. In the hundred yards she had to contend with to reach the incongruous diagonal of South Molton Street, she steeled herself against the following advertising and marketing assault. A sale sign at the first store (black and neon pink print, twelve feet tall). Leaflet distributors, Christmas lights and music, seasonal discounts and its consumer symbolism, sign carriers, closing sales, clearance sales. Targeted paid media ads placed into her ear canals via her headphones and the pings of personalised marketing arriving into her phone. Two buses passed, and their respective shell advertising streaked by. Movies, games, streaming services. Discarded pamphlets screamed messages from the gutter.

This gave Annabel an itch and her arms shuddered as she reached the quiet. She chose to hypotenuse the throb and throng and cut across parallel to the main drag and head toward Liberty. She passed a favourite knitwear shop and wanted to drop in, but pushed herself on, refusing shopping as leisure. The environment weighed.

On a whim, she sought the calm and space of the Photographers' Gallery, an occasional twenty-minute escape. Pushing hard on the heavy glass doors, they cleaved under her light push, and as they glided shut behind her she felt relief. She handled the clerk with a smile, confirming entry for one, her clipped English voice indicating education and an unworried upbringing. Handed a small coloured disc sticker to confirm proof of entry, she pinned it to her coat. She tried to make a mental note (whatever they were) to remember to remove it on the way out, and thought through how this might unfold. Wandering the streets, figuring out why girls were looking at her chest. Feeling a fool, uncool. Stop. She caught herself to desist from burrowing any further into a pointless mental meander, which she was inclined to do.

She took the lift to the top, so that she could make her way down through the three floors with their separate exhibits, unwinding herself from her swirling thoughts. She felt safe here, in a way she didn't in large galleries, which may one day become a target, and from which there appeared no escape. Trapped, the white cubes perfect canvases for the blood spatter of innocents.

In the art world the pop of a yellow or a mauve with the right stroke lifted Annabel. With photography, black and white carried the heavier weight and message, as seen with a present collection of street photography from post-war London. Although most of the people would be dead now, it was always the dogs that touched her – in photography, and classic works of art - they were without question two feet under. The finality and impossibility of life. She wondered how stressful the dogs' lives were, seeking food, fighting, initiating play. Whether they had homes, regular shelter. Where their bones were now.

The next level down, a couple on a first date, cheery and positive, close but apart. They were in a fix. Their conversation needed to flow but reverberated around the hard walls and wooden floors. They needed privacy but had none, and the few others sharing the space knew it. Annabel hoped they would make it to a café or bar before too long and wondered how they were matching. Steven had theorised once that everyone had a dating DNA of ten attributes scoring ten; where would this pair level out? Which talents would she be able to signal to counter her flat flat shoe choice? Would his saxophone abilities counter his self-conscious hand movements? Annabel felt flat shoes would be brutal in her assessment, and expected this would be their last meeting.

Despite it being a short visit, gallery legs began to set in, so she whizzed around the final floor and breezed out the door, which had been held open for her, and she remembered to pluck her sticker as she hit the street.

On to a pit-stop at Whole Foods, and then home. Fresh coffee, a £4 aubergine, some hand-shovelled pulses, spirulina and acai berry nonsense powders, wild fennel pesto, a bottle of Viognier, a garlic and rosemary marinated Halibut fillet, and a small 70% cocoa chocolate bar. A long-standing vegetarian haunted by her choice to eat fish and eggs, as if gasping in death on the deck of a boat were not merciless torture.

"Hey, how are you?" asked Robert the cashier.

"I'm well, thanks," replied Annabel as they entered an automated talk cycle.

"Doing great, thanks."

"I didn't ask, but thanks for the update."

Coming from Steven, this would have been a harsh sneer and unappreciated, but Annabel smiled it off, and Robert rolled his eyes at the ninetieth person he had interacted with in that way, that afternoon. She parted with £82 for her ten items and left. Robert looked forward to the fantastic Sunday he expected to enjoy, on account of the number of weekend well-wishers he had served.

Annabel reached the underground platform, and as the tube rumbled in, she narrowed herself to enter and nestled her cuboid shopping bags in between her sneakered feet and cast her eyes around. A male model implored her to try the vitamins that made him *feel great*. That will be the vitamins, not the lucrative contracts, the TV presenter wife, the Surrey home and the satisfaction in every mirror. Annabel pulled up her top lip on one side, gave a feint shake of the head, and removed a classic novel from her tote bag.

The hand that fed Jess (*Crystal Palace, fox-hunter (unemployed), home kitchen, Wolters*) presented premium food, various 100% natural meat or fish dog treats, priced like Belgian chocolates, and now and then a portion of pasta or paella. Jess spent her evenings lounging in her pocket sprung memory foam mattress, before retiring, to *the big bed*.

All of which culminated in a healthy and peppy five-year-old Parson Russell Terrier. White, and small to medium in size, with tan ears, and patches on her face and body. Straightforward, honest, possessive, and proud. As she walked close to home, her local streets dispensed a heady mix of odours, which drew her in, and pulled her nose in this direction and that. The whiff of ground snacks, litter, neighbourhood cooks, and territorial pissings, upon which she checked for allies, newcomers, and familiar undesirables.

Known to all dogs, their owners, and every refuse collector, everything at dog level in London has received hot jets of piss, and to those that hath been given, an abundance shall follow. The tree trunks, lampposts, fly-tipped sofas, gates, walls, dustbins, fences, traffic signs, sandbags, fallen branches, and occasional human legs, created a rich media feed of local personalities, and their health and other news. Moreover, fast-food containers, trash overflow, squirrels, rats, cats, faeces, sticks, balls and bedding plants had to be re-prioritised with every head turn. All distractions from her owner, whom Jess needed to keep tabs on. Each walk to the oft-visited local green space an automated checklist, each day the same. Routine. She cherished the variety of the proper, extended walks.

On that afternoon's patrol, Jess had been trying to follow the scent of a new entrant to the local turf, keen to establish social hierarchy. There was always eau de chicken bones in the air, but more than usual, that evening. To her chagrin, they lay outside the walk zone. While sniffing with dogged intent in one area, and relieving herself one final time, her pack leader made toward the park exit as if to leave and Jess bolted over to make the way back home. The nose could now be powered down until their next excursion.

10
CHAPTER 2
Steven and Marina restaurant date

Dinner was booked for seven thirty and they had agreed to meet for a pre-drink. On a date like this, agreed for seven o'clock, the man should arrive ten minutes early and his date should arrive two to eight minutes late. She should not arrive first and be stuck on her own, nor should she be too behind without good reason. Lateness wouldn't cause any hardship in itself, but it would create a power imbalance that would get things off to a bad start, and from which the night may not recover. Trajectory was everything.

Steven was kicking around at home ahead of time, clean and fragranced, dressed, shoes on, coat and scarf over the back of the sofa. He was ready to go. While his date was getting ready for *him*, *he* was going through the motions with other women at earlier stages in the workflow. Dinner may go awry after all, or indeed well. Either way, the hunt continued. His pre-date checklist consisted of: nose-hair trimming and ear fuzz removal (that morning), nose and teeth checks (before leaving), and in the taxi a quick mental run through of amusing things that had happened, *just that very day*.

As befit his age, he wore light blues and navy, and this night was no different. He was dressed in a white and powder blue floral shirt, skinny fit navy jeans with a dusky light pink belt and a pair of dark purple leather sneakers. Urban urbane. A navy and black chequered jacket was a long-term go-to, and to contrast the overall dark look, a cream and turquoise linen scarf for an accent colour, giving him some pop. One of the clothing items he wore which drew out praise. A light spray of fresh boutique cologne was given flight as he prepared to leave home.

It was a wet, black night but Steven loathed to use an umbrella -

bad look, better to be hands-free. He wished he had taken a bath to warm him through to the bones. As it was, he felt a chill and lacked energy, and was grateful it was local travel tonight. He had been on so many dates in the last few weeks that when he lost track, which he put down to tiredness, it was pointed out that he 'wore that shirt last time.'

He shrugged and reminded himself that tonight was an opportunity. Although he felt like a man with half his life ahead of him. The sedentary, greying, pale or sallow one at that.

His date, in her photos, wore black, contrasting with her favoured red lipstick and auburn hair. The artworks in her bedroom were in similar hues. He could not decode this, so didn't dwell.

At seven fifteen the cuff was seeing a lot of action, glancing in turn between watch and phone. No holding message or apology was forthcoming, leaving him miffed. He looked around, watching the rotation of workers around one of Kensington's better restaurants, white table cloths, spongy light green seating, large circular mirrors. Old money sought reassuring fashion. A place for seniors who were driven the walking distance. For Steven, a choice of convenience. Location, location, location, such a driver in middle age.

Ten minutes later and onto a second drink, he was becoming annoyed. The world was watching him, spinning back and forth on a tall bar stool. It would not do.

He decided he would phone her around seven thirty, until he received a message, to say she was five minutes away. Ten to fifteen minutes then, he thought. He checked with the staff that the delay wouldn't be an issue, and made some noises and gestures to convey he wasn't put out, just that the two of them led complex lives, full of demands.

After some time, he watched Marina Sokolov walk in, a black mac covering a black trouser suit. Black boots. Trademark.

A double air kiss. He smelled her lipstick, applied in the taxi. No apology. She chewed gum, which he'd never seen before on a date, and the freedom with which she did so suggested this wasn't an oversight which was going to be rectified.

"Like the scarf," she praised, in her Russian drawl.

"Thanks," he responded, taken aback to receive a compliment from The Attitude Itself.

Marina dumped her cappuccino Mulberry Bayswater on the stool next to him and excused herself. "What can I get you?" he asked.

"Glass of white, dry, not Chardonnay," she replied. As she swished off, Steven ordered, "one seven five of Chardonnay."

Steven dismissed claims that people knew wine, and so for the last couple of years ordered whatever his companions asked him not to, if the possibility arose. He had not been caught out yet.

She returned and they had little choice but to go straight through. Marina pushed on first as they were shown to their table. This allowed Steven to eye her up, as any man did in that situation, always.

Saturday evening in a London eatery. Staff swarmed around the floor – take Tomas. At home in Portugal, waiting tables was a vocation – a proud profession of standing, which could constitute a life's work. Watch the professionalism on display as a handful of staff run a large restaurant in Lisbon, and their skill would be clear. Here, restraint was their best asset.

Tomas had to handle customers like Steven with his endless requests, the table changes, the wrong type of tumbler. The commentary on the un-inspirational side dishes, as if Tomas had any say. How the menu lacked the *wow factor*. Although it was rare that the food went out cold any longer, it could be under-seasoned, over-spiced or the portion *too* sizeable. *Too many* menu options. These were never complaints in the nineties. Feng shui and *flow* through the restaurant may not be up to snuff, the art curated without imagination, cutlery too weighty. The annoyance of an *on trend* or verbose menu. Tomas' service may be judged to be inattentive, unresponsive, discourteous. Or involve too much chat, be judged too obsequious, the operating speed too pacey. There may be some language difficulties in question or objection handling, or just a straight balls-up of an order. Slow de-crumbing in between courses or, The Cardinal Sin, above all others – no notepad. Amid the heat and the booze-fuelled din, Tomas had to keep an eye on his dispersion of tables, catch their eye when they needed it, avert from their eye-line when they didn't. He would be envious of his diners if so many of them didn't look so bereft. This international, professional crowd had eaten at places like this a hundred times, leaving them with deadened eyes. The repetitive dreariness of their umpteenth rib eye, buttery mash, parsnip puree baby food or beetroot and goat cheese starter. He had to juggle the trays of drinks, the order and request grenades lobbed while passing, and a myriad of disruptions and interruptions, while he calculated how close he was to making rent that month, to leave him enough for a trip to his dealer and a plane ticket home in the new year. His childhood dog had died, his father was ill, and they were expecting the landlord to inform them they needed to up sticks again, any month now. The city beat him every day, and he fought it or took it. In the evening he would smoke a few spliffs, go down on his girlfriend, and on his own terms, in the final moments, go to sleep *very much the winner*.

In a half full room, they were offered one of the inferior tables to get those allocated without challenge, but Steven unlocked several better options. A succession of round tables (which blew in restaurants as much as they did in business) were turned down until they were presented with a square table with proper real estate for elbows, water jugs, condiments, patron bric-a-brac. The landscape menu was printed on one side, with sides, desserts and wines all visible. Steven was compelled, as always, to confirm that the reverse was blank, when he knew it with certainty.

The waistcoated Tomas had to interrupt them several times before they were ready to order. The pair were on form, enjoying the preliminaries, and in no hurry.

Marina decided on a main and dessert tonight as her choice courses. Never three courses on a date. Fish would be light, and keep the calorie count from going off the charts. Steven decided to eschew the choux, swerve the hors d'oeuvres, and went with the modern cliché main, and looked away from Tomas as he did so. In return, Tomas dished up the patronising 'good choice' with an insincere beam. This grated as much with Steven as the automated response 'great question', that he heard all day long in the office, to any question of any quality.

Marina and Steven exchanged dating experiences. Steven had been on dates with the same person a mere three years apart, and she didn't remember. He wouldn't tend to share a self-destructive anecdote like that, but he felt relaxed, and that it would amuse her, which it did. And he didn't care if he made a mess of things. There would be another along any minute.

Marina mentioned to a man that she had a dog, to which he responded that he had three children. 'That's not the same thing,' she had replied, vexed that he hadn't mentioned it before, and hadn't saved her three wasted hours.

The time Steven turned up and his date indicated she would have to be on her way within two hours to return to work, a timestamp that he then felt he was unable to shorten. A situation that became desperate as she revealed herself to be a loquacious bore-talker. He therefore chucked question grenades at her, let her wear herself out, and begged for time to do its thing. That's the thing with time.

"How's the wine?" Steven asked.

"Very good. What is it?"

Steven ignored the question and resumed recounting his day.

At this point, it would have been legitimate for Marina to have asked for the bill, paid half, and left. Instead she let him carry on. Because she wanted to be out, he was attractive, and she hadn't had sex in a month. So he had wiggle room. Not a lot.

They spoke at length about the general time-wasting, which was different for the sexes. Women had to establish who wanted more than a fuck, whereas men could be strung out on multiple dates by women going through the motions, pushed into it by friends tired of seeing them single. The vintage dater, post-divorce or separation, dipping a toe in, two generations on from when they last fought a dating duel. Rusty, inexperienced, like an American joining the second world war. They discussed the idiosyncrasies of nationalities, and which ones were more dependable than others.

"Divorced men, crying like infants," Marina mocked.

"Older men who have just come out of a twenty-year marriage, and their heads are spinning at the modern dating landscape."

"The lost time," she bemoaned, "the cancellations, the last minute changed plans, endless chats without meeting, the photos."

The photos, yes the photos.

Steven began first.

"Group photos. Who am I looking at? Photos a few years old. Before the lockdown kilos. Endurance athletes, with their Lycra and bad sunglasses. I've been to Machu Picchu."

"Tiger selfies. Big fish. Topless muscle boys. Sports cars. Dick pics."

"It's modern nonsense, the whole thing. The commoditisation of relationships, the sexual marketplace. It's successful in some ways. It gets you out and meeting people," Marina opined.

"Doesn't often turn into anything though, right?"

"Same faces going around and around for best part of a decade. They'll never find a match," she commented.

"What's the alternative? Can only die trying. It's about acceleration, speeding people through the disasters via a numbers game with no end point."

"Masks in photos," Marina reverted, cutting in.

"Do men do that?" he asked with an eyebrow, "I mean, women do that a lot, but men?"

"Oh yes," she confirmed, "and they get a 'no' from me. I don't know who the women are that get turned on by that."

"Whatever happened to the bad boy?" he commented.

"There are no bad boys. Take punk, or any of the rebels of the art, music, movie world. When the plandemic came, DO WHAT THE GOVERNMENT ORDERS YOU TO."

Heads turned on the next tables.

She took a large slug of wine. Half the glass.

Marina was a throwback to a previous time. She had no truck with the ideology of the day. Steven weighed up if she was right or right wing, letting this loop in the background and he slugged back wine, trying to stay focused on her words, planning how to interject in interested and smart ways.

Her horizontal political leanings took an unexpected turn when the environment raised its head. Steven expected climate denial and received instead, "Well, the environment is fucked. Don't bring any children into the world, hunker down, build wealth, dark times are coming."

She paused to eat.

"And don't think you'll escape ever going to war. I don't. Even at our age."

"Population migrations, well that's going to be swings and roundabouts. People scrambling to come here, others getting away.

Some distant outpost, with a hut on beach and internet. If that's still functioning."

"You're trained in weapons, aren't you?" he checked.

"Of course."

Her English close to note perfect, with a charming accent. Bar the odd dropped article, with the drink.

"So, what's next?" he enquired, captivated.

"Do now all the skiing, scuba, adventure sports, city-hopping. Build those memories. Everything ends. If one can still afford it with the hollowing out of the middle classes, the pressure on salaries and bonuses for those fortunate to keep their jobs, once they are working alongside AI. And try to enjoy diving among all plastic, billions of disposable masks and testing kits that rampaged through middle classes seeking safety after years of hectoring about single-use plastic. We went from hundred percent masks on tube and vaccine mandates for health workers, to zero masks on tube and you can't get a vaccine. Within eighteen months."

"But, you know, *it's about the virus.*"

Wine.

Steven wished he could have frozen her look of utter disdain. Black and white, framed. It would go on his wall.

She finished her wine and called Tomas over for the list.

At certain points in the night Tomas had been *in the zone*, handling all comers with aplomb, bobbing along the tides of the night, when the speed and noise picked up the pace. The calm moments when they dropped, and the diners became aware of themselves. At least he was not at home arguing with his girlfriend or their flatmate. Steven couldn't put him off his stride. Nor Marina with her extensive demands, with curt, cursory thanks.

Marina looked through and found a suitable bottle, which she checked with Steven. She snapped the old fashioned menu shut.

"Sun explodes anyway, everything is gone."

Steven was enjoying the paths the conversation was taking, and it served as a welcome change from running off Patter 101, despite the implications for humanity if true. He thought of the two of them, on a beach, living wild and free, fucking off the world. The beach in his head, lifted from a hit movie, the two of them edited in. A false memory built from the familiar.

As any singular dog breed may encompass a whole range of personalities and types, so all individuals within a group, a nationality, a business, can be on a wide spectrum. Yet her strident views were what one might expect from a Russian, determined and assumptive to be correct. Or at least, *you can think whatever you want, this is the way I see it.* It countered his English demeanour and worldview, creating a frisson he felt within him. Exoticism-eroticism.

To Steven, this was proving to be an enjoyable time, as he was able to soften into the conversation, comforted beyond the seating and gentle acoustics. He felt free to say what he thought without judgment, and didn't have to play to the audience. *Know your customer* and all that. He expressed political and social views on current affairs which could have got him date-cancelled with another. Even when he stepped close to a line, some remark she took against, he hit the nerve, she reacted, took a drink and things carried on as before. Indeed, he felt like reining himself in would be the mistake, that she appreciated straightforwardness, honesty. She knew men. Conceited tales and lines to meet an objective would be exposed.

The control and self-confidence she had, gave him these freedoms, yet also made him behave. This was someone who wouldn't put up with any shenanigans, unlike many dates where they let things go. Small things, yet indicative of toxicity, which were not seized upon and used to consign him to history. *Because they liked him.*

They took a breather and looked around the room, adjusted drinks, cutlery, kept an eye on how the staff were doing, took in the décor, watched the people. Steven took a drink and measured if this silence was *good* silence of progress, or *bad* silence, nervy and exposing, and that which should be filled right away.

He thought the former.

A course was left in front of each of them, the contents of which were explained at length. Steven thanked Tomas.

As they ate, Marina asked where he liked to go out, setting a test, at which point Steven took the opportunity to name-check various bars, members' clubs, a couple of his favourite *areas* of London, central or off-the-beaten track. Pleased with his answer, he returned the question.

"You?"

"I don't go out much. I don't have many friends."

Total control, and unwavering truth. She cared not a jot what anyone thought.

"Done all that. Clubs, hotel bars, done it to death. I stay in, cook, just me, cat."

He was charmed by the mention of a cat among the virtues and vices of town life. He gave his cutlery a wry smile. Yet while he appreciated her honesty, this was truth permitted to a female beauty. In contrast, it would not get him on with most to convey an ungenerous, anti-social lifestyle.

"I can't go out on my own. If I'm sat at bar unaccompanied, men approach me. They think I'm hooker."

She amused him, as she dropped articles with the wine.

"I used to be dominatrix, you know."

Oh, here we go, thought Steven, one for the memoir.

"Men used to come around and clean my house."

"And that was it?"

"That was it. I gave them bit of abuse, left them to it. My house was *exceptionally* clean."

She put her right arm out in front of her. It was a thin, white arm, with slender wrists. She indicated to her forearm.

"How much of this arm do you think I've had up guy's ass?"

He didn't need to think this through.

"All of it."

Steven was outside the comfort zone of his own experience, but decided to go with it. They ordered coffees. They ordered whiskies. Steven felt the hangover ahead of him, as the smoky, cloying sweetness hit his throat with the hit of forty percent as it evaporated away its fuel.

They had reached the point in the evening where the food was long gone, coffee cups contained rings of deposits, and the rhythm had them sunk, talked out on full stomachs.

"Do you want to go on somewhere, for a drink?" he ventured.

"Sure, it's still early," she said. It was 10.50pm.
She looked at him, inviting him to come on to her.
"Or we could get a drink at my place?"
"That's more like it. Do you vont to have sex?"
Her directness caught him off guard and he let out a smirk, which was out of his control. He had met his match, his female better.
"Yeah, sure. That'd be great."

About five minutes after the drinks were poured and they had made themselves comfortable in Steven's lounge, Marina climbed on top and began undressing him. They went at it and when they were done, they lay about half naked on the sofa, drinking whisky, saying little. Marina called it, and they went to bed where they screwed again. Steven went to go down on her and she pulled him up, encouraged his dick into her. Getting too personal was not on the agenda for this high energy, sweaty and desperate encounter.

Marina rolled toward him and he was expecting some sort of hot, awkward cuddle with surplus arms. She kissed him, and rolled back over away from him and said goodnight. Genuine or faux post-sex intimacy was not required. He didn't anticipate cuddles and brunch in the morning.

They sunk into their restorative health hormones and slept the night through, dreaming on full stomachs.

The next morning, they had turbo sex, Marina took a shower and left. It was ambiguous as to whether she expected him to be in touch with her. He smiled to himself and assumed not. It crossed his mind to chase her for another night out, may as well, but he caught himself on. It was to be left, history, framed. Like that image of her from the evening. Like everything else.

11
CHAPTER 3

Monday: Annabel and Barney take lunch: Francesca and Helen get tapas

It was a grotty winter Monday; one which felt like the first of many to come. The influx onto each underground carriage brought with it fresh slush and grime, with further gasps of exasperation as heads and brollies were shaken out in time. The occasional warm apology; cooperation and pleasant exchanges for such days, despite the unspoken fear of viral transmission added to general winter woes. The huddle at least offered a collective warmth which felt like some substitute for dryness. For the majority standing, thoughts of how to self-organise to best alleviate the back and knees, or how to accommodate expected leavers at future stops with minimal movement. Decisions were taken on how to finish coffees, hold books, turn pages, complete exam revision or handle a free newspaper with little intellectual content – a true *page turner*.

For those living near the start of a tube line, a choice of seats begging. The seats near the doors looked good – easy to get out, less chance of getting stuck. Not hemmed in between two people. Some fresh air. Alas, the wily, heartless old pro recognised these to be easy pickings for the elderly, the disabled, those with child. Take the middle of a bank of seven, safe with a three seat cushion on either side. To exit, don't rush and push. Wait for someone else to stand up, get in their slipstream, and let them part the waters. As in many sports, one had more time than one thought.

The carriages and the system were over-burdened by the weight of passengers, ageing infrastructure, and all manner of uncontrollables that a city life dished out. A passenger *under the train*, an unattended bag or a signal failure could scupper achieving an average commute time to or from work. See the freedom with which a lightweight tube carriage moves at eleven o'clock. Never leave the office without checking the route home first. Barriers to entry at temporarily closed stations could create a log-jam, as could construction hoardings, which when they appear, could be expected to hold people up for years, not months.

A train lurched, then stopped in a tunnel, moved again, pulled into a station. Where it was held. It picked up some speed at the next section and then came to an unplanned hard stop, whereby the passengers' quads were tested and those not holding on were flung. One must always hold on, or find oneself as a tourist, flying at a yellow pole. As it started up again and approached the next stop, that unnerving feeling as the carriage pulled in, and stopped, inch by inch, as their bodies yearned for standstill.

The automated instructions and apologies came over the carriage and platform speakers across Underground, Overground and mainline trains throughout the south east. We are being held in a tunnel. Mind the doors. Please mind the gap between the train and the platform. This is a Hammersmith and City Line train to Barking. We are sorry that this service to London Victoria is delayed. Apologies outsourced to code. If train arrival time greater than train planned time, then apology message three.

The garrulous, commentating platform staff. Please stand behind the yellow line. Will the woman in the grey coat *please* stand back? This train will not depart until you stand clear of the doors. Mind the doors, mind the doors. There's another train right behind this one. They are not the only ones who like the sound of their own voice. The 'chatty' tube driver. Such lines. What a character.

It had rained hard overnight and there were puddles and pools of murky water, so it made sense to choose footwear with care on such a day. At predictable spots, lakes had formed, deep enough that queues formed to slip around the edges, with a crowd backed up to the station exits, from whence they came.

Wireless zombies in giant headphones stepped out at crossings into the paths of cyclists who had jumped red lights, to get to where they wanted to go *even faster*. What they would do with the seconds saved was anyone's guess. *It's PR, not ER.*

The office automation started nationwide. Welcome to the meeting. Press one to join the meeting. Please wait while we try to connect you. The caller knows you are waiting. Then press the hash or pound key. Out of office reply. Thanks for logging a ticket – your case number is #1547856. Your timesheet is overdue. Press four to hear these options again.

The human automation followed. How are you? Do you need a bag? Milk, sugar? Add your own milk and sugar, over there. Tap here. Good weekend? Fine thanks, you? Yeah, fine. You? Still fine. Great question.

Years ago, talk of stakeholder alignment, *driving* revenue, thinking outside the box. Guys. Matters spoken *'in terms of'*. Architects designed buildings, engineers planned their construction. Now it was tickets, trackers, *sequencing*, deployment, backlog, support providing none, development 'environments', reaching out, levelling up, leveraging. Numbers weren't low or down, they were *soft*. Set-ups were *exotic*, issues *thorny*, downtime tolerance critical, essential to resolve if we were to *scale*. Open the kimonos.

Morning. How was your weekend? Great, mine too. Here's your branded lanyard. Get to work.

Annabel queued, as she did each day, in the same *Pret a Manger*, for the same half baguette with free-range egg mayonnaise & smoked salmon. Most mornings she waited behind someone who *needed* a new bag, to ferry a single protein pot, tub of fresh fruit, or a yoghurt and granola bowl, the two hundred yards to their desk. Women with large handbags, men with rucksacks or manbags. Within three minutes that paper bag would be in a waste paper basket. This drove her crazy, and she would get a little lift whenever a bag was declined, and a baguette dropped into a deep coat pocket. Annabel envisaged the fuel costs in the transportation of said paper bag from basket to depot, and on to a recycling centre (she hoped) where extra fuel would be expended to break it down, and turn it into pulp. Further energy to move it on to be reconstituted, re-coloured, re-printed, and sent on, back to a central *Pret a Manger* depot, and then onto that same store, to be given to the person in front of her in the queue, who *needed* a bag. She looked down at the card and plastic film surrounding her breakfast and knew she too was part of the problem.

Barney Greene *(Crystal Palace, IT Manager, his local family-owned Turkish place, Gant)* was filling up his reusable water bottle from the tap in the office kitchen after starting his morning bamboozled by the new boiling hot and cold water taps which had been installed. He was just shy of five foot eight, in his late thirties, his boyish face was clean shaven every day, and his brown hair combed. His average looks were weighted down further by a lack of any cool. Although dumpy, he was always tidy and well presented, like a disciplined child. He almost always wore a jumper over a shirt, regardless of the weather. Others wondered if he were comfortable. But he was comfortable; he knew who he was and who he wasn't, what he was capable of, his limitations, and he rewarded everyone he came across with an honest smile and a sunny outlook. An attentive listener, he never had a girlfriend, though women felt at ease around him. Annabel felt he would hit his stride, yet it would require the right person to come along, and for him to push himself. Barney, famed and loved around the place for his environmental fads, his diligent but slow working pace, and his lingual clumsiness.

He apologised for being in the way of the cleaner, Monica, who was waiting to tidy the dirties and wipe the sink, and mentioned the weather should be calmer the rest of the week. "Izzit?" Monica replied, as she did to any statement which was news, followed in response by, "Innit," to anything she agreed with, in this case Barney's prosaic observation that the shortest day was looming. They Izzit and Innited their way through a few cycles until others joined them in the kitchen.

"Morning Barney," said Annabel, placing her hand on his shoulder as she passed him from behind.

"Hey, good morning. How was your weekend, up to much?" he asked.

"It was OK. Went into town on Saturday, popped into the Photographers' Gallery."

"It's ages since I've been there. Since we went."

"The Flower Market on Sunday, then had lunch and drinks with Gemma," Annabel continued as she made a fruit tea.

"How about you?"

"Yeah, fine, you know, the usual. Took Jess to Burgess Park, lots of crows to chase. And we saw the stunning mosaic of the Camberwell Beauty butterfly. Helped my neighbour in the garden yesterday."

"Got to dash to a meeting, can you do lunch today? Sushi?"

"Yes, absolutely."

"I'll come get you around twelve fifteen?"

"Works for me," Barney confirmed as Annabel left.

The famine charity they worked for always had appeals for this and that, and Barney checked the noticeboard while he dripped tea onto the floor. A colleague from Finance walked through in a Christmas jumper. The C word. He felt sure that Annabel would get in a state at lunch over the Annual Environmental Disaster.

As a fundraiser, Annabel had enough people skills to navigate the office politics without too much bother. In a technical role, Barney could be in the line of fire, but no-one knew how to do what he did, so he was secure enough. Others, friends of theirs, were not so fortunate, and were exposed. An outsider would think the charity sector was all kindness and collaboration, pulling together, making a difference. Recent scandals had put paid to that misconception. The insider knew it to be a political pit. If you weren't stabbed in the back, you were knifed in the front.

Annabel picked up Barney behind schedule, which he had anticipated, and they strolled to the homogeneous Japanese chain restaurant they had decided upon. Barney braced himself when he heard Christmas music as a coffee house's heavy glass door was swung open. Opposite, a girl wearing antlers stood outside a pub, lighting a cigarette.

Inside, banks of refrigerators, where the healthy lunch chilled. Salmon heavy, classic, vegetarian, the dragon range, platters of rolls and nigiri, and salads of superfoods, chicken, salmon upon salmon. Elsewhere, hotter options, buns, gyoza. Odd flavoured waters and racks of junk, crackers, seaweed thins, packaged sliced fruit. All sliced, arranged, pre-packed conformity, the future of pod living and food as sustenance. The dazzling, snazzy, yet soulless energy of collectivism. The servers saw the same faces day after day, with the same orders, for months on end before some switch. Automated rotational foodstuffs, habits prime for further automation and processing, whatever that might look like. Someone, somewhere was working on it.

They placed close to £30 of sushi and sashimi on the counter.

"Just these?" their server Marcia enquired, who self-declared as Brazilian, via a small flag that had been added to her name card. It must *enhance the customer experience*.

"Isn't that enough?" Annabel volleyed back.

Marcia gave her the 'keep job, pay rent' smile. Annabel felt mean, shut her eyes, shook her head a little and apologised. She knew Marcia was trying to get by, a long way from home.

They took stools on a curved section. It was a calm, welcoming environment and would remain so, up until the food was gone. Then it would morph into something cursorial, shuttling patrons out the door, the clock ticking as they took up real estate. Significant planning, design and testing had gone into creating this impact.

"Wrong side of the bed this morning?" enquired Barney.

"Fucking Silvia is working from home again. Doing her chores, organising the kids, watching girl porn. She *has* managed to get the secret Santa going. She knows I abstain every year but called me out on the email."

"And?" Barney pushed.

"Christmas, Barney. A billion Christmas cards sent every year, saying nothing. Wrapping paper. Do you know how many Christmas jumpers are bought every year? The impact of making them?"

"Can't say I do," he responded, focused on organising and dividing their lunches, so that he was crystal what he had in front of him. He garnered soy, spicy sauces, chopsticks.

Annabel consulted her phone, checked notes. "Fuuccckkkk. Ten million."

"Endless presents no one wants or needs. The food waste, the gluttony. Putting aside the human cost, the stress, bringing warring family members together, the drinking, domestic abuse. The poorest, already living hand to mouth, sourcing debt to offer their children anything bar misery. The sheer awfulness of it. If at any other time of the year I suggested we ate turkey, Brussels sprouts, shared a box of mince pies... then the gyms are packed for two months, and it's all smoothies and herbal tea. Every single year. Pathetic."

Barney made steady progress through his 'wealth & wisdom' box and spicy dragon rolls. Annabel was lagging.

"I know. We have this same recurring annual conversation. The jumper data is new news, remember that for next year. I like sprouts," Barney admitted.

As each clear lid was removed, the sea of plastic took over the table top, a tide which wouldn't recede. A wad of too many napkins for two people were provided by Marcia to be sure there wouldn't be another interaction with Annabel.

"Imagine the waste this place produces every day," Annabel despaired.

"Every hour. And the fuels used in recycling. Whatever small proportion that accounts for," Barney added. Misery did indeed like company.

"We can't come here again."

"Agreed," Barney accepted, "let's find somewhere old fashioned with plates and cutlery."

"With dishwashers going like the clappers hour after hour?"

Annabel stared at a rectangular piece of salmon with its white marbling, unable to connect it in her mind to a live, spirited being.

"I'll make us sandwiches and we can go to the park. No cling film, I promise."

"Yes. Thank you."

He always got her to a better place, it just took longer on some days.

"You can only do what you can, OK?"

Between them they were left with eight separate pairs of plastic trays, clear and black, disposable chopsticks, paper chopstick pyjamas, several small plastic fish individual soy sauce dispensers, with accompanying plastic trays to receive soy sauce. Tough wasabi packets. Fake grass.

They sat in silence with the same thoughts. To desist, they started to tidy, to pile. Annabel picked up a plastic fish that may indeed end up in the stomach of a fish or bird. She turned it in her fingers, bereft with irony.

"Hey," Barney said to snap her back, "focus on what you can, things at home, set yourself the best rules to live by."

"I know, but. The bad flu seasons looked like an opportunity for us to step back, reconsider things, but it was just a waiting game before normal life could resume. Nature was forgotten when the shops reopened. Counting butterflies lost its appeal."

"I felt like this, years ago, the big picture despair. Spend this weekend looking at your life, try to make some positive adjustments. It'll make you feel better. "I know the plastic problem is about food. Do you know how? Every time there's the rustle of plastic and packaging, Jess comes running."

They discussed work and plans for the next year, and made sure each other were informed on documentaries, books, movies to catch up on, before they were interrupted by the cleaning of surfaces, the final, deliberate nudge, showing them where the door was. As they left, Annabel had something to pick up and they went their separate ways. For a few moments she thought about what she could grow outside, improvements she could make to recycling and composting practises, whether she could put any old clothes to better use. However, the pneumatic drills were hammering, the cranes were pivoting. Resources, materials, construction, growth, more, always more. Resistance felt futile.

After tipping and rating her driver, five stars the reward for zero conversation, Francesca Cremonesi (*Marylebone, Auction House Sales, The Ledbury, Coco de Mer*) swished into her favourite wine bar in Fitzrovia, improbably situated among a less than salubrious parade of tatty shops. She wore a navy dress with an asymmetric white slash down the left side, black ankle boots and a leather jacket.

Forty-seven years old, her dark brown hair had body and bounce, and her eyes were deep brown pools. It wasn't clear, without leaning in, where the pupils stopped and the irises started. Her body was shapely yet modest, boosted by the confidence of her movements, which gave her an edge. This smoking smoker wore navy or black in the week, colour at weekends. She spoke English with a soft accent. In her native Italian language, business was interchangeable with affairs. Francesca was the business and, yes, she had indulged.

She used the gym to jet herself to a discrete orgasm in the Jacuzzi, sometimes when others were present. Of all the things that set her apart, she listened when someone revealed who they were.

Francesca was due to meet her friend Helen for tapas and had made the booking this time. An odd pairing, they met years ago on a cookery course and had remained friends. Francesca had enough elite arsehole friends, and Helen was such a decent person, although she was a struggler.

The venue had exposed brick walls and solid wooden tables with dark red leather benches. A single Tiffany lamp sat in the corner opposite the bar and wine bottles thick with dust were dotted about the place. Large chalkboards displayed the wines by colour, sherries, the food plates, snacks and *boards*. The décor was like a hundred other places, but everything was on the money, just so. As was the sound. Acoustics and ambient noise mattered. When busy it was boisterous but a table could talk and be heard, whereas when quieter, one never sensed the next table was party to the conversation.

Francesca was ordering a glass of orange wine and olives as Helen arrived. Helen Steele *(Tufnell Park, Marketing Manager, Iberica, Cos)* was thirty-eight years old, with shoulder length light brown hair and mild green eyes. She would be the first to admit that she could make more of herself. If she could get to the gym as much as she'd like. If she could afford the time and money for shopping at weekends. Her glasses were a couple of years old, were due an update, the lenses showing some wear. She would love to lead a life of order and wasn't one of those who couldn't live without chaos, yet it did tend to find her.

They were both running behind for different reasons. Francesca had to take a client call in front of physical paperwork, while Helen got her work done on time and then her sister called about their parents. There were tears and Helen felt awful for having to rush the call to get going.

After greeting with a kiss on each cheek, Helen dumped her bag down on a chair and began to rummage. After three cycles she gave up searching for whatever it was. She had maybe just forgotten. She shut her bag upon which she folded and placed her coat. After her coat fell off, she stretched to retrieve it and placed it back. This happened again. She was still clutching the Penguin Classic paperback she had been reading on the bus. She turned her phone off so she could focus and enjoy herself.

"What's that, Aperol Spritz?" asked Helen, pointing at Francesca's glass.

"Don't be *pointy*," Francesca chided with a wink. "No, it's orange wine. Here."

"Orange wine, eh?"

She tried a little, "That'll do."

Helen gave it the thumbs up, referencing the last thing about wine she learned from Francesca, that the Romans and Greeks judged wine in binary terms.

As Helen settled down they covered their respective days, and how Francesca knew of this place.

"Let's order, are you hungry?" Francesca asked, as she beckoned over a passing waiter and he leaned down.

"No one is ever hungry any more. I do want food though. You choose, it all looks lovely," said Helen.

"We will have... the almonds, some more olives, the peppers, nduja croquettes. Anchovies?"

Helen nodded.

"And the octopus, for good measure. Thank you."

"Amazing," said Helen as the small cream menus on textured paper were whisked away.

"People tell me things, you wouldn't believe," shared Helen, "I don't even want to know and I don't even ask, they just open up and out it all comes. I was turning the projector off earlier, and Sophie said she was seeing a married man. That was five minutes gone, listening to all that. Yesterday, I had to hear about problems at home with someone's boys – one took a machete into school. The day before, someone wanted to know whether he should sleep with this man he met. He's not even gay."

"You have a gift," Francesca confirmed, tilting her head back with laughter.

"I can't do anything with it," Helen bemoaned.

"You could become a counsellor, a psychologist?"

"I have enough problems of my own. I just wish they'd keep it to themselves, close friends and family are enough at the moment."

"This town. I'll give you the gift of not sharing any of mine."

"First world problems don't count."

Francesca excused herself. Helen had been there ten minutes. She was the sole woman Helen knew who still smoked throughout the day. And so few wrinkles – cruel. Helen sat back and took a few moments to people watch, this good-looking set. She felt self-conscious in these places, but Francesca gave the pair enough cool for her to feel welcome and worthy. She thought of some of the people in Francesca's circle, and liked that she was a small part of it. Francesca never thought about such matters, though many of her friends wouldn't be interested in what Helen had to say, and would make themselves scarce at a party. Brutal. The city was watching.

"Whatever happened to patio heaters?" asked Francesca.

"Remember them, after the smoking ban? Everywhere. Now we freeze."

"I do, and I also remember you saying you would quit when you were forty," replied Helen, calling it out.

"Oh c'mon."

Francesca swatted away an imaginary fly, "We'll plan for fifty."

"I want you to look after yourself," said Helen.

"I want *you* to look after *yourself*," Francesca volleyed back, as she got serious.

She eased herself in.

"Are you getting exercise?"

"I get to a class once a week, midweek."

"How about the weekend?"

"Gym's near work."

"That's a solvable problem, you just have to figure it out," Francesca challenged, frustrated at Helen's blockers.

"How are your parents?"

"The usual. Honestly, I don't even want to think and talk about it right now, I've had such a tiring few weeks with work, and everything, quite frankly," and Francesca believed her.

She looked run down.

"Can we just have a laugh tonight, please? That would cheer me up."

"Of course," Francesca replied. She would have another go at this next time, once she'd plotted an approach.

The plates came in batches, every few minutes, and they dug in. Francesca ordered a bottle of white Italian wine. They discussed Francesca's insane clients, Helen's friends whom Francesca had met, some whom she hadn't. What they'd been reading. Francesca brought Helen up to date on Simon and their on/off thang; the update being that they were both too busy and lazy to be off, so were on. Francesca read between the lines within Helen's update on long-standing boyfriend Phil, her family, the job.

Once they finished most of the food, they put their cutlery across their plates and signalled with some crumpled or balled napkins. Helen then continued to pick at the leftover almonds and olives.

"What is it you always say?" Francesca asked.

"About?" Helen paused as the cogs turned, and as Francesca was going to help her out, it came to her.

"Oh, little pickers wear big knickers," and her face lit up as she chuckled. Francesca always laughed at this and found a way of raising it. A pattern friendship joke.

At the end of the evening, Francesca looked up and caught the server's eye and punched four times with a finger on her palm to signal she would like to pay.

"I've not seen that done before," laughed Helen.

"Move with the times darling. I'm behind, it's all tapping now."

As the bill was left and the machine brought over, Francesca took control. "I chose the place, I'll get this," and as Helen protested, "I'll claim it and say it was clients."

Helen knew this was a lie, and Francesca knew that she knew. But they did their little dance, and Helen was able to thank her for a wonderful evening. Francesca would convince her to take them to a cheap eat next time.

Francesca held the door open for her friend, the shorter of the two, and leaden with bags.

"My ride's here."

"Lovely to see you, let's do it again soon."

"Yes let's. Onward and upward," said Francesca, in a whisper.

"Onward and upward," Helen repeated as they embraced before

Francesca stepped into her car and Helen trudged off to Great Portland Street station.

100
CHAPTER 4

Winter in London and beyond: Steven and Andrew drinks: Steven and Ladbroke Grove

Winter in London was well under way. A mix of sunny or overcast days, mild to bothersome winds, with a low sun holding its position on many mornings, uncomfortable for those underground passengers starting above ground. Celsius temperatures fluctuated from the low single digits to the low teens during the day and might drop below zero overnight. The worst would come in the new year, yet as any self-respecting senior knew, *the winters weren't as harsh as they used to be*. Generation X enjoyed the odd white Christmas in childhood.

Elsewhere, the world was burning. In Australia the mercury hit forty degrees day after day, with *minimum* average daily temperatures hitting levels not seen since those records began. No matter how the data was cut, sliced and diced, cleaned, trended, analysed and dredged, there was no escaping the pureness of the heat. Yet temperature records were set at airports, high on runway, low on trees. Counter-narrative data, even if they were looking, seldom published. Global warming hit home harder when it was hot, at home. Now there were terrifying segments to be made, the media applied focus on these events, and as public perception was shifting, the media feasted upon and harvested that fear. Weather maps recoloured to a sea of red. The outcomes in much of the first world were distant after all, yet encroaching. But to some, the unidirectionality felt undeniable, and the timeframe stark. This wasn't *news*; not now. It was news in the seventies, back when today's grandparents were *courting*. Now the public is expected to believe that the elites want to save the whale.

Bushfires raged beyond the bush leaving households and livelihoods devastated, blackened ex-homes expelled weeping families who in turn abandoned burned out motors. Regional fire & rescue truck workers left overcome by dusty dark grey orange skies, sheer mountain rock faces on fire. That clichéd red earth, and that most iconic of fauna, and a public, begging for the rainfall that was charted to be so distant. Smoked koalas, fleeing kangaroos, all victims of a devastating Aussie *Force Madge*. These monstrous displays should have silenced the convivial jokes of Kent *Champagne*, or burgeoning staycation options. To handhold the infantilised public, small increases in temperature were paralleled with the outcome of a four-degree rise in human body temperature.

California too, had had another tough year. Americans could see the graffiti on the wall. Humans woz 'ere, once. The first world was bearing some brunt, and this couldn't be outsourced to African or Asian communities like plastic exports, toxic or e-wastes. This demanded commitment of investment and political action. Any excuse for control.

Was it worth it? That replacement cappuccino maker, the quinquennially-upgraded sofa, the *even flatter* TV, the unread and discarded books, the downloads, the streaming, the glassware, the décor, the year-round asparagus clocking up food miles, the bags of corn and mixed veg, seldom touched but kept at minus 15. The kitchen gadgets *marginally* better than the last. The thousands of acres of data centres fanned cool to traffic endless search engine queries. What is my IP address? How to tie a tie? How many ounces in a cup? When is Mother's Day? How many weeks in a year? What time is it in Malibu? Do penguins have knees? Why is your face on your head? The second car, the second wedding, the fourth child, the third dog, and their enormous concomitant ecological paws. The cheap flights to *another* bridge and design museum, a *slightly different* pastry.

Steven was on his way to meet his friend Andrew at a pub in Notting Hill. It would be busy, but not *central London at Christmas* busy. That should be avoided at all costs – the horrors of workplace parties and out-of-towners, out on the town. Drunk by seven, roaring and screeching by eight, doused, high on discount nosebag and freedom from spouses. Press rewind for a night of noughties fashion, stilettos, bodycon, zebra print, hair gel, rosy flesh and nowhere near enough black. Wrapping paper suits. No good ever came from tequila. Ever. For anyone with any taste and sensibility, zone one was a war zone, a strict no-go from the start of December. January: now that was a choice month to go out.

Two things happened to Steven on the way. He cut through a residential side street with some low hanging trees, and a cobweb consumed his face. Schllooooop. And the bitter cold had created icy spots and he hit a patch, his heels backpedalled, suspended, as his arms went out and each circled for stability. As he landed upright, a thick tingle shot through the soles of his feet, from back to front. Whenever this happened he always recovered, and acknowledged the miracle of the human body.

He entered the tavern, tucked behind Notting Hill Gate. A quick recce to check he had arrived first, and it would be standing room only at a sliver of bar while he waited. After getting attention and being served, he absorbed himself in some digital auditing, while he put away his first beer in hearty gulps. He was happy to knock back a loosener before Andrew arrived, and then they could align themselves anew. An ex who he was still in contact with had got in touch – drinks and some dinner? He smiled at this *friends without benefits* arrangement he had landed himself with, but sure, midweek could work.

Andrew White pushed open and hustled through the small and heavy-sprung doors from another age, fitted long before the world piled on the pounds. Under a three-grand wool coat, Andrew demonstrated the funnelling of fashion toward a fitted shirt and a thin silk tie. Outside of the usual in and out cycles, some elements of style had found their perfect note. Box fresh white trainers, tapered jeans, the white shirt. Here to stay. Blonde, grey eyes, six foot, lean, strong. Exacting, punctilious, gregarious but focused. He knew the world didn't revolve around him; he chose to act *as if it did*. He had a clear image in his mind of how he looked going about his business, as if he were watching this life unfold live from behind a floating drone camera. Watching the delivery at new business pitches, the flirting with powerful clients, the *perfect* career laugh. The old razzle-dazzle.

"Stax, you old rooster."

"Watcha. Pale ale?" Steven checked.

"Yeah. Cheers."

"Let me focus on getting served or we'll be here for hours."

"Sure."

Steven drained the remaining third of his pint so that an empty one sat signalling before him. Still, it took a while. As the beers were left, he tipped the staff with a spare fiver to reduce future waiting time. 'Time *is money*,' he thought, as he weaved across the room and placed their beers on a prized piece of shelving Andrew had managed to sequester.

They shot the shit for a while. Unexceptional. Steven indicated a well-known soap actor sat in the corner with an acquaintance. Don't look. Andrew gave it the full swivel, and didn't know who he was referring to. As in New York, you did see famous people around, if you could call him that.

"How's the sex life?" Andrew probed. Steven's kinder friends would ask how his *love life* was.

"Been on a fair few dates with a Christina," he answered.

"Posh? Been giving her the *good news*?" Andrew asked, and to which Steven answered with the manner of his laugh, an audible puff through his nose, as his eyes smiled while his lips did not.

Steven had a small number of friends in his life who would support each other in their quest for the opposite sex, knowing this to be their best approach for overall peer group success. However, most men couldn't abide the victory of others, and it would be all out mutual destruction, with no winners, save for the women spared. Andrew was Mister Sabotage and wouldn't get near Steven's other halves, except maybe twelve months in and if she were made of stern stuff.

"And... any potential?" Andrew pushed, probing for a weak spot and a *way in*.

"Good looking, fit, smart" Steven began, the physical attributes always kicking things off. This was the natural order of language and male thought, like big fat Greek wedding. He continued with his outline, "sex is good, she's a laugh, good job, good family."

"Forget the good family, everyone's living to a hundred," Andrew declared, "there's no money coming down any longer. No grandparents giving up the ghost at seventy, leaving the forty-five year olds with proper cash. Extensions and conservatories going up all over suburbia. Now the government will have that to pay for the home.

Once the boomers have done their last cruise."

"Better than a bad family, imagine."

"Oh fuck yeah, don't go near one of those, no matter who she is. I'm presuming there's some downsides, which you don't want to go into?"

"Not many," Steven replied, as he gave his head a wobble.

"Are you picking up the tab for everything?"

"No, she's been contributing."

Andrew nodded his approval.

"When they buy rounds and their share of dinners, we can discuss the pay gap. It's natural market equilibrium."

Andrew reverted to Christina.

"Listen, once you start weighing it up – the good, the bad, it's done. If you're talking a proper relationship, at least. You know this. If it's just sex, that's different," Andrew opined. He pressed on, "I know people, you do too, that have weighed things up for years, the balance sheet. Truth is, their partner has good sides, and they don't want to cause them pain and go through all the hassle. But those downsides, they stay downsides."

"I barely know her."

"Doesn't matter."

Steven had no option but to agree with this arsehole. The secret to Andrew's success was neither brains or talent, nor looks. It was his sheer shamelessness, the ultimate attribute anyone can possess in the twenty twenties. He was so thick-skinned; he couldn't be offended. It bounced off. In business this made him a killer. Even Steven in his Sales role would balk at some of the propositions and demands Andrew made of his clients and colleagues. All balls.

"Of course, the best looking available women are the single mums," Andrew offered.

"Yeah, why is that?" Steven asked, not expending any effort delving into the cause, as the stomach filled and the beer fug descended.

"Any childless top grade Group One filly has her pick, and she can go for the superstars; no offence Stax," Andrew declared without pause, "but with a kid or two in tow, they have to bat lower down the order. This is where you come in. I've heard you talk before about your ten attributes."

"Women have their ten for men too," Steven interrupted to underline.

"Kid count is the eleventh factor, which can down-weight a score by twenty points out of a hundred. This is your plight. Some advice..." Andrew paused and supped a couple of times.

Nodding, and turning over his right palm to face up, Steven indicated that he should continue.

"If you do take on a mum, they must be young enough to have one of yours also, and they can have one daughter already. That can work. One of hers, one of yours, you're the man of the family."

While Steven mulled this over, and again, it made annoying sense, Andrew just rolled on to the next topic.

"Oh, Stax," he continued, as he recalled something else, "I was talking with this guy at work earlier, total dick, Carl, you've met him. He mentioned his kid, and I don't have a clue why I asked because I don't care, but I asked how old the kid was," Andrew recounted, beaming.

"He's a twenty-two month old," Andrew declared, laughing in a booming, self-confident manner, surfaced from deep.

"Could have just said two, wanker."

As they chugged back some £7.70 American Pales, Andrew had to confess his mate Rob would be joining for a couple later.

"Oh here we go, conspiracies, the environment, Russia, China, fraudulent voting, state-sponsored doping."

"He's all right," Andrew shrugged, loving being able to land a grenade into Steven's evening.

"Orderer of broosh-etter. Pistash-ee-oh. Paninis, plural."

"You're such a fucking snob. Jerking off over your food blogs."

"Oh, fuck off. You know he's going to have a company backpack, wearing mountain-wear brands, a fleece," and Steven threw his head back and laughed as they ratcheted the volume up and the language down.

Andrew stood up and walked off, and Steven realised he *never* announced he was going to the bathroom. Steven thought this was a good way to go about things and made a note to do likewise.

"All right Steve?" Rob greeted him, having stealthed in, lurking and giving Steven a feeling of unease before he had even taken a seat.

"Steven," he corrected, choosing to refrain from shaking hands.

Steven marvelled that he was one degree of separation from any number of people he couldn't stand. Friends of his good friends, he thought, *should be* pretty sound. Rob was one of many examples he could cite. A media wanker, just like every other white, single-syllable, Gen X/Y Dan, Sam, Matt, Ben, Joe, Jon, Tom, Pete, Will.

Andrew returned, slapped Rob on the back, and enquired about the prevailing chemtrails.

"You can joke, Andrew..."

"Get the fucking drinks in Rob, I'm gasping here."

"Shafted, again," complained Rob as he threw down his snow-gear branded beanie."

"Two of the most expensive beers on the menu."

Rob returned with beer and Firecracker Lobster, Jalapeno and Dill, Aberdeen Angus Beef and Suffolk Ale Ridge-Cut hand-cooked crisps. Andrew and Steven tore open the bags and handed him the floor to regale them with his latest doomsday scenarios. Who knew, but environmental disaster was incoming. There had been a further nuclear situation that had been hushed. Tensions in the East China Sea were concerning. *They* control everything, see? The usual trite whistle-blowers name-dropped in plus a whole bunch of new names, modern day fighters. Drone technologies, the vulnerability of the water supply. An impossible to follow Middle Eastern act before the curtains closed. Andrew enjoyed this theatre, pure entertainment, and applauded the knowledge and taut arguments. The hours of theories gamed out with like-minded souls. Rob was informed on these matters, and the commoner was outmatched. He became exhilarated with the drink. He fizzed, crackled, peaked and troughed with his relentless inner energy, panic, despair. It kept his motor running.

Steven and Andrew had their digs and their laughs, but they knew *some of it* was true, and in the post. And only some of it had to be. 'You heard it here first,' rang in their ears, as he left to meet up with other acquaintances, for more of the same, into the small hours, fuelled by spliffs and paranoia.

"When do you think he last got eight hours sleep?" Steven asked.

After putting away one for the road, they stood, spun their winter coats on, looped scarves, hooked bags over shoulders, and left.

Steven put on some tunes as he walked home, and confirmed he would spend Christmas with his brother and his wife in the country. They didn't have kids and they liked a drink and a smoke. This was against his normal instinct that Christmas was the one time above all others that London quietened down and was bearable. Easy to get around, visitor numbers made sights bearable. The *right* number of people for a city of this scope.

Before the bitter cold forced him to put on gloves, he despatched a few work queries, pushed as many date matches back by a day with a couple of pre-set questions copied and fired off to each, and checked the news before focusing on the push for home on foot. He thought of how Rob viewed the world, and how he could choose to view it through the same prism, or focus on what was in front of him. A bourbon and a movie when he got home, another week's work, dinners. He was late thirties after all, yet the shit seemed to be hitting the fan. The last decade had wound up, and already with each passing year, a multitude of social, health and geopolitical upheavals.

The rawing twenties.

He could relocate, but where could he go? The pressure and heat was universal. Civil wars in civil nations. There was no safety, no shelter of boyhood. He went into a mind hole, running plots, scenarios, the drink prompting him to start a dialogue with himself, aloud, on the quieter stretches. The worse for drink, oblivious to passers-by, should his surveillance let him down. The bright signage of his neighbourhood fast-food joints injected in him a childlike buzz and snapped him out of it, and he turned off the main street for home.

Halfway through a movie, after he poured a second bourbon, tiredness overcame him. The fog of the Christmas run-in descended as he sank the drink and headed to the bathroom. He ran the hot tap over a flannel until it was piping hot and he wiped the day and the night from his face, before applying creams to his face and hands. It would take too long to masturbate, so he turned the radio on and was sleeping like a top within a minute.

The next day after taking measures to ease a dull, flat-lining, lingering hangover, Steven was at home sifting through work when

Christina messaged him. He skimmed the message, aimed at prompting him into making some plans, and he tossed his phone onto the firm sofa beside him, where it landed with a dead cat bounce. They had seen each other a couple of times in the last week or so, a dinner out, and an evening at hers. Christina was keen, Steven not so much, hence his dating of other people, but he *was* keen on the sex they were having. This kept things ticking over while he explored other options. And reset the sex clock each time - how long it had been since the last time. He had been mulling over Christina all week, and would continue that weekend, and he knew he wouldn't be able to desist. The pros, the cons, the balance.

What with work pressures, his mind was busy, churning, figuring out angles, approaches, replaying conversations. How it all fit into the limited plans he had on his direction of travel. These situations and problems washed over him throughout the day as if he were prone on the shore, with the stubborn, existential questions pinning him to the sand. He didn't want to be an employee into his forties, but he couldn't see an alternative. He had no obvious friend or colleague to co-found a business and to figure it out with. Few could go it alone, the first time around. And how could he decide what he wanted in a partner when children at times felt like a natural rite of passage, and at others an exhausting bind. The latter position gaining traction across society as home ownership and career stability seemed intangible concepts. Prior generations bought a home, popped a couple out, and they amused themselves and each other in the neighbourhood.

He was put off when a girl didn't want children, that was for certain, but he couldn't unpick why he felt that way. All his life, he had seen those with clear direction, setting their own clear goals from a young age, go on to succeed. The curious nine-year old who knew the career she wanted, or his friend who dated the same girl over and over until he decided on one.

In his life now, thanks to technology, the sheer choice on offer was dazzling. Tall girls, shorter girls, those in between. Slender, medium build, fuller figure. Postgraduate, bog-standard degree-educated, or out of school earners. Marketers, vets, office managers, caterers, teachers, business owners, finance managers, salespeople, nurses, solicitors, doctors, landscape gardeners, bar staff, interior designers.

CEOs, entrepreneurs, professors.

He could go older or younger, stay in London, meet someone out in the country, someone with family ambitions, someone without. His life could be different for each of these combinations in what was *expected of him*, and the lifestyle each might supply. Tennis players, sailors, walkers, skiers, readers, members of the literati, political animals, crafters, cooks, power-consumers. Somewhere out there was a vegan, non-monogamous former barrister with a helicopter license and alpacas, waiting for their one true love.

He had to form a view as to whom he wanted to date, who challenged him, turned him on, and provoked him in the positive sense. What would the shape of a year look like? To prevent a descent into a new thought hole, he accepted that he'd know when he found her, and the peripherals could be solved or handled. An easy out.

He put his left hand over his face which his thumb below his left eye and pulled down as he looked up and exhaled into his palm.

He wished he didn't feel compelled to check email over the weekend, for when did they ever bring good news? The thirst for the unread suggested new mail might inform of a surprise pay rise, bonus or promotion. Instead, news of the *challenging environment* they were facing [which may affect bonuses if we are to retain all staff], a deal gone south or the promotions of peers. As he connected, a litany of complaints about a project behind schedule ticked down in front of him. People with twenty to thirty years in business, still expecting a project to finish right, on budget, on time. As if that *ever* happened. Wailing about how their business, which had coped for over one hundred years without the service Steven's company provided, but who MUST land this project in March rather than May. Some C-level name dropped in for good measure. Steven knew that if all the delays caused by the customer's inability to provide the information asked of them right and on time, were added together, this would come to... two months. He sipped his metaphorical tea and left it to the project manager to handle this tirade. Another future *detractor* for our Q2 customer score.

His personal desktop computer hummed in the background so that he had to get up and put it to sleep, and the washing machine drove a vacuous gurgle through the pipes connected to the kitchen sink.

Feral children in a neighbouring garden were going wild, in the house which turned over families every year or two, some noisier than others, but all of whom either sold or smoked drugs on the street.

It felt stuffy indoors and he was gasping for fresh air, so he grabbed his winter coat and some headphones and bolted out the door for a Lebanese café around the corner, for a falafel wrap and mandatory *bants*. The shared corridor full of leaflets for pizzerias, cleaning services, airport taxis, Asian takeaways, ironing services. He had heard the door slam several times already that morning, so he figured he would need to pick these up, as per. At least the corridor was bike-free since those upstairs acquired a car.

Turning into Ladbroke Grove, he negotiated a couple of crossroads where it was straightforward to cross on red, the wind and light rain imploring him to do so. A car he recognised from the area had received a parking charge notice, fifty percent off if the money was paid without fuss or delay. Parking restrictions, parking suspensions, controlled zones, permit holders only, temporary cycle lanes, permanent bus lanes. A local shouldn't have been caught out on this one. Perhaps the parking rules were changed that same morning, and the warden came along for the inauguration, to slap the ticket down at 9.01am.

A new car, with a new registration and a green flash on the plate, signalling virtue, was stuck at the lights, waiting to turn right. Steven saw the squared lines, the boxy look, sleek and angular, and moving away from the curvatures or the last five years. A fashion that would bounce back and forth on rotation, forevermore. He closed his eyes into a relaxed squint, turning the car into a blur, and he was able to see how he would view the vehicle in ten years' time. How out of time it would appear. The modern was of its moment, nothing more, and never absolute.

As he strolled on, he passed a young brunette girl with a coat open at the neck, and the perfume of a favourite ex-girlfriend trailed her. He closed his mouth and breathed it in. It was a common scent and he appreciated when new dates wore it as it came with pleasant associations of better days, and superior sex.

He changed his mind on the café as he spotted a new place and steamed in. He ordered a pastrami, cheese and pickle toasted sandwich and a *lartay*. He felt irritable, combustible. Some reminders, nudges had followed him from home; auto-renewing car insurance at a higher cost than last year with an extra year's no claims, plus a response to a request he made to his freeholder. He imagined all the tasks he had to do in his lifetime, for every task he completed, two seemed to appear. At a run rate of thirty small or large tasks a day over a lifetime, he would have half a million tedious, routine, vile pieces of admin to complete.

Two solitary males sat either side of him. They each had small round tables with insufficient elbow and forearm room. Steven could hear the man to his right chewing, before he stopped to suck snot into his head, rather than blow his nose. Steven winced as it happened the first time, and expected this to continue every ten seconds thereafter. He had wanted to sit and slouch, to check some publications, for a change of mind tempo. Now he just wanted to get out of there. To his left, the gentleman had a ballpoint in his hand, and he started to click, second-by-second. There's a reason dog trainers used clickers - it was abrupt, and disruptive to pattern behaviour. The man had headphones on, which incensed Steven further. If the snot cunt wasn't also a problem he'd say something to click fuck, but he didn't want to get punched so stood up, went to the counter and said he'd wait outside. More petty annoyances than he could shake a stick at. He took an outside table in the freezing cold, and scarfed the food under the dirty, frayed awning, unattended to since opening. The daily automation of a familiar homeless girl making her requests interrupted his snack and made him feel queasy with guilt.

He thought he might be able to reset at the Italian bar with an extensive beer selection, a long row of pumps. Cushioned seating, well-spaced tables, attentive but not over-bearing staff, and close to opening time, he should be one of few occupants. He had paced around his flat that morning like a dispirited animal, failing to settle into any one task. Now he had taken to prowling the streets of Notting Hill, unable to find some calm and solace. Unable to escape himself.

It was open, and as he pushed through the doors and selected a favourite pint, he shed his coat in a heap next to him and sat back. The cool alcohol would deaden and sedate his bloodstream. As he quaffed the first third, his head slowed, his brain slumped, and he turned to the women in his life. He set up for Christina to come over midweek. He confirmed a second date with Sophia for Monday. He went long on a first date with a fashion editor, suggesting they chatted toward the end of the week with a view to meeting up the following Sunday. Nothing like an unhurried and nonchalant advance. The pipeline could become overwhelming. He cancelled a couple of conversations which he would have pursued, if he didn't have sufficient better options. Appeal was all relative, as he noted to himself in consolation, whenever he was ditched without word or apology, after having made some positive inroads.

He had been turned down for a second date that week after what he had perceived to be a successful first. It jarred and reminded of prior elbowings. After he had reinitiated contact, he had had a good time, would like to do it again, blah, messages received back began with the positive, "I had a good time too, it was fun," and descended, "but not the best fit for me." This felt a high-low pointed blow. And dominating behaviour.

By the time his second pint was brought over to him, he had got on top of things, and when that was sunk, he took himself home for a nap.

101
CHAPTER 5

Barney at the supermarket: Helen at home: Annabel in bed on Sunday

    Barney left home to drive to the big Sainsbury's as he did by rote each week. Upon arrival, he had to park his modest hatchback a fair clip away from the entrance. Although this did allow him to avoid any difficult manoeuvres, which might get him banged up in a scrape. He had owned the car for some years, and while reliable and cheap to run, it was becoming a mental burden, as he pootled around running the odd errand. That which he might be able to handle on public transport, and thereby reduce his per capita emissions.

    It had been raining throughout the day, yet it seemed to have been amped up upon his arrival, whereat it monsooned onto the windscreen, the wipers stuck in flagrante, mid wipe, once the engine was turned off. He feared giving it five minutes would invite tougher circumstances. He grabbed his shabby, scuffed *Bags for Life* from the passenger footwell, took a few breaths and flung the door open to make a swift exit and bolt for cover. The door swung too hard to its limit and came back on him, and he was held in place, legs and head out, absorbing the rain as he extricated himself from the car's grip. Once free, he slammed the door behind him, zapped a few times with the fading remote key to lock the damn thing, and tugged his jacket up over his head with carrier bags swinging, and ploughed on. This served to expose his midriff chub and he took some water on board.

    As he made it to the entrance he gave a shrug and an expression of inevitability to a huddle of customers gathered outside at the edge of the covered section, like penguins massed on an ice shelf.

    He pulled out his list, ordered by item location so he could snake once through the store, up and down the aisles. Fresh first, meats, dairy, household...

He picked up some loose apples, baking potatoes, mushrooms and peppers, a chilled pepperoni pizza, a few cheeses, lemon surface cleaner, shower gels, branded cooking sauces, rice, pasta, crumpets, some cans of beers and a bottle of wine. Two a day of his five, at most. 'It could be worse,' he muttered to no-one, surveying the beige. If Annabel was coming over, he would buy fresh. Nothing for Jess - he wouldn't feed her mainstream junk, though he never applied those standards to himself.

He moved through the chilled aisles. A cause of discomfort, where his clothes were wet, and they blasted him with their icy ecological footprint. When Barney felt hot or cold, he thought of heat.

The household products aisle with its heavy plastic and bright branding, seeming to both scream their brand for recognition and also signal warning as with a bee or exotic serpent. Their dangerous contents exclaimed and underlined by a cross in orange and black. The toxic envirohorrors of the micro-crystal, the wet wipe destined for a trip from anus to fatberg, and that old staple, the aerosol. He harked back to innocent days. Days of CFCs and two-star leaded petrol, where the masses thought that a few changes would suffice.

His choice beers came in cans conjoined by a solid plastic holder which looked dense, tough, single-use. Their grainy, matt finish with their colourful design weighed on his mind – the processes and compounds which would have gone into putting those together so that he could enjoy a lazy armchair drink. Bottles were heavy and weight cost in freight, and he knew nothing of how they were created or the recycling percentages of each. He selected the bottled beers he liked less and would research at home to make an informed decision next time. He expected going to the pub for a kegged beer would be the best option, but couldn't face it that evening.

He queued for the cashier he knew to be amiable, despite the longer line, and stood behind a well-dressed man around his age, who followed every move the cashier made and fidgeted with his feet. The man wore an expensive-looking piece of wearable tech on his tanned and hairy wrist, onto which Barney could see a bright green light being projected, flickering, at a constant rate. He figured this was taking measurements of his physical condition, as he queued for his oat milk and raspberries. Millions of trackers all beaming away throughout the day, needing a charge from the mains at night. Fuel. Heat. Everywhere. After the man hurried off to maximise his output, Barney swapped pleasantries and smiles with the Sales Assistant, sufficient enough to show her he cared, but stopping short of annoy his pursuing queuers. They too had their maximum outputs to chase. The guilt of the automation forced upon her felt heavy on him, but he preferred she had work than he adopt self-scanning, and the economy had extra labour units to redistribute, into bleaker circumstances.

He left and ran through the pouring rain, and after some fumbling, sprang the boot, dumped his bags and got into the driver's seat, where he blew his nose and made a poor attempt to wipe dry his glasses. He wrestled his phone from the left pocket of his wet jeans, and chucked it on the passenger's seat where it collected white dog fur and specks of mud. He sighed, left it, and drove home for a reset.

He opened his front door within the shared corridor and Jess was sat in front of him, eyes fixed on his for a mere moment, before she moved forward toward the food. After the food had been assessed, she fussed around his legs and sprang up with her paws, until he encouraged her down, upon which he crouched to greet her.

Barney's aunt had chosen Jess as a puppy to keep her company and to improve her own wellbeing. When her own health deteriorated, Barney promised during her last days to give Jess a good home. He had felt a darkness in the animal, uprooted and unmoored from the company of her devoted owner, and the upheaval of her routines. They had no choice to better understand, to seek therapy. Dogs found a way to adjust.

He paid a retired neighbour to look after Jess the few days a week he needed to be in the office. Otherwise, the routine she needed gave some structure to Barney's evenings and weekends, and helped fill some long days when he had no plans.

The relentlessness of the schedule did become testing after a few years. The walks, the feeding, the water bowl replenishments, the vet visits, the grooming, the pet shop trips, the treat-giving, the long walks, the same short walks. To Barney, dogs were life-enhancing, with the odd horrendous exception; the moment she was out of sight for a little too long, when she found shit to roll in.

He slept better since Jess arrived, and he considered that his mind switched off with an intruder warning system. Though he could be startled if she heard something and went wild in the middle of the night.

Jess missed her one previous owner for some time, but she was young when things changed, and that was behind her now. Always forward-looking, she was dedicated to Barney, and the comforts, exercise and food he supplied.

Jess swarmed around Barney forming a picture of his movements from his scent map. He had been in the car, wherever the shopping came from, and hadn't met with anyone she recognised. The smells of those she knew were no stronger now than when he left earlier. He had passed roasted rotisserie chickens, cheese, and fish.

Switching his computer on, Barney sat down to find out what he could about cans and bottles. He wasn't surprised to find the usual toss-up between ocean waste, production and transportation fuel, degradation rates and recycling costs. There was no immediate, clear winner from an independent source, inasmuch as independence was possible. It wasn't. He cast a suspicious eye over bodies and their research, their motivations and funding sources, recalling that seminal courtroom moment of the sixties and *'he would, wouldn't he?'*

He huffed and resolved to do some digging later that evening on that and related matters, and figured if he could decide upon a small lifestyle improvement that would make some difference, then that would be something.

It had cleared up a little outside and Jess watched Barney change into something dry and weather appropriate, some mid-range department store staples. An animal logo, neither a horse nor a crocodile.

After Barney issued the 'walk' clarion call to Jess, there followed the low, rolling thuds of paw on floor as she scamped toward him. She presented her neck to speed things up and held still, hoping Barney wouldn't start getting fuddled and slow progress. The big walk at the start of the day had extracted much of the energy stored within her terrier cells, to calm her for the day ahead. They could stick with the local park for the mid-afternoon outing.

They executed the oft-practiced, choreographed manoeuvre to leave the flat, and Barney held his breath as he walked past his neighbours' front door, omitting even when closed a damp odour and stale cigarette smoke.

On this drab, dreary day in North London, and with Christmas and New Year in the rear view, the time had come for dieting, cutting back, saving, re-joining the health club, making smoothies. In theory, the one time in the year for *less*. Instead, the advertising messages and consumption demands shifted. Gym rats and bunnies the country over groaned at the annual pasty porcine influx, hogging machines and swilling in hairy sweat.

Helen Steele, like many, had put on some weight over the holiday season, as she did every year, and this year, as ever, she would lose it by the end of January, but fill herself with concern in the meantime. She was never her ideal weight, always *a little over*. Yet if she put on too many pounds, she would feel uncomfortable, and her unconscious reflex was to cut back until she felt good in herself again.

As she looked down onto the street from the main bay window, a dumped, lifeless Christmas tree. She visualised the couples she had passed in the street weeks before, carrying a tree and shopping between them, excited for the holidays. The contrast, the purity of the waste.

It had rained on and off all week, but the winds had whipped up, providing a soundtrack beat of the large raindrops hitting trees and outdoor furniture, whereupon an occasional hard gust would push a sheet of rain from the side onto her living room windows with a splat. Her home was a common or garden Victorian conversion flat, and not one of the better ones. Despite the footprint they were thankful to have adequate light, high ceilings, and a window in the bathroom. It could be a lot worse. Those who weren't *top earners* in London (AKA people with a staircase) could choose between living on top of each other in a poky flat, vacating to Zone four plus, or even south of the river with that riskiest, most disruptive transport mode, the train.

Her other half, Phil, had gone out with friends, and she had decided to do some sorting, some tidying, some auditing. Throw out some clothes, question the levels of joy.

A common way to spend a January day, repeated year after year. How she thought they would have children by now. How she thought they would still have a decent sex life. It was never an adventurous one, but it was nice enough.

'Nice enough,' she thought, looking down. Now it happened every month or so, when it felt like it had been too long. Although not discussed, neither of them wanted to be the couple that *never* had sex, and Helen at least had this card to play when necessary with some girlfriends. Helen estimated that ten times a year put her above the median of her social circle. She got to hear about it, because *people told her things*. The tiredness, the children, the exhaustive duties, the evening bottles of wine to transition from sofa to slumber without any threat of rumpy-pumpy. The existence of two people who continued to see each other naked, slept next to each other, but just didn't want it any longer. With each other. The sex toys used while partners were away, wanking in business hotels or at the office. Tims and Sarahs, Daves and Claires, Emmas and Staceys, Teds and Mikes, Dans and Martas, Denislavs and Gabriellas, Dales and Sandras. Getting into bed without fuss, making the right tired noises. Quick read, lamp switched off.

"Night."
"Night. Sleep well."
"You too."
Flatmate zone.

Helen went to her wardrobe, bursting with squashed and crumpled garments. Storage space was a constant battle, especially without a garden. They now operated a strict one-in-one-out policy on furniture, kitchen appliances, electrical items, plants; anything with a square footprint, shoes included. Nothing threatened domestic balance like *the new hobby*. Pilates rubber pick'n'mix, racket sports, art and crafts, slow-cooking, camping gear, ski garb. Bikes.

She dreamed, not of walk-in wardrobes, but of a mere half an inch between items, so something she liked could hang free, un-creased. She dug into the melee, testing herself on when she last wore something, whether she was still comfortable in it, would she wear it again? A small pile began to form. Thoughts interrupted her, the jacket her sister liked. Her sister. They needed to speak, she could call her now, get it out of the way. Or later, it could take a while. Then Phil would return and she wouldn't have got anything done. Except Phil could be out until all hours if he's out with those mates. He stayed out longer than he used to. Her sister. Clothes, Helen. Her thoughts swirled in loops. She needed to eat something, so wanted to know if they would get a takeaway, or did she need to cook? Should she eat light now, have a snack? "Jesus, Helen, stop," she chastised herself out loud.

Helen thought she would speak to Phil later about doing some sorting himself. She thought through how she'd open the conversation, or just move into it after asking how his day was. 'I've thrown out quite a bit of stuff today, you should have a look through your stuff?'

A mumbled response, 'Yeah, could do, later.'

How could she manoeuvre 'later' from 'never' to 'at this specific time in the near future?'

Helen entered another thought hole, gaming this conversation through to its natural conclusion – the same argument. The one about energy and motivation, maturity. Whether it was about going out for a meal, the household, time with friends, division of labour, it all swung around to the same thing. She could scenario this conversation with accuracy, she had thought it through that many times.

'Stop!' she again called out to herself, questioning why she was allowing herself to become wound up, tight, from simple thoughts. She had to figure out how to desist; it felt like it was burning through her brain cells, her wiring. That this would slow her down long term, like a worn-out laptop that took forever to get going.

'Can't it *just stop*?' she thought, and then said the words to herself as she put her hands on her thighs and leaned forward. Concentration at work was one thing; the endless dog-whistles and re-prioritisation of tasks. But home life shouldn't turn into the same battle. She gave herself five minutes to bag some clothes, then would crack through her must-dos and cover off family and plans for tonight. And get an hour to turn everything and everyone off and do some reading.

On Sunday morning, Annabel woke from a recurring dream about her father. It was never the same dream but variations on a theme. She would be trying to tell him what she had done that day at school, and the words wouldn't come. He would be playing with one of her sisters, or in the middle of something, in the garage, the garden, his study. She would stand there trying to force it out, mute. He might mutter, 'Out with it, Annabel,' or words to that effect.

A dream like this could stay with her all morning, not replaying in her thoughts, but affecting her mood, becoming the negative background music to her day.

A day that was not planned ahead of her, a relief for many city dwellers who were at it hard all week, working their thirty-five to sixty hours, depending on fortune. Commuting up to fifteen hours, travelling overseas and overnight, and filling in all the administrative gaps around and in between. The sheer breadth of options manifest within a large city for each individual with their own menu of things to observe, experience and consume across any given year. For those less active, it may be a list of ten things: cinema, pubs, the lido, park walks. For the energetic extremes, this may be a list of a hundred - beyond the fundamentals, the pottery classes, the wild swimming, the charity trusteeship, the ballet, barre Pilates, occasional touch rugby, an interest in cryptocurrency or NFTs, plus all the seasonal events, and on, and on.

For each of these items, the frequency and depth of engagement and time expended, adding next the element of change, how these flexed over time, as interests gathered and waned, or from seasonality. These rotated throughout the year. Restaurants perhaps each week, theatre once a month, weights three times a week, attending a choral performance every six months. The total activities a reflection of one's natural, genetic energy and drive, the exertions and demands of work, partners and children, and the enthusiasm one had, depending on how they felt the world was working out for them, or not.

Annabel's mix of twenty included more talks, fewer gigs, stable cooking, fewer work-related weekend charity events, less time dating, rare (yet stable) theatre trips and museums, to name a handful. She would run through her mix list and conjure something for the day ahead.

Throwing on some jeans, a sweatshirt and a big coat, she grabbed her purse and brute forced herself out the door for coffee, morning goods, the left-wing newspaper and one of the right-wing ones.

Within ten minutes she was back in bed, naked, ready to re-fuel and do some world-watching. After shedding the papers of packaging, flyers and ad pull-outs, and low-rent travel brochures, she had her ready pile. The *bad* news was extensive. *Rail companies cancelling trains at a record rate. Woman held after baby death. Man stabbed to death in nightclub. Men charged with people trafficking. Animals seized in welfare raid. Bullying and harassment revelations. Kidnapped daughter investigation. Lawman savaged online. Intensive Care wards see patients spill onto corridors. Party sex scandal trial begins. Anti-Semitism crisis, major data breaches, demands for better funding for community services, victims failed by inquiry. Election interference, diversity problems within our national institutions. Toxic traffic fumes, waste incinerators impacting the poorest, rhino poaching, coastal flooding from expected sea-level rises.*

She slurped her coffee from the takeaway cup, which gave her pause. And fingered a pain au chocolate, the flakes dropping on her duvet. Stickiness that made her have to go and wash her hands.

Returning, and with serious matters out of the way, she moved onto the fripperies. Restaurant reviews and their metaphorical nonsense: the punctuation-shaped offal, foodstuffs which shattered or dished out a happy-slapping. Slow-cooking their personal journey for the reader, week-by-week. First-world problems sent into an auntie in agony. My life in driving, my life in food, a day in my life. Me, me, me.

A double-spread: The Top Ten Leaf Blowers.

The news compounded how unsettled she felt. Annabel didn't mind feeling out of sorts when it had one root cause. However, there were several things at play, overlapping, and she had no way to decouple and understand the relative contribution of each to her pain, and where she should focus corrective efforts. She felt queasy.

She hadn't had sex for three months and had been experiencing a wave of horniness that week. It came after a few weeks without, then would dissipate, then return a couple of months later. It would pass in a week or so; it wasn't summer after all. As she flicked through the final lifestyle section, she came across an article on threesomes and recalled a boy from a distant holiday in France, failing to persuade her and her friend. She reached down and imagined that scenario unfolding in the heat. With her, but not him. He didn't have it. She substituted another in for him. A quickie, for the relief. It took her little longer than a minute. As she came, she kept her eyes closed, tilted her head back, bit her lower lip and curled her toes. She lay motionless for thirty seconds, then threw back the duvet and sprang out of bed to get on with her day.

110
CHAPTER 6

Annabel sensory overload: The waters aisle: Annabel hosts Helen midweek

A month beyond the shortest day, the night began in mid-afternoon, haunting the populace, who locked away the joy of long days, for several months each year. The next hours saw an inexplicable paralysis to the streets of west East London, within mundane midweek, with no obvious cause.

As Annabel stepped off the bus, her small feet splashed in a shallow puddle which had formed alongside this smart bus shelter, self-illuminated, with the next bus times ticking over. The doors hissed shut, like a shaken up bottle of pop, trapped shut before opening. The next bus that could take her the stops remaining to her destination was twelve minutes away, so she opened her small black umbrella and it popped and fanned open to cover her for the short walk. The traffic was heavy, and she took care to stay away from the roadside and to sweep ahead to spot for large bodies of water, which might be tyred, and crash over her ankles, knees or worse.

The lights came at her, from oncoming buses, cars, motorbikes, lampposts, traffic lights and zebra crossing beacons. Cyclists approached in lines, their bright white rapid fire lighting, harsh and dazzling. This made her look down. She saw a bright green image of a bicycle icon floating and jumping in front of her, projected by a bike coming up on her shoulder. A well-lit urban environment was important for her general personal safety, yet in mitigating risk of a physical assault, she instead received a visual one. The traffic was backed up, and she left the bus behind, unable to pull out, rooted. Horns were parped and words were exchanged from windows wound down by inches, to allow expletives to flood out, but little rain to pepper in. The puttering of cars idling away for minutes on end, their exhausts shaking with a low hum as they puffed their fumes. Mopeds zigged and zagged their way in between the static traffic streams, the riders heaving and weaving through, with their precious farinaceous cargo. On their way to grateful young families, the rotund single, the sexless coupled, and gaming stoners. A pointless cacophony, to little end. And the aural attack on her senses to go with the light show.

Everywhere she looked, she saw fuel. Down at the exhausts, up to the lit advertisement in the bus shelter, the flashing bus times, the bus destination signs, the engineered doors and ramps, the vehicles burning themselves out, heading for scrap. Litter bins emptied by the local authority van crew, street lighting maximising safety, but at what social cost. Electric cars and now bicycles. H.G. Wells turned in his grave. Her head low, a discarded white plastic coffee lid winked up at her from an earthy corner atop a low wall. London felt filthy right then, and it was a relief that it was cold, for these thoughts came darker in the heat. Regardless, in her head she saw the blazing heat of the Middle East deserts, that most masculine piece of destructive engineering, the pumpjack, wanking its raw seed from the earth. Everything polluting, nothing ever cleaning.

A delivery driver tried to sneak through and clipped a wing mirror. The driver went to open the door and get after him in disgust, but got in a tangle. Annabel turned away, focused straight ahead and ran a short while to get away from what might be a wrong time and place. Aggressive situations that brewed in nightclubs in her youth had never left her, when a spiralling ball of violent men formed and sprawled, looming to overwhelm her group. She took flight at the sign of any trouble involving strangers. There were her female friends, tough, who wouldn't shy, but she couldn't control a physical situation like she could a political one.

'Know your limits,' she reminded herself. The possibility of a kerfuffle of doors and bodywork, of fists on wet helmets, of verbal abuse, she left behind.

The shopping centre gave shelter, but the bright white interior dazzled her, as she shook off her umbrella and went into the hypermarket for some staples. After which she would pick up some prepared salads and cheese from delis closer to home, for Helen's visit that evening. Annabel's sister called and the timing, without preamble or forewarning, made Annabel take the call. She checked there was no emergency and said she'd call back in an hour when she was at home, and was that OK? It was. She was relieved but wary of further stresses in the post, snoozed for one hour. She tried to deal with things there and then, but she longed for home and to get settled in.

Annabel stood immobile in the waters aisle. The glaring strip lighting was harsh and penetrative against the white floors, the white ceiling and the light grey walls of shiny bottled water. She was staggered by, and in awe of the choice available to her for the most basic commodity. Still water, sparking water, soda waters, tonic waters, light waters, full fat waters, vitamin waters, *smart* waters, hydration waters, magnesium waters, fruit flavoured waters, Scottish waters, English waters, French waters, Italian waters, Fijian waters. Plastic bottled waters, glass bottled waters, canned waters, 24 packs, 12 packs, 6 packs, 4 packs, single waters, 2L, 1.5L, 1L, 800ml, 750ml, 600ml, 500ml, 375ml, 300ml, 250ml, 24 x 150ml, 6 x 250ml, full price waters, discounted waters, pallet-stacked waters, screw-top waters, flip-top waters, cylindrical bottles, squared bottles, smooth bottles, ribbed bottles, thin bottles, fat bottles. Dizzying brands. Buxton, Highland Spring, Sainsbury's, Evian, Nestle Pure, Volvic, San Pellegrino, Harrogate, Aqua Pura, Ocean Spray, Nexba, Perrier, Dash, Hildon, V, Glaceau Smartwater, Schweppes, Fever Tree. And the combinations of type, format, size, brand. Putting aside blue for still, green for fizz, and the exotic flavours, they were unrecognisable to a consumer in a blind test. For a product delivered just fine out of the tap. Of course, she knew what purpose all this differentiation served. As it ever does; to move money from the person to the corporation, from pockets to dividends.

Conflicted and scarred by a streak of self-hatred, Annabel herself had a favourite. Evian 1L. Crisp, clear taste, good size. Four bottles filled her lower bedside drawer.

She picked a bottle of Sainsbury's 1L soda water, 60% cheaper than the near identical branded product, and fled to check herself out of the self-service tills. She felt the crush of the world closing in on her, thudding her with their relentless messages. How many bags? No bags. She imagined the machine spitting at her, 'Scan it yourself bitch, you're all checkout slaves now', as its cousins were being developed for war, prepared for termination. Unexpected item in the bagging area. The red hazard went off, but the ringmaster was occupied. Automation, technology, all speeding up the rate the planets resources were sucked from the earth, consumed and trashed.

The young man came over to help, and with a flurry of screen work, this human repetition, she was free. He acknowledged her but without a smile, as he sped around to others needing help.

"Have a nice evening, look after yourself," he replied. 'Cute,' he thought, as he watched her gather her things, turn and leave.

Back at her place, after putting things away and readying herself for Helen's arrival, Annabel poured white Italian into a tall glass, wide around the middle, then fizzed in some soda and plunked in three cubes of ice. They gave that low pitched wobble as they splashed about in the glass before settling. She tilted her head to one side over the glass and swirled its contents around, enjoying the sound. Anticipating that they might get through a few bottles, she opted for the hydration support of the spritzer.

She put on a movie she had stopped midway through earlier that week, and tried to press on. A woman lay in bed at night next to her husband, and the moon and outdoor lights lit up her room, and she woke with a start, bolting straight up and gasping. She'd had a nightmare. She got up and dressed herself, and left her husband asleep without stirring. People slept in the dark and they woke from bad dreams by opening their eyes. And no-one slept through their partner leaving. So lazy, and they had a budget. She turned it off within a minute, dismayed. The mopeds and the lights returned as she considered whether to put the radio on, try streaming something, do some stretches, read. This endless restlessness that had taken hold of her dog whistled her attention here and there, all day long. She reverted to Twitter for the umpteenth time, somewhere she went once for humour and joy, and now for misery and division.

She levelled the glass so the cold wine mix ran to the back of her throat and she took a long glugged slug. This wouldn't help her concentrate on a book or a magazine, but it would turn off some of the noise, slow the whirr. Her head felt soothed, as if the wine had soaked straight through to her brain. Immediate, cocaine hit speed. Although overall a depressant, that joyful first glass, first pint. People turned to drink for a reason. As they do drugs, from which she had only (herself) had positive experiences. She knew herself to be fortunate on that one. If she listed the best ten nights of her life, most were drug nights. Although long behind her, she replayed these times with pride and delight.

Her family began to whirl around her head as it spun, as she put the radio on and an American new wave hit from the past came on. When it was replaced by mainstream grunge, she switched off and called her sister, feeling she could either despatch her within twenty minutes now or an hour tomorrow. Helen gave her the out she needed. Call with an out, or create one. She listened to her sister whine, dropping in the requisite acknowledgments and recognitions. Trying to make minimal noise, she went about things in the kitchen, nudging her own life on a few tiny steps, pouring herself a bigger wine, and muting herself every time the drink made her belch. She pretended Helen had arrived and had to go, and left her sister a hot mess.

The shrill of the old London doorbell in Annabel's hallway startled her with a jolt, as it did every time no matter how much she expected it. She could change it for something softer, but it was classic, iconic. A sound of the town. Annabel opened the door to a soaked Helen.

"Oh no, come in, I'll get you a towel!"

Annabel darted off while Helen struggled out of her boots and coat, dropping her bag to the floor, and shovelling an umbrella into the corner, half open and sagging.

"It wasn't too bad when I left home, and it's just chucked it down."

"Give me a hug then," implored Annabel and she threw her arms around Helen. They squeezed a few times and separated as Annabel told Helen she would be given a drink, and disappeared into the kitchen.

"Here's the bumf you wanted me to drop off," said Helen, as she dumped a brochure and some articles she had kept for Annabel. Trad.

"Chuck it on the dining table," Annabel advised, before checking, "white wine spritzer OK?"

"That'll do," Helen confirmed as she went through to the kitchen, where she leant back on the counter. Annabel poured the soda and unshackled ice cubes.

They clinked glasses and met eyes, "Cheers."

"Cheers."

They went through to the lounge and put their drinks down, and Helen let herself flop hard onto the sofa.

Annabel made the call to expunge Helen's problems, to break her down like Commando training, allowing for a rebuild, and a couple of fun hours later in the evening. She felt guilty for having coping strategies to handle Helen. She muted the TV and turned *6 Music* on, hoping to get thirty minutes of decent output before they played something jarring. Once Helen had unloaded, Annabel could relocate them to the kitchen to prep food and change gears.

"Root cause?" Annabel asked, reverting to *workese*. "Cau*ses*?"

"Work's been shocking this week, home keeps ticking along. Home home is no better, with dad. Money's tight, I haven't had a holiday since March last year. I've fallen out with my sister again, I want to move. That enough for you? I forget things, I'm always behind, and I can't focus. Thoughts thrashing around my head, morning, noon and night. I haven't been to my gym classes enough."

"You can only do one thing at a time, so you need to work on your focus and cut distractions. Make time for the gym, it always makes you feel good. Write down some goals for the next few months. And see the doctor if you keep forgetting things. Early onset and all that."

Helen laughed.

Annabel choked on her own advice, as she dished out a plan which she would do well to follow herself, to someone oblivious of the inherent hypocrisy.

"I'm not as organised as you."

"Just write a short list of things to do each month, which will focus you on ticking them off. If you get half of them done, that's progress. Life is just a giant list of steps. Tick some off each month, *jobus donus*."

"God loves a trier. I suppose."

"How's your mum and dad?" Annabel ventured, braced.

"We're trying to get them to move to the coast," replied Helen, wincing at the reminder, "better air for their breathing."

Their breathing. Both of them.

Annabel sensed the reticence to continue and steered away.

"Why do old people head to the sea? I guess it means they just have to worry about what's lurking one side of them, instead of all around. Halves the risk when out and about."

When at the coast, Annabel would watch the breaking waves, whispering her mortality. In sinister English seaside towns, with their hushed criminality, the tides that would ebb and flow long after she was grounded. To the sea, she was never, ever, even there.

"How's Phil?"

"He lost the fucking car in a multi-storey last week; he asked for help at information, he thought they might track it or something. They told him to look harder. Took him half an hour."

Helen laughed but the drops that collected in her eyes and would not fall, formed from some greater loss.

"I don't want to be childless, Annabel. What am I going to do?"

"Talk to him, make him make up his mind, tell him you need this. Or else..." Annabel paused and angled her face, "he'll have to go out on the pull again."

"Imagine!" Helen exclaimed.

The baby lock. Helen looked at Annabel, needing comment.

"Timeline, Helen, deadlines. I'm going to set you a deadline to set him one."

Helen nodded. Her woes continued their world tour, and received consistent responses from the audiences. Was it within her power to listen?

They went through to the kitchen, poured drinks, cracked open the beige snacks, dished up cheeses and salads.

Annabel ferreted about to take a step back from Helen, and lamented having to toss the latest bag of rotten spinach in the bin, bought two days prior. Her principle food annoyance, along with honking fish fillet plastic.

Annabel grilled asparagus to serve with hot butter.

'Fresh food,' thought Helen.

"Did you hear about Sam and her friend's wedding?" Helen asked, referring to her boss. "She's going to be a bridesmaid, at forty-four!"

"Oh god, that's so funny. Bridesmaids should be no older than twelve, it should be the law. Hope to see some pictures. Toe-curling. The traditional wedding, isn't that over with yet?"

"Apparently not," Helen confirmed.

"Occasionally. O*cc-as-ion-al-ly*, I have been able to attend a wedding of a genuinely sweet couple who want to share their happiness with their favourite people. Largely though, it's a marketing event. Either the couple themselves, creating and pushing their new shared brand, or it's family PR. Look at the wonderful families we have, haven't we done well? Pah. The last wedding I was at, my friend elbowed me when the bride was coming down the aisle and said the bride shagged her boyfriend at university. And the one before that, I know from multiple sources, the bride had a threesome with one of the bridesmaids and another bloke."

Helen was chuckling away into her wine, and came close to seeing it disappear up her throat and down her nose. She cried out, "Classy!" and they both lost it.

"How's Lydia?" Helen asked, giggling while they recovered.

Lydia had realised the upper middle class dream. The large house in outer South West London. Large. Second home in France, a Porsche wagon. Many iterations of home extensions, multi-bi-fold doors, a summer house, rear roof terrace, walls of *Pale Hound*. Coordinated labradoodle. When Annabel last saw her, she wore expensive-looking calf-length, light green suede boots, signalling a different level of expense. They went with very little. £2,400 for five outings.

However, she did fail, and that was what Helen was after.

Lydia had London covered for a decade, in her back pocket. However, the Tiger Mums had landed, blessed with superior resources, and a pure untrammelled determination, the likes of which Lydia had seen in few competitors. Ice picks for elbows. This compressed demand even harder in the top schools, and pressed upon her a devastating rethink. But what Annabel was able to recount for Helen was the selection of the puppy. Sent photos of the young pups, Lydia and her 2.4 children (third on the way) made their selection.

Annabel explained that the dog breeder set her straight.

"That's not how this works; you come and meet the puppies, and we see how you get on."

"Yes, yes, yes. But we want *that one*."
"Cheers to them!" Helen wooped.

Annabel put dinner together.
"I haven't seen Barney to speak with all week. Any new mixed metaphors?"
"Like the project that became a nest of worms? He did mention his sister and her husband were going through a new round of UVF."
Annabel poured fuel, then remembered, "We were at the garden centre last week, where he asked if the indoor plants could go outdoors? He put forward a scrambled argument about suitability to English conditions. But he was reaching."
"So funny. I'll bring that up when I see him."
"Someone at the park told him they'd lost their dog and he asked if they had placed a notice on this or that site, put up posters. It had died. I wish people wouldn't use euphemisms for dying. We lost our mum. She passed away. Unless it's done properly - he circled the drain for days, before he kicked the bucket. If I die, Helen?"
"You *will* die. No if about it. Annabel's in a better place."
"They'll think I'm in the Seychelles. Got canxed."
"I could do with a couple of weeks in the baking sun," Helen reiterated.
"I'd lie there soaking up the heat, while my brain played a movie reel of images of forest fires. I'd find it hard to enjoy, like having sex while the dog's farting," Annabel offered, remembering an ex.
"Dog poo bags are the latest thorn in his side. The mountains of bagged up shit piling up each day, the millions of warm, scrotal sacks. Sealing their contents, unable to decompose."
"Yes, that's a problem."
"I said they were exported, unwrapped and segmented by hand. And he looked at me affronted. He didn't know if I was making it up, and I didn't know if that would be a better net solution."
Helen surrendered, "I cannot think about all that at the moment, I have too much on my plate, so if you and Barney with your simple lives can figure some of that out and let me know. Things just seem to get worse and worse. Nothing changed after the pandemic..."
"Bad flu seasons."

"Bad flu seasons. We had all that time to reflect, and everyone just waited for it to pass. That and nine-eleven, the two moments in my life when *things have changed forever, life is never going to be the same again*, blah blah blah," Helen ranted, flapping a hand in the air, putting away a good swallow, before continuing.

"It couldn't be more the fucking same. Any fucking more the same. However you say that. Landfill, forest fires, plastics, fracking, mass extinction, rhinos under armed guard. I despair. On a long enough timeframe, it all happens. Nuclear war, killer robots."

While Annabel went to the bathroom, Helen reached over for a newspaper, announcing 'TRANS ROW' on the front page. As she brought it closer, she read 'TRAINS ROW' and chucked it back and huffed. As Annabel returned, too quick to have washed her hands, Helen thought.

They were becoming quite drunk, and as tended to happen, Annabel drifted to her father.

"Dad got another new car the other day, and he's going on about how green it is, all proud of himself, doing his bit etc. He'd be helping if he didn't buy a new car every three fucking years. Imagine the energy and resources used in mining, transportation of parts, all that R&D, so that something happens without him having to press a button," and as she began a new despair list, she just ran out of steam.

She stopped to knock back some drink and turn up the music. They moved onto their youth, and Annabel gave Helen a schooling in hard drugs.

"What I imagined drugs to be when I was young, disorientating, numbing, fracturing. Weed, coke, pills, not like that. Weed I suppose, if you'd already been drinking. Ketamine, that's the one. I took it once in a bedroom at a house party, and was unable to get down the stairs. LIMBS UNRESPONSIVE! Conversation not forthcoming. A lot of standing around, waiting."

"Doesn't sound worthwhile," Helen checked, raising an eyebrow.

"It is," she confirmed, as they both laughed.

They sat in the kitchen, getting colder with the hours, until Helen's mouth was so dry she knew to be on her way, and ordered a car to leave.

They exchanged goodbyes as they hugged.

"Enjoy your Sunday, text me when you get home."
"Will do. Thanks for everything," said Helen as she walked away.

Annabel didn't drift off. She lay there turning and churning, listening to the town sounds. The strangles of foxes outside, the random huddle of two people a few doors down, drinking or dealing. A helicopter passed overhead and hovered for some time, locating a miscreant, whose trail had been lost. She thought of flies on the car windshield when they drove to the coast as a girl, and when she counted daddy long legs with her brother. Which switched her to her family, and the angst of middle-class middle England. What to do tomorrow. Some nagging work thing that she knew couldn't wait until Monday. Her list for the weekend, and it was Wednesday. It would end up a long night.

CHAPTER 7

Simon at home: Business and wider interests: Simon calls Francesca: Escort delivery

Simon Knight *(Borough, CEO/Entrepreneur/Investor, Claude Bosi at Bibendum, Tom Ford)* stood still, smoking on the wraparound balcony of his top floor apartment, taking in the three-sixty views. The City of London on one side, and with a short walk along the decking, The Shard, glowing in horizontal bands, strips of harsh white light. He faced the green glow of Tower 42 and its financial neighbours, dotted with acne lights. From a specific spot one could catch St. Paul's if one leaned into the corner, something he never pointed out; too desperate.

This London, overseen and managed by his people, his high net worth network. Even if his capital was laughable to the global ultras, who owned and ran the place. He would need to marry into wealth like that, and he had tried. Not easy; the first hundred million was the hardest, before one even got into the right conversations, let alone drew in the heiresses, who were surrounded by those who already had it.

He thought of the financiers or bankers, working that minute on the Americas. The consultants pulling all-nighters on that Friday evening, in pursuit of more. More. Oh, sweet more.

It was a bitter evening, but he had always enjoyed smoking in the cold. A trip to New York in December, where he could duck out for a draw and cool himself away from the heat of the hustle and throng. The smoke balanced and soothed on its way down. He handled his cigarette in a number of ways, and when alone, liked to form an 'OK' sign with his left hand, using two fingers to meet the thumb, in between which he would pinch the Lucky Strike and pull the smoke in a long breath, air hissing between his fingers. Nasty. The ice air cooled the heat from the smoke as it filled his lungs, like an ice bong his nephew might enjoy. As he took his hand away, he held it six inches from his face and observed the fading orange glow at the end. Fiery orange dappled with black points. He didn't flick off the ash; he let it build so as to tap it off a handful of times across his smoke, rather than give off any nervous, compulsive signal to the world. For it was always watching. People like him, alert to all signals. The air still, he exhaled and watched the smoke jet out ahead, widening, before being swept up, rising and separating.

In his early fifties and with three business exits behind him, a highest achiever, with all the companion trappings, peccadilloes and indulgences. That he had played his cards right, there was no doubt. But what cards. Born on third base. To successful parents, both lawyers and then entrepreneurs themselves, handed the genetic gifts afforded by such breeding lines: IQ, pure ambition, vigour, natural charisma, easy charm, and the classic and dark looks of someone women sense would be hot in the sack. Ready to spoil, spank and soil, in equal measure.

Given all the resources one could hope for to get ahead, the shared experiences of an immediate and extended family and friend networks, mixing him with the elite from toddlerhood. The predictable educational journey this background determined. And being around all that business from such a young age, picking up things over breakfast, that most take years to cotton on to, via painful career *first attempt in learnings*. An arc of long-term failure was unthinkable. To fail in youth at all, where success across the board was in one's control, likewise.

He leaned forward on the balcony railings, stomaching the cold, finishing his tab. He had light brown hair, parted to one side and with length at the back, cut every few weeks by a mobile stylist at his home. Blue eyes fading to light hazel at the edges, set straight. He held everyone's eyes, unflinching. The unwavering gaze of a lawyer. His nose was a tad off centre, yet this signalled a rugby injury and boosted his appeal. His one complaint, and this was beyond his influence, was that he stood at five foot eleven. This continued to make him feel inadequate, and forced him to super-charge the competitive bullshit when among his taller peers. The American financiers. But these top

0.05% of earners had been sniffing out weakness their whole lives and they got him on this whenever they could. He sought out a tall heel, and to anyone but his tailor and his doctor, he was six foot. He had begun to pay attention to the emergence of leg-lengthening surgery.

He wanted to check the time, and he went through the options. The Patek Phillipe watch on his left wrist, but it was dark and required movement other than of his eyes. The wall clock, the digital displays on stereo equipment, the television, too distant. He checked his watch, turning it to catch the moonlight. Just gone 7.20pm.

He finished his cigarette and stubbed it in the sand of an outdoor ashtray, which his cleaners plural dealt with each week. He went inside for the next twenty minutes at least. Closing the tall, heavy door behind him, he walked through the mixed space, part office, part lounge area, with its sliding walls, complemented by the select interiors and artworks, procured with his advisor. The draft from outside would take a few minutes for the air conditioning system to overcome, and bring the temperature back to an across-the-floor twenty-two point five degrees.

The kitchen and a reception area were situated on the level *above*, and he moved through to the central space, and took a seat. Bloomberg was on the wall-mounted Ultra High Definition television, and it was a red sea. Markets sliding, negative, global shares indexes bearing down in crimson, in sidebars and tickers, while a report on wildfires in Australia filled the room with a dark red glow, transporting him there.

"Fuck that, looks like a nightmare," he said to himself in cut-glass English.

Down red. Fire red.

He glanced at his share portfolio summary, and hissed and clenched through his teeth at the size of the falls. This may postpone the third home in Italy, after he'd narrowed down the location with Chiara, the local property contact who charmed and despised him in equal measure. The office distress was piling up, a leadership team he wished would show some, and desist in asking him to provide all the answers.

'Set ambitious stretch targets. Beat them. That's all. Just be better than you are. Stop being so fucking average. And you might keep your job.'

Jesus. This middle manager was looking at five years' salary if they could exit this fucking thing in the next 18 months. If the world would stop falling apart, turning to ashen red. It was because of *Simon* that he was looking at paying off his and his parents' mortgages, buying whatever car he wanted, maybe a second home by the sea at a stretch. Simon's idea, his starter risk, and he a mere executor, drafted in after a proof of concept and strong sales. And he would detest Simon for pushing him, and once Simon was gone, he would rejoice. If he kept his job beyond recommendations to the new regime.

Texts came in from an investor; these could not be ignored. He dealt with it via a lengthier response at his desk, and went outside for another smoke, this time pulling on an overcoat. He looked back through the large windows, at the live global outlook screen: demonstrations, public unrest, this time in America. The. United. States. Of. America. Futuristic guards and police, in urban black-grey warfare garb, tooled up, shielded and up for a ruck against smaller groups, yet this was a vast combative turnout. A modern, informed response comprising big, muscled-up guys, wily and wiry young experienced males with nothing to lose. A heavyweight resistance, not the puny workers from the seventies. Two forces feeding off each other, growing in size, aggression, weaponry, powers legal and moral. This could be an ass-whooping for the dissidents, while the foot soldiers of the regime would be along at night to burn the city to the ground, unabated.

He checked his watch again, waiting for his Finance Director to send through the scenarios for redundancies he had agreed with his investors. He loathed redundancies. Not making people redundant, there was too much at stake. This wasn't three grand a week to pay the rent and bills, this was real money. And real money meant real power. The higher the stakes, the less he could care about the human angle. Starting from a low base. For most it would be six to nine months of cutting back, painful job searches, networking, and then they'd move on. No, he loathed the communications after to the rank and file. And the protracted, formulaic process of the whole thing. The feigning of regret, reticence, friends of theirs will have left the company, we are all sorry that this has had to happen. But this is what was necessary for the business to continue (subtext: their jobs to continue). Simon knew there would be disquiet. For about a day. Then everyone would settle back to doing what they needed to, to stay looking essential in case there were further rounds to come. There would be faux concerned calls and texts between the remainers and the departed, and then they would be forgotten, moved on from. Within minutes of people boxing up their stuff and saying goodbyes, the remainers would send their next emails. Open their next files. Check the next report. They wouldn't just sit there doing nothing, staring out the window. And with each task, each act, it got easier, like falling off a log, until it was business-as-usual. It wasn't them, that was the main thing, and they knew it when they looked at each other.

Say his business went to the wall, the departed would just get another job, and he'd be shafted. In reputation, at least. Fuck the lazy lot of them, swinging the lead. He'd seen the employee monitoring software stats. Something he'd asked his FD to build into her scenarios. He valued those who over-delivered versus their cost, and if that changed, it all changed.

The communication channels, people networks, organising his assistants, organising his home help via the assistants. The gym workouts, the golf, tennis and squash with people to stay close to. The dinners and charity foundation events, the Oxford shindigs. Women. Fitting in regular sex. Endless questions, one after the last. Endless reprioritisation. Each business sold was the formulation of thousands of decisions, tasks, annoying, difficult, painful, most of them. The large yellow rug in his first office perhaps the most overwhelming of them all. Twenty-grand. He took it with him whenever they moved, a memento, and a link to earlier times.

His eyes roved around the room as he flicked through a lifestyle magazine left by an armchair, which contained an article commenting on the habits of billionaires. Billionaires weren't billionaires *because* they get up at 5am for gym circuits, they do those things *because* they are billionaires. When there's tens of millions to be made in a day with the right decisions, why stay in bed? When there are so many games to win, the finest of everything to enjoy, why choose to be out of shape, to risk an untimely curtailment. While some of his contemporaries had opted for the *power paunch*, he fitted the modern stereotype of the ripped high energy leader. Cliché, touché.

Simon *could* switch off. Skiing, fashion, the arts. Being out on the boat or at a shoot. Restaurants, most of all weekend lunches, when things were calmer. With a beautiful woman or one of his select cluster of equals, those *on side*. Mayfair, Fitzrovia, Marylebone, Chelsea, even Soho or somewhere East. He could never get his hands around the scene, always moving, ever alluding him, never acquired. Eating well, the best, was like having a superior sex life. Against the backdrop of all life's vile day-to-day tasks, moments of culinary and carnal pleasure, for those needed and well-earned boosts. Fleeting moments though they may be, yet they strung together a harmony. The downing of an oyster, a spoon of the clearest cold consommé of tomatoes, duck roasted to its sweetest point with a sticky jus, and some sharp dessert to turn his cheeks inside out. The tall youthful professional in colourful Agent Provocateur lingerie riding him hard, the shaved Iranian side piece sitting on his face, the buzz from coming hard in a competitor's wife. The girl who leaves her panties behind for him to breath her in. All moments to savour, until the food is taken away, the lover leaves his home, and he is left sated, full, or empty. Later, the hunger would return. These moments across a lifetime were colour, but they could never be an end in themselves.

Speaking of billionaires.

*** BREAKING NEWS***

Billionaire found dead in London. He turned up the news. Suicide, they alleged. Or as Simon would say, *syoueeside*. Simon expected it was. Despite being worth a cool $2 billion dollars, this industry titan was worth $20 billion until some bad moves and state intervention. Simon imagined the climb down, the lower level players in the circle he would now have needed to move in. The previous contemporaries now out of reach. Busy. The parties happening without him. The conversations and moves he was now not privy to. Nothing but an $18bn downer.

Simon imagined himself losing what he had, starting again. His peers, most of all Piers, no longer striding over to exchange a few words in the best establishments. The locker room hush as he walked in. Fuck that. Thoughts like that fired him up, raised his energy levels, thrust his mind back onto money matters, and away from lifestyle trimmings. Pressure, pressure, pressure, from himself, his competitors, the banks, the investors, the market, his network. It all *helped* – carrot *and* stick. Keeping up with the softer activities – the endless awards, charity and alumni events, cultivating his media presence, to fight obsolescence. The low return long games to be played with potential investors, with their flighty flight capital and pony sensitivities. Each dinner a delicate dance, a constant balance and recalibration, every word carrying meaning and risk. A lifetime's work started watching his father as a young boy, absorbing. He had accumulated enough business nous in his teens to leapfrog any MBA graduate. Not in the academic detail, none of those action distractions. How to talk wealth, how to listen, how to dress and fit in, what shoes to wear, what to omit, the chicanery. From youth he had found a voice that was clear and unrestrained, just the right side of over-bearing, but which could range from soft and influential to thump-the-table dominant.

Despite the altitudes he cruised at, he wished the little people knew the work involved, the never-ending list of administrative tasks and decisions, as dull and endless as their five-figure managerial positions. The constancy of directions to be given, calls to make, schedules to be aligned, the covering of cross-functional bases, consumption to keep his properties' interior-décor-magazine-ready. To keep his art collection on the rise and his wardrobe functioning. Maintaining the past-times and personal habits. Even with a support team of assistants, home help, fitness trainers, whole teams of C-level and SVP professionals, the finest investing minds, accountants, legal professionals, and lifestyle advisories, it was as relentless as any London life. Less nine to five, more five to midnight. At least the opposition needed to sleep too. And while the hoi polloi were driven to madness by government diktats from those they looked to for safety, while they masked, tested, doing their bit for community health, he went about his business. Untested, unmasked, without question and interruption, as an elite with important things to be getting done. In his world, the *pandemic* had been navigated, except in the technology stock valuations, the engagement KPIs from an atomised public, and his personal wealth. *That'll do nicely.*

He would *get there* one day. He *was* there, others would think. But there was no *there*.

Restless, he poured himself a glass of Scotch, which he carried outside to smoke once again, annoyed to keep having to put on and remove an overcoat. He reflected on Francesca and their unofficial arrangement – not an item, but available to each other. A personal stone in his shoe all day had been that he couldn't take her away the following weekend as planned, and he had to tell her. He saw Francesca as gutsy, terrific fun, independent, high-minded and busy. All good things. Sincere, but never earnest. Sharp of mind and tongue. And he was content sat opposite her, looking, drinking, eating, listening, taking her in. She messed him about too; their relationship was on an equal footing, despite their situational differences. This kept him itchy, his blood hot, had her rotating through his thoughts among everything else. There was plenty of high society ready to give him everything he wanted, and *she* made him wait. Francesca, with her historical art and movie knowledge, her obscure book references.

Like Simon, she had been given good base materials to work with, knew her worth, and had always spent time with fiction and non-fiction, understanding how the world worked and the interplay between people. Conscious that the older she became, the less she felt she knew. Of the old world and the new additions.

Francesca had no mantra, but her life had a sure rhythm and style which led her in colourful directions with interesting people, and helped her ride the bullshit without too much internalised stress, nor too many wrong turns. Like Simon, she was shameless and didn't dwell on missteps.

He called Francesca and said the trip was a non-runner. She was blasé. It wasn't a big deal – it wasn't the one big weekend from the kids they'd been looking forward to all year. The money was coming in and things were happening for them both; it was pleasure deferred. No matter how much of a rotter he was, she took it in her elegant stride. For she didn't care that much. She accepted him. Sure, she enjoyed the ease with which Simon was able to make things happen, and the trappings of dinners, time on the water, new high-end connections he was able to help her make. But she never saw him as a potential life partner. She rolled with the punches and enjoyed the moments, and saw no need for rancorous dramas.

She hadn't lost anything, least of all her own money.

"What are you doing?" he asked.

"Drinking wine, smoking, much the same as you, I suspect," she responded, "and listening to opera."

Simon glanced down at the ashtray as he tapped, looked out at the glowing towers, and asked her to come over.

"I'll send a car for you," he nudged.

"Call me tomorrow, take me for a terrific lunch," was her offer.

"Sure. I'll text you a place and time. Bye for now," and he disconnected the call with her name and photograph staring at him. Then they were gone.

Francesca chucked the phone down next to her, muttered 'wanker', tapped the ash from her cigarette and picked up her book.

She paused to sketch out Saturday, and outlined a trip which would take her through a couple of local book stores, Luigi's - the Italian delicatessen on Fulham Road, and somewhere to buy a gift for a friend. She texted CHELSEA with a full stop to Simon. She thought of nudging him to bring some coke, but it was Saturday, he wouldn't need reminding. The seductive idea of a perfect Saturday was forming; some shopping, a beautiful lunch with good wine, and driven to whatever they would choose to do that evening, some members' club, and ending in bed. One thing Simon could be trusted with was organising a good time. Saturday would be of release and letting go, and Sunday would be waiting for her, to recuperate and pull it together again.

He wished that Francesca would come. The way she would lean back on the pillows, self-contained, after he had finished inside her. Light a cigarette. Shut up for a bit. Then share an indiscretion of one of her art contacts, or their comical shortcomings, while he let his body melt into the bed, and his head swim with hormones, nicotine and alcohol.

He smiled at the memory of something she said after sex.

'I love it when you come, because for three seconds you're not tortured.'

Lunch. Yet another task. He had a recommendation for a new place from an old friend which he hadn't tried out yet, and it was in Central South West London. Simon was <u>very</u> careful from whom he accepted recommendations; *will I like what this person likes?* Likewise, he might caveat a suggestion he made himself to another – *I liked it, you may not.*

He would want to try it before he saw him again, and he tended to see him at this time of year. Said friend was on his whitelist of people with impeccable taste, who could be trusted to give high quality recs when planning to visit a strange city for the first time. New restaurants aged before you knew it, and he was surprised to catch a booking for 2.30pm, and he informed Francesca.

He was horny. The nagging switch had been flicked. In his twenties, he could hang out with anyone unsuitable as a partner if the sex was good. But now if they weren't on his wavelength, no matter the quality of the sex, once he came he just wanted them to disappear. And come back in an hour. No face-to-face time. He would finish and roll on to his back and stare at the light fittings, and if they rolled over into the crook of his armpit, he would shiver and it creeped. That's where escorts came in. With a clock on the side in the bedroom he could time them to an hour or an hour and a half if he was feeling it, and come for the second time around, as time was called. Gentlemen, please.

An hour of flesh pleasure and they would scramble their lingerie back on and vanish. *A phone call away, and it's too easy.*

"Hello, can I order a delivery please?" he quipped, to a familiar voice.

"What can I get for you tonight sir?" drawled the coordinator of services.

"Sophia or Isobel, if they're available."

There was a pause.

"It's a little late for that. You can get them both sometime if you give me notice. I'll find something comparable."

"Yes, well, make sure they're ballpark."

"Ciao."

No superfluous words. They hung up in unison.

He poured another drink, changed out of his suit and into something comfortable, shook the duvet, and put some cash in an envelope which he left sat on the edge of the long, clear table close to the front door. Money and pleasure was all he had time for. Sure, if without time or if in poor health, priorities would change. With time and health on side, it was the money that called the shots, and from money, flowed the pleasure. And as he learned at school, be the best at whatever you chose, and success would follow.

The news cycle reverted to wildfires, and while he wished they would stop, they were bad for business after all, they were not his concern to solve. His priority was shifting ever more of the global supply of money in his direction. Share of pie, better quality networks, favours, ever more oblique and lateral operations. And while the pleasures of sex and food were levelling off in what they could supply at the margin, better artworks, new homes, finer women, greater bragging rights were all ahead. And it all waited for him. Whether on a choking planet, or a healthy one.

Yet others were all moving forward too. And this pushed him always.

He stepped outside again and looking across the London skyline, knew that although it had provided the platform and given him the start, he would need to make global moves.

He was made to wait due to the hour. He buzzed up a new face.

1000
CHAPTER 8
The Wyatts: Iva and Julian talk: Fiona and Francesca out: Julian and Iva phone sex

Waitrose in South-West London on a Saturday morning, and the scene of a devastating fresh family shop by the Wyatts. Fiona Wyatt *(Wandsworth Common, Part-time Consultant, Balthazar (New York), Dolce & Gabbana)* led the way, brood in tow. Tall, with that blonde-brunette mix, the culmination of fifteen years of salon highlight visits. Blue eyes and freckles sprinkled over her cheeks and a sleek nose with a flattened section in the middle third. She managed sufficient gym sessions and kept a disciplined, healthy fridge and larder, that her stomach had squared off flat between her bony hips, widened an inch by the years. To see the whites of her widening eyes, and to hear her throaty, dirty laugh, was to understand and take in the mischief of her youth.

Her husband, Julian Wyatt *(Wandsworth Common, Banking Analytics, Hawksmoor, The North Face)* languished behind, with their daughter, Florence, twelve, and their son, Theo, nine. Julian, all mountain-wear and worn jeans, his sole choice each weekend in autumn or winter: *fleece or gilet*? Upright, rigid, tight, freer and easier with his views than his money, but with an unexpected sense of humour that caught Fiona off guard when they met, and charmed her. Dark-brown Lego-haired, with a large narrow nose, and rangy hands with long cold fingers, which had a few habitual ways of expressing themselves when making a point, both in the workplace and at home. Men meeting the couple today would say that he did well for himself, a measure which seemed to increase each year, as he relaxed further into the easing skin of his lean yet dad bod, keeping up racket sports as a getaway from the noise and home hassle, and to keep a touchpoint with acquaintances.

A man who flourished in a society with ever increasing rules and layers of complexity, with its busywork and multi-step security. The nuances of corporate jargon and networks requiring *navigation*. He *was lanyard man*. Once he swiped in of a morning, he was on home turf. To somewhat gauche and conflicted Julian, everything was either fantastic or utter dog shit. Ridiculous middle-class nonsense, or essential product. He would turn between excoriating a colleague or neighbour for the banality of their choices, while sitting among square yards of *Railings*.

Fiona began collecting asparagus spears, baby sweet peppers, baby aubergines, baby courgettes, bell peppers, spring onions, several types of tomatoes but never just 'tomatoes'. Large garlic bulbs, dill, rosemary, coriander, flat-leaf parsley, mixed chillies. Thyme and basil in pots. She chucked in some organic versions, so that Julian felt the pinch. Sweet potatoes, ginger, pak choi. Next she tore into the fruit aisles.

Each time digging to the back, for those with the longest life.

"We already get £200 worth delivered in each week," Julian protested, "poor knackered Ladislav and his onion van."

"That's ambient and non-food. You must select your own fresh. When you can be bothered."

"So we're close to putting away £1,200 a month on supermarkets."

Fiona refused a discussion and threw in more to underline her position.

"If you brought half that in in consultancy fees..." he pushed, referencing how part-time her contributions had been in the last year.

"Deb has something big coming my way. Anyway, money darling, that's your job. It's your one big special contribution."

The children trailed, their eyes darting across the brands and colours, missing nothing. Scanning the aisles like the widgets on a tablet page, consuming each item, looking for anything sweet and new. Florence, smart and well-educated, chose white nectarines and apricots, and a couple of smoothies, and added them to the trolley under Fiona's watchful eye. As expected, the smoothies were refused, 'we make our own, without all the shit they put in.'

"And sugar."

"Exactly."

Florence deposited four onion bagels into a brown paper bag, which she could just about reach, and picked up some live yoghurt with rhubarb. All items were approved.

"Do you think the checkout man earns as much as we spend on shopping?" Julian asked.

"Oh yes," replied Fiona.

"Are you 100% sure?" Julian manoeuvred, vanishing around a gondola end, disappearing the conversation with it.

When Fiona was distracted, checking out some packet content analysis, Julian removed a continental cheese she had picked up, and dumped it on a shelf behind a box of dog biscuits, retrieving a packet of snacks for the dog, before re-joining the pack.

A girl not unlike a youthful Fiona walks toward and then past them, carrying a bottle of vodka.

"Eyes front!" snapped Fiona, as Julian looked down to start the swivel, which he was made to stop. "Fuck sake Julian."

"Already on the hard stuff," he commented.

"Good for her."

They passed some shelves with baking accessories, and Julian picked up a large glass mixing bowl and, checking the kids were a suitable distance behind, wobbled it, reminding her of when he shaved her pubic hair into her mum's mixing bowl in her parents' holiday home.

"When we had sex more than twice a month, yes, I just about remember," she replied.

"It *was* 20 years ago," he justified, laughing and nudging her.

She didn't dwell on it too much in that moment, but she knew that twice a month meant one of two things – a lot of wanking at work or in the bathroom, or someone else was getting fucked.

And yet Fiona already knew he was seeing someone else.

The proud owners of a whole house, in an affluent and waspy area, with several bedrooms over three floors, and a decent garden. Over various cycles in the last decade they had extended, reconfigured, added extra rooms, replaced kitchens (plural) and bathrooms, and erected a summer house. Texting each other from around the home was standard operating procedure. Tech projects ensured capability throughout, and allowed for easy luxury working and schooling from home during the *pandemic*. No sweat for the laptop lockdowner classes, while within a mile radius, victims of domestic abuse were jailed with their tyrants, and poor children, four to a bedroom, struggled to concentrate on their analogue schoolwork. All the while, immigrant and working class skivvies dropped off consumables, while 'Liberals' reconnected with nature.

"Julian, can you deal with this today?" she asked, thrusting an automated car insurance letter at him, "I just don't have the bandwidth," she added, workspeak now permeating their home life, as cheffing parlance did in the kitchen.

Julian groaned at the price comparison rigmarole, and potential phone calls she had just assigned to him, just to get their quote for next year in line with the previous. With another year of no claims, up to nine now, it was no surprise their quote for this year had increased by 15%. Automation here was no great leap, and he reflected that the world needed to figure this out, and someone would become wealthy when they did. The insurance gig was due another tranche of disruption.

Despite his handsome salary, any opportunity to be lean on the outgoings *he* was in control of, at least, would be seized, even to save six minutes' pay. Fiona had his number on this, and delegated it to him while ordering a £460 pair of Olivia Von Halle silk pyjamas up in the bedroom.

"Esther's eldest has been bullying," she informed a Julian who wasn't listening, as she reappeared in the kitchen.

"What was that?" he mumbled, and she repeated herself, louder, like a nurse raising her voice for an elderly patient.

"Bullying child. Dog bites man. Why are people surprised by this? Children are small people, and people are dangerous," he opined.

"Keep *those* opinions to yourself at drop-off," she ordered.

He got up, collected and fluttered the insurance documents, and left to move to the office, on the face of it, to do what she asked. Instead he checked his two choice porn sites for any decent uploads that matched his varied tastes, and which he could come back to later. With the screen facing the window behind him, children came and went while he did so. Trying to engage their father, he fobbed them off with some free screen time, handing them some technology.

Once he got the insurers on the phone he walked downstairs so his effort was recognised, whereby Fiona shooed him away for bringing that dull chat into her world. She opened some strawberries, washed and kitchen rolled them dry, and Florence joined her at the island, bringing the black pepper to crack over the top, one taste of many that they shared. Florence looked at her mother and her features and style, blessed by what she had received from her, with that competitive work ethic. She would watch her mother for her influencing and manipulation skills, and her hard edge. Absorbing. And dissect her cutting remarks, so she could understand their components and practice reassembling them herself.

Fiona flicked through the papers and commented to Julian as he re-entered, of a film they might catch in the week, task seven of forty-one completed for the day.

"Oh I've seen that, it's fucking terrible."

"Mark said it was good," she added, referring to her brother.

"That's about right. Why can't stuff be plain shit anymore? Everything has to be caveated, it might not be aimed at you, others may enjoy it, blah blah blah. You watch it, *you'll* probably enjoy it," he snarled, loaded, as he grabbed an apple.

"Where's the cheese?"

"I got cheese."

"It's not here."

Fiona validated this.

"I'll pop back in a bit," Julian volunteered, checking his watch while trying to sound pained. She didn't thank him, but neither did she nix his plan for a walk.

Julian left home, grabbing a carrier bag from the hallway hooks, and strode back to the supermarket, while thinking who he could bump into that couldn't be checked and which could buy him time to speak with Iva, should he need it. A pure tactician. He hurried in, picked up some fruit, a random yet pricey bottle of wine and three continental cheeses, to bolster his story and defences.

Julian hurried out and round to a spot at the end of the car park where he could sit down, behind a Jeep, on a low wall, which was ice cold on his bony arse through thin jeans.

Iva Jovanovic *(Greenwich, Analyst, Restaurant Gordon Ramsay, Jimmy Choo)* paced around her apartment, tight throughout with stored energy, like a young dog in the morning. She owed her exuberance, crisp looks and symmetry to her Russian mother, and her education and drive to her successful Serbian father, long separated from each other. Her straight, fine, darkest brown shoulder length hair was kept tight in a pony-tail at home, at the gym, and at work. A *Cotswolds facelift*. Inherited also from her parents, her love of finer labels, continuing from the branded gifts bestowed on her when a young girl. Fashion labels, junior labels of the real thing. Parents who knew that desires like these would drive her on to high earnings herself, or to seek out someone who could plate the best for her. To those who like nice things, money must flow.

Her international schooling, absorption at home of the languages of parents and nannies, and time working abroad, left her speaking three native languages, five languages to business standard and another few for travel. And gave her an accent of nowhere. A *du jour* type who would describe herself as a 'world citizen'.

Annoyed by the wait for his promised call before going to work out, she turned the ringer volume up on her phone and got about doing some prep in the kitchen. All sorts of nutri-fashion shiz; bitter green smoothies with powders to consume now, a workout drink with *electrolytes* and hyper hydration qualities beyond water, for later. Julian was on a deadline here as she had a class to make. She applied moisturisers, plural, *before* her workout. Men didn't understand the cost of maintenance, the reason she felt nothing of letting men pay for everything. She checked her kit for her post-workout lotions, and in case anything was running low.

Gym classes happened five times a week, three lunchtimes and two evenings. Tennis twice a week, once with her coach, once with a friend or a competitive match. On an ad hoc basis she would fit in a couple of runs, when her head, always full, needed an attempt at clearing. Meditation and yoga several mornings per week, or some stretches if against the clock. In her free time, which meant any feasible gap in her schedule, reading, writing, life drawing, fashion, sailing, online courses. Journal before sleep. Doing an MBA.

Julian Wyatt appeared in full on her phone, and she took the call after wiping clear a rogue smudge from the precious screen, that needed to be spotless.

"Yes," she answered, catching the background noise of wind and wheels.

"Hi, what's happening?" Julian asked.

"Off to a class; I don't have long, but sounds like you have a shop to do," she responded, as a train of trolleys collided with a post.

"It's done," he said without thinking, until it had been said. Don't give her an opening, he chastised himself.

"How about call me on time. Are we on for this week?" referencing the expected work trip.

"Yes, leaving Wednesday afternoon, but it's going to be Frankfurt," he said, bracing.

"Frankfurt. Dreadful. God, what are we going to do for food? You better get them to book a top hotel, and not a business brand. Make Paris happen next," she urged, taking a muscular approach.

"Yes, yes," he answered, though the thought of Paris already had his mind and his gut swirling. Too close to home, too many networks rubbing against each other. He and Fiona both knew people in Paris. This would start troubling him already.

"And later, you're..."

"Out tonight. I'm seeing my therapist this afternoon. You should try it."

Out, he thought. Whatever.

"Once you start that stuff it never ends. If I thought I'd go and after a couple of years be in a better place, I'd do it. Everyone I know with a therapist will see them forever."

"It's a process," she replied.

"The process of relieving you of money, in exchange for old rope," he fathomed.

"That's not my narrative, Julian," she responded in a controlled manner, looking at herself in the full-length mirror, ensuring she looked athletic, professional, and expensive.

"And no one uses expressions like that anymore," she chided, "you need to do some reframing."

'Reframe this' he thought, cupping his balls in his mind, being in view in daylight.

"I've got to go," she said. Four magical words to Julian.

"Oh," he responded, all fake abandonment. "OK, have a good day. I'll text you tonight," he volunteered, as Fiona would be out on the tiles.

As he walked in, the predictable questions about the supermarket.

"I wanted another bottle of that wine I bought last time for tonight."

"We've got stacks of wine."

He shrugged and went to leave to end this pointless to-and-fro, tiresome, even without the jeopardy attached.

"Here," she said, thrusting a bottle of bleach at him, "give the toilets a go around, would you? In the spare room ensuite too," she ordered, tasking, thrusting the heavy, smooth-rough-feel plastic at him.

Fiona was readying herself to meet Francesca for dinner, choosing an outfit; moving in tight direct lines around the light and soft toned master bedroom. From their walk-in wardrobe she pulled skirts, cashmere sweaters, plain and floral dresses. She felt sassy and shoved it all away, going with a pair of classic, well-cut mid-blue jeans, a white fitted shirt, one of her black leather jackets, and a pair of white-cream boots. The showpiece.

Florence sat on a chair looking at herself in a mirror. Family photos showed the likeness between her and her mother at that age, in looks and physique. She was tall and lean, yet although blander in looks than many of her elite school friends from even better gene pools, she possessed an inquisitive, sparky mind. Observant and a good listener. Fiona had no worries about her per se, save the myriad of externalities and uncontrollables.

Florence had been flicking through *The Guardian* in the kitchen, and had some things on her mind she wanted to explore. Oils – crude and palm. On this rare occasion, Fiona was focused on her evening out, and away. Leaving it behind.

"They're complicated issues darling, which is why they remain problems."

"How long have they been problems?"

"Palm oil is newish, I think," she offered, powdering her face in rapid fluffy strokes, "oil oil, that's been in the mainstream for decades. Long before that for those in the know."

"That's ages. You were young then. And what's been done about it?"

"You like the car don't you, and going on holiday? And the nice warm house. And the technology. And the blueberries."

She had been trying to encourage Florence to do something else without saying so, but Florence was missing her physical cues.

"Happy to discuss tomorrow, or why don't you get Dad to put on a documentary for you tonight? And get him to watch it with you, don't let him plug you in and get on with other things."

Florence left. Fiona perked up and picked up the pace.

Julian encouraged the dog out (two guesses max to nail the breed, it could be one of two), opened a bottle of wine, reached up for a cut glass goblet, and filled. The combination of the bright spotlights and the black outside lit up his reflection in the large window at the sink. He paused to see himself, aware the mirror got a look to check for parsley in his teeth or before leaving for work in the morning. After lunch before a call. He contrasted this with his youth when his reflection was a dear acquaintance.

He fixed himself a cheese and pastrami sandwich, with some salad leftovers after a validatory sniff.

"Can I have one?" asked Florence.

"When mum's gone, if you and your brother settle down," he replied. Forever a negotiation.

He let the dog back in, checked his personal and work email accounts and the dozen social media, news and info apps for updates, which took a minute and revealed nothing new from half hour previous. Nothing much happened on the weekend, he thought. News is politics. He locked doors, pulled blinds, closed plantation shutters. Shuffled sofa cushions, replaced pillows, collected the newspaper from around the ground floor. Had a look what was *happening* in Frankfurt, and then had to peel a young boy off himself when Theo's squeezing arms relaxed. A heap of tasks for Sunday were filling his head, some taking up to an hour, and he felt his free time compressed to little already. Then it would be Monday. The dog looked bored and the children had too much residual energy for this hour. He swallowed half the glass of wine in one gulp and felt the harshness hit the top of his throat, the light of the glaring ceiling darkened for a moment, and his thoughts eased. He scrolled through the TV listings, and when Florence chose something, he stopped. Between the three of them there were four screens live, feeding them content. Returning to his sandwich, he flicked through the *FT Weekend*.

This was how they spent last Saturday, each in the same spots. This gave Julian the reassured, eased glow of fatherhood. On the television, a character was returning home from Amsterdam, things hadn't worked out.

"Mum's friend Angie came home from Amsterdam. They always come home from Amsterdam," Florence confirmed.

Julian could name a couple of acquaintances who had also returned from Amsterdam. He couldn't say the same of Paris or Milan.

"It's the kind of place that's fun for a while, when everything's working."

"That's all the..." and she made a smoking gesture, as Theo was with them.

Julian tried to resist a smile and failed, puffing through his nose.

"You'd like it, lots of bikes, eco stuff."

"We should go, just us. We can get bikes, and you can..." and again with the smoking.

"When you're 21."

"If you make it that long, deal."

Fiona's car pulled up at the Fulham bar just after 7.45pm, and she entered and spotted Francesca among a sea of similar faces, from quite a distance. Most people were on high alert while waiting for someone to join them, but Francesca was engrossed in something, and oblivious until Fiona pulled back the chair opposite. Francesca stood and they leaned in to kiss three times on switching cheeks.

Surveying the condensation on the inside of the windows, and through the gaps, the slick black roads outside, Francesca asked if they should keep the reservation she had made nearby for 8.30pm.

"Can we stay here and drink?"

"Sure, we can eat here anyway," she added, grabbing the attention of the staff.

"Wine?"

"I haven't eaten. No. Vodka martini for me, please."

"Oh," she said, "I see," raising a signature eyebrow, before ordering two. Francesca caught herself, about to knock back her remaining white wine. Cocktails meant a ten-minute wait, plus.

Francesca pushed her small clutch bag to Fiona, "I have some coke that Simon left behind the other day," she said, "help yourself."

"If you insist."

Fiona chuckled.

Once they started *catching up*, Fiona figured they would be waiting a while for drinks, so made an efficiency move; she stood up, picked up the clutch bag and sought out the bathroom, heading toward the back of the restaurant and looking down. In London, most times, back and down.

When she returned, drinks were waiting.

"Timing, Fiona," she said, congratulating herself as she lifted the spirits yawing within the cocktail glass, a classic yet predictable straight Y.

"Rewards. Chin chin," she offered as they lifted their glasses, meeting eyes as they did so.

As she put her drink down with great care, Fiona sniffed hard a couple of times, and savoured the chalky sharp moment.

"Get another couple of these in progress."

They didn't so much shoot the breeze but gun it down, with uninterrupted, competitive garrulousness, a litany of interjections, at a heightened volume. At times, the use of one mouth and zero ears. It did not go unnoticed on an adjacent table that they seldom stopped for air, and had weak bladders.

"You remember Ellie from the picnic a few years back?" asked Fiona, "she split up with Jack."

"Is that a shame or not?"

"I told her we *always* thought he was a nob. Several other people the same, which prompted her to ask why we kept this crucial information to ourselves? Obviously, we have to keep this to ourselves for the duration, watching them see out twelve long wasted years. As if she would have been interested in the news in real time. They did split up, they got there in the end, bless 'em."

Fiona stopped for water, then ploughed on. Francesca observed the occasional user.

"A guy at the school gates asked how many of my female friends, if their father won the lottery, would walk out on their partners the next day? I said: many."

Fiona expected this to turn into a discussion, but Francesca didn't offer a view, and the conversation reverted, as Francesca groaned, "*I* always told you I didn't like Julian."

"Yes, you've always been consistent on that," Fiona replied, laughing.

"Still think he's seeing someone else?" ventured Francesca.

"Nothing concrete, but there's a definite caginess. A different air. He's thorough though. He's not been hitting the gym or dressing up, so he probably can't be arsed with her already."

Fiona dialled it down, wishing to confide, but not to commit in her reveal. She kept the phone hacking to herself.

"It all bloody works, for both of us," she explained, "and our rows, no matter which angle they come from, always converge to the same argument, at which point it drops." She paused for a glug of water for her drying lips, then continued, "And that's without bringing the children into the equation."

Francesca had no doubt that a buoyant Fiona would stay afloat, as she watched her knock back half her cocktail and hold up the empty glass in front of her face.

"Did you want to get some food?" checked Francesca.

"Maybe later," said Fiona as she segued onto other topics. Small plates of lobster croquettes, steak tartare and duck salad would later go half eaten.

Francesca handled ordering another round, in between updating Fiona on the latest art world high jinks, and progress with Simon, whom she had met through Fiona and Julian. *Not* Julian and Fiona.

Julian ushered the children to bed in turn, and teed up Iva for a late phone call.

"We have some time for *rewards*," he confirmed, requesting some pictures.

Iva waited ten minutes and sent through a few she had taken prior and had not sent him. She remained make-up free in her soft cotton pyjamas, on her sofa. She put headphones on and ran through a fantasy of his for him, while finishing off some tasks in her living room. Julian took less time jerking off as he got older, but made an exception for phone sex. As she built him up and started to receive louder, excitable feedback, she sauntered through to the bedroom and took out a sex toy from her bedside drawer. She turned it on next to the microphone and told him what was going to happen in no uncertain terms, and in the coarsest of language. To her, this was about the outcome not the journey, so she tugged her bottoms down and brought herself level with him, indicating so. She was not an individual who hadn't mastered her own orgasms, and ability to hit the on switch. When they both finished, she made her excuses, which he feigned disappointment about, and they both returned to drinking wine and pottering around their respective homes.

Fiona and Francesca continued until they were boozed, the coke had been nosed, and the laughs had been exhausted, and they took separate cars home. Fiona opened the heavy wood and glass door, knocked a couple of coats off their hooks, careered into the hallway table and stood on a dog squeaker, greeting its owner before heading to the kitchen. She opened a bottle of rosé, poured a large glass and hit the sofa so she could get beyond drunk and work off the energy to be able to sleep without being gnawed at.

The three quarter bottle of wine, imported from the west coast of the United States, sat open all night.

1001
CHAPTER 9

Steven late night deal: Walking date cut short: First dates and sexual preferences: A bad date

Friday night. It was approaching eleven and Steven had had to meet with prospects on the American west coast, who were about to sign. He had the final draft v29 final final over to them that morning after his in-house legal counsel had finalised the terms. He was satisfied yet astonished to be in this position. This had spent significant time in limbo and he had assumed they were going to go with Do Nothing Ltd, yet it had picked up again with a change of personnel at higher levels. Which tended to lead to a downward turn of events.

The face-to-face meetings had been predictable. The intimations of budget limitations, what was on offer from competitors, having to hold his line against a faux-bolshie procurement grilling. The callow managers who looked at their boss to see how to behave, which reminded him too much of his younger self, and which made him shudder. He caught the glances seeking the brand of watch, the writing style, the tightness of the shirt creases, the cleanliness of the cotton.

Things brightened up when the CEO joined for 30 minutes. Whip smart, mind like a trap, snapping with the right questions. She was so attractive with such restrained power, that Steven couldn't stop smiling at her. He forgave himself; *she gets that a lot*, and his mind wandered for a moment to imagining some brutality or other she might subject someone to in her leadership team. Unmarried. No time for inefficiencies. Few available betters. He speculated upon her house or apartment and its décor, what her *look* was. And who she slept with, and what they did together. And *how long it took* to roll off him after riding him to a finish.

There is always someone better than you.

She began, "I and Jason had some questions on *purposiveness*," and this registered with him as he had come across that word, for the first time, just the prior day. He had searched for it. She then arrowed into the specifics, and was proving to be thorough. Legal background, he mused. He satisfied her with his responses and segued the conversation to one of reporting needs. She took this to be a suitable exit point and left. Reports, reports, reports. So much effort leading to so few decisions.

Back to the evening call which was wrapping up with timing commitments for signed copies, and how much they were all looking forward to working together. Looking forward, Steven foresaw, to misaligned expectations, missed milestones, lack of perceived value, finger pointing, endless trackers, update meetings with minimal progress, and some killer emails. Perhaps an escape hatch agency resignation or an exercised out clause. As they began closing pleasantries, a client reached inside himself and managed to extract a salient question. Steven felt winded, and the whole thing was kick-started again, and went around for another fifteen minutes until they had ironed out the wrinkle. Steven imagined the client asking one final last question, and him going postal, losing it, resigning, leaving professional office life. Goodbyes and empty weekend wishes were exchanged with career smiles, and it was done.

He triple-checked everything was closed, powered down, and when all the lights blinked their last, he wrapped his fingers around the top of the laptop lid and brought it down so that it puffed air out with the satisfying exhale. This was no Sales Animal big deal, yet he felt a surge.

"Pleasure doing business with you, arseholes," he said to no-one, continuing, "glad I won't have to deliver that fucking nightmare." That's twelve K for me, and nights and weekends for some lackey or lackeys. So be it.

He reached the wooden box on the coffee table, and removed a wrap of coke-lax mix, and eased the powder onto the surface of his laptop, being careful not to knock the paper limbs, the gentlest nudge of which could disperse (and sacrifice) a great deal. He used his choice credit card to organise these into two thickish lines. He continued to take care to fold it closed without loss, and returned it to its home. He would repeat this careful process within three minutes to put the edge on. He poured a bourbon. He turned the music up and drunk it down.

As he moved the music on, his eyes wandered between potential mates, messaging services, photo stores, emails, maps, social feeds, news, and muted tennis matches involving sovas and kovas, the court casting purple into his dark lounge. He strolled in laps from bathroom to drinks, to the box. And his mind wandered to establishing his favourite three historical lovers. This became harder as he became increasingly gone and kept losing mental track, at first of the lovers he had recalled already and then of the whole topic itself. It took some back-cycling through a chain of thoughts to retrieve it. Now he had to resolve this so he could let it go again before it disappeared on him. It was too stressful. He had his three, and his last reflection before he let the tennis take control: *the best, and yet they weren't the best looking.*

He drunk hard with large measures to overtake the high, to stand a chance of sleep, and after finishing his last tumbler to the warming vibes of the Mamas & The Papas, he folded and turned in.

The next morning, he struggled to reach full consciousness and regain bodily control as he woke from a long, anxious dream. One he had experienced before. He had been running late for a flight to South America (always to South America, or home from) and he was dragged through a journey from home to a slow underground to the switch to car and jammed up carriageways, through to the inability to run in the airport, no matter how hard he pushed. The final desperate lunges through security and the minutes-to-spare struggle through the terminal. For nothing but to wake up at home.

This kind of dream tended to drain and gnaw away. Accompanied with a hangover and regret. He tried to shake it off with a full personal refresh: quick teeth brush, floss, shave, long shower, full teeth brush, mouthwash, shaving balm, moisturiser, anti-perspirant deodorant, spray deodorant, cologne. He slugged back his medications, vitamins, headache pills, and downed a pint of icy water, from the tap. Coffee, several cups. Out for some fresh air and a newspaper, and home. Bacon and smoked salmon sandwich. An apple, grapes.

At noon he left home, well wrapped up, yet omitting some of the items he would wear for comfort – hat, gloves, warmer shoes.

He approached a street cleaner, bedecked in orange and reflective silver, as if a felonious menace to society, rather than the key worker champs that they were. The pavement wasn't narrow, but a large tree was rooted in their path, causing the flagstones to lift and bend. He didn't recognise this legend, his pale white round face blotched with the purest, cartoon pink welts. A face which looked like someone had inserted a nozzle and pumped it up like a football. It was pot luck the response he could expect, but he volunteered a 'morning', and football face looked straight through him and continued brooming away, as Steven navigated his cart.

Steven continued a fair few strides and chastised them both with a muttering of 'cunt'; castigating himself for trying to bridge the class divide. Yet to ignore would be to invite the warmest, friendliest 'good morning!' delivered to a now churlish snob. An unwinnable game. *Never offer, never refuse.*

He was walking to Kensington Gardens to meet a younger black girl for a walk. Educated, looker, political advisor, potential. And that best of dates – short and cheap. He passed a battered old car on Pembridge Crescent. An ancient Renault, with aching flaky paintwork, one flat tyre. Rust. Plants and weeds were growing up through the tarmac in line with the end of the car, front and back. No parking tickets, no doubt the pride and joy of an owner of a £7m villa.

This elbowed him to take his car in to replace the handle on the passenger door which had been giving him some problems for some time and needed a bit of welly. When he picked up a recent girlfriend, he thought it best to open the door himself, lest she should struggle. Chivalrous too (win-win). As he pulled hard yet with subterfuge, the whole handle came clean off in his hand, and it ended up near his face like an antique telephone.

"I've never seen that done before," she quipped, and he had to re-enter to open her door from inside, tossing the handle on the back seat. A shambolic passage of play.

He met up with Dominica, dressed in style, weather appropriate, postcard cosy. They wandered a path some distance away from and circling the round pond. Behind his companion, at the edge of the water, swans, geese, shovellers, and moorhens shuffled, dabbled and haggled about. The conversation was so-so, and Steven handled the standard stuff (job, hometown, blah) with a smile on his face, enjoying the clarity of her features, her fit – dark coat, colour splashes, and the gentle movement as she glided around, looking across at the right moments. This went on for around twenty minutes until Steven indicated they could get a coffee from the unit north of the Palace, and walk to the south-west corner from which she had transport options from the high street. He would even pick up the tab, he thought.

She answered, "Yes, we can do that," and took a few steps before pausing. She turned to him and went on, "Actually, I'm just not feeling it, sorry. I'm going to head home."

He fumbled some directions to help her on her way, and stumbled in the other direction. Yet as he walked off, he congratulated her on her attitude, nodding and applauding in his head. Why waste any time once he'd been discounted? He reviewed the subject matter of their conversation, and couldn't pinpoint a specific error or problem. Still, he thought of some of the women he'd called it a day with, and why.
High scoring looks, smart, doctor. Dull.
Fun, intellectual, cultured, in good shape. Too intellectual, too cultured.
Music industry type, all personality. Name dropper.
All good, across the board scoring. Two kids.
Entrepreneur, a multi at 32. He was lagging.
Good looks, thin, amusing, close proximity. Posh uncool, loud with it.
Good mix, promising. Widow, it being a happy marriage.
They total scored the same, good match. She kept repeating a couple of bad stories.
Outgoing, fun in a random way, good drinker. Too into the theatre.
Gym bunny, in terrific shape. Always at or talking about the gym.
He was all-in at first. Incompatible in bed, kept pinching his nipples, hard.
Never paid for anything. Cost him a fortune.
Older, beautiful, gentle, sassy. Divorced from a superstar.
Independent, good lover. Not dependent at all.
Young, spirited, high energy. Journaled.
Hot sex. Bad denim.
Connection, warm, kind, sensual, top sex, kinky. Too hippy.
Slender, supple from yoga, stunning Latin looks. Yoga, yoga, yoga, yoga, yoga, yoga.

Oxford educated, titled father, beautiful home, go-getter. Exhausting.

A slew of women in turn thought him one or many of: full of smarm, unambitious, dull, uncultured, tight, under-buff, childless, a drunk, a novice skier, cutting, misaligned on worldview, just *no*.

He continued toward home, and passed a restaurant where he kissed a favourite ex-girlfriend for the first time, on the street, at night. He stared at the filthy bare grey pavement slabs peppered with chewing gum stamps, and the dog-eared frontage of flaky olive green paint surrounding the large windows, and he saw the shortest clip of it, that night. Seconds, no longer. And the palms of his hands itched for her, this memory, trying to reach out, as if the body didn't know that what the mind saw, was gone.

Thoughts returned to that day's park walk flop, as they would for the next few days. Although he was amused by the episode, he wouldn't be telling that story in future dates. Likewise, he wouldn't delve into the date where he felt a bad fit within seconds, and she set his expectations that she 'had two hours', as she had to return to work that evening. Trapped, for the duration; he didn't respond on the spot to conjure his own restrictive time limit. The zoomer who flipped out about some story he recounted and who was so angry she couldn't even stay calm enough to tell him what he had done wrong (still clueless). The teetotaller he got too drunk in front of, the vegan he ordered steak with. The awful first date incompatibilities resulting in hustled drinks and joint agreement that heading off was a good idea. The older woman who would not stop talking, and who kept him outside the bar on the street, listening to a barrage he couldn't escape from. The passionate dramatist who figured out he hated the theatre an hour in.

Times there wasn't a physical match, despite personality and humour compatibilities. The girl that was tardy without apology on a Saturday afternoon. Peak time. A host of women that he had invited for date two, and received no response.

He had a further first date lined up for that night, so there was more to play for, he wasn't a busted flush. Yet. Plus, another had lined *him* up for midweek, and with her open, flirtatious and racy approach, had been getting him steamed up all week. Although he wanted a life partner, failing that, he tried to tick things off his sexual bucket list, be it a body type, a kink, a nationality, a race, a sexual style, a place, a fantasy. And while his sexual mores had remained level over the last decade or so, things had begun to morph, to shift. Various sexual peccadillos remained evergreen, like a favourite classic film. Rich bitch white shorts, hair tumbling down to the lower back, pierced belly buttons and nipples, the big hooped earrings, open knickers, no knickers, girls who showed too much, bratty types. Cold, slim fingers. Ridiculous swimwear, lower back tattoos (where did they go, they can't have *gone*?)

When it came to the sex itself, old staples included octopus hands over his hands and bottom, progressing to an inserted finger. Rimming (him on her, not reciprocated), spanking (her by him), edging, filthy talk, shared fantasies, face-sitting, masturbating while having his balls licked. The moment a girl produced a sex toy *box* from under the bed. To some partners, this was a hot list, to others, this was tame stuff, entry-level, limited. Welcome to the world, find your people.

In recent months, he had noticed things enter his head as potentials. *Being* spanked. *Maybe* pegging. He never before liked being tied up but maybe he *would*. One thing never changed, his dislike for being rough and dominating. Some gentle holding down of limbs, some light spanking and coarse dirty talk, sure. But never the rough stuff, this always felt like he was being asked to inflict *further* damage.

Having an appetite and wishing to commiserate on another dating fail, he stumbled into a favourite pub, ordered a prosecco and the pan-fried hake with buttered greens, and planned to take a nap after dessert. *Find your pleasures where you can.*

Charlotte Yu was just hoping it wouldn't be a disaster, this first date since her divorce was finalised. She wasn't overwhelmed by the prospect, but friends had nudged her, in a way verging on the annoying. Swiping and selecting men for her, taking her to water and forcing her head below. Steven wasn't what she would go for either, but she figured it would get the ball rolling, keep her friends and sister at bay, and you never know (except *you do*). As long as they didn't split the bill (cringe) she figured it should be pleasant enough.

They coordinated en route to arrive together, and after a stuttered greeting and off-timed air kisses, went in. A few dining gripes were identified right away. There was some booking system issue, which wasn't resolved by a phone being presented and waved in front of the front of house. Neighbour proximity, limited beer options (lager), and wine glasses shaped to rebuff the attempts of his nose to get in them, were further things Steven had to contend with. None of which were as off-putting as his date's numerous references to her ex-husband throughout the evening.

They picked up the small specials menus at the same time. They both noticed this yet neither mentioned it, and they focused on the options in silence.

He glanced up and gave her the once-over. She had removed her luxury cream woven jacket which sat on her chair back. Her chic, slim fit little black dress bared her lean and tanned shoulders and arms. Her ultra-thin black eye-liner drawn out from the centre toward the ends of her eyes, providing a pointed, sharp finish. Minimal make-up applied elsewhere, except her pink-red lipstick. Her cheek bones creating shall pockets either side of her pout. Her well-manicured eye brows, symmetrical and a shade lighter than her medium-length dark chocolate hair, parted in the middle. In turn, as he reverted to his menu, she too looked at him. She preferred the smart over his smart-casual, and didn't like jewellery on men.

"*How special* are the specials?" Steven asked.

"Sorry?"

"*How special* are the specials? Are the specials additional menu options, or something unusual, stretching? I went with a mate to lunch, out of town mind you, and the specials were salmon or fish pie. I ordered the fish pie. She said the last one had gone. Written on a blackboard, but not rubbed off. Infuriating."

She laughed because it was signalled for her to do so, not because it amused her.

As if on a sunny autumn Sunday walk, he strolled through a selection of historical date convos, London neighbourhoods, the restaurant scene in the US, active holidays, the south of France, film. Nothing worth writing home about. A few of his theories, none of which hit the usual humorous notes, not even at his expense. They discussed wine.

"Judging a book by its cover is one thing, but selecting wine by its label? Any new, untried wine is bought blind."

He expected her to *have to* agree to this, but she took an opposing view, offering that the information outlined on the label, plus its design, indicated a lot. He didn't disagree, but this contrarianism wasn't sexy. He felt both had to pull in the same direction. Up to a point.

When she used the bathroom, Steven ordered her the wrong wine.

Being American, Charlotte began discussing her education, whatever she majored in. This was volunteered information. She studied in Boston.

"Have you been to Boston?"

"Yeah, I've been a couple of times. Work," Steven replied, and left it there.

"You like it?" she pursued. *This* felt like work.

Steven hated Boston. *If you've been to New York ninety-nine times and never been to Boston, go to New York.*

"Love Boston."

Expecting she would keep on this track, he took a long pull of Valpolicella. It warmed him and turned his alcohol dial up a little, from 6.0 to 6.3.

"What do you like about it?" she pursued.

He tried not to lie, "Great seafood, huge oysters, easy to get around."

"Do you miss it?" he asked without interest, retaining her gaze, while turning off audio, and thinking about what he might drink when he got home. What quality of red wine could he tap into when already drunk, without disrupting his tomorrow self. She answered at length while Steven bobbed his head, and pursed his lips.

He went to take a leak.

In the bathroom, dick in one hand, phone in the other, he looked around at what was out there, rattling off some standard copied questions and responses to other women, distributed across London, all sifting, panning. What was next? And next at work too? His boss wasn't going *anywhere*, and there was no vacant level in between. He would have to leave, but he had accrued bonuses which were to be paid, and moving created gaps in payment. This could be thought about on Sunday, or over the rest of dinner. More pressing was what he was going to do once he'd unshackled himself from Charlotte. He felt like he needed noise, some din, somewhere rowdy.

As he sat down he noticed she had taken control of the questioning. In this instance this reflected his ambivalence and not her interest, which it might in other circumstances. Bog standard stuff. Had he lived abroad, hobbies, that sort of thing. Dating one-oh-one. Now he was doing the talking, which he wasn't motivated to do. This wasn't going anywhere.

After answering, he turned it back to her, "Let me guess. You work out, yoga, enjoy eating out, bit of a foodie, podcasts, flower markets, city breaks, skiing."

"Pretty much. Pilates though."

"Everyone's the same now. As London is the same as New York is the same as Berlin is the same as Shanghai."

A large pause, and some looking around the room. Steven felt eyes on him and knew the restaurant staff would pick their lack of rapport.

"Is this somewhere you've been before?" she asked.

"Do I come here often?"

"Yes."

"Just the once," he replied, looking across to the wall on his left.

The waiter dropped off a thick and inky Syrah for him, and a Pinot Noir for her. It was dark enough that she didn't pick its clarity. With new drinks appearing the date was over in spirit, if not yet in time. Steven made a comparison to dates with Marina and others, with shared experiences or a similar sense of humour. He was becoming bored with and uninterested in this datee, and absorbed in the way the wine was heating him and making him feel. New interests in philosophy, maths, and futurism were coursing through his system with the punchy red. He thought of the probability of any date turning into a nonagenarian armchair veranda scenario, overlooking some warm retirement spot, with the perfect mate. Not with Charlotte, that wasn't just a zero percenter; that had a 0.0000000% chance. He thought of the chance with anyone, of meeting someone in the next year. After all, being single, he had a lifetime relationship failure rate of 100%. In terms of longevity, that is. He had had successful failed and short term relationships, judged against other criteria. He slumped into his chair and cradled his bulbous wine glass in the crook of his opposite arm. This was not a good look. He was not *full of industry*, as he had heard a footballer described the previous night.

Steven chose to fire one question after another at her, and let her do the talking, while he nodded, and made appropriate noises based on the tone of her voice, rather than the words themselves.

Charlotte continued on about some work event that was being planned, and it made Steven want to reach up and pull his brain out via his nose, uncoiling and dumping it on the table in front of them like a supply of white sausage. If he had any drugs he would have taken them. He didn't have any drugs. *Not yet*. An oversight, but he didn't want to tempt himself if it was going well, and get himself cancelled.

He put forward an argument on the impact of modern capitalism, something he could recount from umpteen conversations with Annabel, knowing this would push some buttons. Give it some needle. Ecological carnage, overpopulation. Inasmuch as we had any control over how we were fated. Her views and values were otherwise.

They did laugh about something, and as they shared a moment, Steven recalled an ex who loved a restaurant high five. He loved that too, with her. He would be mortified if Charlotte offered him. He was by now misbehaving, offering opinions he wouldn't to someone his speed. He referred to religion as mumbo-jumbo, and dismissed the value of travel at their age, for the sheer waste of time for the travel itself (seven hours each way to Europe, a day either way to North America give or take) and the sameness of big cities, a point he had now made twice. He shook his head as he realised. The drink swayed within him.

Charlotte bristled at his abrasiveness.

"Did you know it was a mistake to marry your husband?" he chucked out there, and she choked on the brashness of the question.

He went on. "On the day itself, the big day. You knew it wouldn't work out, you voiced concern to friends, and they dismissed it, *it's just nerves*. They were the same on their big day. Standard. I've heard this time and time again. Come on?"

Silence.

"I'm right," and he drunk to his awful self, signalling for the bill, as he did so.

The bill was left, and she was furious, yet tried to hide it. If there was any karma for this, he figured he was in surplus from having his car keyed the previous week, so this might level things.

Charlotte was shocked at how this date had unravelled, and descended into a bad date story. The first of many. They had exchanged nice enough messages over the previous week, and he had been nothing like she expected. Her head heavy with disappointment as she gathered her things and they left, whereupon she felt lighter.

They managed 'bye' as Steven strode off and Charlotte walked to her waiting car. She longed for home.

1010
CHAPTER 10

A hangover: Annabel at Tate Britain and Sloane Square: Annabel on a downer: Columbia Flower Market

Oh no.

Steven woke up and it was dark, save for the pale blue-grey glow emitted by his bedside radio system. He knew he was in trouble. Seeing the doorway via some residual lighting from the bathroom light, he had to think to recall the layout of his room; how his flat was configured. As he oriented himself and this fell into place he moved on to physical matters. The problems he had first to resolve were twofold. He had been asleep for some time with his mouth wide open, catching flies, and with both his arms above his head. He had to park the pain from his pounding head, the nausea and the noxious breath, and focus instead on re-hydrating his arid, barren tongue, and the recovery of his dead, heavy arms. He wished he could suck his thumb, to help produce the saliva required to solve problem one, but this was prevented by problem two. His cracked, sore, geographic tongue felt swollen and covered with alligator skin. He closed his mouth and started to suck, drawing saliva around the floor of his mouth, and as it circled the base of his tongue and crept up, it was absorbed with relief, and his tongue was reborn, and before too long, was operational. He opened and shut his lips, and grimaced in the dark at the residual taste and the vague memory of both tequila *and* Sambuca.

He lifted each of his shoulders in turn, and moved his head from side to side. This told him that while his left arm was without response, there was a little life in the top of his right arm. He was able to rotate his right shoulder blade so that his right arm began to move clockwise, until his elbow was in line with his head. As his elbow continued on its circular path, and as his hand levelled with his head, the nerves in his arms began to correct themselves. Blood flow was re-introduced to his limbs, with light pins and needles. He gave it some time to recover, and then took that arm back behind his head to retrieve and winch his remaining lifeless appendage, holding his warm but deadened hand and pulling until it was over his head and then by his side, at which point he released and it thudded into his goose down duvet without a ripple.

He turned to his clock and was unsurprised that it displayed 4:52am. Five o'clock, that habitual time for a body abused by alcohol to stir back to life. That unfortunate truth that when the body needed rest, it failed to supply it in full. He reached into his top bedside drawer for the old Ibuprofen–Paracetamol one-two, the double, those most complimentary of bedfellows for the hungover. He reached down for bottled water, kept at the edge of his bed for moments like this, and knocked back the pills before gulping several large mouthfuls, as large air bubbles rose through the neck and into the body of water.

After removing the suckled bottle and casting it to the floor, he gasped and exhaled, and his head started to spin and pound with his heart. At moments like this he yearned for sleep. To sleep was to ride out the trauma, to allow the body to recuperate, without struggle. But he was bolt awake. And horny. He realised then that this might become a painful, long, sleepless, four-wank morning.

If history was anything to go by, and why wouldn't it be, there were two ways today could go. If he could put away and keep down water, coffee, toast, the meds, and get to sleep for a couple of hours he should wake late morning and salvage something from the day. If he failed to sleep, or threw up, he could be in for a long day, on his back, staring at the ceiling, his head receiving an unrelenting pile-on of broken, interrupted, meandering thoughts covering all matters. Recounting work issues, girl problems, an ever-burgeoning task list, holiday plans, thoughts and ideas ingested from the range of media flowing content to his cortex that week. If he was sick, that worst of fates, the empty stomach filling with bile which needed regular emptying, could see him stricken the whole day, coming back to life in the evening, when he could consume a delivered pizza and watch a movie before turning in to recover lost hours. Should he be fortunate enough to fluke a midday recovery, he could organise a night out, whereupon he would be protected from another hangover, bulletproof after that first big night.

The night before had turned to black, twisted through drink. He tasted bourbon and some dark spirit in the background notes beyond the shots. He hadn't been clubbing or he would still be out, yet he saw rays of colour and felt soul music. A couple of girls and their boyfriends he spoke with while smoking. East London. It could be difficult to improvise somewhere decent so late, he would check his messages to retrace who helped him get there, but not now.

Annabel had sufficient time, if not the requisite energy, for an enjoyable trip to Tate Britain. She hadn't committed herself to it, in case she went on somewhere with Barney after the park, but she felt she had to catch a photography exhibition before it closed in a week's time. A show not enough of a draw to visit within the first few weeks, but a lingerer in the diary, pushed back, now ending, last week.

About two miles as the crow flew, yet a painstaking fifty-minute journey by public transport, bus, train, foot. She decided to suck up the cost of a car, as she wouldn't have spent much over the course of the weekend, and excessive public transport at the weekend sucked. Although dropped off nearer to the side entrance, she preferred to walk around to the front, and enter via the original portico. For the romance.

A corporate sponsor list made her shudder, from banking, consultancy, energy, technology, automotive. Not places you'd find artistic soul. Strategies for growth via oblique means. A donation here, an opened door, a meeting there.

As she passed through a great ceilinged hall, she looked up, extended her arms out to her side, and spun, oblivious to a few greying visitors from afar, to the young couples from the city. She didn't give a shit. In this place of living and historical artistry, full of the masters of soul and craft, what would they make of what this had become. Had it always been thus? The richest person who ever lived was not in modern times. And how the twentieth century artists must have whored themselves around for any deal to establish and elevate themselves, to enjoy the finest. Wasn't art, like horse-racing or boats, just another arbitrary tool for the competing elites? Yet she felt the hollowing out of London, New York, from conversations with older generations, from what they were. Places of ideas and lives centred on fulfilment of those ideas, to rack and ruin. The gentrification of *out there* boroughs. Selling out now standard operating procedure.

She spun a little more, and then stepped the length of the building, picking up a ticket, climbing the wide winding staircase with heavy legs, and entering the exhibition. It was full of people, and she felt quite bitter. That was last week for you. But caught herself, and considered this reflected well on society, until she was knocked by an elbow as she squeezed to see a large photograph of a crowd circling a monument. Behind, a London so plain, so dark, ubiquitous, in shades of black, grey and white, with no advertising, save the shop signs, many protruding to face on to the oncoming walker. A simpler life, but not one that provoked any envy. The polluted, colourless city. Yet today on the other side of the world, perhaps a better life for the poorer nations, with, on balance, fewer externalities. The words from a recent talk rang in her ears, the world, humankind, has never had it so good.

Skipping the clogged first third, she found some space in room three, and let these thoughts stew as she took in the history before her. With space she found physical calm, while she tried to relax and unfurl her tight mind. She saw an old colleague some distance ahead with a boyfriend, and she hung back, not wanting to talk to her. Grasping the perceptibility of the unconscious when in the proximity of known others, she had to move further away and put others in between them. Still, she could see her searching, looking behind in a way one wouldn't expect of someone focused on the pieces, as everyone else was in room five. Millions of years of evolution of our ancestors and beyond, at play right there.

She took her time to finish off, reading her mini booklet, seated, before loitering back and around some favourites, until she needed air and her legs needed to get going again. Following an older man through the heavy doors, and then leaving through the sliding doors, she figured Kings Road was a good a place as any nearby to pick up a new cookbook and a replacement French press, and avoid the centre. She feared this turning into a wild goose boondoggle, but went anyway.

Dropped off at the bookshop, she found what she needed and made her way up east to the department store at Sloane Square and descended to the kitchen department. A targeted trip which didn't take long. Bag for you? Would you like a bag? How would you like to pay? You can take your card now. She winced at the ubiquity of payments, as the populace shuffled to a cashless society and total government control of money. A problem to fret about another day.

At Sloane Square she waited for an underground train, Eastbound, three minutes away. Beside her two girls were sharing the latest. "So I was like 'I'm gonna need a refund, yeah?' and she goes 'I can get you a credit, or a gift card' and so I go..." and Annabel walked further down the platform to remove herself from this interaction of butchery.

Opposite, weighed down by their purchases and worn down by the years, an attractive and still young couple stood in apposite silence. Laden with shopping bags, there were out of words. They had nothing further to say, after having discussed the kitchenware they needed, and negotiated at length their bespoke needs. The potential usage occasions and storage limitations. He checked his phone, scrolling and scrolling, as she looked down the track. He even glanced the wrong way down the track, and there they stood, looking in opposite directions, tagged forever in Annabel's memory. A dead relationship, still walking, waiting to deteriorate to its inevitable trough, whereby they could agree to bury it. Awaiting an event to wrench them apart forever, one fast approaching. A Westbound train trundled toward them, in the distance, thirty seconds away.

"Are you hungry?" he asked, the evergreen question within any dying relationship.

"Yeah, shall we get something on the way home?"

The question tennis has started. A meandering debate through a multitude of variables (spicy/not-spicy, cost, meal duration time, nationality, locale) until one of them acquiesced to make it all stop.

He looked up and straight at Annabel, and their eyes met, as the train coughed, slurred and rattled in, in turn cutting off and then allowing their stares with each passing door and window, until it squawked to a standstill, and the pressure gauges puffed out and the doors forced themselves open.

The closing doors consigned them to Annabel's past, and they were gone, back to Chiswick or Richmond.

Steven lay for hours that day, awake, staring at the ceiling, unable to sleep, reforming some of the night's images when they returned, recalling amusing conversation. He endured the longest of waiting games, horizontal except for bathroom trips, made doubled over to keep the head at waist level, thereby minimising the pounding. Boredom that wasn't worth it. He wouldn't feel right again and ready for food until six o'clock that evening. He felt ready for change. In that way that he had felt ready for change many times before.

Once home and changed into something comfortable, Annabel picked up a novel she had started during the week, and which had been recommended to her by a reliable friend. She had covered many of the classical authors when studying English Literature, and benefitted from their lessons in her own life. She loved to re-read some loved classic or other by a pool somewhere hot, warming herself in the nostalgia of the words. Perhaps a memory of a Drama teacher she might have had an affair with, had it been the seventies, not the noughties. She fell now into contemporary authors and their improbable tales, distant lands. Most of all she loved to stumble on something which felt real, close to home.

The novel was causing her some discomfort; the tough subject matter, and a style that she found grating. She tried to push on, then stopped, and again. Until she threw the novel so that it skidded and scuffed across the kitchen floor, grating on the specks of mud and grit. The first step on its journey to recycling.

She attempted to find something appropriate, yet that couldn't be something that better fit her present mood, as that would take her further down. But something positive, uplifting? No, that wouldn't work either. She sunk into the sofa as a wave of numbness and a distant ache in her shoulders sunk her, and she put her hands to her head. She had to keep moving, so she grabbed her things, and left her home to walk, somewhere. A predictable local loop.

The evening was a fug of red wine and a home-made lentil dish. Cooking was an active distraction, with a minor sense of completion. A gardening show and a section on water features, something her dad had installed, pumping to no end in the clean English back gardens, powered by coal burned somewhere dirty out of sight.

Round and around the water flowed, outside hospitals, train stations, modern city concourses, calming the lucky first world. Up and away the bi-products rose, into the beyond, unfurled.

A film she'd seen before streaming in the background, the internet in her foreground. Data centres whirring and buzzing, lights red and green highlighting, validating, cooling fans blowing. Temperature monitored, air conditioning responding, in warehouses beneath the American sun.

And bed at nine-thirty, misery paused, to bring tomorrow forward.

The next day, waiting for the kettle to boil, Annabel stretched up, in her white vest and soft light pink pyjama bottoms. She felt spring and its light was coming, which made her glad. Winter this year had been a bitch, and she had felt more disconnected and uninterested than ever. The discussions of the re-imposition of limited restrictions. Tyranny without end suffered in other countries. It wasn't enough to be satisfied that it wasn't on these shores. For suffer there today, suffer here tomorrow. Keeping up with the world around felt like a chore, and her media consumption had shifted away from satisfying inquisitions, curiosities, or the wonder of the new, to a barrage of political and current affairs commentators reinforcing her isolated chamber. Being single had removed one usual distraction, but she didn't have the inclination or the energy to supply the answers to two people's needs and wants.

She stood on the end of her toes and leaned into the counter, pressing her palms flat on top, and took a good look at the sky and the light. She opened the windows and felt she needed some colour, some prettiness and delicacy. She took a long, hot shower, cleaned herself several times over, and moisturised. She put on no make-up, but she did put on some favourite underwear, something she had worn on first dates, just in case.

Dressed in a light beige wool coat, a thin black roll neck and a long, hippyish patterned skirt, she left home and walked the length of London Fields park. Boys played basketball on the court in two groups, a separate game happening at each end. Others played football in spots on the grass, a ball rolling in front of her as she stuck to the main pathway. A whiff of spliff smoked across her, and she looked around at who was puffing at this time. It wasn't clear, with or without her prejudices. Shiny laughing gas canisters congregated in a grouping just off the pathway, next to a bench.

Broadway Market was as appealing as ever to the sensibilities given to her by her fashionable middle class upbringing. She looked into the window of the closed bookshop which was decent for picking up something offbeat, before grabbing a coffee. Passing the pavement breakfasters, she reached the bridge and looked left toward the gasworks and the still, dark canal water. Nothing moved, the boats all moored with local residents. People jogged on by, cyclists passed, and the odd electric scooter zoomed along, rushing its owner to their next tasks. Two women walked toward her, laden with plants and flowers purchased at her destination.

She hacked on down Goldsmiths Row, through the residential sections with high walls and hatched wire fencing, and along a peaceful pedestrian section alongside Haggerston Park, to reach Columbia Road Flower Market. She hustled the rest of her coffee down lest it should burst the lid off in the crush.

Passing the hangers-on on the fringes, she was sucked into the throng and being inched along at half a mile per hour. It was like being at a bar two hundred deep, and one of the few places young parents couldn't tackle with a pram.

An environment dominated, owned by young couples, with their mutual protection and mobility, able to dive in and out of tight spots, to survive the puffing and buffeting. Annabel liked to wonder about one thing they might do behind closed doors. A game she played also when watching *A Place in the Sun*. She saw an odd couple, not good-looking, yet who looked connected and, she imagined, might have a wild time. She compared this with the tight, buttoned up couples, put together, but who might never drop any barriers, and let each other in. Things that turn them on, words each of them may have said with others, left unspoken. Maybe ugly couples just did it better, putting in the work.

Annabel was surrounded by people. And behind the people, were peonies, lilies and orchids, roses, tulips, fuchsias, sunflowers, hydrangeas, and trays of bedding plants. Yellow, purple, white, pink, fuchsia, and orange explosions. Verdant green lines of yuccas, crassulas, areca palms, rubber plants, lipstick plants, snake plants, cotton plants. Lemon trees, and deserts of cacti. She went the full length, deciding that on her return, she would negotiate a couple of indoor plants and a bunch of yellow tulips, even though she could get those anywhere. Then she worried about the flower miles.

As she made her way back along the pass, amid the crush and the push and the shove, there was a rumble and some shouting ahead, and the bodies in front moved back. Her foot was trapped under a large boot and she fell back. Someone fell on top of her, and the plants went over. Words had been said, spaces had been invaded and a melee had broken out. Men were separated, women too. A couple behind her helped Annabel up but as they did so, her jaw knocked into someone's knee, also trying to right themselves. It was a rough experience, and it shook her up, plus the embarrassment of being grounded and the disarray of her shoulder bag which had shed some items. The lack of control. Peace was restored, and the couple helped her to the pavement with her things, and made sure she was all right. Her eyes welled up as she tried to convince them she was, enough at least that they could be on their way.

She insisted they left her shaken, and she took off, calling a car for home and away from people.

Spring

1011
CHAPTER 11
Helen and family: Annabel meets Steven for lunch

Helen was WingFH and approaching the end of her day, normal hours at least. She sat on a call with two other people, so had to pay attention and be ready to jump in.

She begged for the call to end, and made closing noises in her tone of voice as things appeared to be getting near to wrapping. Influencing the removal of air from the online room. Exasperated as a final can of worms was opened by one of her colleagues, as they were closing in on the closing of laptop lids at the close of business.

Once dispatched, the machine whirred in the background, while she curled her legs, tucked beneath her bottom on the sofa in her patchy, threadbare tracksuit bottoms and smart work sweater. Yet it whispered and winked at her: check me, I'm watching. The paranoid survive, so Helen assumed her every move was tracked, screenshots sent to her manager, summaries of her *interactions*, emails sent and read, time spent active tracked via mouse movements. So in downtime periods, she would check the odd application, open a few things, view a few meeting invites, whatever. Her pièce de résistance, however, was to make a note (on paper) of videos shared by the team and put one of them on for an hour or so.

She would start to leave the day behind in the early evening, check in after a while, send a few late emails, look like she was still online, and cared about doing a thorough job, *into her own time* if necessary to *get the job done*. She had mentioned a headache to a couple of people during the day, buy herself a little wiggle room if needed.

Should one be sick, the questions on *how one was feeling?* [subtext: when will you be back at 100% and doing your own work again?]

In the background, on low volume for company, *pandemic* spillover debate continued unabated as global hotspots suffered new political low points, and tactics at home continued to align the country to a form of globalist centralised control under the banner of health protection. Helen and her loved ones had been heavy net gainers from the National Health Service, and she understood this, and had wanted lives to be saved and people to be kept safe. Being a good person. And yet here was someone who was straight with people, who balked at the ongoing fearmongering. At times, she thought, spread with the best of intentions, she questioned if the ends justified the means. One could, after all, convince a child to eat their greens by threatening to kill the dog. She grabbed the remote off the floor after lunging at it and knocking it off the table's edge. And turned the TV off at the mention of this 'evil' virus; a virus was no more evil than a kidney nostalgic or a liver benevolent, she pondered. Human hands may have been tied a little on carbon emissions, but left behind were a tsunami of masks, protective equipment and precautionary plastics in countryside hedges and swirling in ocean trash centres. Memories of across the board overreach, toddler masking, old people dying alone, people kept apart at funerals if they even had one, made her *smh*. A year later you couldn't even get a jab if you wanted one.

Helen wanted to spend some time with the thousand-page historical novel she had become involved in, sucked into. It connected her to great stretches of summer freedom as a young woman, when a pile of books could be conquered, studying History and English. School had been a tough place for her for some years, but these were bright spots. She shut the laptop lid, fixed a cup of tea, her tenth or thereabouts that day, and knew that she had the best chance of putting thirty undisrupted minutes into her tome if she went to the bathroom again.

On the first page, it was clear that her eyes were scanning the words but they weren't going in. She worked back over a couple of paragraphs three or four times and stopped. Her head was full, and she replaced her bookmark, dropped the book on the floor next to her tea, swung her legs up and lay on her back, staring at the white ceiling, tracing the edges of its cornicing and light fitting.

In rare happier times, when motivated, she was as forward looking as the next, figuring her route through whatever obstacles, casting the past aside. However, tougher days had brought with them much intro and retrospections, and allowed the long list of regrets, missteps, and an embarrassment of humiliations and low moments, to hove into view. A spiteful act by a friend at junior school. How she initiated and handled the break-up with a first boyfriend. Brought home drunk by the police for her own safety. Forced out of a job by a manager. Some toilet incident, like everyone. And worst of all, the one moment at school she joined in with the bullies' laughter at a poor girl's expense. If she could erase any one moment, that would be the one. *And of the eight worst mistakes you've talked us through today Helen, which is the one you would choose for us to take away from you, forever?*

She took herself for a walk, being a cursorial animal, happiest when in motion. She thought to leave her phone at home, pinging away to itself, but there was too much randomness in the streets, so she took it with her swirling troubles. Financial calculations and the lack of money *put aside*. Ambitions to move. The burden of sisters with children, all popped out in their twenties, consistent with suburban life. The eight pensions she had vowed she would get around to consolidating. The financial adviser she had been recommended who she never got around to calling. Sister-she-likes stress. Sister-she-likes-less stress. The reality of mum and dad, the memory of cherished grandparents. The pain of calling home. And what in fuck's name to do with her career. She wanted something new, but what? Eating too much processed garbage. A barren social calendar. The last two she could do something immediate about, so she bought some bagged salads, and texted a few friends to put something in to look forward to. For she needed to begin to look forward again.

A brisk walk to the local park and beyond was spoiled for Helen by her telephoning sister. An ominous notification made Helen tense up, her lower arms and gut clenched, answering with a light swipe, as if a feather-like touch would lead to a gentler outcome. Her immediate concern was an emergency or bad news, which was assuaged by the tone of her sister's voice. No panic, no fear, no urgency.

Surpassing that first hurdle, Helen nudged her concerns on to how much she was going to have to give her. Sibling donations. She was right to assume there would be some preamble, and after a bit of back-and-forth, it would go a little quiet and then a soft voice would exit a sentence beginning with, "Helen, I was wond..."

Helen ticked off the prerequisites; how she was, how Phil was, how work was, how the others were. And was figuring out a number. A number that would be fine, say £100. A number that wouldn't, say £500.

"Helen, I was going to ask. We're a bit short of the mortgage this month. You couldn't help us out, could you? We'll pay you back."

Always the mortgage. Never short for the cigarettes or cider or weed.

"How much?" Helen braced.

The line was bad and her sister was calling from a busy street, kids shouting in the background. "... hundred be OK?" was all she heard. She assumed this was not the whole request.

"Phone me when you're somewhere quieter," she shouted, and cut the call.

Helen walked home, blood coursing with new stress hormones, something she knew would affect her all day and in all likelihood hang over her attempts at sleep. She wanted a clear day or two, maybe a week, where things were easy, something good happened, forward movement. No new obstructions, obfuscations, obligations to deal with. Obstetrics was something she *could* handle.

The council were parked up on a corner, where, surrounding a large litter bin, were two sets of drawers, an ironing board, a mirror, and a child's bike. A pile of dirty, sodden clothes was heaped on top. A man picked up the detritus chunk by chunk, and heaved it over the caged rear of his van. This common spot was hit every day by fly-tippers, over and over again. The worker felt it, the pointlessness of it all. Helen looked at him with a half-smile of sympathy, and a shake of the head to communicate her distaste for the way people treated the community. It would be the same tomorrow, and the day after.

Helen had escaped the suburb in the town which held her relatives via its gravitational pull on the powerless. And like the need for humankind to fight to retain its freedoms, so she too had to scrap the crap town, desperate to keep its lifeblood. Old friends who missed her. Family who needed help and support, incapable of self-sufficiency, unable to figure their way out of problems. The lower cost of housing when coupled with a new hybrid working norm, meant these places became attractive again. Return. Once age had dulled and taken the edge off the need to go to live music, arts, theatrical events. And the numbness of a fifth Van Gogh exhibition.

It was one fight she continued to win. If a town captured her in the future, it would be elsewhere, further even, somewhere the other side of London, where the capital would become a further roundabout obstacle, and add a convenient inconvenient extra ninety minutes to any journey home.

Wherever she remained, their expectations that Big Time Helen, who knew how things worked, who could help get things done, spare a few quid with her 'big job' down in London. An accolade she found laughable.

Her better living never led to respect or admiration, but spite and manipulation. She never understood this. And she succumbed to requests for help. It was a small price to have escaped, to have put it behind her, knowing that with each handout she would have respite, a month or two, before another request. The price of quiet.

As she paced for home, she was now hurried to get back, take the call, find a resolution, kick their canned cider down the road. She recalled previous beefs, anticipating the detail, of an argument that may unfold, and found herself concocting arguments with herself with information not given, for a situation not yet real. She kicked herself for it. For becoming angry within her imagination. Her thoughts flipped between real history and imagined possible outcomes, as she flicked between each of her mother and two sisters, hearing their problems, their criticisms of her, when she was young, now into middle age. Her father scowling in the background.

'Jesus Christ!' she cursed, struggling to unlock the two locks to enter, dumping down bag, keys, gloves, scarf, and coat, before she boiled from the twenty-three-degree heat indoors, as her phone rang.

"Hold on a minute," she said, taking the call, grabbing headphones while trying to sort her stuff, before sitting down.

She slowed her sister down. Stop. One thing at a time. Her

concentration wasn't there. She sat with a biro in hand, hovering above a blank pad, as she heard her sister break, beginning to cry. Something she thought to be genuine. And the tug of sympathy, of familial compassion, overcame her, and she too welled up and choked a little. Something for which she never forgave herself.

She heard her out, and they agreed a sum of three hundred pounds, which Helen transferred while they were speaking. Then the ended call would end matters.

"That's done."

"Thanks Hel. Also, mum's emphysema's flared up."

"I've told you umpteen times, you need to get the council to move you away from that main road. And Dad needs to stop chuffing. Or do it outside."

"It's winter though."

"Emphysema's a serious matter, if he can't smoke away from mum, what the hell can any of us do?"

"Could you call the council Hel, you know what to say?"

"You're thirty-five years old. You live there, they won't listen to me."

There was a long pause, a telephonic stand-off. Helen had done a sales course, and knew not to give into the silence. She was not going to commit to resolving this.

"OK, can you find the number at least?" her sister requested.

Helen begrudged the internet search, conceding ground.

"I'll text it to you now," Helen confirmed.

"Thanks Hel," and that was that.

She took the L, and with there being many a bigger L out there, she considered it a W.

Helen had to take a conference call from home, with a contact from a partner business. They were both distracted and put upon by having to have the conversation. Helen was pushing back a slew of meetings to the week after, wherever she had the option. This freed her time for this week to get some non-work done while at home, and moreover, were she to *die suddenly* in the next week she wouldn't have wasted her time doing the damn things. Her contact was nodding as Helen spoke, looking attentive, until she garnered from the reflections in his glasses, of female images zipping from side to side, he was in fact swiping away on dating apps.

They finished up and she left home to get some milk. She kept moving, too much, getting up, moving about, picking things up, going for walks. Like a hyperactive pensioner, she felt safer on the move, no sitting duck.

She walked past her neighbours, who were retired and owned the full block, as opposed to an individual flat like most others on that strip. Four storeys bottom to top, bought for a song in the nineteen eighties, for a year's wages for the two of them with their ex-government jobs. Now worth £2.5m. A generation that never saw war, handed everything if they were savvy enough to get on the ladder.

Helen, while bitter about this, was conscious that they to her, were the same as she was to a millennial. Stuck in an endless cycle of handing over a huge chunk of their wages as rent to a professional landlord or buy-to-letter in their forties or fifties who got on a rung and climbed a couple.

They said hellos, in that way that people did, who have known each other a long time, were different people, and of little use to each other. In case they ever needed urgent help, but with little enthusiasm. The couple got into their five-year-old BMW, the wife getting in the passenger door, giving it firm closure, the door giving a satisfying whump as it shut. Tens of thousands of man hours, all to engineer that fine, quality acoustic, which served no practical purpose. Yet it shifted units.

At the corner, an ambulance with its ear-splitting sirens, stuck, immobile. She recognised the van in front, and figured the owner had his jungle music up so loud, and was so deaf as a result of that vicious cycle, the cyclical ramping up of stereo volumes, that he hadn't clocked.

The sun, having struggled off the horizon from its low winter level, now sat halfway up the sky, and was head on into his eyes. He hadn't taken the care to pull down his sun shield. A few passers-by waved at him to draw his attention to life-saving matters.

He cursed and pulled over, gesticulating. The ambulance, heavy and from a standing start gave it the big heave to get going.

Helen hoped lives wouldn't be lost, but for every few seconds of delay, and across enough incidents, in time they would be. The *pandemic* saw national and local governments roll out long preferred schemes, and Helen saw the tangled impacts of low traffic neighbourhoods and cycle lanes on the emergency services and their now less than rapid response. Pollution shunted from one location to another, pushed from pleasanter to nastier streets or to the main arterial roads. Cars, vans, lorries, lined up, idling rather than moving. An ongoing pinch-point for the last two months, a sufferance every time she went to the shop, due to temporary lights, and no works on the roadworks. Guaranteed. Trade-offs, always with the trade-offs, complexity beyond that of her childhood, with its bare roads with minimal markers, signs and local exoticisms. Now, when making certain trips near the end of a tube line, she might start her journey travelling in the wrong direction, to be able to change and get on at all, maybe get a seat, before heading in the direction she needed to go.

Watching the news, seeing others' convictions and determined stances, their untrammelled vision for what the world should be or become, the unwavering confidence that *they were right*, made Helen feel weak. Apart from views at the extremes upon which many concur, Helen sat as a centrist, wavering about like an old fashioned radio needle, scanning left to right in search of somewhere to settle.

On occasion, she even took heat for not making up her mind. Sensed and preyed upon weakness from flailing in the wind, with no sense of right or direction.

She challenged the views she heard from all sides, testing opinions by turning around the circumstance. Imagining what the other side were thinking, how they saw it, going against the flow. Something which could pay dividends on the underground, following 'No Entry' signs against the grain of people, and avoiding large unwieldy loops in the interest of the planned flow of human capital.

She could fill her spare hours and walks with opinion piece podcasts, from different wings or thoughts, otherwise having some talk shows on the wireless or in the car. Oftentimes, however, it built up, the gradual weight of opinion from the sheer number of issues.

She wasn't in prison and knew no-one in prison. So allowing her ears to fill with the strains of a debilitated justice system, crying for reform, creaking, maddening itself under mental health issues and drug abuse, left her exhausted. Yet, she didn't have children either, so should she show no interest in education? Spent no time in the Middle East. Whatever?

No, she felt everyone should have an opinion for a functioning society.

From her centrist positioning, lockdowns must have worked. Keeping people apart must have been effective. Yet plenty of data showed that they didn't. Some countries with no or light lockdowns fared well. Who didn't want a better environment, but people needed food, transport, jobs, clothes, a good time. She saw too much binary thinking. People made up their minds, then found the data and reasoning which entrenched them further.

This agonising constancy, balanced, stuck between two boats was tiring, yet she found some solace in her perceived moral superiority of being able to countenance both sides of the argument, to be able to challenge anyone on their viewpoint. However, it led to much churning, even in the most peaceful of circumstances. In the early 2000s, a swim would have been a sound way for Helen to clear her mind, to meditate, setting her body in repetitive motions requiring muscle energy and memory, and little mental input. Now, she never switched off, and the silence and mellow she found beneath the surface as she dived her head under with each breast stroke, ran alongside her whirling thoughts, chewing over the week's political, economic, world fat, plus her career and personal woes.

In her full body swim suit, by reliable old Speedo, she walked the width of the pool to her personal lane. Without thinking, she scanned the pool, noting a high female to male ratio. That never meant absolute safety, but removed the not insubstantial stress were it to be majority male.

She sat on the edge and checked her hair was tied back well enough under and behind her cap, rinsed and applied her goggles and took care to lower herself down into the warm cool of the disorienting pool. High on chlorine, buffeted by substantial ripples by the muscular man crawling in the adjacent lane. She pushed off the wall with a froglike spring, the soles of her feet feeling the small tiles, slippery from a thin layer of water squished between them.

Despite the waves, she was relieved her neighbour was swimming a crawl, head rotating from side-to-side, rather than approaching him during each length, head on, moving toward her and eyeing her up and down, should he choose to.

The swimmer was powering away in bespoke goggles, his large shoulders and arms, upper, lower, working in symmetry, with force and balance. Helen figured he might be a triathlon type, training ahead of the next competition, for he lacked a certain grace that a dedicated swimmer might possess. The wrong kind of splash. Something her swimming team years at school gave her an eye for.

She considered how disciplined and obsessive he might be. The powders, the supplements, the sleep, the nutrition, shakes, special menus, the sacrifice of fun, to achieve his goals. The possibility of coming, for the first time, in the top fifty of some regional event. And how to be the best, to hold a place at the top table, most must sacrifice all distractions, remove all the noise beyond that one objective. Something that needn't concern *her*, yet she knew there was a general lesson in there for anybody, around focus, determination, and sacrifice outside oneself.

Absolute ruthlessness.

This meditation and mental meanderings passed the time as she automated herself through the first lengths.

She relaxed, and the mental space created from doing so, became engulfed by worry, and matters which needed attention. Her consolation that being active meant she at least isolated one problem at a time, times three, until she had completed her thirty minutes, upon which she left for home.

Steven had been in touch with Annabel to organise breakfast on Sunday. She regretted this when she woke. She was becoming atomised, begrudging dependencies and commitments.

Her overnight began with a fitful start, struggling to drift off, then waking. Then she was caught into a period of sustained deepest of sleep, which left her grasping at the storyline of several dreams. The most prominent an emergency situation as she passed dark smoke up-pouring from an apartment window, and her inability to get help. When connected to nine nine nine, she didn't know the address, and couldn't continue to talk with them while trying to checks maps. No street signs. Familiar streets and a lost memory. Waking was a relief.

They had agreed upon a casual corner joint on Marylebone High Street, with high ceilings and good air flow. The food was beyond passable.

"Belle," he called as she walked in, removing headphones, searching.

She walked over, and he vacated the banquet seating for her, which she thanked him for, before plonking her bag down, and casing her headphones.

They didn't kiss, that wasn't always their style. Different farings for different pairings.

He admired her figure from the front, and as she turned her back to him to fix her bag, he took his time to run his eyes down the curves of her hips to her bottom, in skinny jeans, and then back up her slim body, in a classic, box clean white tee. As she turned, the photography on the wall grabbed his attention. Did she know his eyes were on her, or did women assume something else? She straightened her hair and settled.

"They have a *breakfast* menu," she commented.

"Yes, they do. Comprising *brunch* items. Granola, smashed avocado, eggs four ways. Brunch 101, slopped out by some junior. I just like being somewhere you can breathe."

"Agreed."

"We can have a coffee and a drink for half an hour, and then get some lunch plates."

"Yes, let's."

It was little effort for Annabel to get the server's attention, and he came across. They ordered coffees and a prosecco.

"I'll have one with food," she appeased.

They spoke about family; who they'd seen, who they'd heard from, who'd gone underground. There didn't seem to be any news, not even of their comical, outrageous uncles. The humorous familial edge cases.

Coffee and drinks came. Steven caught the female assistant giving Annabel a good onceover.

They spoke about work. While they didn't have any strong mutual friendships, they both knew many of each other's friends, through party and get-together osmosis. This gave them sufficient range for update fodder, at the crazy end of the spectrum if need be.

When the clocks were striking twelve, Steven called the assistant over and they ordered some lunch.

"How's dating?" he asked.

"I saw a guy a few times, he kept asking me out to do things."

"Bastard."

"An exhibit, walking, the races. I was busy. Haven't heard from him."

"Funny that. Brad Pitt theory. Or Ryan Gosling theory, for the millennial."

"How does that go?"

"I get this all the time. You're interested in someone you like, who you aspire to. And they leave your messages hanging, or they're busy for ages, and it's one excuse after another. And what they're really saying is they are too busy to do whatever it is with *you*."

He expanded. "Say Ryan's calling her up, wants to take her out clubbing. Is she going to knock him back? Got quite a busy week with work, have to visit my mum. Gosling Theory – you're not interesting/hot/appealing enough, it's nothing to do with the demand itself."

"What other theories ya got?"

"Not so much a theory, but I've been thinking about how each of our lives could break down into ten phases, or roles, even the most uninteresting of people. Memoir sections. Let's take you."

"Oh, let's don't."

"Come on."

She indicated she wasn't going to protest any longer.

"So there was the swot phase."

"Obvs."

"Mini rebellion phase, but nothing to push you off course. Literature phase?" he suggested, counting on his fingers now, "Festival and Ibiza phase. Bad boy old men phase," he laughed, swigging his prosecco, "Now you're in art and green world peace phases."

"So I've got a few phases left?"

"Well, you should be a mother, pass those genes on."

"And bring children into this world?" she asked. "What are your phases?" she added, not wishing to be probed further.

More finger counting.

"Films & TV, Hollywood. Golf. Weed stroke music. Drugs stroke clubbing. Business. Serial dating. Drinking has been a constant source of comfort, an ever companion."

"Wholesome."

Some *plates* they ordered turned up, with drinks, and they both stopped talking for a while, enjoyed the hum and the drum of the cars sloping by, the posh chatter, and chavvy natter. The background kitchen clanks, the hisses and whooshes of the coffee machines. The shutting of teapot lids, the gathering of cutlery.

"Give me some dating funnies then."

"One girl said she liked waterboarding on holiday," he answered. "You know, girls at work said they'd like someone to ask them out in the street. That's got to be something that sounds nice in theory, but really?"

"Oh no. Awkward," Annabel confirmed with quizzical eyes and a sour mouth, "Gosling, maybe. Don't you do it. You'll get arrested."

"If she's a siren, it may need a ballsy move. How's the focaccia?"

"Bouncy."

"If you or your friends ever need a male opinion…"

"Thanks, I'll remember that," she said.

"Never let a man answer a question with a question. Obvious enough, right? But the things you can get away with. Why would you ask if I love you or not?"

They enjoyed their drinks, and Steven clarified for Annabel in no uncertain terms how Helen and Phil were going nowhere, and why Helen needed to move on, while they shared a kale Caesar salad, mackerel pate with toasts, and polenta chips.

"What's the difference between Italians and toast? You can make soldiers out of toast."

Annabel couldn't help herself and let out a laugh. As the food disappeared, so their conversation slowed, before it stopped. They sat in a Mutual Assured Fug. As noise levels increased as the place filled up further, and sticky Bellinis were sunk, Annabel surveyed the pairs and groups surrounding them. On the surface, so much happiness, warmth and support. Or was it a sea of games, power and dominance. Neither women nor men in abusive relationships walked around with a sign hanging from their necks. Children crushed by the ambitions of domineering parents were able to eat Eggs Florentine without incident.

Annabel didn't need to check with Steven, and caught the server's attention.

"We'll settle up, please."

Once done, Annabel shuffled and scooched along the leather seating to freedom, and they paused outside, where she gave him a quick hug that he wasn't expecting.

"I'm going to an art event with Helen soon, one of Francesca's. You *like* Francesca, you should come, I'll check it's OK. We'll get noodles after."

"OK, see you."

"Ciao."

And they went their separate ways.

1100
CHAPTER 12

Steven work meanderings: Josie date-shopping: Steven and Josie first restaurant date

It was Friday afternoon and it was spring-cool, a slight sun tentative in the distance, with a breeze to refresh any passers-by not flanked by tall buildings. After an unhurried lunch with some colleagues, a pint and some casual spicy Asian, Steven had returned to the office and slumped, reading through a pile of pure madness, busywork and arbitrary deadlines and *needs*. It wasn't long before he felt warm and sticky, oozing the sweat from chillies and beef, and so went to the bathroom to wash his face, hands and forearms in cold water, twice, and felt the pull to go outside.

A frantic client, coming back to him, post-sale. Hadn't got the memo; you're in another team's hands now. Bonus accrued, and on he had moved. One of the ten percent of dysfunctional clients that can be found in any supplier or agency-side roster. He considered these lot to be one of the worst he'd had to deal with, until he checked himself and this recency bias, and played back some long forgotten nightmares. In the ninety percent, one would find the tight, the witless, the slow, the unorganised, the finger pointers, the plain liars, even some decent, fair people. The ten percent comprised the moon-on-a-stick lot, the power abusers, the direction-changers, and the time thieves. The worst, for time was the most precious commodity. What use were millions with months to live. With enough time, even the destitute had hope and an upward route.

He put his headphones in and began to walk, tapping and swiping away, clearing backlog. Direction-changers and time-wasters. He was just relieved to reside in the city, where the prospect well never ran dry. Always some people churn, as relationships, affairs and flings ended, and the markets shook out the incompatible or those over-reaching, as they found their equilibrium. He couldn't believe what life was like in the shires. A taste he got during the odd weekend away outside the M25, and it could be a couple of potentials, a day, piped into his device. Here, it never stopped. Like 4am traffic or the 6am tube, there was always plenty going around. Room at the top, middle and bottom.

Walking and talking (to himself) he checked his email and saw the ominous 'Catch Up' put in by his boss for Monday. He wondered for a moment if there might be an HR person in the meeting too, but he'd been putting the deals away left, right, he was bullet proof. No good salesperson goes punished, no matter the misdemeanours. It'll be some petty bit of feedback, something his boss doesn't give a fuck about either, what with Steven's driving her numbers too, but which she has to pass on. Whining techie teams, again. He looped over a few theories, and fluctuated between being concerned and feeling as free as a bird, content he had other options. Past bosses who had made their numbers from his deals, were just waiting out there.

In sales, one could work an hour a week if one made one's numbers. So he returned, picked up his things, and went to float around Marylebone and buy a couple of light shirts, as brighter days were coming. This was speedy stuff, tried and tested brands for some plain yet well-fitting threads. A few shirts selected, two sizes of each demanded for the changing room, and out within five minutes, snaffled. He stretched his legs and pinged down to Carnaby and Soho, grabbing shaving creams and a new fragrance.

He texted Josie to ensure she was set for Saturday night, and she confirmed that they were. Too soon. This already did not feel like a challenge to him. In years gone by, nothing wrong with a sure thing, or close to. That meant success. Nowadays, this meant wasted time, hurt (for them) and the sex just didn't outweigh the dumpings, avoidances and general misery. Putting aside the humdrum, unimaginative sex one had to endure to get to the premium stuff, the soul-shaking goods.

Approaching his forties, this could be the optimal time to meet someone. Young enough to enjoy fun times, and less time to get bored of sex with them. And with less energy, the sex wouldn't have to cliff dive from five times a day like it would at twenty-three. It would decline from a couple of times a day the odd weekend, to a couple of times a week, then down another notch every few years. Maybe it was unfortunate to miss a whole lot of youth together, like some were able to enjoy, but what use was that when the sex tank was empty by thirty-two and both are horny as hell for other people. That wonderful couple, so good-looking, so good-together, so not having sex any longer.

He de-tangentialised his thoughts and returned to Josie, as manscaping crossing his mind. It was doubtful it would be important on this first date night, and if he was a bit unkempt, he shrugged, it wasn't the biggest downside in the world. And besides, he got into grooming at the request of an American ex-girlfriend, who encouraged the smooth look. Three years later and a Russian girlfriend criticised him for it, preferring the hirsute male. No shrinking violent, she criticised his jewellery. Men didn't wear jewellery.

There was no right, only *right for some*.

He had gone tasty but mid-range for the venue, preferring not to drop a couple of hundred quid on this one. Simple economics.

He phoned his boss to check on the vague meeting, not wanting anything hanging over his head on the weekend, and it was something minor and un-troubling that could be straightened out on Monday. He bought a bottle of Japanese whisky close to home, and passing a white sports car, decided to get drunk at home, watch *Vanishing Point*, and search for white sports cars, the next job, the next tech and the next girl.

In her head, Josie Porter *(Battersea, Barrister, Chez Bruce, Diptyque)* would have liked to have been sashaying around central London that spring day, yet she didn't quite have the chops, and so settled for some mild swanning. Smart, academic and accomplished in law, the limitations of her teenage years remained rooted in her foundations, lacking in the cool and fizz many of her social peers enjoyed, however comfortable and modern she now felt in her legal circles.

With muted, shoulder length blonde hair cut straight, parted, she had moved on from the fringe that had dogged her twenties. Her foremost physical appeal was her thinness, which could go either way depending on what she wore. If she chose wisely and accessorised well, she could look quite the companion. Thin light eyebrows and hazel eyes led down to faded freckles spread out from her straight, pointy nose and across her upper cheeks. Her pale pink lips were narrow and tight. She smiled as much with her eyes as her mouth, which didn't give too much away.

With the long hours and weekends her work demanded, she felt a couple of steps behind in the latest fads and trends. Sunday newspapers were insufficient substitutes for active monitoring of fashion, fitness, and culture. Her friends would describe her as dependable, trustworthy, and trusting. The city hadn't hardened her edges outside of work, as it had within.

She felt optimistic and apprehensive, a typical way to spend the day ahead of an evening inching closer. As she shopped for an outfit, the words of her colleague and friend, Victoria, rang in her ears. *Don't get drunk, don't sleep with him.* Not her habit, but always worth reinforcing, should a relationship be a potential outcome.

Wanting something new to wear that night she went to a shopping centre, which had a choice of middle of the road brands she liked. She felt like the better part of looking good consisted of acquiring something new, and avoiding items tired in the fashion or threadbare senses. Could a typical man outside the fashion industry tell how expensive or couture clothing was? She tried to concentrate, but failed; thoughts pervaded of her caseload and what she had to get done on Sunday, let alone Monday. Furthermore, one of her unmarried friends had just announced her engagement and drinks to celebrate, and she felt the walls closing in. She was behind schedule for the first time in her life. A number of her friends were on the 31-33-35-37 track. Engaged, married, first child, second, done.

Within her circle, Josie was one of the most successful, however, like water, group dynamics and reputational criticism would find the paths of least resistance, zeroing in on points of weakness. It didn't matter what you said, or what you had achieved, only that which they purported to value mattered. Ask anyone who has made a mint in business but their parents valued the academic and professional career path of their sibling. She flipped over her friendship Rolodex, over some of the remaining friends and successful colleagues in her situ, mental support, backup. The single colleague and one of the brightest lights of her generation, the industry leaders dedicated to work and eschewing family life. Women who would have no truck with peer pressure. Josie knew she was kidding herself that she could opt out in this way, and gave up with this thought track.

Trying several of the obvious stores, she was running dry, until she found something dark and uncontroversial, with good lines. Threw a bit of money at it and surrendered. She picked up a few make-up peripherals and hailed a black cab once out onto the street, as it was right there. She always had an acute sense of the value of her time. The taxi was new, roomy inside, large enough to take a wheelchair, but which left one individual and her bags rolling about as if on a listing ship. She organised herself, and was able to settle bags next to her which she could then lean on, and got to work in the back. Like most complex things in life, a case was a thousand tasks, so getting numbers 593-594 done in the next twenty minutes could be helpful. And with many road closures, albeit with minimal actual work happening, she ended up with time she hadn't banked on.

Back at home, a large apartment overlooking the water, two bedrooms, a study, she dumped everything down, did an hour's work, then went to the gym to sweat her stresses and thoughts out, see if she could tire her mind. And try to reset for the night ahead. She dropped by the Battersea Flower Station for something to brighten the kitchen, and went on to get what she needed for breakfast the next day.

Figuring out her timings, she squeezed in a little work, then got started. A third shower that day, finishing by cooling the water to take her body heat down, which still glowed after the workout. She put on some of her better underwear. Not her best, but getting there. She wanted to feel good, and well, *you never knew*.

She remembered something important to make a note of, and sat in her study in knickers and bra, trying to get a handle on some of the detail which had been sent to her that day. She caught herself in the reflection of the tall window to her left. Cream silk with black lace trim. She had to stonewall some email and phone messages. Working on it tomorrow. Personal family messages. Tomorrow. Dealing. She turned everything off, churning over how on earth she could re-prioritise. Not her current work. The big decisions were waiting for her, and had to start being made. Or they didn't.

Both living west of centre, Steven had booked a place in Fulham, halfway. This had become a habit. Modern European; in other words, bog standard fayre. Casual smart. That they lived two miles away from each other, driveable, cabable, even walkable, was a massive plus, should this turn into anything meaningful or failing that, regular. Dating someone who lived in Hackney meant writing off a great section of a year, days of travelling, lugging, ongoing mental logistical gymnastics involving clothes and tech; flexibility Josie, in particular, couldn't tolerate. Steven could wear a shirt and jeans, chuck a laptop in a backpack and be OK for three days, with the right coat. He could do Hackney, for a premium.

They met beforehand for a drink at the bar next door. As Josie walked in they gave each other quick scans up, down and around, their nervous systems sizing up how each other moved, confidence levels, eye contact. And both were pleased with what they saw. They were in each other's ballpark, which settled them, and took off the edge. Steven had had situations where he was reaching and under pressure within seconds, every move and word under the microscope, exposed to that inevitable first false move. Not tonight.

Josie ordered a rosé champagne. Steven followed suit, and they walked over to a free high table with tall stools.

While Josie was organising herself, Steven gave her more than a once-over, and thought she looked the ticket. Sophisticated, although she had played it safe. He noted her Cartier watch, which looked like a gift on reaching adulthood, and a good signal of future comfort. With her head down, she was assessing what she could of him, giving him points for his dark green shoes. Pleased he looked well put together, in case she knew anyone out tonight. As improbable as that was.

Steven remembered the last time he drunk oodles of pink champagne and was still drunk the next morning, feeling fine, before being sledgehammered at lunchtime when it caught up with him. He wouldn't expect her to have ever experienced this, so he kept that to himself, together with some of the less classy details of what took place.

He asked after her day and let her have the floor. Don't talk too much.

Steven listened at first, enjoying the efficiency and precision of her language, concomitant with her job, and contrasted this with all the nonsense he had to put up with at work. He complimented her on it.

"You should have heard some of my clients years ago, it was an effort not to absorb their colloquialisms and tics."

"So I was like, you know, like."

"Yes. I had to deal with all kinds of people. In a previous life."

Steven appeared to be *actively listening*, while ruminating on the usefulness of a lawyer wife, should anything go awry. The money in and the money out saved in legal fees.

Josie thought he looked engaged and felt listened to.

"Required a lot of dogged probing and cutting to the chase. Singing like canaries they were not. People respond to pressure, so that's the angle everyone uses, the police, the lawyers."

"Taciturnity is underrated. Most of our meetings are a fight for air space, everyone gasping to jump in after any pause, switching off their ears in the meantime," Steven added.

Their drinks turned up and there was a natural pause, and both felt comfortable riding it out. With a bad match, one or both could end up spinning their wheels in the mud, trying to get some purchase on a next topic. This could lead to an onset of dumb panic. The conversational date clock, not dissimilar to that in chess. They sipped their flutes in turn and looked around them and back at each other.

"OK place," Josie said, and Steven nodded in a way that concurred but conveyed the emphasis on *OK*.

Steven said there were a few around, one in Notting Hill, and the conversation moved on to their respective neighbourhoods. Josie outlined a few of her favourite local places. Steven retorted with a couple of places local to her that he knew, as opposed to validating her thoughts, and she hadn't heard of them. She felt this to be dominating behaviour, something she was used to, so just threw the topic back at him, and focused on her drink.

They covered some preliminaries, ascertained that they both had connections to Suffolk, loved the south of France, and neither was in a hurry to leave London.

Steven mentioned something in the news that day, self-aware that average people talk about events, and smart people talk ideas.

"I don't follow the noise, there's too much going on."

"I'm not sure it's *noise*, it's the world around us."

"People fascinate themselves with things that don't impact them, and which they have no interest in influencing. It's curtain twitching," and she pointed to her watch. "We should be going," she added, ending the conversation.

They downed the remaining warmed swill at the bottom of their glasses, and both wished they hadn't, and after Josie collected herself, went next door.

They were shown to a table in the middle of the floor of what was a busy joint, so Steven didn't check for a better option with cover. No side offered the 'good seat' but Steven spotted a hazard he was keen to avoid. The attractive woman facing them at another table. The guy she was with looked kind and poor. Of course he didn't.

As a younger man, Steven would have taken the seat with her in his eyeline and been distracted all night, but he moved to take the seat with her behind him. He could have a look during bathroom breaks, regardless.

They made themselves easy, ordered drinks, reviewed the menu. Steven felt compelled to say that the menu was unimaginative, and that he wasn't expecting it to be leading edge.

Unspoken, they parked any serious topics until all this had been put away. Not an occasion where they were so engrossed in each other the menu went on the backburner. They executed, then moved on.

The server angled toward Josie.

"The soup to start, please."

"Mushroom soup with truffle oil," was mirrored back to her, a low-level negotiation and bonding technique, Steven noted.

"And the fillet steak. Please."

"And how would you like that?" she automated back in reflex, her voice going up and down like a shop assistant in an eighties sitcom, as she cocked her head to one side, scribbling.

Steven wanted to say 'Oh, I *do like* it."

"Medium."

Steven winced. Judgy.

"And on the side?" pushed the server.

"Triple cooked chips and a green salad."

Steven opted for the rabbit and pistachio terrine, and the Dover sole. Sole never failed to disappoint, but he wanted something clean.

They began to probe each other's histories, personalities, desires, attributes, over the next couple of hours. Both with the capacity to reveal themselves to be a great number of people, once class, race, profession, wealth, age, politics, had set a baseline. Steven trotted out some of his loves-his-job-loves-his-family patter, as per.

Josie thought Steven to be entertaining, if negative and dismissive: "If you want to waste breath, give people advice."

"So, are you a glass half full, or...?" Josie ventured.

"Oh, glass half empty, hundred percent. Fifty percent," Steven confirmed. "If you ordered a dish or a drink, and they gave you half, you wouldn't be grateful for having something at least."

"I'm not sure that's the right context."

"There's no official context. That's *my truth*. I *set my own context*."

"Very millennial."

"Millennials are done. Youth is fleeting. Days past, in the elevator of life, you went up to 27th floor then back down, to drooling in the basement in your nineties. Now you're past it at 24. The next generation pushing you out, mocking your ways."

What Josie didn't cotton onto, is that these weren't *the right answers*. How easy it would be for Steven to trot out the I'm-a-positive-person-young-people-are doing-great-things stuff, and be honest later. This was a signal; he was too relaxed. He wouldn't let it all hang out like this with a woman he *aspired to*.

Gender wars came up with some predictable positions.

They meandered about.

"I'm being facetious, don't take me seriously. Look, we're all thrown onto this world with different assets, talents, difficulties, and then we add some we make for ourselves. We're all trying to muddle through, whether it's putting food on the table, getting a movie produced, or taking control of an oil refinery. And when we criticise those with different values, you'd be surprised to what extent it's a genetic position, beyond upbringing and what is absorbed from those surrounding us."

Josie gave his monologue some consideration while she put away a slug of wine which didn't taste like the Cabernet Franc she ordered.

"In the war on language," Steven continued, "people who excitedly use the word voracious, they're first up. Unforgiveable."

"Eclectic," added Josie.

They clinked glasses, and moved on to modern dating.

"Discounting someone for a minor language error. Wearing dodgy shoes. Whatever happened to something building up, bubbling away, or people surprising you, warming to them?" asked Josie.

"Grinding them down, you mean? In the seventies you'd hear all the time about someone punching above his weight, wearing her down, until she couldn't fight any longer," which they both recognised and found funny.

"Probably a good thing."

"I've dated people who might not have been an option had I not got to know them through work or wherever, and grown to like them. Slow burn type thing."

He wouldn't want to break up flirty preliminaries with a bathroom trip, that would be a duff move, but some semi-serious chat allowed him to do so. Josie checked up on work, reviewing some documents sent through by a colleague. The bathrooms were spotless so Steven sat on the toilet out of laziness and swiped away, keeping some dating conversations going, which could then be picked up again the next day.

He returned and sat down, and Josie leant forward, and Steven followed. She flashed her eyes left, and mentioned, "Those two are discussing star signs."

"Nice. What sign are you?"

"Taurus."

"Ah, horny?"

"Borderline Gemini."

"Double horny."

"In the peak of summer."

Food arrived. The terrine was bland, and no-one was going to photograph soup to share with the world in real time. One habit that seemed to have disappeared, *just like that*.

As the alcohol worked its timeless magic, the oldest joy, things loosened up, and for a while, pinballed around.

"During the pandemic, a friend of mine in a super long-term relationship would encourage her boyfriend to go out for things, so she could masturbate in peace. Then she realised he was also encouraging her to pick things up from the shops."

Steven laughed, "Classic. No mad scrambles to get dressed and chuck the toys away?"

"I forgot. My wallet," Josie mused, producing a stern impression and voice, her face blushing pink, imagining a returning boyfriend.

"Porn, like the crossword, best done alone."

They skirted his career, beside the fundamentals, yet dug into the law which Steven was interested in, finding themselves discussing the States, and their rougher justice. This interest in her career, her wheelhouse, was genuine, and she sensed integrity.

Josie explained, "Life without parole for being part of a group who did something heinous. Who it was was irrelevant. Who *wielded* the knife. The police would suggest in passing that 'you were hanging out with them, but *you didn't do nothing did you, you're innocent?*' Coaxed it out of them. Gentle. Once they agree, the cuffs are on, and they're staring down barrel at a life sentence."

"My, my, my, a life in the big house."

"In the big house."

"I know the drill," he assured, "I ain't *saying* nothing, I don't *know* nothing. Get me a lawyer."

"That's the one. You stick to that," and they nodded and drank.

"There's still time."

They made their way through pedestrian main courses. Steak looked the better option, as Steven chased around underdone segments of sole, liberating shiny slivers from bones.

The restaurant was still taking new comers late on as coffees were ordered, so the hush never came. Orders piled in to cause the clanging of an understaffed kitchen, and the natural silent stress aura from put upon floor staff.

Over coffee they discussed the altering dynamics of friendships and how one must adapt to them. For Josie, accommodating new life stages and new members to the family, while also presenting grown-up options to reprise a sense of short-lived freedom. Steven complained about the male friends who had moved on, save a cursory annual text, or those whom, once you got them out for lunch or an early bird dinner sat there live nervous cats, checking the time, unable to miss whatever arbitrary deadline had been agreed with home. *Must get back for three thirty on a Saturday afternoon.*

On the controlling nature of human relationships, from different viewpoints, they concurred it was a cancer of the age. For both sexes, though with different outcome risk profiles.

Josie summed up that the food was good, and Steven agreed out of politeness, and to preserve the mood.

Josie insisted on splitting the bill.

"I'm not splitting the bill," he said, "I'd rather let you pay for the whole thing. That heavy feeling of anxiety, judged by the staff."

She thought for a moment.

"I'll pay, you pay next time," he suggested.

"OK."

They left to figure out whose Toyota Prius was whose.

"Thanks for a lovely night," said Josie.

"No, thank you," Steven replied.

They came together and kissed on the lips. Steven put one hand behind her neck and eased her into him, and she reached down to hold his other hand. She was a good kisser, as thin lipped girls tended to be, and Steven became hard.

"We should do this again," she said, first, signalling he was in control.

"Yes, we should," he followed.

They broke away and separated as her fingers trailed away and left his.

On the drive home, among the cacophony of bright street lights, red tail lights, and the stop-start of jostling, somewhere-to-be night traffic, Josie felt a quiet calm she hadn't felt in a while after a date, with many disasters in between, and thought perhaps she had *met someone*. Steven ignored the London views in his car, head down, swiping through dating profiles, exchanging questions by rote, and seeing what he could line up for the next week.

CHAPTER 13

Simon and excess: Trip to the Scottish Highlands

Simon Knight's scent arrived long after he did. No cloying, dominating, overdosed after shave, but a richer, elusive trail, which spoke of the care he took in the selection of grooming products, and time spent with experts curating that knowing smell of success and luxury. Spend time with me, it whispered. You'll enjoy it.

Long weekends in Modena, Copenhagen or Catalonia. Saturday afternoons at The Waterside Inn, luncheon at Core by Clare Smyth, or safe in the hands of someone other than Gordon Ramsey. Firing on all cylinders on a Thursday night at Sketch or cutting loose at Bob Bob Ricard. Dropping in at Eleven Madison Park. Top-end Japanese to retain some civilisation and decorum. Chinese leaves, tonka beans, kumquats, a fruit consommé, a mousseline, salsify, mahogany clams, sea lettuce, corn miso. A tranche of turbot, a flambé of quail, a poach of lobbo, a crisp of tilefish, a tang of calamansi, a squid ink shooter. Sixty pounds sterling per course; super. Supreme nights rounded off with an open Coco De Mer playsuit, a black mesh mask, and a snakeskin paddle. Two girls in tulle suspenders, wrist cuffs and bunny ears.

Bi-coastal in the true American sense, and a budget domestic version. Holiday homes in Cornwall for golf and the sea, and Norfolk, for country pursuits, the odd shoot, in his hunting *syute*.

Simon had well established methods of consumption.

As he came across restaurants, luxury hotels, adventure trips, home furnishings, booze, anything legal at least, he would photograph or screenshot, or send on a link to Marie, his suffering assistant. He sent her an email years ago to cut out any long term preamble, which read: "... every time you receive a photo, link, request, please assume it is preceded by: 'Dear Marie, it would be wonderful if you'd look into holiday options, reservations...' and tailed with 'and come back to me with dates and options. Grateful as always for your wonderful and devoted support, Simon'..."

From that moment on, just the photos, landing at all hours. Mishaps with photographs *have* occurred. When it came to drugs, his nephew was a godsend. The last thing he needed was regular connections with undesirables, and exposure to threat. For his nephew, a similar briefing: You came up here to borrow music, right? The Doors. *Who the fuck are they?* You ever get in any trouble, call me, whatever it's connected to. I *am* your uncle, after all.

It chipped away at Simon that at some point Knight Drop-Offs will not pay back any longer. And he'd need another solution or an appealing offer.

In adulthood, as in childhood, he tidied himself, preened, flicking flecks of dirt from white sweaters, a speck of imaginary dust or dandruff to be removed from a dark suit. Looking to eradicate any negatives, irrespective of how minor they might be. For he knew that at the highest levels these could cost. A run-of-the-mill business person could turn up with a small coffee stain on a shirt and couldn't be taken seriously, regardless of what they went on to convey. In the highest echelons, the criteria were exacting. That's what the £400k Rolls Royce was for, with its impeccable leather, the result of farmed beasts and their antioxidant rich feed. That's what the £1,600 cashmere sweaters were for. One mark or a pulled thread, replaced. He made the absolute best of any situation, for the world was watching at all times.

His parents watched him negotiate, even as a four-year-old, testing his father, trying to get *any better* deal than that on the table. And he watched the signals his father gave off to other men, and those from the wives, the gentle directional nudges to push things in the direction of their partnerships. He observed and then questioned his father about conversations with other men, at the weekends when he was along for the ride. Seeking those indicators, tricks, traps and pitfalls. Now here he was curating his various club memberships to hit the right signature notes, like an artist of perfumery hitting the olfactory senses. A soupcon of business mastermind, establishment, on the up in the newest business sectors, artsy and physical elite, at home on the water, and a high society hedonist.

A giant with an ecological footprint to match. Flights, business travel, pleasure travel, the large home temperature controlled twenty-four seven three six five point two five, thrice weekly sushi deliveries, run out of milk or mixers deliveries, exotic food miles. The open plan office flexing between heating and cooling, the exacting wine storage facility. These, managed over multiple homes, when in residence or in absentia. The cars. Never buses, trains, the underground. Occasional helicopters. The white goods and dry cleaning handled by home staff, with their excessive usage of cleaning products and electricals. The extensive wardrobes of fine materials, exotic wildlife leathers, shipping through to binning. Nothing wrong with them. And industry, via his own businesses, and where he invests. Businesses with no signage on central London offices, lest they be targeted for protest. Index funds, pension funds, crypto, as any modern investor down to the private individual with their enough-to-get-by private pension. Accelerating the mining and pumping of whatever resides in landfill one, five, ten, twenty years later. All helping humans on their comfortable journey from cradle to grave. The production line of highest spec design and materials into top grade weaponry, to be fired, exploded, detonated against the competition of his peers.

He was scheduled to schlep to the Highlands, a trip he made every two years for deer stalking, and when a real back to roots reset was called for. An opportunity to enjoy the pleasures and leisure of an old friend, Fraser, who exited his final business for mid seven zeroes, and who, in theory, had left *the game*. A way-back acquaintance not to be confused with any of the small number Simon would consider trustworthy. This get together was the one time their competitive energies could clash and spa, where they could share ideas, learn from each other, within reason. To nudge a scheme or design, or urge a rethink on a potential banana skin. A five percent gain, the removal of four percent risk there, compounded. Moreover, it did not help to sow a seed for another which might get them onto something big. So ideas were cloaked, safeguarded. They might hit on something appealing, and could assign one of their team or a consultant to do some exploratory legwork.

Fraser's place afforded the space, views and nature to allow the mind to stretch, let the granular distractions dissipate, and to enjoy the produce of a working estate, with staff on hand to whip up whatever their whims wished. Wine and spirit stores to make the spirits soar.

Workouts from a custom-built gym with a personal trainer, sterile in light wood and nickel-plated steel, mirrored walls and daylight skies, windows never opened, conditioned to nineteen degrees. Footballer social media post chic. Home advantage for Fraser. Tennis, weather permitting. Stalking, or terrorising rabbits.

An email sent to Simon from the kitchen staff the previous week checking on any personal requests, allergies, and outlining what they were planning to put on. Fresh, local produce, as if there were any other kind. Foreign produce on the turn, anyone? An indication of seasonal bounty received from local streams, fields, farms or picked from the sky.

Two older men, with the most premium of educational and genetic resources, upbringings and a lifetime of walled gardens, striped lawns, tended roses. Shepherded through to a platform of wealth re-distribution (to them) and the opening of the curtain to how the world worked, from infancy. As a young man, Simon assumed it was the young who were the toughs. Boxers retired like footballers in their thirties, after all. That as a physical peak at twenty-seven was surpassed, so the body declined. However, it became apparent that age hardened men even further, that there was no softening. Added layers of what lay beneath, toughening further, petrifying.

Age amplified confidence, reinforced by one's achievements, or led to withdrawal from lack thereof. The grizzled older actor didn't cease to be the cool focal point, they just played a new game, re-aligned themselves within an older generation. The ex-hard man footballer that, in his elder role as manager, could give any young player a battering, for it took a couple of good leathering and weathering punches, and no longer a full brawl. That was, before the power dynamics in football changed.

Simon hardened with the years in business. As his wealth grew, so too, his intolerance of errors, mistakes, backward steps, poor moves, costlier in dollar terms as he progressed toward the rich list. The young Simon with his quick successes, all smiles and moments of victory, the babyface of celebration and private excess. Bubbles and awards and PR. Cleaved to reveal the solid, terrifying, dissatisfied modern business leader. Yet the billion ate away at Simon. He knew the moves it took to make that kind of money. If you weren't lucky enough to have that one huge unicorn idea, setting up a viable competitor to someone who had already cracked the principle solution was possible, though a hard ask coming from behind and matching the intellectual property. Always chasing. He knew he had it in him, yet the first billion would be the hardest. Fraser hadn't made it, but Simon might. And while Fraser had impressive assets banked, Simon had the potential and the legs, and should surpass. To fail would be failure. Fraser's bird was in the hand. Simon's plumper birds were bushed.

Each year a new report on the number of the world's richest people with the same wealth as the poorest half of the world population. Billions of *them*. And an ever shrinking number that could fit into a drawing room for flutes, toots and canapés. The masses could not think in terms of big numbers, and the billion had become so commonplace and trite as to become a mere large number. Half the world's population would fill 50,000 large football stadiums. In a generation the explosion of paper millionaires, created by age and property ownership, relegating the multi-millionaire to *well-off*. Now at the government level it required a trillion here and a trillion there, to be classed *real money*.

It was a flight and a helicopter ride to the estate.

Fraser Andrew strode through the open twelve-foot doors onto the striped lawn, the lushest of alternate light and mid-dark greens. Six foot two, fair hair, thick arms and a broad chest, which had the cut of late-life gym work product, rather than a natural build. A gingham checked blue and white shirt tucked into heavy-looking dark navy denim jeans, with a burnt sienna leather belt and dark tan shoes. A look of casual strength, but also rigidity when still, and from a stiff gait when on the move.

The grass blades leaned toward him in unison, pushed out by the rotor blades on his custom helicopter, in white and royal blue. The colours of Andrew Enterprises, now sold, but living on. He planned to determine some new colour scheme. Get the respray. Move on, he told himself. Always be moving. Could be £30k, something he wasn't in a hurry to say goodbye to. Hovering close to the ground, it went the final yard to touch down, carrying out a satisfying springy wobble as the landing skids cushioned into the spongy turf, well-watered by nature or technology. The rotors started to slow, moving from ongoing noise, to a manufactured pattern of whirrs, as doors were opened, to get the show on the road.

As Simon stood off onto terra firma, he took a deep breath to ready himself for the domination which would start from the get-go. He tightened his core, drawing to raise his energy, ready for genetic and learned war to travel in both directions. Pressure, immediate and continual for the duration of his stay.

The big hand thrust out for an eighties death grip handshake, the booming voice, raised even louder to cut through the transport noise, while subsiding. Simon felt queasy from the trip and kept this to himself, but Fraser scented it, and challenged him on his constitution. He talked a while about the logistics of helicopter ownership, dropping in some monetary amounts, the kit itself, salaries, maintenance. Signal banter, indicators.

Fraser held position as the unit prepared for flight, informing Simon that they would be watching this spectacle. A spectacle that he wouldn't need to endure if he also possessed one. As it distanced away to a small spot, Fraser held firm for emphasis. He inspected the turf, "Gaet somewon tae saught that oot," he ordered, while staff fussed about.

"C'mon big man, let's get yae a draink."

They stepped inside onto the slate floor tiles by the entrance, the distinctive heavy tread from male heels of bespoke shoes clacking as they strode through. Simon knew his way around, but expected there would be new additions.

"Need tae show yae aroond the new wing, aye. New gyum, sorna, spa, aw lookin' oot ontae thae hulls."

Simon's head nodded. Eyes side-swiped to avoid the roll. They continued through as the help stepped back, ensuring they were afforded ten feet of radius.

As they entered a large drawing room, Simon realised Fraser had done it. The full bar had gone in. Simon had to applaud an art deco masterpiece. A pure white wall, with no mirrors, with thin shelving in stacks, reminiscent of a bee hive, narrow at top and bottom, wide in the centre. Every necessary spirit, with shining plinks of blue and green among the whites and brilliant ochres and umbers of hard spirits, backlit by brilliant white lights. All framing a young man ready to conjure something.

Sweeping his hand toward the bottle bank, he uttered, "And us ae waise Scort wunce saed, *yea cun draink us much us ya leek*."

Some bites were left on the bar, and Fraser dove straight in, as he indicated they had wine from his vineyards in France for later, and some superior whiskies from his distillery to try now.

Simon was keen to understand what they had planned for the next few days, but was not going to ask, like some expectant child.

"Yer probly wunderin' wit wae huv plunned fae thae weekend, aye?"

"Surprise me."

Golf. A ride further up the coast from the course to see his beach house under construction. Via the castle where *the wedding* would be held. This was news to Simon. Wife four. Once you had the first divorce under your belt, subsequent ones were like falling off a log, with the right legal protections in place. A payout that would give future independence for the escapee, proverbial chicken feed. Deer stalking. Fishing. Wreck diving.

The kitchen had been working on Scots-Nordic, which would be the broad dining theme.

"Very 2017," Simon snorted, muttering under his breath at the staff behind the times. They weren't in London now.

Fraser led them on to the newest addition, indicating that there would be additional spa staff coming each day for massages, treatments. Before leading Simon through to the games area. Snooker, pool, movie theatre. Even darts. Darts. Simon was always taken aback by the fetishising of pub sports, films, among people of all walks of life, right up to the top. The unexpected pastimes of people, notwithstanding illuminations of class or lack thereof. The incongruous wonder of the joy of a catwalk model for racing cars. A prime minister with an irresistible zeal for a game of arrers. The top chef who loved a Pot Noodle.

"Quick frame, aye?"

"Sure."

An unexpected set of commonplace magazines set in a neat fan on a low table. *Stella, Evening Standard magazine, Hello!* Until Simon noticed a familiar face peering from the bottom magazine, grinning through his creamed stubbled whiskers, in front of his highlands eco-home.

Simon looked away as if he hadn't noticed. Fraser noticed.

On a distant wall, the awfulness of the celebrity, political, business, awards photos. A lifetime of the man.

The host broke off, in a classic right side break, applying right-hand side, to return to baulk. He started a latest well-rehearsed monologue, presented with fine élan, on the greatness of his lifestyle. An unequivocal, unchallengeable guide to modern life in the highlands. Away from the distractions. Allowing pure thought. Remote living. We were all as connected as we needed to be these days. Cities, pah. All the same. Been to New York and Tokyo, been to them all. Same shops, same restaurants, same new architecture, same fashion, same thinking. Simon thought he'd stick with holidaying on Lake Como and Ibiza, the clubs and networks of the old towns.

Simon was no slouch with a cue, and it turned into an alpha baize hazing.

That afternoon and evening they loafed about like man boys, drinking outside with a view, sharing information and views, eating the evening grilled seafood and charred chard, served outside surrounded by patio heaters. Cigarettes, cigars. Smoked meats, smoked out lungs.

There were predictable moments of Scotch Scotch melancholy. Fraser lamented the potential impacts of sea level rises on his favourite resorts and lagoons of the Maldives. Simon fucking swore about how it might mess with his ski season plans of the future, yet reminded Fraser how at their age they should escape unaffected. Unless Fraser were to be on his ninth honeymoon aged 108, which wasn't an impossibility, given his interest in life extension science therapies. Simon reminded him of the money he made in energy. Old energy, not new energy.

The impact on the hills surrounding them. Nature, wonderful nature. Damaged coastline, weather extremes, threatened species, agricultural challenges, wildfire risks. These were Fraser's new local concerns after coining it from the old damage.

Simon could not believe his ears. Fraser. Even Fraser, existentially concerned. He thought of some of the brutal things he'd pulled off in the past, ruining people, livelihoods, their towns and farmlands. Even the hard cunt turned soft. Now he had sold up and no longer in the chase, he'd got himself a conscience. Take it away and the game would be back on, chasing the dollar, pollution flying out of his erse as he tore about, leaving gutted properties and twisted families in his wake.

Halfway through the autumn of his existence, edging at speed to pushing up the daisies, and now came talk of renewables, sustainability, lost habitats of all things. This could be the influence of fiancée four, well, nine. Simon knew men who had been married so long that as time added the layers, as they became portlier, rotund, suffering compounded lunches, their wedding ring had been grown over, absorbed into their fry-up sausage digits; wedged on, unmovable. A new ring every seven years or so meant this was no issue for Fraser.

As the evening went on, the message revealed itself. It was not one of saving the planet. It was that *there was even more money to be made*, and Fraser knew it. And while Simon knew this about all matters relating to professions and the economy, Fraser was underlining a truth as old as time. That for the winner in the green race, in driverless cars, zero carbon, carbon capture, renewables, lay great fortunes, behind the facades of cleaner air and road safety.

Fraser's narrative, for his words were always part of a story with an agenda, was to continue to exploit the challenges of his time, to lever another share of the world's capital in his direction. There was no nudge-wink about it, even with Simon. The world was a stage and this was a new act. The green developments were 'off the chain,' a curious Americanism, suggesting Fraser had spent too much time with foreign investors and private equity. He was looking at levelling up. From the tens-millionaires to the hundreds-millionaire. Late fifties, and revved up to go again, energised by a young wife and the lucre lure.

If the eras of global destruction and pollution manifested the profits of the past, then if the clean revolution heralded the future of carving the great cake, so be it. He was wherever the action was to be found. While Simon's image leaned him toward cooler industries, du jour, he would settle for being a wellington boot billionaire. Not ideal from an image point of view, but easy enough to shrug off as he was buying up islands, and behaving like an international rogue. Many of the biggest businesses started with people who wanted to create anything huge, nothing specific, until they got started. Then it became the great story about how they wanted to solve this or that problem, improve the world. Passionate to the last until the business is sold. Then, well, whatever. Don't spit in the soup, but with an adroit pivot, they're off to the next shiny avenue.

Fraser raised the pain of letting people go, of putting bread winners out of work, a current issue for Simon. Simon was sceptical until he turned it into a yarn about an HR Director who was effective at levering people out at Fraser's whim. Asking him his secret, they revealed that they saw things happening ahead of time, and began to put together a dossier on each potential problem employee, then when he got the nod, he had the material. When it was time for *him* to go, Fraser had been building up the dossier on him for some time.

To Simon, this was a problem for department heads and lawyers to resolve. If he wanted someone gone, they were gone. Their stay was untenable, even a stay of execution. Remove them from the office pool, send them home. It was just a question of *how much*.

They exchanged and competed on their investment portfolios, biggest gains, properties at home, properties overseas, their future property *needs*. Their tastes in wine, food, whisky, travel, exes and currents, their wins by age milestone, cars, modes of transport, celebrity connexions, business networks. Their club memberships, networks, press attention, online profile, attention from business publications, from national press, educational history, consumer assets, antiques, auction acquisitions, large but failed bids, charity auction purchases but never their time donated. Fraser had been getting into Urt (Art), and *ennefftees*, assisted by a contact of

Francesca's based in Scotland. They went through the full gamut, gazpacho to pistachio.

There were occasional lighter moments, at the expense of some fallen mutual acquaintance or foe. Guard never dropped, for there was always the matter of what each other knew. What was in the public domain, what could compromise a source of information, or indicate insider information or problematic legal issues? Whereas Fraser, when full of the drink, would become the garrulous Scot, Simon was guarded when drinking, having come close to making a misstep at twenty-four years old at a company function. Long-term a profitable lesson. Loose lips cost greater ships, the later mistakes were made in the lifecycle of a business elite. In some matters. In others, an earlier error could be catastrophic, disruptive to the passing of the hardest first million.

As the whisky kicked in with a brutalist thump, and as they reached halfway over large cigars, a smoother smoke, Fraser knifed in a remark about a deal Simon put always to the back of his mind, and which haunted him. And Fraser knew as much. He looked across with base intent, and but for the rule of law, lord knows what might take place. Simon ran through calculations he had done a hundred times, of what Fraser knew, in the balance of probability, and what he could prove. He shifted about as Fraser's cheeks hollowed in as he sucked, turning the cigar in his fingers between puffs, before opening his mouth, emitting a walled sheet of rising, creeping, oscillating smoke, which cleared his cheekbones before splitting, as he blew out a solid stream ahead. He laughed hard, at Simon's expense, but a laugh which gave Simon cause to believe this was a matter of the past. Just japes.

They finished up and stood, both rising in full, with stacked spines, Fraser looking down by inches. Simon took the fullest breath, and they shook hands, and retired.

The weather was patchy, which led to haphazard golf, played for £250 per hole. Fraser's superior drives and course knowledge countered by Simon's putting and mind games. Fraser left £750 the better, which Simon accepted with some grace, given the minimal costs he incurred from the weekend. They realised many of their initial plans, which changed on a dime with the weather. As their whims switched, people scurried around in the background smoothing transport, dining, visiting plans and timetables. Deer were eliminated and fed to them. The masseurs were kept busy.

"Ah'll be seein' ya then, sunshine?" said Fraser, as Simon took his extended hand. He felt the aura of the man, and the fear other men had felt in that position. In his way and crushed in the hard decades ending the twentieth century.

Simon said nothing as they locked into final eye contact, and gave the one-inch nod in the affirmative, before turning and heading into the waiting transport, buzzing on standby. He never looked back, while Fraser stood tall with folded arms.

As they hovered and rose, and took flight, Simon considered that the future could be green, or it could be black. Clean or dirty money, it was all ones and zeroes on a statement. Money was unprincipled, a true lawless meritocracy. And it was never, ever, enough.

1110
CHAPTER 14
Steven and Josie second date: Garden Museum lunch and walk

Managing to wrap up things on Friday evening by seven o'clock, sufficient to hold *them* off until Sunday afternoon at least, Josie lugged herself, her laptop and papers down toward Chancery Lane Central line station. She noted, as she did every time, the mainstream shops, the dingy pubs, set against the wealth of workers in the area, yet reflecting within her and her set, an over-indexing of mountainwear clothing and activity sunglasses, and minimal, practical jewellery.

The work and the billable hours were paramount. Life's accompaniments - the hobbies, the domestic weekends away and fripperies like friends and family, the picnics, the bridal showers, cousins' birthdays, were scheduled with caution. Presence and excuses in equal measure. Little time for *the current* in fashion or culture. Holidays could be restricted to short high end trips - a week skiing, a yoga retreat, ten days diving at a push, an opportunity to exit the burgeoning coffers, and keep up with colleagues and their pursuits, shared in passing, when in or on court.

While friends were decked up in edgy athleisurewear brands and by-invitation boxing gyms, Josie was stuck with Nike sweats and her local independent gym with its grey demographic. Getting there was a constant nagging bind, and while energy was elevated in her job, it was resigned to the floor with her mat in classes. It all felt like keeping up, *just about managing*, until she would be old enough to give it up altogether.

Josie would try to expand her leisure horizons, but whether an exercise fad or getting into an author, she was a few years behind, when the taste makers were long gone, the book prize writer no longer in the discourse. In the rare times anyone discussed books. The notion of which itself dated her. While looking across in envy at the early adopters, those setting the agenda, she had to console herself with the last resort of any middle-class Englander, that she had no thirty-grand a year issues, and she had an enviable home, replete with houseplants selected by nature to thrive on neglect.

She hadn't seen much of what had been a hot day for spring, although she had suffered the residual heat and clamminess offered to her within the old buildings comprising her place of work. Unlike her management consultant friends, chilling away in cardigans throughout the hottest days of the year.

Taking the underground steps with great care, she descended into the low ceilinged vestibule where she was met with a sweet cloud of warm air, which had been pushed around all day below ground, shunted in and around and through underground trains and human bodies. She wanted to draw a deep breath but did not want to gag, and hustled herself through the gates and through the artificial respite of the long, deep escalators and their sticky backdraft. In further recurring thoughts, she considered the odd positioning of west and eastbound lines, set at different depths rather than beside each other. Followed by the automatic recollection of the office cleaner informing that Whitechapel was the one place in London where the Underground was over ground, and the Overground under ground. Now an oft-repeated city fact of hers. Observations gained at work remained on a loop, and would do, until such time she might succumb and sell out to in-house corporate life, and leave the area.

This was a brief mission, she hoped, to get something to wear for lunch with Steven the next day. She went to check the weather until it registered that she was seventy feet below. Stressed by the unpredictability of a spring afternoon, and the horror of dressing inappropriately for the weather, roasting away in something dark and heavy in the sun, or soaked through in a light summer dress.

Once on a train, it with Sophie's choice between a gross out from the warm, germy hand poles, or some sort of lean where one's clothes could absorb a day's grime deposited by others. Her black jacket was old enough to sacrifice against the Perspex dividing windows. She had three stops during which to calculate the options she already had at home, and to justify bailing south at Oxford Circus and calling it a day. It needed a little thought but was a done deal, one she reached with herself by committing to doing some yoga exercises on her mat at home for twenty minutes before organising herself ahead of time for Sunday, and having a glass of cold Gavi.

Dumping her bags down on the long corner sofa, she texted Steven to check the plan, failed to get any clarity on the weather which looked changeable hour-by-hour, and resolved to do some yoga in the morning, while deciding not to postpone the wine opening, thanking Bacchus for the screw cap. Her long-term plan was to retire somewhere the weather was sunny and hot, every single day, and a light, cream mid-length dress or a white vest and navy shorts would see her through any plan, happen or circumstance.

Emptying a bagged salad just short of the turn into a bowl, she revived with olive oil and balsamic, chopped up some tomatoes, and added mozzarella cherries, which always kept, and after her first glass of wine was sunk, put a pizza in the oven, before getting into a comfy slump.

Waking on what had turned out to be a bright, warm day, and one which promised consistency from the off, Josie left home in a favourite *go-to* summer dress, dinner plate shades, a cream, flouncing wide brimmed hat, and a tote bag sufficient to ditch said hat in, when required. The day itself chimed with the optimism she felt, encouraged by Steven's plan for the afternoon. A surprise choice, lunch at the Garden Museum in Lambeth, one of any number of places she had *meant to go to one day*. After a pleasant luncheon, they could wander around and then trace a walk along the river.

Josie was punctual, being a few minutes late, and Steven was waiting, looking into his phone, stood in the open courtyard beside the road, beside Morton's Tower, which would fit into a historical setting of expansive majesty. Misplaced, alone against a main road and the dingy river, the backdrop of postcard London ugliness that Steven had come to loathe. The beige and greying Hs of P, the mud banks and the charmless bridges. He stood with buildings cornered behind him, a defensive position protected from moped robbery. He glanced up, not wanting to be approached by Josie without realising, something that seemed to be a general human habit.

She waved as she approached the road, conscious of the hat and glasses disguise, though he picked her. She crossed and they met, and kissed on the lips, after exchanging hellos and good afternoons. It wasn't obvious to Josie how they got to the café, but Steven led the way. A classic new glass extension bolted onto an old church, completed with sympathy, in an odd locale of the capital, surrounded by new builds, workmen, traffic.

Inside, light wood tables and chairs, a level of beige one might find unappealing. Yet its simplicity worked against the mix of bright and dark greens from the gardens outside, and the blues and greens streaking in the reflections of the eight foot windows opened throughout, creating gentle air tunnels, flowing over all. The staff loved their place of work, which gave it a delicate lightness.

At his age, dating executives and other professionals, Steven couldn't take them out three times to the pub to drink. There needed to be variety to a set of three dates, to paint an optimistic picture of a future life of variety and beauty. Josie was charmed by the place. He had been here with maybe half a dozen other women over the years.

They were welcomed and seated by a neat and good-looking young European man, and Steven watched Josie, intrigued to see how much she checked him out. While she didn't appear to, Steven theorised that women were good at taking in the goods unseen, compared with their lascivious male counterparts and their lingering eyes.

They settled in, chose waters, and took a look at the small A5 menu on textured paper, crumpled from previous uses, dotted with entries of ham, clams, monk's beard, pink firs, rhubarb and honeycomb.

"Well done, looks good," commented Josie.

"Yes, got lucky I guess."

"Sure you did."

They chose a bottle of wine to share and gave their food orders.

As he returned with drinks, Steven decided that if he were bisexual their waiter would be a suitable option. Josie appreciated the fit of his black casual wear around his torso and below, and his tanned arms, which appeared to be perfection from genes, not gained in gyms.

Fortunate boy, she thought.

Sneering at their neighbour a couple of tables over looking at the wine list, with their 'holiday shirt with the parrots,' Steven took a long pull of wine as he put the boot in further, 'favourite wine: boxed.'

Josie looked at him without waver, everything ticking away in the background, as it would at work, focused on her prey or competition. Sat with a straight back, she possessed high poise.

She complimented him on his brogues of the darkest blue, "Good to see a man in quality shoes, everyone's so comfort oriented these days. I'm still wearing heels to and from work every day, but as much as my feet could do with the break, it just feels like giving up to do otherwise."

"Yes, the smart, suited professional lady in *Reeboks*, married and easing. Saving her energy for the evening quarrels back home. Her unmarried counterparts slicing themselves up. There's no winners on that one."

"Semi-comfortable boots in winter gives us a break."

"Yes."

"Trainers with a suit. Shame."

"At first. Then it's like water off a duck's back," Steven finished.

"Right. A habit seen first-hand when dealing with the tight legal spots politicians and other elites get themselves into with the press."

She paused for water.

"Front page scandal the first time, then once the family have been through the ringer, it's old accepted news."

"Business as. London's a mature, permissive society when it comes to sex, despite clichés about the English purporting otherwise," Steven finished.

"Another example of things the police, as an extension of society, aren't interested in any longer. Together with burglary, cyber-crime, drug dealing," Josie lamented.

"Assault, robbery, theft..." she continued.

Steven diagnosed her commentary for sincerity and earnestness, and decided it was matter-of-fact. That was the world she lived in and which she accepted. He couldn't see himself tapping out lines for them both in bed. Though, *it was always the quiet ones.*

"Our dealings with the law tend to extend to contract disputes and if you're unlucky enough, dealing with HR on the way out. One day they're welcoming you to the *family*, sending out the introductory emails, so excited that you are joining, here's some company swag, happy birthday messages! A year or so later it's cameras off, stern voices, legal present, without prejudice discussion, offer, sign this NDA, and managed out the exit."

Like dating, Steven reflected, though he daren't say so.

Josie nodded, and acknowledged the truth in his words, yet they dripped with cynicism. Maybe keep that to yourself for a while, she thought.

As she scanned over the mixed foliage in the centrepiece garden surrounded by the café, Steven had moved on to impersonating some colleague or other and their corpspeak, "... sounds like that could lead to positive revenue impacts. Does that narrative resonate?"

She was amused despite herself, tried not to show it, and instead focused on the occasional bird noise over the chug of buses doing their business, and the whooshing compressed air release of truck breaks, liked snapped opened cans of urban transport pop.

"Endless business metaphors, under the bus."

Starters of sea trout and artichokes, were left without fuss, the staff making themselves scarce, yet within view and on the scan for queries. Steven approved. Supporting the starters, some tranches of spongy and moist sourdough with soft butter slabs topped with flaked salt, and which lounged over the rise of the plate edge, employed as a chaise longue.

As they sunk into an afternoon bathed in sun, Steven swirled his large glass until the white wine climbed toward the brim, teetering with jeopardy, before he caught it in time, and let it slow and settle before knocking back the warmed nectar. He poured glasses for them both. A full one for him, a top up for her. Value for money.

They discussed their respective friendship circles, how they evolved. And how they both experienced that when re-invigorating a friendship which had derailed, the previous issues surfaced again before too long.

"Great to see them again the first time," Josie offered, "enjoying the best of them, then by the third meet up, the hierarchies and annoyances are front and centre once again, leaving one to wonder why the re-engagement at all, and letting the connection disappear once and for all. The reason Christmas is so painful for so many. That pervading hope that things will be different this time."

After Josie finished making her point, raising family, this association unlocked for Steven to one of his oft-told stories of yore, about a comical uncle. As he paused, he approximated how many times he had aired this story. He figured it came out on most first or second dates, of which he's been on at least a hundred over the last couple of years. He added ten percent for the times he repeated himself and his date was too polite to mention. He figured a further fifteen years before that since the event itself had occurred, and an average of a couple of times daily down to weekly then to monthly over the years, perhaps meant it had been trotted out the best part of 2,500 times.

Repetition, repetition, repetition.

A period of silence followed as they looked around and soaked up the quiet, both calm and subdued in each other's company. Steven's mind was elsewhere. After the previous calculation, he looped onto previous mental peregrinations about the limited number of filters within dating applications. How if it allowed him to filter for his exact requirements, it would amount to nine people from nine million. Within four miles of his home, aged within five years either way, English, French, Italian, Swedish, Canadian, no children, non-smoker, no large extended family, no low or medium income, fit, high attractiveness, no divorce baggage, pro drugs but *not too pro*, good sexual fit, open-minded, not *too open-minded*, sparkling personality, a list of careers and roles which weren't going to work, and harmony in their future plans and wants. Short girls, although manoeuvrable in bed, had an off-putting inability to (one) reach his balls during sex, and (two) reach for things in the kitchen. The former the pressing issue, and the true discounter. He refocused.

Dating itself raised its head. Steven laughed at his own observation of the ridiculous frequency women highlight confidence as an attractive quality in men, whereas that was a given. "Who are the women out there who *love a nervous man*? Oh, he lacked confidence, such a turn on for me."

Josie commented in turn that whenever she saw 'open-minded' she thought swinging and not intellect. Steven concurred, linking with his previous meanderings. She put her hands on the table, pushing aside the side plates, and turned then palms up, encouraging him to hold her hands. She gave him a lingering look and opened her lips, a potent combination when added to the touch of her cold, satin hands. Steven stretched his legs under the table, finding his way around the legs until they were connected – above, as below.

They leaned across the table for a quick kiss, both feeling turned on.

Yet, as hot as he felt, as lunch progressed Steven became aware of *that feeling*. A heightened awareness of his surroundings, flicking the eyes left, right, beyond, and now and then, with a swivel of the head, behind his shoulders. Looking, checking for anyone with whom he was acquainted. How Josie reflected on him. For most people he knew, she would pass scrutiny well enough, however for his more elite friends, her personality may not pass scrutiny, versus some of his sparkier exes, scene movers, despite their accompanying flightiness. Rough with the smooth. He loathed this feeling and himself, for how this uncontrollable measure had a grip on him. That others' perceptions mattered so. When these thoughts kicked in, quality of conversation became paramount; should they be overheard, what would they be discussing?

This was an angst he felt when stuck in the wrong group at work drinks, or wanting to be speaking with *other people* at a party. Yet some of the most connected, gregarious types he knew would feel nothing, carried always by their confidence. It was a British disease, condemnation by association. Ducking out of groups, fighting to be seen with the right people, pure social ambition. Swivelling with every appearing champagne tray to upgrade company.

Josie noticed he was distracted before and did not mention it. She went to, and stopped herself.

With the *right person*, his focus would be on her. Fearless of who might approach from any angle. This wasn't yet a problem; he had been on shocking dates where what he had not expected had turned up, and then it was dark corner, two drinks and off time. And a ready excuse: intimations it was a client, a distant cousin, an old friend.

Main courses were brought to them. Cod and bavette hovered as they confirmed the his and hers selections were as anticipated.

As they chatted away into the breeze, and as the spritzered wine was sunk, Steven relaxed into it, felt drawn to her, and stiffened. His eyes roved around her face, down to her exposed neck, displaying her thinness and delicacy. He couldn't smell her but wondered how she would smell in that exact spot, and if the skin on her neck was as wintry and soft as it looked. And how she would respond to him kissing her there, nibbling her ears, the biggest bang for buck he had identified.

He fancied her, that was assured. And he anticipated the sex would be powerful, that they would match well. At least for a few weeks or months. As she talked about something – her family, friends, whatever it was, his thoughts drifted as he nodded away, to a few of his favourite lovers. And they weren't the best looking girls he had dated. For there was a match beyond looks and status when it came to sexual attraction, and preferences. The high status women could be vanilla, and had their eyes on and invested their energies in other prizes. Whereas the upper middle could be open to experiencing the moment, revealing and conceding their desires, quirks and kinks. By his mid-thirties, a man knew what he liked in bed, many fetish or peccadillos had developed, and what he was hoping for in a partner. There might be some additional flourishes, or changes in direction later in life, but the foundations had been set for most.

Steven was interested to understand how accommodating she would be to his wants, and what she would want from him. In due course. He looked for other couples in the room as a reference point, wondering how they matched to outsiders, how did they *rank*?

As Josie circled her fork around in the air while thinking and voicing her way through a point she was making, Steven employed this distracting movement to look away from her, in search of in real life examples. He saw a couple behind her to one side, a young blonde man in his late twenties, with a modern, neat, well put-together look and plentiful hair, with a younger redhead. She had paid her long hair much attention that morning to great effect, bending and twisting down the back of her armless cream dress, a hint of freckles down her white arms. Sideways to him, he could see she was short, petite framed.

How does a man commit to one type, he reasoned with himself, as

Josie rabbited? Steven was guarded for a question thrown his way, but continued with his thoughts. The redhead was a catch, yet could that young man eschew blondes, brunettes, tall girls, tanned girls, strong girls, Japanese, Indian, Somalian girls, high echelon Europeans; cast away the variety and devote himself. Adding in factors other partners may offer – familial wealth, career status, *their* connectivity and social circles, how they held attention with humour.

"Is something up? You keep looking around."

"Oh, sorry. A habit of mine, seeing who is about," he replied, turning a negative into a connectivity brag.

"On an adjacent note, I was out with a male group once for steaks in London Bridge, and we were pretty hammered, and in a high backed cushioned booth, private, on the face of it. A couple of the group were gay, and the chat got spicy, as they regaled us with their exploits. At high volume. As we got up to leave we filed out and saw an older out of town couple, jaws on the floor from what they had learned over the last hour or so."

"Mum texted me earlier to say she was tidying the front garden, which I hope is something I can take literally," Josie replied.

Neither laughed at each other's comments as much as either of them hoped.

Professional life arose, and they took turns educating each other in aspects of technology and the law. Steven felt outclassed, up against the qualifications, the dedication. To the boomer generation and priors, the respectable aspects of that triumvirate of law, medicine, and that poorer cousin, finance. Josie, in turn, felt isolated between narrow horizons when around business people, who she perceived could have a flexible range of roles, and experiences across diverse industries. Whereas for her, and her peers, it could be laser focus on a specialism, and everything within, though there was always much to learn, following changes to the societal landscape.

Things weren't *too* off balance, though Steven felt pressure.

"Things ease as you work your way through spring. Clients realise there are other things in life. Lighter evenings, better weather, reasons to leave work on time, to forego the evening email. To take holidays. Summer. Now you're talking. Clients off on rotation for two months, and while your colleagues are off too, it doesn't net out, and it's the best time to be working. November to February, though. Killer. Everyone's miserable, no sign of change, end of year business financial pressures, Christmas personal pressures, everyone grumpy in January, on diets, going to a gym they hate. Months away from their first holiday. I've a friend, contractor, he just won't work the winter months. The contracts are too demanding – all bang for the same buck. Takes the time off abroad."

"Nice lifestyle, if you can make it work. I have friends like that. They're so skilled, they go travelling, come back, pick up where they left off, or clock up hours on some huge government case where there's an extensive team required to review, summarise documents. And my work has a seasonal shape just like any other."

They were having parallel conversations.

"And the clients in winter. All strung out, none of their superiors on holiday either, mounting pressure. Doing what clients in big corporations do best – little or nothing, push emails around, do their one report per week, work 9 to 5 with an hour at lunch, hitting the canteen at twelve noon on the dot every day, like prison. Bloated teams filling their days with repetitive busywork; the updates! Changing the brief or scope, failing to complete the dependencies we rely on, correct and on time. Blame it on the agency! Still, I've worked client side and that can be no picnic, outsourcing control. Agency wants to charge for every single change or new idea. The worst are the nickel and dimers, their hands shooting up for money with any slight change to the spec. Always working on other clients at the expense of your project. Lousy communication lines. Put up a timeline which assumes everything happens on time, in order! Imagine that. Still, they make us do that. To hit their arbitrary deadlines. We're giving them something their company *has never had before* since it opened its doors in 1878, yet they must have it in place for the end of Q3. Or whatever."

Josie laughed in a gentle and amused way, as Steven's monologue became more ranty.

"No matter what sizzle we give it, they're always underwhelmed. Never... whelmed?"

"Oh yes, lack of whelm."

"Overwhelmed. Give a client nine things, they complain about the tenth. Give them ninety-nine things, they're missing the critical hundredth."

"Human nature. What have you done for me lately?"

"Exactly."

Some acknowledgement of their dialogue before he continued.

"Cracks me up when the CEO calls out someone's work, how they worked so hard, nights, over weekends on some project. Applauds the dedication. What I hear is: 'this sucker worked for us all weekend for free, for nothing. Free labour, we love free labour.' Free labour to a business is as free beer to the man in the street."

Steven had strung together a mass of work related tales and issues which didn't flow from one another, like he was unloading an area of his brain in which it had been simmering for some time.

"People complain about the British culture of the desk lunch versus European culture, but this is a more capitalist economy. Or was. Many people have to work a hundred miles per hour, all day, forty-five hours a week, so they don't have to work until midnight or over the weekend. The market demands it. At least it's a couple of notches behind the American model, the relentless *I must work harder* ethic with ten days holiday a year. Thanksgiving, a few random days plus one week away."

Steven would prefer to avoid extended professional talk on a date, but with a successful woman this was fine ground, and while she shared some of her experiences, as the date progressed he did much of the talking. This didn't register with her as perhaps it should, being used to working with men who liked the sound of their own voices. That it was something she had grown used to, shouldn't have lessened the strength of the signal.

From his dissatisfaction Josie could see he was driven, from his monologues and expressive gestures that he had vital energy, and that he required more. She could see success ahead for him, and said so: "You're going to do well," and felt any future together would be one of security, comfort and a not unenviable lifestyle, "you should start your own business, start seeing who is out there to work on something with you."

"Right," he agreed, "one of my colleagues left to set up her own thing, got the right technical partner and off they went. She was a high-performing, tough salesperson, drunk the kool aid, then once that resignation's gone in, it's over. She had checked out, focused on her new venture. And after four years telling all and sundry that *our* business had the greatest offering out there, her contacts are all about to hear it wasn't so hot after all. I don't hear from her now, but continue with a rolling LinkedIn feed update, her like addiction, and 'that's great Divi', 'awesome news', 'congrats Jeff!' updates."

They agreed to get the bill, which was left with them. Steven went for his wallet, and Josie took the receipt from the small silver tray, "I'll get this," in such a way that Steven had to say, "thank you," it being apparent to both that she earned more than him and he had paid on the first date. An imbalance that may become a difficulty in the future.

They collected themselves, left and strolled down toward the river, agreeing to walk the short distance to Westminster, over the bridge and up through St. James's Park before they could figure out their respective journeys home. Ahead of them a jetty for cruise goers and a shabby café, made them both think, though it went unspoken, how tatty and unappealing London could be. Josie thought of the clean beauty of New York and a stroll along the High Line. Her disdain at photography of postcard London, the dark and grubby Houses of Parliament. Steven thought of being young and stumbling off a work boat party, in his cups, watching a colleague throw up the buffet into the water, hugging a mooring bollard.

Steven decided to get her talking, elevate the date, and opened her up with questions about her work, appear interested, and to do some semi-active listening.

She gave a brief run through of her career progress to date, Steven noting she talked in general, rather than in specifics, about some of the cases she had worked on. He could imagine this discretion falling as she began to trust in a partner, when extras might be revealed, yet for now it was public domain stuff, before she moved on to approach and strategy.

He asked smart questions, which garnered her respect.

"Just before you go on," he broke in, "I met a client the other day who said they had twenty-two strategies for the year ahead. In fairness, I called this out and they laughed. Sorry, go ahead…"

"Yes, well we have to settle on one strategy at the start, which may well change once the case evolves. The law's open to interpretation, and can be subjective. Which is why the judge assigned is such a big reveal. Everyone knows everyone, it's like backstage at the theatre getting ready to go on. A judge's record, preferences, and, ahem, idiosyncrasies, known to us all. And the Rule of Law is a myth when politics decides what gets prosecuted and what gets a pass."

"Oh yes, subjectivity. The boss who asks your opinion on the best strategy, as if he or she is open to suggestions. Test upon test, it's my job to try to figure out what they are thinking and go that way, half the time. Opinions and feedback, shit flowing down. Anyone in charge can pull others' opinions to pieces, it's an abuse of power."

A passer-by approached with a poodle, and as they went past, Steven mentioned the comedian who tweeted about the death of his dog Macy, and who lived a few streets away, "Who I've seen around maybe fifty times, and not once was he accompanied by a dog."

"Ah, modern media grief."

This moved them on to talk a little about first impressions. Josie felt for the most part she got the measure of someone. Steven had noticed that a number of people he had grown to admire and enjoy the company of, he had at first taken a dislike to, so he had learned restraint in judgment.

A speedwalker strode toward them, a faded cap on his head, his tanned levver face stretched tight over his bony features, pointy elbows and forged calcium knees, moving through their repetitions. A man so energetic, tense and taut, his body unable to build much in the way of fat reserves due to the exercise, let alone the doubtless always-on activity of his hyperactive nervous system, never resting, least of all in the four hours of sleep, when it fries away making sense of it all.

By this stage they were alternating between linking arms and holding hands, as they crossed over Westminster Bridge. The Houses of Parliament, enjoying at last a relief from scaffolding and opaque sheeting, while tourists with no seeming understanding of beauty or composition, snapped away on large cameras, tablets or phones. The filthy bridge pavements hemmed in by protective barriers, there to protect from the terrorist people plougher. A local nutter or two added to the flavour and the vapour.

Steven acted the goat as they walked in between snapper and

snappee which made Josie laugh in spite of herself.

Westminster did not set a romantic tone, yet the park bridge in St. James's with its double aspect view of the lake offered that much. Buckingham Palace nestled behind copses of weeping trees and the still lake, spattered with floating greenery and gentle carved by the chevrons of moving ducks, their ripples dissipating to keep the surface calm. Looking the other way, the clustered hotchpotch of government buildings of Whitehall and environs, with turrets, peaks and spires, like a Disney castle for the manipulative, crocodile-skinned players of domestic and foreign politics. They paused either side to take it in.

Pashing in public made Steven self-conscious as the years ticked by, but they forged a path into the green spaces of the park, with tree cover, and stopped to kiss. Steven ventured that he didn't have anything planned for the rest of the day if Josie wanted to hang out and get cocktails. She agreed and they kissed further.

They headed toward Notting Hill for drinking options, and although it was their second date, it was a long one, and Josie stayed the night.

1111
CHAPTER 15
Squirrel kill: The Wyatts and Iva: Planetary project

Jess stirred early. Standard. The light that came through the shutter slats of Barney's bedroom, coupled with the overnight temperature and her sense that it had not rained, told her this was the perfect morning. She moved about on the bed, stretching into some drama to wake and shake Barney from slumber. This took a few goes, and it worked. A true influencer. She moved up to his face, to give it the personal touch. He put a hand over her head and gave it a ruffle, down around her chin and to her chest. She jumped down off the bed and shook herself, as if she had been swimming, going after another of Barney's senses. She then paced, nails on wooden floors, clat-clatting across the room and back, before sitting next to the bed, staring into Barney's eyes. A quick bark, arf! And another.

He relented and swung his heft out of bed. Jess continued in energetic fashion while he boiled a kettle, prepared an instant coffee takeout, and pulled on the dog jeans.

As they left the house, Jess was filled with heightened optimism, having called it dead right; optimal conditions for the hunt. When she stopped to do her business she jetted it out and hurried on. Leaves rustled as the clock ticked. She pulled Barney onward and he too knew that it was on. En route were pizza crusts and bones, but for once they weren't distractions; the stomach was shut, there was work to be done. The window would close before too long, as other dogs hit the park and flailed about in their amateurish fashion, lumbering without any real hope at the vermin.

He released her as they entered the park, and she rounded the walled path taking her to the first open space. She smelled squirrel. And she spotted them. A handful, dispersed across the lawn, each of them close to a tree, and busying themselves inspecting the ground in a blinkered fashion, pawing, collecting. Jess held still, and assessed and prioritised based on proximity, direction, face of travel. She could advance on those looking away, reduce distance, ensure proximity before launching. As with a lion on a prairie, she kept her head and shoulders low, having learned to reduce her profile from experience. No longer the youngster who would throw herself with abandon at any prey, garnering no success.

Jess knew the first run was critical. After the first attack or two, the targets would relocate to the trees, and the odd one would venture down. Now she had choice. She focused on the larger squirrel, fatter around the body. Weightier, slower, preoccupied. The larger size made no difference to the kill, once she had it in her jaws for that first time it would be over. It had started to wander from the nearest tree and toward open ground, whereas the others had remained close to a vertical escape. As it moved around, turning, whenever it faced away, Jess took a step or two forward. As it turned sideways, she froze. There were no other distractions. Everything else in the world went away. There were no smells or calls from Barney that mattered. The clearest head in London.

The squirrel strayed, inching further from the narrow trunk of a young tree. And it was near the tipping point. Jess would allow it a few steps, and with the next turn of the head away, strike would be approved.

Go.

Jess went, scrambling hard as she went for maximum speed. Her silhouette a mess, now immaterial. This was a ground race, and one Jess was winning. The squirrel fled without a plan, and realising the grave threat used its one advantage in this situation, that of a tight turning circle and the ability to pivot. It turned ninety degrees and Jess had to dig her paws in, shift weight and readjust, but got on top of things. The squirrel hesitated again, and as an aircraft is brought down not by one failure, but multiple, so this further hesitation cost it. Jess gained and went low with the head and scooped the animal up, her jaws closing around its belly and drawing her own head up to take the squirrel clear of the ground. Pressing hard she had it locked. Now the death shake. She thrashed her head from side to side. Those first dozen shakes were the severest blows which rendered sufficient damage to make the rest a formality.

A mother and her young daughter had been watching and the child gasped, and the mother cried out something at the dog.

A snap of the neck, of vertebrae, a punctured organ, a broken leg. Any of these would do. Incapacitated and unable to mount an escape, the squirrel sighed its last breaths, its eyes closed, as Jess thrashed it to death. The endgame. Jess dropped it on the ground and the mother tried to shoo Jess away, as if it could recover. Jess stared at the squirrel as it flinched, twitched, breathed great heaves, and scooped it up again, and walked it off to a quieter spot, devoid of voyeurs. Barney followed and as Jess dropped her quarry at her feet, Barney moved in to collect. He accepted that as he himself ate meat, pushing animals through the tortuous farm supply chain, he could have no truck with Jess for what humans had put into her.

A live squirrel has a tight profile; it is a petite ball, extending with a flick of bushy tail when on the move. A dead squirrel unfurls. It stretches out to its fullest extent, its body astonishingly long, its tail as long as its body again. As Barney bent down to pick up the victim by the end of the tail, it hung with dead weight, at least two foot in length and he needed to hold his arm at waist height so that it cleared the ground and also the jumping Jess, eager to retrieve her bounty. He also held it straight out, away from his body, in case it should lash out in any further, final death rattle. There could be nothing discrete about what had just occurred as Barney looked around to calculate how close the various litter bins were, and if there was any preferred path to steer away from young families. In profile, there was no question that he was a man disposing of one dead squirrel.

He looked at the ground ahead, shut the world off for the next twenty seconds, and as he reached the bin swung the deceased in an arc, aiming the head for the letterbox opening. The head hit the side a couple of times before it disappeared in, and Barney let the tail go and it dropped into the black and gold litter tomb with a soft thud.

Jess acknowledged a fellow white terrier and Cocker Spaniel she was on good terms with, then had a snap at an unfamiliar dog as it came close to Barney. And then she moved on, trotting to the next area of the park where she hoped a new grouping of squirrels would be waiting. And on.

The rest of south London awoke in waves.

The elderly, the restless, the preoccupied, the heartbroken, the bereaved, the fittest, the natural risers and those with building work next door, or doing the building, started first. Knickers were flicked out of the bed with feet, dressing gowns were donned, and bottoms were scratched through pyjama bottoms once out of the sight of other halves. Parents to young children had been awake for hours or were scheduled to maintain routine. Young children appeared, wandering in on parents, or helping themselves to entertainment. Kettles were filled and flicked without thought. Radios, televisions switched on, phones unplugged for the first of many five minutes of hate. Toast and crumpets were toasted, muffins were plunged, eggs were whisked, bowls of sugar rush supplemented with fresh milk. Fresh coffee tablespooned into French presses, instant coffee teaspooned into mugs, tea bags divvied. Milk in first, milk in last. Households in harmony, households with varying tastes requiring bespoke preparation, handling preferences, allergies. While the suburbs were stirring, somewhere people were doing coke to banging music. Young house-shares were skinning up, grogged out on pills taken at 5am. Sex people were still going at it, some in groups, some harnessed, some in A&E with explaining to do.

The concurrent themes of lives lived were hard to fathom.

The next waves woke, until the lazy, the teenage, the hungover, the earlier clubbers, the unwell, were all, too, reborn. Some would not wake this morning, nor any other.

One of the first true days of spring, at first a cold chill, but with a spirited clear blue sky and a sun which would warm in time. A day which required smart dressing, something which would become apparent to those who dressed for the cold, and would later overheat as they walked about and their dark coats and quilted numbers trapped their warming armpits under layers.

London, one of the greenest cities. Parks splayed the first stretches of daffodils, mixing with crocuses. Yellow, white, purple, standing out against patchy grass, bald, muddy, mucky. Crows and skinny squirrels on their missions. Pigeons took tubes. The place lifted and the air tasted fresher, coming out of the downer of winter, and before the storm of summer, with endless picnics, park parties, litter mountains that couldn't be dealt with in the time it took to produce them. As gym fanatics felt about January, so the year-round park devotees felt about spring.

Elsewhere, in the US, a *weather bomb* saw historic blizzards and snowfall hammered a group of the central states. Hurricane-force winds, and the follow-up floods broke records as it did people. Whole feet of snow. Extremer weather, worthy of a news item on the mainstream news. Now that global warming was on the agendas of governments and news agencies. Weather maps with land once displayed in green, now an angry crimson, representing identical temperature levels. Hmmm.

The majority white population of Wandsworth Common began to emerge and grace the common with its young, organising themselves by hierarchy via the looks of the parents and the brands of their baby gear and toddler clobber. Julian walked the dog among them, confident that he had the house, the career, the wife, the children and all the spoils to hold his own. At home, while the children were downstairs, his wife was enjoying an empty bed, and affording herself the luxury of a peaceful morning orgasm, after having a sex dream overnight. She was given the cover of creaky stairs and went undisturbed in the process.

As Julian arrived home, Fiona was buzzing about downstairs, and said she was jumping in the shower, darling. It would be long and hot, to put colour in her cheeks. Julian set his hearing to standby mode, alert for keywords or intonation which demanded a response, filtering as the children went about their Saturday morning tasks and activities, while Fiona was behind a locked door.

They had little planned together that day, which suited them both.

Fiona came downstairs in casual jeans and a cream sweater. He never got bored of watching her fine arse, which he followed as she walked by and reached up into cabinets, before fixing herself a hot drink.

Radio 4 news mentioned the blizzards in America.

"Think they've got problems. So, when Lily and Tom moved in together, merged everything, they both had a few Staub cast iron cocottes, but different colours. She had the white truffle, he the graphite grey, or whatever. Four years and a marriage later, she still hasn't found a way to resolve this into one large matching set. They last forever, and she knows he won't allow her to replace some for this reason. She has her perfect kitchen apart from this. The family dinners, events. It's taken over, she needs this resolved."

"Hilarious. Stressed out, gnawing away. Reminded every time she strolls past their six ovens."

"You're good at solutions, if you think of anything let me know."

"Oh, you have to let her suffer."

"If we fix this for her, we'll be in her debt."

"Tell her to lend them to us to take down to Cornwall for a party. We forget them, leave them there. Then offer to pay her for them as we aren't going down for a while."

"But we've got a full set down there."

"I KNOW THAT. She can fly tip them somewhere."

"Right. I'll see what she thinks."

"Can't see him swallowing that we don't have eight of them ourselves."

Julian shook his newspaper so it stiffened straight, and to remind that he wanted to concentrate.

Fiona busied herself organising life via technology, notes and the board. School comms, household maintenance and supplies, homework, social events, babysitting, relatives, friends. She had half an eye on proposing a further extension, and surfed some kitchen suites and even larger giant fridge freezers, worthy of super-sized Americans. It had been six years since they last extended. It could be time. She wondered if a darker paint shade in the kitchen, albeit of the same colour, would keep it cleaner looking for longer. She looked up options.

Getting up, she filled the kettle from the water purifying jug, and set it off once again. While that started to scratch, drag, bubble and steam, she filled the purifying jug from the tap, already fitted with a purifier. She took care to fill it to the right level and not go over. Placing it down and stretching, she looked outward. In the garden, little moved except a small bird sat on a low branch of the tree to the left of the large window behind the sink. Birds were not a strong point, and figured it was one of the common ones like a sparrow or a starling, something her father would mock her for not knowing. It sat looking around and looked content enough. The tree had begun to block out a little too much light, and would have to go.

Fiona held it all together, always, and never buckled, even in circumstances where a myriad of situations conflated, when nine seas met. The relentlessness of the pressures energised and pushed her, as she burst through endless task lists, challenging her as new situations arose, with her eldest child encountering things for the first time, which she then did in turn. That of the latest generation. A compounding pounding which toughened her further, requiring extra resilience to fight the competition they were up against from her brood's globalist counterparts. Fighting too for their Joai, for their Camille, for their Alima.

She made a fruit tea and sat down.

She wasn't so deluded that the nonsense of it all was lost on her. She allowed herself limited self-awareness, but chose not to look too hard. The world was as it was, and it wouldn't change for her educating herself in philosophy and human rights. She could play its tune and its games, by the rules as they were printed in the box. She had a five to ten-year window to set her children up, that was all there was to the matter. Impressing on her children how to shape the rules they lived their lives by for positive societal change was a side-benefit luxury outcome. A frippery.

Florence's teen years and young adulthood were in the post. On the one hand this terrified Fiona, knowing the risks she took at that age. The scrapes, the lies, all in the name of fun. Yet Florence was balanced with a calm head, maturer than the comparable Fiona. When she considered this, she dismissed great worry. Then she would remember her late teens and early twenties. Drunk and on drugs at parties, getting lifts home from drunk people with whom she wasn't acquainted. Sleeping with people she didn't know. How can one know anything of someone one met that evening? The time she acquiesced and let sex happen, because the risk of being forced was apparent, and she could grit her teeth through the former and not the latter. When she covered for her friend, who went missing. Missing enough that police were on it with a rare urgency. A taxi ride with a friend when they forced their way from the car, kicked off shoes and ran. She shuddered and distracted herself. Not Florence.

More thoughts of this ilk swirled as she sipped tiny amounts of piping hot tea.

From where she was sat on a bar stool at the kitchen island, Fiona shook her head a few times in one swift flurry and sprung up, all energy. Something her mother had watched her do since she was a small child, amazed by her pep then and beyond. The juggling, the coordination, the efficient modern mother, retaining her upbeat way and humour with it. Drunk too much, swore too much, maybe, but that was rife across her gen.

Her mother had hoped for her that she would form a closer relationship than she had with Julian. A hope based on the limitation of her own marriage to Fiona's father, one that also comprised security, comfort, financial health, and nice things, in the end. For each generation, hopes for the next, to build further, to plug holes, to eradicate problems, addictions, compulsions. Yet she saw that Fiona's untrammelled mission was for her children's attainment and happiness. A success of motherhood and a failed marriage, was a couple of coin tosses Fiona would settle for. Her mother had wanted success at both for her. The money flowed in for both women, and they each passed on a taste for the finer things in life, and some instruction on what one had to do to achieve them. The holidays, the ponies, and all that.

To Julian, the children's successes were his success, a necessary reflection of himself, to round off his own not insignificant accomplishments. Something to crow about. Fiona was ambivalent to this side of him; he put the money up and that was his reward. The pressure of fatherhood for him, the worry of failure. That he should be quizzed on how they were doing, as they fell behind, and a lifetime of deflecting, covering up, changing the subject.

Fiona had sight of a couple of jet-set rich marriages, and the accompanying toxicity, and assumed that as most things, her family was on a spectrum, and she and Julian were doing damage to their young ones in turn. And when others dismissed how much children took on board, Fiona remembered the adult thoughts she had at ages five, seven, ten. The grasp she had on the world back then, what her adults were getting up to, that one would not presume youngsters to have, looking out as adults, at a group of young children. Adding further the declining innocence and naivety of twenty-twenty living and their informational and mis-educational access.

Julian took the dog out to allow him to text and if needed, speak with Iva. This was routine at home, yet he tried not to be too transparent to the away side, varying the contact times. Iva would pick up on the rhythm of 8am, 1pm, 5pm, 9.30pm and it would be a hoo-ha. He tried to phone from home whenever alone, as the open air call from the common was maddening for both parties, given any wind. He would collect a few thoughts at home, so he had something to say, beyond 'how are you?' and 'looking forward to next week'. Variety mattered when contact was fleeting. He knew too well that she had youth, looks and options, and while he was a vine that could help her to climb, her availability to him could bubble burst. Her pushiness with him reassured and threatened him in equal measure.

He had his own lot to juggle, and while he was organised at work, sat rigid among a spotless desk, he was a step behind Fiona, and had to be watertight with Iva, with planning, communications, expenditure. Traceables. Fiona got everything she wanted, and Iva was his peremptory reward. Perks. Fiona's dad was the same, so Julian would hope she knew the deal, if it was exposed

He texted Iva, got some grey ticks. Walked on for a potential twenty-minute loop, stopping every twenty yards for the dog to sniff every trunk, post, section of wall, pavement stain. Every instrument of dog messaging, their own grey ticks.

Iva soon responded, reminding him she was out *with a friend*. 'I told you this already.' In one eye, out the other.

This was a short term result for Julian, meaning the dog could be hurried around in as long as it took to overboard the urine stores, while they were prevented from a lengthy and challenging conversation. Yet *the friend* would nag parenthetically that evening. He wouldn't know with whom she was enjoying herself, or otherwise. Whether she was hunting for someone with better availability, total access. The not knowing made him hornier for her.

He needed to walk that off before getting home.

The prepared conversational topics could be filed away for a later evening, having taken up some mental time that shouldn't be wasted.

Arriving home, he unclipped the dog's collar, who sped off in pursuit of the pack, to check them off the register, then placing the dog paraphernalia on the wicker basket under the coats in the hall.

He hadn't woken his ears up to Fiona when she started to assign him some tasks. Wine bottles, putting away outside furniture, moving the patio heater.

As Fiona passed in front of him in her comfortable house jeans, he thought about what Iva might look like right now, what she might be wearing. Yet right in front of him he saw the control, the balance of power Fiona held. Iva was mere entertainment and folly; at least he was honest to himself about *that*. Swap the two of them around, married to a mid-forties Iva with young Fiona glamming up for nights out, and he'd be lusting after *her*. He didn't believe in *the one*, any more than people finding *their career thing*, but he never regretted his choice. It would be a waste of energy to throw that away and start afresh, no doubt kicking off a new cycle.

Julian picked up some paint brochures assigned to him by Fiona, and commented on a few tones he liked. A week after mocking their neighbours for updating their décor schemes for the sixth time in a decade. Not a marmalade dropper, but upper class overkill nonetheless.

Florence sat in her thin pyjamas on a cold evening, as the stifling gas central heating warmed all floors of the house, the boiler pumping away without pause. Julian grew up in a cooler household with parents who liked crisp air, and so he had to fling open windows now and then, cooling the warm air rising from radiators underneath the windows.

Fiona's body temperature was at loggerheads with his. In the day she preferred warmth, forcing them to play windows wars. At night, it reversed and she preferred thinner, cooler bed linen to him. She would sleep half in half out, while on his side, Julian would be buried.

Florence had to make a decision about a school project. Titled: *Planetary*. The theme was of her choosing. Julian sat in silence, half listening as Florence talked through her ideas with Fiona, who couldn't help but feel a depth of loss with the topics Florence was running through, all relating to planet earth, and the absolute fucking state of the place. She thought this and didn't voice it. She tried to guide her elsewhere, "Why not try something leftfield, about Saturn or the moon? Something hopeful."

"What does left field mean? The moon's not a planet."

"Unusual, unexpected. I know that, but it's in a planet's orbit. Get creative would you! You can't do plastics like everyone else. Originality."

"You think I should ignore everything going on here, that we can do things about, and start, like, colonising mars?"

"Colonising. Good word. Some return on our £23k a year. Cut out the likes please," Julian huffed, himself turning over murmurings at work about business performance, in energy, on top of what he knew from official figures. They were behind others in following the green money, and had been caught on the hop. This might have serious implications on his bonus next year. He couldn't even countenance redundancy and what chickens might come home to roost in that scenario. Polar bears and fish stocks were not his concern. Keeping the boiler and his loins pumping away were.

"Oil, gas, coal produces all this stuff. The tablets, the TVs, this roasting hot house, the food transportation of your cherished avocados. It pays for Daddy's bonuses, the holidays, the homes plural, and that school you go to."

"Give it a rest, Julian, she knows all that. You've mentioned it once or twice."

"I'm trying to be helpful. Weave that into your project."

Florence looked away from both her parents, she knew the fix she was in. All the shiny stuff, the fun here, the fancy gear, created misery and caused havoc elsewhere.

"Maybe I'll write about the carbon footprint of a second home," Florence offered.

"Oh, I can sell that. Someone else will buy it. And you won't be learning to surf anymore. And that's not *planetary*."

Florence puffed, mirroring her father.

"Is that what you and Dad were talking about the other day?"

"What was that?"

"You were talking about selling something."

It dawned on both the parents how much she absorbed, as they went about their business, talking as if in private, about a family property they had to make a decision on with Fiona's brother.

"Oh, no, that was something else. Don't worry about that," and Fiona distracted her, returning to the focal subject.

Fiona watched her compute, as she stared in concentration and then looked up as if in a cartoon, as she had always done. Fiona imagined her pulling this face at a high court judge, at some judicial misstep.

Florence watched Julian stabbing at the remote control with a fading battery, and Fiona flicking through a fashion magazine, tearing things out for later.

"Mum, you can do something for me."

"Oh really. *Even more*. What's that?"

"Stop running the water while you brush your teeth."

"Ah, yes. Good obs," she concurred, "sorry, it's just how we did it when I was your age."

"Move with the times, mother. Or the times will leave you behind," Florence tutted, before looking stuck.

"You could do something on the water supply. There's water on the moon. Your father might even be able to help."

"Tenuous! Giles does water. Not me. Sorry," Julian said, stamping that out, refusing to pay and do the education himself.

"You're not helping."

She didn't have anything further to say. Fiona stepped toward her and touched her shoulder.

The parents had both passed the stage of being willing to help on that day.

"We'll figure it out. It's all going to be OK," reassured Fiona, her habitual response, repeated to encourage acknowledgement and acceptance. A mental trick to turn off the cogs, and which might have worked in her youth, without the distractions, but which had less impact now.

"Sleep on it, you'll know or figure out what to do in the morning," Fiona reassured. "Or you won't, and we'll look tomorrow."

Julian went outside and he saw a light on in one of the large houses that overlooked theirs. Something he heard a lot about from Fiona; options to move, build a wall. A bedroom light was on, and he could see an attractive silhouette closing a small window, in a robe. He was careful not to step further forward to avoid triggering the outside light, and took a moment to appreciate the sight. Sex thoughts to pile on top of the hormones circulating that day. He would try to fuck Fiona that night.

The figure disappeared. He stepped forward and clanged and clonked things around to ensure his effort registered inside. Stepping back into the kitchen he opened and decanted a heavy red. Fiona heard the winefall into the large, flat bottomed vessel, and thought 'sex tonight then,' doing a quick mental scan of her cycle, and concurring it was as good a time as ever.

"Pour me a large glass, would you?" she urged, and Julian looked up, paused, and then glanced to one side.

10000
CHAPTER 16
Phil and dinner with Helen: Steven gets sushi: Soho drinking

Phil Sheffield *(Tufnell Park, Web Designer, Domino's, Levi's)* got up around eleven o'clock and lumbered through to the kitchen in a T-shirt with armpit holes, and greying white boxers. Not just fresh stubble, but another day's batch, the rare personal growth within his living corpse. Unwashed yesterday, let alone today, his body varnished in a layer of gig grime and arse gunge. Breath steeped in stout and rum. Another session, sticking it to the man. And to himself.

Sleep appeared to have exhausted him, to have taken everything that remained, leaving little for him to apply to the rest of the day. The act itself took more from the man than it gave.

The previous night was a night like any other. Ale and a couple of small-time bands at a local boozer with mates from the record label. The price of entry was the price of a beer, yet getting in for free as Jez knew the bassist in the second band, felt like an enticement and small victory. Work had been a swirling mess of scum all week, plughole circling, and it was time to put it on the backburner, for alcohol and noise to burn through it. IT problems, A&R pressures and hot-headed label team meetings, and *musical artists* with visually artistic pretentions, at loggerheads with his ideas.

Once dressed, in the same grey lounging hoodie and faded-to-grey black jeans Helen had seen him wear now for a run of consecutive weekends, he went through to the kitchen without thought or direction, while the cogs began to ease themselves into a turn. Great wooden gears driven by water in olde canal-side homes. The hope that the bodily movement would kick-start something, a plan for tea or breakfast, at the very least. Helen wondered at the total lack of any pressure he applied to himself, a mind void of troubles and fear of the future. The pure clarity of little thought. He passed the clothes horse Helen had put out to air the clothes of his that she had washed. A jumble of black, grey and primary colours, beer, sports and band logos and emblems. Alcohol or music logos, record labels, never a high fashion label. She paused as if it might register and she imagined him turning and thanking her, maybe countering with something he might do for her in return, later that day. He continued to saunter, but it didn't escape his notice that the jeans were positioned to reveal the growing holes where his hot balls had burned through, either side of a thick seam and rivet.

"We've got no plans for tonight, we should go out for dinner." Helen opened.

"We could see if Chris and Sati want to go for a drink?"

"We can do that in the week."

"We can go for dinner in the week."

Helen looked sideways and huffed at these exhausting debating loops, "Jesus. It's Saturday night, we're a couple, and I want to go for dinner. If you don't want to, what the hell are we doing?"

"OK, calm down. It's no biggie."

This annoyed Helen further, chucking in slang, a metaphor itself for the position in which their relationship found itself.

"We can go for a curry," Phil continued, unaware of the oil he was throwing on the flames, thinking this was helping.

"We're in London, we can go *anywhere*. I made a note somewhere of some of the places Francesca's been to recently."

"Fancy places."

"Yeah, fancy places. Why not?" Helen continued, then added, "you could wear a jacket!" at which point they both laughed. For no matter the disagreements and the disconnection, there was underlying affection.

Helen picked up the newspaper magazine and waggled it in the air, "I'm tired of reading what *other people* are doing."

"OK, well you find somewhere, and we'll do it," he offered.

"Right, I will."

"Can we make it North London, though, I can't be bothered with Soho on a Saturday."

"All right."

Helen listened to the toilet seat clang against the cistern as Phil took a long morning piss, and it piped down into the bowl. Helen thought he could at least run it around the rim. She waited to see if the shower went on, but he wandered through to the lounge instead and loafed on the sofa to appease his muscles built for laziness, and he put on a music TV channel, like some throwback relic, while Helen looked for small night out options.

Once that was done she stood helpless, in front of her wardrobe, pulling favourite tops out one after the other, each one tired, pre-worn on too many nights out, days at work. Dark cottons with too many washes under their belts. She chose a lighter material with a brighter design, undimmed from previous activities, and resolved to buy a couple of items in the week, cheap but nevertheless new.

That evening they made it to a new local restaurant in Kentish Town. Mexican. Uninspiring. Helen proceeded to raise a couple of friends and relatives who were pregnant or with young ones, and which Phil showed zero interest in, choosing instead to reminisce on what the parents got up to when they were younger. As their conversations paralleled, Helen felt a baby showdown coming, it was in the post, but not tonight. She had not the energy or the inclination other than hopeful probing.

Phil signalled his sexual frustration by picking away at his beer bottle labels, water torture to Helen, who showed hers by going heavy with the make-up and wearing a low cut top. She tried to focus, but in spite of, or to spite herself, she looked around at the other couples, admiring the younger couple enjoying their evening together, touching hands. She reached across and put her hands on Phil's.

As the drink kicked in, overpowering chips and guac, Helen went for footsie under the table, and Phil figured it would have to be sex night tonight or an argument; weighed it up and went with it, and at least figured he could enjoy the alcohol first.

The music was boisterous, matching the cocktails. There was an abundance of food gripes and they didn't care. They got drunk, they had unglamorous yet functional sex and with the precious sex endorphins chasing around their systems, slept as logs.

Needing to clear the mind clutter, Steven booked a single spot at the counter of a choice sushi bar. Exceptional in its produce, precision, cleanliness, interiors, service, mixology. Crisp and clean in its linen, lines, cuts, paraphernalia layout. As close to pure uniformity as he could find at this price point. Local and European caught langoustines, scallops, oysters, clams, crab, eel, mackerel, squid, plus Asian imports of wagyu and yellowtail. Provenance added in fine italics beneath each item. As he would scribe the menu himself.

He followed the chefs working in front of him, watching their hand and knife work, the efficiency of movement, the sharp focus, no sense of the distractions and dirty hubbub of a European kitchen. Their knife work. The knife work. He thought of them sharpening their knives each day, disinfecting, applying care, putting them to sleep in their soft wrappings before travelling home each night.

The scallops served in their shell, with a gentle waspy yellow and black char, set against a green garnish. Tempura oysters and brill. These were the jabs that hit his taste receptors. Yet it was the nigiri which gave him the ASMR buzz he sought. The pleasurable itch and buzz inside the base of skull, which stretched out down his back, as the precise items were formed and left in front of him. The front of his brain hummed and tickled as consecutive courses were eased in front of him, in an assured but not strict manner. The simplicity of neat white rice and protein.

He was aware of the treasures of the sea he was lucky enough to indulge in, plundered with industry from the oceans. Driven by the division of resources between parties in competition. Yet he was a fatalist. Humans were going to do what they were going to do. Two earths with similar human populations would end up in a similar place, there or thereabouts, despite the odd temporary breakthrough by a top zero point zero zero zero zero one percent individual. The emptied oceans were as fated as the egg dropped from height was to break. And a meeting of the G20 was an interlude akin to the paused recording of the egg halfway on its descent.

He shook his head to stop that train of thought and returned to what he saw in front of him. The knife work. He wondered when the last Japanese kitchen knife was eased deep into human flesh, and did it enter a blade, an artery or organ. Where, and for what reason. Japan itself the most obvious answer; that internal, inward nation, 99% Japanese, 1% Other, an island free of the grip of wider states and commitments. With their well trotted out idiosyncrasies and perversions, and *if you pay for it, it's not cheating*.

Case in point behind and to Steven's right. A middle-aged gentleman and a younger girl, both Japanese he figured, from their conversations with staff. No ring on her bony fingers, but a gold and silver watch sparkling with her every movement. Diamonds on the wrist and not the finger could mean one of two things. He smirked and continued to eat. He was at peace with his food, not a complaint in sight.

To the other side of him, a young family, comprising a smart and good-looking couple, both looking successful in their own right, and their two daughters, under ten. They had finished their meal and were all reading books. An unbelievable sight. Inside, he thanked them for the peace. Tranquilo.

Over lunch he worked out that Andrew was in the area.

He left and strolled down central London's wide arterial boulevard with little traffic save for buses, rounding the substantial curve of Regent Street, and looked up to trace the outline shape against the glaring, cloud-covered white sky. A number of women walked toward him, looking away, down, behind him into the distance. A British curiosity, showing up the palpable fear and risk women felt, in the middle of the day, in the middle of town. Women would look him in the eye in New York, Paris, even take their time with their assessment.

He chicaned his way between buses and bespoke raised footways, and elevated central reservations, cutting into Beak Street where he passed Kingly and Carnaby Streets and restaurant brands, until he reached the clustering at fragrance corner. At pace, he weaved right, through the cold, shaded, empty street toward Brewer Street, and beyond through Old Compton Street. An enclave for tourists, in a city for the rich, personality and idiosyncrasy stripped away year-by-year, supplanted by the gloss of new exterior design and tropes galore. Neon signs hung off back walls, minimalist black shopfronts with dialled down white lettering, the puns of future mass chains, proving their concepts to Private Equity.

Faces face down, following map tracks, handling their digital backlogs, looking for feet, lampposts, fallen bicycles, unaware of paired moped muggers, all geared up to snatch at machete point. Global people, firing in all directions, taking up whole paths with their bulk, forcing strident Steven into the street, dodging tuk tuks and the ubiquitous car of the hired driver. The city, where the sheer volume of cars meant every corner could offer an interruption to the walker, the flaneur, crossing a road, walking the road, taking a shortcut. Now threatened further by the pavement cyclist, electric scooter, or powered skateboard. New agile menaces which could whizz up to the thirty miles per hour at no physical cost to an owner encouraged to minimise activity further, adding heft and tonnage, ready to flatten a passer-by.

He met Andrew at their mutual members' club in Soho as dusk set in and the street lights took up the heavy lifting.

They were into their second drinks and both water torture distracted by the best looking girl in the room. The soft buttoned armchairs, endless lamps, ornate fireplace, modern chandelier, midnight blues and turquoises. Steven could sense an overhaul coming. Her gregarious, girlish laugh, hand movements with her slim wrist, jingling jewellery which would get annoying. She had the unspoken attention of most of the male majority room, something she enjoyed over the other women present, as they went about their drinking and networking, many conscious not to give away their interest by attempting to restrict their glances. Instead, she received the ongoing attention of eyeballs on rotation, enjoying what Andrew assumed were professional model looks.

And then some divine intervention.

One of a small cluster of girls nearby stood up, arms wide, to welcome a new joiner. This was someone at a whole new level. The most beautiful girl everyone in the room would see all year. Even radiating kindness, generosity of spirit, and warmth.

"Holy fuck," Andrew said. Thirsty male and female eyes all around, as he caught the previous best looking take her place among the hoi polloi, deflating into herself and sucking on a straw, bewildered, damaged, lost in harsh thoughts.

Steven was delighted at this turn of events.

"Remarkable," he commented, noting to himself that he had overused remarkable/unremarkable that day. At risk of becoming a verbal tic. Something he chose to keep a close watch on.

"What's the latest office wank at your place?"

A recurring theme for them both.

"Fireside chats. Round-tables. Give me my pay check, give me my bonus, don't interrupt my weekends. Fuck off. Home working, hybrid working. A whole generation lost to *A Place in the Sun* repeats. A renaissance in the viewership of *Escape to the Country*. Unmuting to interject with a career laugh, for the *right* colleague. You?"

"It's all user journeys, tailored, personalised, the capability to integrate sources, next generation touchpoints, channels, chatbots, workflows, to harness and democratise access to technology. Pays the bills. Cheers."

They clunked glasses and drunk in the chaos and the bizarreness of it all. The way the world determined the game's values.

"Oh, tell you what though. I got one fucking switched on client, this guy's got the lot: young, smart, tough, high energy, always working, always on. Robust. Towering. Four languages, networked, on the rise. Cunt's got the looks too; from premium moneyed stock, the education, all of it. We're going through the ROI numbers for the year, big numbers. *Happy* numbers. And he stops us, even takes a few seconds, as if he needs them, which we know he doesn't. And says: 'Numbers look strong, as they always do with you, but I've got four or five of these big ticket projects going on, and each agency is coming in here and putting up the millions of pounds, euros, dollars they're making me, and we're not seeing it in Finance.'"

Andrew regaled, "I couldn't help but smirk at the cunt, and he had the temerity to smirk back. No pretence, it's all in the game."

"Nice."

"Then he started talking about some other department he's not responsible for. And that's it. The subtext. Keep the numbers coming, on the rise, get me my next move, that next department and you can keep taking our money."

They agreed to move to spirits, and as Andrew got up, Steven rotated his thoughts to money. Running through bonuses owed and quarters due, and a few other purchases he had in the plan for the year ahead, he figured out when he could make some mortgage overpayments and how that would affect his outgoings. He felt a slight thrill at the potential leftovers and what he could splurge those on. Himself. Yet in front of him, Andrew, worth more. He could tot up based on the apartment, car, best guess salary, plus some of the chat of investments and property, that Andrew was well ahead. From a similar baseline start. And of course, while Steven was growing, developing, earning and burning, Andrew was in parallel. A hare he would struggle to catch. The acridity of his pain at the success of others didn't reflect well on him. Yet for most, grace was something to offer after one had realised one's own dreams.

Andrew was attended to.

"What can I get for you?" asked the Australian *mixologist*.

"G'day. Two bourbons and cola, Hudson Baby Bourbon. Doubles, few cubes of ice in each."

"Heavy tumbler," he added, bouncing his palms up and down in front of him.

Charm and disarm.

The mixologist turned around to face the wall of alcohol before grimacing, checking with furtive eyes that there was no mirrored backing, which might get a complaint raised, or a helpful review left online. He accepted the grind of delivering twenty-eight-pound drinks to over-valued dickheads, busy in his spare time educating himself, so that he might become one himself.

"Bowled 'im," exclaimed Steven as Andrew set down the drinks.

It was Steven who would be quizzed first on women and any sexual success he might have enjoyed. With most of his peers married, for what that was worth. As one put it, "Any recent luck finding women with sufficiently low esteem to sleep with you?"

However, in Andrew, he at least had a fellow single soul, so he asked before it came down to a question aimed at him, which it would during a drinking session. First mover advantage counted. Asking about latest news, he received a rather rambling, philosophical response, musings on the general state of play.

As his uncles told him when he was young, women wanted two

things [youngster hanging on every word]: security and kids. Little he had seen himself in adulthood led him to disagree, until the Zoomer generation arrived.

"No new squeeze for a while, too much going on elsewhere. When I get horny I call someone."

An ambiguous reference which could mean escort or casual sexual acquaintance. That it was ambiguous indicated toward the former, and Steven didn't want to clarify, and risk revealing his naivety. The sound of Andrew crying out at his expense played out in his head. Andrew elaborated but did not clarify either way, muttering about a recent lover (sexer?) that he was *balls deep* in.

This was a dated conversation from the nineties, set within a pub full of hostelry ephemera, copper kettles, fishnets, boats fixed to ceilings. And even Steven felt uncomfortable with much of the content, characterisations, misogyny, yet Andrew was iced in time, unthawable. Many drinks in he decided to go along with it, to *have a day off*.

"I saw someone for a while, but she ghosted me," he revealed, which was a bit much for Steven, given Andrew was a seasoned phantom, "hot single mum. *Mums need fingering too,* old boy."

Orbiting the stable staples, huge variations in what was acceptable and non-deviant sexual practice. Nowadays, for some, rimming was table stakes, and required no manoeuvring or encouragement. For others, not so, ergo in the sexual arena, there was no Rule of Law, merely what was consensual and enjoyable. A maelstrom of awkward ambiguity for new lovers without a strong natural connexion.

Andrew looked Steven in the eye, and shook his empty glass. He expected the ice to shake back and forth, clashing and clinking, but instead they chased each other around the circumference, ringing as they did so.

Approaching the bar, Steven ordered two *Godfathers*. "Equal parts scotch and amaretto, couple of cubes of ice."

"I know what it is, mate."

Steven confirmed a scotch brand.

Another fifty quid, gone.

Steven gave a brief update on Josie and expected digging, but Andrew's mind was somewhere else, on himself, and the unconnected thoughts he wanted to expel.

"Guy gets on the plane at Istanbul, it's delayed, I'm at the back queuing for the lav. Cunt's been over for hair implants, with a couple of mates. Bald heads, red raw to fuck, ten thousand pin pricks, red and purple soreness. Daft cunts. Starts asking the cabin crew where 36F is. Fucking plane goes up to 32. She asks him for his ticket stub, he handed it in to the guy at the front, fuck off, who does that?!"

"A 36F error."

"Poor bastards, having to deal with morons like that."

The drink dragged his language further into the gutter.

"Squaddies too. Say what you want about the squeezed middle classes and their tax burdens, but it's the uneducated, low classes sent to die in our wars."

They bounced around topics for the next twenty minutes, as if the conversation were a mix of related and unconnected search terms, whatever sprung into someone's head, segwayed via some general conjunctions, 'you'll never guess who I saw / what happened the other day / did you?'

Girls, work, investments, cricket, film, recent news, spirits, despised politicians, legs, restaurants, Japan, brain tumours, classic horror films.

Steven looked at his Apple Watch. 10.23 blinked back at him. Configured to show a small ten and a giant twenty-three. The time that had stuck with him since childhood, a time that he perceived had appeared more than it should. He wondered if one day it would reveal meaning, that the 23rd October would be an important date, that a child would be born at that hour, or his body to decommission itself into the longest sleep. A reminder for tonight at least, that it was time that he scarpered.

Time to *go-oh-oh-oh-oh*.

They stepped out into drizzled, drenched streets, which mirrored the street lights and shop fronts before them, and squeezed and swished the rain out from under the tyres of all types wheeling about by the gutters. Bad night to wear suede shoes, thought Steven, looking across at Andrew, who had *chosen unwisely*.

He nodded at Andrew's shoes, "36F error."

They might sometimes get scran before heading home, but they had both had their fill of each other, and it wasn't floated. Steven had had some sly coke, which had not gone unnoticed.

While Steven picked up a car, Andrew delayed confirming his pickup so that Steven could disappear, leaving Andrew free to go walkabout, as his mixologist might say. The rain had ceased at least, so he strode along to the circus, then down Piccadilly to Green Park tube, ducking into a side street halfway to snort a couple of lines from a bullet which he had been enjoying himself that evening.

10001
CHAPTER 17
Chez Iva and the gym: Simon & Francesca steakhouse: Bad news

Saturday mid-morning chez Iva Jovanovic, and an intense, full day ahead. She had tidied and freshened up the gleaming white and light grey interiors of her modern apartment, and the light streamed in via the kitchen windows and balcony doors, both facing toward the river, up several floors. Plants in an array of vibrant, rich greens (well looked after) and a short book stack broke up the clean lines of monotony. Art prints, positioned to splash colour in the right directions, led the eyes around the light furnishings. She had hung them herself after she had a friend come over on the pretence of lunch, to hold them up and move around as she directed, while she eyed and pencilled the positioning marks.

Dressed in Alala black, cream and gunmetal leggings and a dark blue muscle tee, her hair just dry from her first morning shower, tied back, she was bursting to get out for a run. However, she was hamstrung by the confirmation that her new Apple Watch was out for delivery within the next hour. She paced around, making slight adjustments to kitchen item alignments, checking her white laptop and white phone, trying and failing to find a playlist to stream to fit her mood. She tinkered with her to do list and calendar, ensuring everything was covered for the rest of the day. That the time and connections between tasks, events, journeys, all made sense, and were achievable. Slotted, a massage, mani and pedicures, and a few things to try on around Bond Street, at Chanel and Alexander McQueen. A late afternoon session at her gym, followed by a swim and a steam. She regretted feeling too pushed to hit a boxing class in town. She adjusted calendar slots here and there for the following day, changed the colours and tags, added small edits to notes, punctuation that she alone would see. Re-ordered tasks, undid the changes, made a redo, settled with the new result. She synced her phone and executed a hard drive backup with a storage unit she kept in a dresser.

She finished a green tea and placed it next to the sink. Then she put it in the sink, and walked away. Returning, she put it in the dishwasher and dropped the teaspoon into the cutlery caddy. She wiped a slight sludge green watermark from the steel sink base, rinsed the cloth, hung it to dry over the tap. And returned to straighten it.

When the door might go any moment, she couldn't meditate. Or journal, which she preferred to do at sunrise, and which she hadn't managed beyond an outline already that morning. She consulted her to do list, and figured she could concentrate on some interiors acquisition, having jotted down some brand names she had picked up from *FT Weekend*, and *HOW TO SPEND IT* magazine. Oh yes, one day, she *would* spend it. The lot.

Synced, updated, she executed a restart. Clean.

She better aligned the remote controls.

Referring to her interiors notes, and searching away, she hoped the glassware producer she was taken with would prove expensive enough, much preferring to discover a choice vase to be seven hundred than one fifty. Price would contribute to defining the quality, not the other way around. She had to come by a few choice pieces to complete the décor, before having a few friends she was competitive with over for a dinner party. This had to happen in short order, as it had been commented on that she'd been moved in 'a while now,' and it threatened becoming a dismissive blight. Of the four friends she had in mind, she rated herself in second place. Elena, the Russian, had money and familial standing beyond her reach, and taste to match. The best she could do was align herself as best she could, and try to carve out a couple of niches, in which Elena took an interest but hadn't invested in to any true depth, for some kudos and recognition. This was going to require some bonus money from January. Iva was finding this problematic, and would use dinner to test some topics for weakness. The others Iva had covered in their standings in the workplace and looks, though an undeserved promotion to any of them could put this under threat. Right place, right time, one of those.

Figuring the answer to be some extra stretching before her run, which she tended to do on the move after leaving and hitting an easy jog, she figured some additional light yoga moves indoors would occupy her until the door went. Yoga was meditative, and in classes she could switch off so that she would miss the call for the next pose, and *almost* have to scramble. This didn't fit with her aesthetic, yet her suppleness and poise were on point, so she made a point to reconcile herself with her higher mental attainment beyond the physical optics, as any class ended.

Fifteen minutes in, the concierge called, her package had arrived, and she could hope to break open the packaging and crack on. The delivery guy was still scanning and beeping when she turned up, turned out in her best gym get-up. He was a fit young lad himself, which she caught but didn't acknowledge, and she dealt with the fuss and disappeared before he did. He got this a lot, but didn't complain.

Fixing the tech and organising the packaging into their respective recycling receptacles, she was out the door, music bluetoothed in, free to start compiling new lists.

Later that day, approaching evening, Iva took a car to the gym. Fifteen quid each way, she was not going to take a bus. On rotation, a mix of cardio sessions, classes, weights, boxing, plus massage, sauna, and occasional treatments at her luxe gym. Holistic, wholesome, wholly energetic.

The gym changing room, a well-lit chamber of light wood, reminiscent of the interior of a Helsinki spa minus the reindeer pelts. Lockers and flooring the colour of antlers. Great mirrors fixed atop marble walls, white with stone grey slashes. Surrounded by tall, coded lockers, and shelves with pyramids of rolled white towels.

Ready with a new weights programme built into her gym tech, she took great care to ensure perfection in front of the changing room mirror. All outlines to her tight gym-wear neat and seamless, lined up in the right directions, hair tied back with no loose threads, no marks from the light make-up applied at home. Shoelaces tied in a risk-free manner, tech operational, headphones charged, self-curated 'Gym playlist – weight training' on, volume set to fourteen. Her clothing brands noticeable to the trained eye, to fellow consumers, able to spot the small logos weaved in the same colour as the stretch fabric. £150+

per item, obtained after she accompanied a finance friend to *her* Mayfair gym and having caught on to their brand vibes, executed a four-figure upgrade. Ready with water, powered by powder with protein and electrolytes, prepared at home.

Iva hoped that the intensity of lifting heavy barbells, executing squats and deadlifts would not just offer extra-curricular muscle strength outside the high stress zones, but also allow for concentration and silence the background thoughts. As she got into it, it became apparent that this was a pipe dream, and like half hours spent on a cross-trainer, treadmill or astride a two grand home-based static bicycle, she was fated to churn over her manifold first world troubles.

She felt two sets of eyes boring into her, from different directions, across the workshop floor. A ripped Latin guy, South American perhaps. They looked at each other, rutting in who could look the most dispassionate and ambivalent. As the woman, she could break and get on with her doings. He had to take care not to look weak.

Elsewhere, a blonde Scandinavian girl was watching Iva with hungry eyes, honing an improbable mix of interest and nonchalance, crafted from a decade and a half *in the field*. Her lingering, cruising look turned into a smile at the edge of her eyes, seeking reciprocation.

'Won't be telling Julian about that,' she thought to herself, but of course she would. If not because he would piss her off at some stage, and not even because Fiona might come up in conversation, but as most things tended to go said, in the end. Except for embarrassments, damage to brand image. At the higher ends of society. At the bottom, daily humiliations and tribulations shared, where laughter, shared joy and trust through openness were the currencies which kept their world circulating.

Warming up for ten minutes on a cross-trainer, she turned the music up to help clear her head, but the lyrics conflicted too much with her cascading thoughts, and she had to remove the cans, placing them on the mini TV screen in front of her with as much care as she could, her arms and legs scissoring back and forth.

Julian occupied her. He had her on the hook. Whereas she was up and coming, he was *oven-ready*. Nabbing him would accelerate her, set the foundations, and take out of the equation all the time consumed with finding a peer at her level, and years of toil and manoeuvres to establish themselves. It could be acquired, off-the-shelf, accelerating her toward her goals. Beyond getting *there*, it mattered to get *there* soon.

No matter what Fiona were able to prise away, which would be substantial, he would be left with significant assets and the future earning power. As for the children, she knew enough from her own experiences and using her eyes and ears that once separated and given a new family to look out for, the appeal of an easy life and minimising conflict would win out.

Pumping her arms and legs away in arcs like factory testing pistons, she drifted to happier thoughts. To skiing, pregnancy, second homes, holidays in their second home, early-stage pregnant and skiing. As he juggled a hundred pressure balls, she would be there organising him, a level up on Fiona. Meanwhile, the self-centred Julian could indulge in his pleasures and rewards.

She hit the free weights for a turn, capturing weights and reps via a terminal, to journal her output, an addendum to the principal. Ending on a final exercise she had been taught for the first time the previous week by her Personal Trainer, she approached the sole member of staff at the desk, and asked for his assistance in showing her the ropes.

This Englishman, the Health & Fitness Manager, looked both ways for one of his charge to be able to delegate to help. He was trapped, by the lack of a lackey, and by Iva's looks. Were she to be average-looking, overweight perhaps, he would indicate he'll send someone over when he could, yet she stared beyond his eyes.

In Iva's league looks-wise, although king of this jungle gym, there was a huge class discrepancy in status and power, and she required high maintenance. He had to acquiesce, and hurried through the coaching as quick as he could, to retain pride. As he finished, Iva nodded at him to confirm she understood and to offer no thanks, for she saw what was at work here. The dismissive and hierarchy-addled English and their systems and games, an ongoing source of contention for her in the office.

While she finished her final sets, she nudged Julian on some matter of financing of some trip or treat, which he parried, while in Wandsworth he was organising the sizeable deposit for the winter getaway, at Fiona's forthright behest.

It was a Wednesday night and what better way for Simon Knight to spend it than taking Francesca for an opulent dinner, light drugs, and a sleepover. However, she demanded simple steak, so steak it would be. Francesca couldn't be bothered with all the tasting menu courses, the fussing, the interruptions. This worked for Simon, as there was an option down the cobbled streets of Borough, and then it would be straight home. A short walk ruined by the tourist hordes, ever increasing, keen to visit the awful market and tourorestos. It pained him to cave to the inevitable, and leave behind the hullabaloo, but he loved his apartment.

It was seldom the case that he could cut too loose midweek in case something complex appeared. Should he be needed to review a synopsis or point of contract, a cocaine membrane would be a barrier to its completion. An evening call from a US investor, and a tetchy, garrulous phone call might raise eyebrows. Every sign of imperfection cost them cents per share. A drug-addled business leader could cost them. And they would be listening. The world listened.

Buzzing her up to his flat, the steel, mirrored lift doors pinged open and she walked through. He went to greet her for a kiss, and received a welcome and immediate hand, roving around below his belt.

"We'll be quick," was all she said as she manoeuvred him onto one of his leather sofas, the large windows open for the night sky to observe. She caught him off guard, as she was quite rough, removing his shirt and trousers, hitching her dress up, inserting him inside her, and then putting her right hand around his throat and squeezing. It was a functional act, devoid of affection, and she rode him until he came inside her. She came first, but was discreet. He wasn't sure, she kept it to herself, and he wasn't going to ask.

They didn't hang around, and dressed themselves while he wondered what brought that on. A combination of hormones, elapsed time since last fuck, and the prospect of a large dinner.

They both straightened themselves up in the floor to ceiling mirrors in the hallway, stood next to each other, suited, in black and white, like tango partners.

Entering the restaurant via a heavy door, the dark wood interior met with an industrial vibe in the reception area, and another layer of darkness inside, candles, sidelights, and muted lanterns, attempting to light a sombre interior with inky leather booths and matching salt and pepper mills.

They ordered eighteen oysters as Simon wanted twelve to himself, and then three further starters between two. A new one to the waitress, who had to confirm she was getting it right.

Spiky, tart cocktails began to arrive.

Simon complained about flecks of oyster shell, and they were removed and new ones presented minutes later. He busied himself with the extra starter of scallops while this resolved itself. He grumbled about the effect a hotter climate was appearing to have on options for late season skiing, and the threat of his favourite cluster of holiday islands disappearing into the sea. Sharing these burdens with a new audience.

Oysters were re-delivered. Simon looked them up and down. "Fine," and the waitress paused as if to digest, and then shuffled away. Francesca called her back and asked for another cocktail, same again, and was polite in doing so.

"Since I saw Fraser, I've been giving the environment some thought."

Francesca huffed her derision, "Since when did you start taking an interest in the environment? Is your dealer pushing eco-coke?"

"The business could do with a couple of years as-is so as to avoid repercussions on our sale potential. Many of our customers are in affected industries. They take a hit, they hit us, or cut us off. And I'm exposed in my investments to old world fuels and technologies. If this is the way things are going, I need to be on board. This is where government money is being spent, and I'll be happy to receive it. Besides, you don't have to give a flying fuck about the environment to make money from it. Wealth creation, that's difficult. That requires real innovation. Wealth redistribution, that's easier. It doesn't matter where the £300 million comes from. Whether it created jobs, or ended jobs. The money is the money."

"What's the big idea then?"

"That's forming. Don't you worry about that."

Francesca could see the truth in his words. The direct speech, the mouthpiece for the high spec brain, never stopping, never tiring. Every conversation a duel, the debating society of college extended out, thirty years later. Francesca found these people draining. She kept up for a couple of hours, then tired, and lost interest.

"It's a shame people like you didn't put your energies into doing some good. The world could be a better place."

That simple and logical suggestion didn't register. For it meant *less*. He looked at her, moving his gaze from eyes to nose to lips and back up, trying to push his own buttons. He cast out wider, down to her arms and chest. And back again. He couldn't quite decide upon what he wanted from her.

"No. Someone else can figure that stuff out for little reward. Are we moving to wine?" he asked.

"White wine," Francesca directed, "I want to taste the steak, not red wine."

She pushed on, unabashed, "You may rule it out now. God may have other plans for you. For all of us."

He knew what she was driving at. He knew his history and a sufficient number of its lessons. There was a long-tail of low probability outcomes, catastrophes among them, enabled by technology. He was in a race against them.

She watched him, turning his cocktail glass at the base, the giveaway of pressure within.

From looking at Simon, Francesca glanced sideways at a couple sat against the wall thirty feet away to her right. A gentleman, dressed in that *old money way*, sat opposite a woman in her thirties, dressed with high-end accessories.

"I hope that's his daughter."

A short time later, the man slid his chair back with care, but nonetheless dragged the feet, which caught Francesca's attention. He looked like he creaked as he rose and straightened his tall, stiff body, before giving it one final push of pride to bend down and kiss her on the lips as he made his way to the bathroom.

"Pre and post wives," Simon outlined, "there's the wife who helped you to make it and the wife after. Politics, business, show business. Unless you were of the highest order to start with, a matter of time. There's pre and post husbands too, believe me."

"Oh yes, I know."

Simon caught sight of a petite redhead, wearing a short dark red dress, swaying across the room toward the bathroom. Following the golden rule, her dress was discrete and covered-up at the top, while stopping well short of the knee at the bottom. The dark lighting took the edge off the white skin of her legs, which looked dreamy. She reminded Simon of *the best lover he had ever had*. The outlier. The one that went to eleven, where even the best lovers scored an eight or nine. The lover that would never be usurped. Not the best looking, nor possessing the finest physique, yet one of the most gifted, and the clincher: the mental fizz and draw, the connection and siren sexuality. Someone he needed to own, knowing he could possess her for a short while. Independent, aloof, separate. There would be men after him, no matter what he proposed. In bed, the one who would bring him close and then stop. Confusing, the first time it happened. Yet after five minutes of nothing except her eyes, and the feeling of her long red hair falling on his shoulder and upper arms, and no words, she would start again, and bring him beyond where he had been before.

He took a few moments to recall a night they had together. Before putting the thoughts to one side, perhaps until he was inside Francesca again that evening.

Bloody steaks were served for them. Although medium-rare in principle, the sensible modern practice of under-cooking meat left them at rare-medium. An under-cooked steak could be corrected; one judged overcooked herded to the bin at great cost.

Salads, greens, chips.

As they reached the end of their meal, Simon and Francesca in turn went to the bathroom to put away some coke. For Francesca, a couple of lines worth (standard) and for Simon, a few lines worth (rock star), something which became apparent when Francesca said something as Simon sat down and he took over, his tongue speeding.

He winced and swallowed, something Francesca caught, as coke residue tumbled down the back of his throat, stuck. The harshness made him gag, yet it then felt like it opened receptors to the joyous powder, and he held it there, letting it be soaked up, not wishing to swill it away with a drink, which would be a waste.

Simon was alerted by his phone, which allowed for notifications from a limited set of people.

He didn't apologise but did bother to frown to convey annoyance at their being disturbed. Francesca understood he couldn't ever just switch off, and instead ordered a glass of wine from the bottom of the list, choosing to enjoy the benefits of an *always on* partner. £33 for 175. Nineteen pence per millilitre.

He made a call and was notified that Marianne Ferguson, one of his oldest friends and a success of her generation, an investor in his businesses and his uppermost legal counsel, had been killed in a climbing accident, in an area which had seen an increasing number of avalanches over the last decade.

He held a hand up to Francesca to confirm something important had happened, as his mind raced through the implications and complications her death would cause him, and what options he had to fill the holes left by her vacated expertise, filing through the resumes of his investor circle and his network of legal advisers.

A waiter came over and began to speak, and Simon cut him off one syllable in, "Not now," and said waiter disappeared himself.

He ended the call.

"Marianne's dead," he revealed, "climbing accident."

Francesca had met Marianna a couple of times.

"My god, that's awful."

Simon swiped to check his stock portfolio, part of the habit web of his circular phone routing, unrelated to Marianne of course, and caught himself.

"Yes. Yes, it is."

Francesca caught the calculations, the mental manoeuvres in full flow, facing this ensemble of psychopathy. Flesh, bone, organs, grey matter and memory, combined in a machine of material acquisition. She saw before her someone who sought the greatest slice of pie. Someone who attended no charity event without a strategic angle for himself, a connection to make, a relationship to foster. Yet, as she cast her critical eye over Simon, she pondered herself if she might join him at the funeral, if offered; an event of the highest echelons of London society. She chided herself for the thought.

"What was she climbing up?"

"That's a pleonasm."

"Jesus Christ," she raised her voice, "with the classical semantics, your friend has died."

She took a long drink.

"I don't know, somewhere in Pakistan," was all he could respond. Climbing did not interest Simon. Too much training, equipment, time out, travel. Though he was bitter at some of the wins of some of his contemporaries who succeeded in this regard, while risking their lives for bragging rights, there was a not insignificant chance that they wouldn't make it home.

Two scoops of sorbet each was served, manageable after the coke. Lychee and lime sorbet for each of them, to give their taste buds a shot, clear their fired heads, and to give their tight stomachs little to handle. A relief to Simon, to disrupt and distract them from the intensity of this situation, in which he was required to show grief, sadness, pain, when he felt, well, nothing. Save for annoyance at the increased complexity of his next travails, not the least of which was the impossible task of replacing a trusted first-class talent. They spooned in silence, both brought close to the edge of brain freeze. They upped the drinking.

He talked a little about how he met Marianne and a couple of memories. Both humorous. Nothing emotional, of complex humanity. And then changed the subject, asking about poker night at Julian's, and who would be sorting out the high quality booze and drugs.

From a young age, her mother observed her daughter, astute, a quiet reader of people, appearing occupied, distracted, busying herself with childhood things, displaying tenaciousness in her puzzling activities, while the adults talked. And later, a quiet question about the content of the conversation, something specific, a business expression, a name she hadn't yet come across. For she was all over the gist.

Francesca observed the man in front of her.

A bulldozing, unidirectional capitalist, trapped in pursuit, hurtling toward death, driven by beating others on the way. Who enjoyed the finer things in life, but would trade them all for the more he sought. A man haunted by the achievements of the richest in global society, the biggest of names. A man high and past fifty, of superior cachet in this capital of wealth and association, the conduit and connective tissue between Europe, the Americas, Asian and Middle Eastern money and investment, culture and cartels. Nothing for broader societal good would come of him, for the proletariat, though many would get wealthy from their labour and trusted investment. Yet she understood that this drove the psychopathy, for should he slip, should he descend, they will take everything he had, as he would of them. Though she remembered his comments from earlier, perhaps there was a green energy route up for him, which could benefit others. She cursed herself for finding a loophole as people did for those they wanted to be around. Francesca needed depth, beyond the luncheons, the trappings and the aleatory pleasures. Yet he always had a foothold in her. A temporary solution which might default to something permanent.

10010
CHAPTER 18
Josie meets a friend: Joined by Steven: Julian and Simon play squash

Saturday was mapped out for Steven and Josie. Josie had decided upon an art exhibition she wanted to see, recommended by a friend. Her friend, who did not make huge rates at work, and was not shackled to her desk to the same extent, had the inclination and the time for extravagances like cultural exploration and development; Josie did not. This friend short cut her on occasion. Josie was to meet a friend, Victoria, for brunch beforehand. This kiboshed Steven's ideal plan for a Saturday lunch of leisure, afternoon wine and a couple of hours at it back at Josie's place. In his experience, the more expensive the lunch, the better the follow-up sex.

He was at least thankful they were going to the Saatchi Gallery, and not over to some industrial *space* in East London. That would be a big ask, and a trek he would only make with any enthusiasm for the right person.

So he had to reframe his day, eat alone somewhere close to home, get the art thing done, then aim to steer her to a bar or pub for some imbibing into the evening, dinner out (it *was* Saturday, and he hoped she wouldn't offer to cook) and then sex back at base. Once. This new schedule and cadence to the day, afforded him the time to enjoy porn at leisure that morning before leaving home. He observed the regional differences in output. The classic American product with their moaning and aggression, or casting day. The clean, young and beautiful creatures from the Czech Republic. The occasional low fi French efforts. The lamentable niches discovered by the Europeans and Brits. Seniors and *Fake Taxi*. The best his home nation had to offer. Yet he marvelled at the sheer range of body types, the extensive tattooing and continual innovation, bringing such new delights as *Jerk Off Instruction*, which all suggested there was a large pool of talent out there, even leaving the amateurs to one side.

And all for free.

He fed the ducks and took a shower, where he mulled over his predicament. An inability to find that someone that he could put everything into, instead of these temporary fixes. Settling down required him to find someone superb he aspired to but with low enough standards to accept him as adequate. A big ask. He wanted to switch off in the shower, to live in the moment, like a dog, enjoy the feels of the rain, but his thoughts spun away, so that instead of taking his time, he hurried through it.

In Sloane Square, Josie joined Victoria, an ex-colleague and now friend, sat outside a restaurant on the concourse of a supposed shopping centre set back from King's Road, all corporate construction beige brick, replete with rich foreigners, new money milf, old money dilf, out for an unchallenging bite. The gastronomy may be average, but they were among their own, and that was the cost.

Victoria had long wavy hair, down at the weekend, tied back when working. She wore large Celine sunglasses in pure black, in a lacquer-like gloss finish, which somehow looked at the same time squared and rounded, paired with black earrings. The sunglasses made her skin look a lighter brown than it was, and when she removed them to hug Josie, her complexion switched up to a darker deep brown. She wore a grey armless dress, exposing her toned arms, emitting the dedicated gym hours, and a chunky black bracelet, that despite working with the outfit, looked clunky and uncomfortable.

They danced around the hottest topic together, in purest cooperation, covering the familiar ground, checking off safe conversational avenues, until Victoria became impatient and dove in.

"So. How's it going with the man?"

"Steven. He'll be here before too long, you'll meet him."

"Are things moving forward, it seemed like things were stuck last time we met?"

"It's hard to say," Josie answered, understanding how weak that sounded, she was reaching, fencing.

"How are you spending time together? Are you going around his for takeaways and sex, or are you getting out and making plans?"

Josie hated being dug into like this, and looked anything but comfortable. Victoria's bracelet knocked on the table top when she made a point, something which she was oblivious to, unlike her companion.

The task ahead of Victoria was to steer Josie toward a path of clarity, to help her reveal to herself some truths without Victoria speaking them, clear as day as they were to her. Like the therapist asking question after question after question without answer, it had to come from within. It was best to avoid laying it out for Josie, as she could, which might spell the end of that particular friendship. Even if she were on the money it could reek of sabotage, and better for Victoria that she pussyfoot around; at least to receive a 'you were right' than 'you've got it wrong about him.'

However, she might feel obliged.

An orange juice and a mimosa were deposited in front of them, plus mediocre, warm Eggs Benedict and Florentine with congealing Hollandaise. Victoria considered sending it back, but thought better of it.

They ate with few words, which was conspicuous to them both, as the dishes that required little mastication half disappeared within a few minutes, and others nattered around them without pause. They exchanged polite if unreliable assessments of the quality of the food, not wishing to drag down the aura a notch further. Josie went to change the subject and as she spoke, Victoria spoke too at that exact moment. Josie backed off, and Victoria leant forward and placed her left hand on the top of Josie's right wrist while her hand flicked her fork about in a childlike manner.

She just didn't have the patience after all.

"All I'm saying, and I see this all the time, is that men do their thing, and act in their way, and give out all these messages and signals, and we need to listen. Pay attention. And I think you need to ask a few questions and dig into the seriousness of this. Or not. If it worries you to do that, well, then there's a learning moment right there. You've been seeing each other a while, right? Couple of months?"

Victoria had a knack of estimating time with accuracy.

"Yeah."

"That's a reasonable time to see if this is something real and worth pursuing. Communication, that's all it is."

And then she layered in the true advice she wanted to give, under the cover of unknown future events.

"And if he's all chill out, it's early days, of course I like you, yeah things are great, blah, then you need to test it by turning it into something substantive. Commit to time away together, and we're not talking a B&B. Talk is cheap, right, what is it they say? Don't tell me your priorities, tell me where you spend your money. You're both successful and free, you should be going to New York, Cape Town for five days. Skiing, whatever."

Victoria was glad she got this out in time, for she clocked Steven without having seen a photo, walking over to the two of them.

Steven was late, and said so. Josie was grateful she was still eating so they were also running behind. She was able to delude herself that they were both on the same page.

He introduced himself to Victoria who shook his hand, responding, "How do you do?"

Steven leaned down to kiss Josie on the cheek. Wrong order, thought Victoria.

Victoria remained passive. Steven took a fancy to the dismissive, sleek, attractive Victoria who looked unimpressed and tough. Victoria noted this right away. She had enough street smarts to know a manipulative hazard when she saw one. Able to leave a trail of disappointments behind as he spun his way across London, a city so large that sexual and relationship reputations never seemed to catch up with its inhabitants, with their numbers of hook ups and humpings, the flings, liaisons and dumpings.

Victoria finished her food and Josie pushed what was left to one side and placed her cutlery at 5 o'clock. She considered a recent meal, scallops, purées, sea bass, mash, cream sauce. No chewing, gums only required. Eaten without challenge, like any cheap high street burger. Chewing was paramount to eating satisfaction. She drifted as Steven had joined them and Josie could tell. Josie interrupted her thoughts to evangelise the art she and Steven were about to see, before they had seen it. More of a live music type, Victoria nodded and smiled. One of a hundred daily micro performances.

She wanted to be getting on her way, so checked her gold watch, which Steven clocked, trying and failing to figure out the brand as it flashed around her supple wrist. She called the lithe young European waiter over to pay, which they did without fuss. Josie had a query about one of the items on the bill, and was put out by the silver plate hitting the table without care, but she left it and said nothing.

Gathering her bag, tech and other ephemera, Victoria gave Josie a brief hug with a *call me okay* in her ear. She and Steven exchanged professional *good to meet yous* and Steven watched Victoria's backside as she strode off to her next appointment. He imagined her hitting the gym, shopping for fragrances or lingerie, meeting up with a married man in a hotel room, gifting her that watch. That she bought herself.

"OK, shall we go?" checked Josie.

"Why don't we get a drink, it's such a nice day? We don't have a time slot do we?"

"Well, no, but. Don't you want to see this with me?"

"Of course," he said, "just while we had a table, that's all. C'mon then, let's go," and he stood up, to show some willing. As Josie picked up her things, Steven adjusted his sunglasses and had a good scan of the moneyed females all around. Assessing too the men when part of a couple or group, the dynamics, wondering what they were bringing to the table.

So much beauty to take in in this world, he thought. The jewels, the fashion, fabrics and colours, the brands, and their characteristics and rankings. Before you even take in the flesh, the hairstyles, the skin tones, the war paint and heady fragrances. A slick updo, a slender back, bright yoof nails, an expensive skirt with a cheap cut, or an appearance so crafted and accessorised with such range as to signal wealth and an abundance of spare time. A handful from an endless list of things which could grab Steven's attention. His gaze was broken by the throaty splitting roar of a yellow Ferrari caught between the gaps between buildings, as it sped from zero and topped out at 26mph before hitting traffic.

Josie felt a deflating twinge from the lack of enthusiasm toward their plans and his seeming interest in their surroundings. She knew this feeling and she tightened, but pushed on like she would do every day in her work.

After the gallery visit, they arrived at hers, and as they were through the door and had deposited bags and coats, Steven wrapped his arms around Josie and pulled her into him. They moved through to the bedroom in silence, as she led him by the hand.

Josie went down on Steven because she liked going down on men and the act was a good starter. Steven let her because it was a good precursor to sex, turning *her* on, as opposed to enjoying the act itself. He let her continue while he was hard, and ran through a bunch of scenarios in his head, some fantasies including Josie, some not, flicking through the playlist of tunes, finding the right fit. And like a jukebox that returned to a crowd favourite, Victoria kept flickering back to him. The tight clothing over thin limbs, the breasts, which he bet would appear fuller in the flesh, freed as she went to work on top of him. He hardened. Josie felt she must be improving her technique with him. He had bumped into Victoria in a club, and they were both drunk, and she came onto him, and they had gone back to his. Don't tell Josie, *she* said to *him*. Steven reached down and put his hands on Josie's back and then reached under her armpits and gave her a pull, indicating to come up for air. She responded and her flushed face, framed by giving head hair, appeared on Steven's chest. She strained and reached up, and kissed him full on the mouth with wet kisses, which tasted of himself.

He put his hands on her hips and pulled her up, indicating he wanted her to go on top, and continue to do all the work. She obliged, wanting his cock in her, and not his tongue. Another time. As she sat on top of him and sunk down, he felt in a state of bliss, yet kept his eyes closed, not to enjoy the moment itself and enhance his other senses, but so he could draw the Victoria fantasy forward.

Josie came first as Steven held the rhythm, pace and force that she needed, letting her ride him to her finish. Steven then flipped her light frame over and picked up the pace he wanted, bringing Victoria to the fore as he took her beautiful black body, repeating in his head her powerful attributes. The thin arms, the full breasts, the pierced belly button, the bald pussy. In cycles he worked these angles until he came hard into Josie.

He rolled off onto his back and stretched one arm to the side and the other behind his head. The length of wait before rolling off one of the best indicators of desire and relationship health. This didn't go unnoticed, "No post-coital kisses then."

"That was great, just need to breath," he replied, panting and sweaty, from the grubby business.

Josie didn't push her luck, fearing rejection. Afraid she might poke at something she would regret. Without digging, no negative would surface. Instead an empty stomach of loss and uncertainty. A lack of hunger and weight loss.

She sought reassurance elsewhere.

"We should go away for the weekend, where haven't you been that you'd like to go?" she proposed, adding to keep it loose, "We could go to a foodie place, San Sebastien, Copenhagen."

"Been to them."

"Jesus, somewhere else then."

"We could go away to the country," Steven countered, figuring a dirty domestic weekend to be much less hassle than planes. And while he didn't fancy holding hands with Josie through the streets of Vienna, he could countenance a weekend holed up in bed down in Dorset.

The knot inside Josie tightened, and she felt sick.

"OK, it was just a thought."

"Yes, and a good one, let's both have a think."

"Do you want anything while I'm up?"

"Glass of wine?"

"Already? I was thinking water, tea," but Josie was eager to please, to try to rescue herself from the slide, "I'll open something."

He smiled and kissed her, and she dragged herself up off the bed, grabbing a robe, and swung it around her back as she walked through the doorframe.

Steven admired her arse.

He heard her organising and cleaning her kitchen, sorting and packing things away, something a previous girlfriend did, whenever he wanted some peace. There was a cupboard frenzy, bins were organised, white goods emptied and then kicked into action, with pods and tabs. It sounded like a kitchen hoarding too much equipment.

He got out of bed, kicked the door so it was ajar, and then, inspired by the meeting with Victoria, and the strength of his fantasy-driven orgasm, Steven grabbed his phone from his trousers and suggested to a black girl he had been chatting with that they met next week.

The mutual understanding between Simon and Julian was that cancellation due to work demands was a fact of life, yet that Monday afternoon phones had remained silent, and evening squash was on. With a final check of the phone as he entered the club, Julian proceeded to the changing rooms, scanning around for Simon or the reverberation of his voice, attending to some last minute matter.

Julian changed into sportswear that made him look athletic and rangy, and added the finishing touches, his squash shoes, sweatbands, water bottle, racket and new balls.

He was a few minutes ahead of their booked slot, and Simon was already on court, hitting in anger, the small black ball thwacking and yo-yoing in lines between Simon in the back court on his forehand, and the front wall. Julian set his kit down outside the glass wall to the side of the door, lined up straight in parallel lines and right angles, positioned in replicate during every visit.

Looking away, the sound of racket cutting and chopping through the ball told that Simon was hitting the ball clean and with power. Julian looked across at the neighbouring court where Bill, the club's best player and hero, was hard at work, putting a pretender to the sword, bullying him around the court over sapping forty shot rallies.

They acknowledged each other, and Julian took a swig of water, ready. Simon watched him take that same pre-swig before each match.

Long-time competitors on the squash arenas of London and the tennis courts of town and country, Julian had the edge in squash. Not by much rally-to-rally, but edge enough over a match, to dominate the competitive table, winning around seven in ten matches. As Simon improved, so did Julian, with some discrete lessons on the side to isolate and target weaknesses. Off the court, Simon made sure to dominate Julian at every opportunity, but Julian knew enough about the life of Simon Knight, to level them off in Julian's mind. And there was the court.

Simon continued hitting in lines to himself for longer than was courteous or necessary and turned it over to Julian who began hitting sweeter, crisper-sounding backhands, in lines parallel and close to the side wall, where the writing was being written.

They sweated and grunted and toiled and ground. They battered and hammered and served and lobbed and dropped and faked. They hurried and slowed and varied their styles. Yet Julian just had that extra cool, and was able to stay closer to his natural style and game plan. The pure execution of his highest standards. A drop in his level of play would give Simon the opening and edge, but without such a decline, Simon had to bring in variation. And the darker arts. Swinging with more abandon than was necessary, creating dangerous arcs, keeping Julian toward the back. Calling optimistic lets on interference. Crossing the figurative lines on where it was fair to position himself when off the ball. Julian knew all this was going on, but just built it into his challenge. To beat him under these infringements, would make it tastier. And they would both know this would represent a definitive, bitter defeat.

The ever upright a noticeable two inches taller whenever they crossed paths in between points. Noticeable to Simon.

Julian knew that if he was a 51% chance to win each point, each additional stroke within the rally, allowed him to move Simon into a poorer position, force a sub-optimal response, to take a shot too soon or too late, to run it at a mere degree or two off along the wall. And these additive mistakes would create the opening to finish and kill.

At 2-2 in sets, Julian made it over the line at 9-6. They were both shot. Simon wanted to collapse on his back, a la snow angel, but couldn't bear the optics, the concession that would represent. So he leant back on a side wall and put his hands on his knees, his body in recovery.

Julian sat down with knees bent, and splayed his fingers behind him on the floor, sweat shining down his neck, his hair clumped and out of place. To win he had to push all the way, as happened most matches. For Simon, this was all in the game. Even he accepted he couldn't win every game, every fight, every move, but to ease off here, in this meaningless encounter, could unleash any number of real consequential let-offs, relaxations, a softening in his business negotiations. Unacceptable. It was all connected, and this man had to have his foot on the world's throat. They sat in silence. Until the next pair tapped on the glass. Time.

They hustled out, and sat beside each other outside, backs against the glass, as the clangs and smacks began of the next pair warming up a cold, lifeless ball. Julian tossed the ball to Simon to return it, as if it mattered.

Defeated, Simon went on the offensive.

"You still seeing that girl at work?"

Julian glanced left and right, ahead of him, checking who was around.

"Occasionally."

"The old business trip, eh," he asked, "as old as time. Careful there. She could be trouble."

"She's demanding, but there's not a lot I can give her. I'm hoping she's seeing that," Julian said, interrupting his attempts to calm his breathing.

"Yes, well. Your perceptions of *demanding* may vary. Some women are more expensive to run than others."

"You've noticed that too."

"You've been married a long time, no matter how fabulous Fiona is. You don't think she still masturbates over you either, old boy. Just cover your arse. Humiliation cannot be survived through, most other things can. Except being jobless."

Simon twisted the knife, "Did I hear about redundancies at your place?"

"Possibly, they're figuring out the departments affected."

Julian figured if you had two or three true friends in your life, you have done well. Simon wasn't one of them.

"A ball ache," Simon continued, "for all concerned. We've got so many people on NDA, the business even has a high rating online. You'll be all right, you always land on your feet."

While that *had* been the case, Julian knew nothing lasted forever, and felt the worry in his guts at the prospect.

Simon had put defeat behind him, hauled himself up, and headed for the showers. "Poker this Saturday still on, right?"

Julian had been taken back down from the high of victory, and wondered why he bothered. He confirmed the weekend plans and remained sat on the hard floor, pained on his skinny arse.

Fiona had caught a fictional reading on the radio. A deep voiced actor, full of gravel, familiar, but unknown to her by name. This gave her mind license to imagine his looks, how he dressed, his talents, and what he would do to her if they had an afternoon in a hotel room. She fed the children, made sure they were busy, feigned a headache and went for a *lie down*.

A sex life for someone in Fiona's situ could involve regular or sporadic, frequent or infrequent sex with her husband. Out-of-hours it could centre around masturbation, fantasy, porn. It could involve a full-blown emotional affair, a poor family outcome, or a dalliance of mutual convenience, with someone who also had skin in the bedroom games. Or it could be the odd fling, the right person at the right time, though this could rack up the numbers which carried different risks. As of yet, she had been faithful to Julian. They had occasional sex, and she took care of her own business otherwise. Yet she was feeling open to change, perhaps reflective of society's opening legs. She had no doubt that the purported oddities reported in the papers as the new normal were nothing like, however the winds of change had been sweeping through for the last decade. Bi-sexuality, female-friendly porn, sex toys, emotional non-monogamy, seeking arrangements, sugaring, cuckolding. And shame wasn't what it used to be.

Her roll-necked fictional reader was dominant, smooth, an entrepreneur yet built like a fisherman, and didn't say a word after he entered the hotel room where she was waiting for him, until half way through the act when he uttered filth in her ears.

As she lay back pleased to get through the satisfying act uninterrupted, she took a few moments to recover, before checking the clock. She put her gown on, and washed her hands in the ensuite. Dried her hands on the soft white towels, and applied a dash of hand cream.

Not much of a lie down, which didn't go unnoticed by Florence, and who assumed she wasn't resting at all.

"Too much to do."

Florence ran through her latest project progress, which felt hopeless to Fiona.

Julian came through the door and was met by the dog and silence. Relaxed as he had been doing sport and nothing else, he dumped his bag down in the hall, and entered the lounge, hoping to generate some enthusiasm.

"You need to sort out the cables behind the TV."

10011
CHAPTER 19
Poker night

Fiona and Julian and Simon and Francesca, in turn, arrived at the South Kensington home of Michael and Carl; a married couple, sceney, portfolio restaurateurs. Simon knew Michael from business way-back, when he was a financier.

Their home a four-storey townhouse. Ground and basement levels painted a powder blue, the first floor well pointed with cared-for brickwork, with a top floor roof extension of vertical tiles added within the last five years, and a narrow balcony fit for little. No matter what you paid, space was tight. Its frontage dotted with a black lamp, a Banham burglar alarm, and three varnished royal blue pots, empty and equidistant on the white sill of the large front window. The three short steps up from street to entrance a chess checkerboard of tiling, tasteful yet deadly in winter.

They were a giant, gregarious pair, built and over six foot three, both. Carl, white, with short greying blonde and spiky hair, ruddy cheeks, dappled skin, and a few days' growth. Blue spectacles, a floral shirt and salmon jeans, boat shoes and no socks. Michael was pure brown, with a shaven head and the thickest black ad man glasses, pulloffable by someone deep in personality and cool. Smooth in his status, dressed in cream jeans and a Hawaiian shirt.

Adored as hosts for their charm and warmth, and self-effacing humour. When it came to business they were serious people, and if the numbers were good, their personal lives were a breeze. They never made life breezy for their employees, always on their toes, toeing the line, the course that they set without equivocation. Staff that showed loyalty and dedication, for they were tough, but they were fair, and had taken others with them, further than they might have gone elsewhere.

Carl took Francesca off to show them some art they had bought, float some names they were thinking of buying. She adored the provocative photography displayed in staggers up the staircase, black and white photography, of black and white subjects. She smoked as she did so, this being a smoking house, despite the owners switching to the vape, after a period stuck on both before the full trade, post-Trade.

"I don't even want to know how much you wasted on those," Julian called out as he watched Carl signing with his hands, embellishing his descriptions and passions as he talked Francesca through their creative process for acquisition.

In retort, Carl gave the finger without looking over, continuing without pause. Francesca realised they might have client potential, now their budgets had improved, along with their tastes. While he was outmatched in terms of expertise, they had the money, and Francesca did not, and in England assets spoke volumes, even up against the critical side-eye of taste. Francesca took the conversation into other artists, adjacent style parallels, and into the video and installation work also on offer from the artist. She stretched the discussion beyond Carl's expertise to counter the dominance he displayed, and assert herself. A European expert in her field, mansplained by the moneyed, this had started to feel like work, so she suggested she needed a top up and peeled off, stepping with care down the stairs, a thick white pile stair runner pinned with matt steel rods.

The hosts went about their business, occupying themselves in the provision of drinks, snacks and high-end drugs. Catered nibbles to support a friend's fledgling food operation. Pre-rolled spliffs, "like anything in life, success stems from a combination of talent and consistency. Rolled to perfection by the gardener," said Carl, "every one the same, like biscuits, delivered from the ovens, pure uniformity."

Simon smirked to himself, delighted he didn't have to cringe at the home-mades these two might produce.

Michael stood up and picked up two cards sat on the mantel of a large fireplace, under an over-bearing, silver-framed mirror. He passed them round, commenting and laughing at the polar propositions. The first, expensive paper, purest white, embossed silver lettering, inviting them to their male friends' wedding, in a castle in Scotland. For the second and alternative marital experience, the invitation had a male couple's bald heads and goofy faces photo-shopped into a bowling alley, captioned, 'Let's Go Bowling!'

"No wedding, just the bowling. My type of invite," confirmed Carl.

"God, I fucking hate weddings." uttered Julian. "Except mine."

"Everyone loved our wedding. I loved our wedding." Fiona confirmed, "Every day since, not so much."

Julian contemplated the person attending the wedding he had slept with not that long prior, which might take the shine off the memory.

"Yeah, everyone loves living it lavish, hotel paid for, the free fucking bar, cost me a fortune, drunk men and posh totty falling about everywhere. I paid for people I dislike to get laid."

"Like the stag do," commented Carl.

"Filter!" reprimanded Fiona, "these people were our guests."

Always keen to understand what was happening at higher echelons, at rarer levels of oxygen, Michael tried to take the conversation onto Simon's territory, money, property, acquisition, second homes, but it slipped elsewhere.

"It's all Somerset these days I've heard, in the right areas. Achievable distance, good restaurant scene. Not considering selling your place, eh Julian?" Simon chipped away.

Fiona exerted optical pressure, at the mention of this sticking point. She couldn't abide the thought that they might give that up, and be stuck with one household in their forties.

"Not for the time being," Julian replied, in such a way to signal he was a man of options, rather than concerned about belt-tightening. In such a tone that might be taken as, 'we might sell and buy in Italy.'

Under normal circumstances, Fiona would segue into something about the children, what options some exciting new venture might have in store for them (her), yet this was a rare environment where children were a weighty ballast. As a result, Fiona and Julian were guarded about when they brought them up. When asked, by someone feigning interest before taking a long pull on a whisky and drifting elsewhere. Letting the alcohol boost the senses while nodding about some childhood project or hobby or whatever. When there was no basking in glories, Julian left it and focused on the drinking and the drugs. Everyone needed a holiday.

Simon relieved himself of a few grams in his jacket pocket, which he tossed on the table toward Michael and Carl. "Never come empty handed."

"You could have brought wine?" Michael joked, laughing from the deep.

"And waste it on you? That is the fucking best. Off colour, au natural. Bet you've got a load of white powdery shit."

"You'd be surprised."

"Well come on then. I'm not gonna talk about myself all night at this rate."

"You'd give it a go, though," observed Carl, before moving on after a pause. "When are you going to host, Fiona?"

"We can make that work, next time, with notice to deposit the children somewhere."

"Yes, well, there will be tighter drug controls, otherwise Simon will be forgetting lines he's tapped out on one of the children's desks."

"They'll have to discover drugs like the rest of us," Simon suggested, "not have it handed to them on a plate."

Fiona shot him a disapproving look.

In turn, they went through to the large kitchen island and topped up on canapes, seafood.

"Watch what you eat if you want to give me a game on the squash court," commented Julian.

"Tough to beat these stiff, rigid, repetitive players with their honed technique. Backhand drive after backhand drive down the wall, grinds a man down with boredom. Hypnotises you. Bit over-seasoned these salads, and pretty fiery, some of this," he griped.

He had all but cut spicy food from his diet, as it tended to add inconvenience, and unnecessary randomness to his plans.

Carl and Michael looked at each other. Carl mouthed 'cunt' first.

Simon swivelled back to Julian, making sure he had given him both barrels.

"Good shirt that, for off-the-peg."

"Fucking company day out last week. Had to put a smile on my face while doing archery, axe throwing. All that shit. Can you imagine? My mistake for leaving it up to the leadership. One thing I'm not participating is the annual virtue signalling charity day. Might have some important meetings."

"You fattening her up for sale?" asked Michael.

"Couldn't possibly say."

"Yes, that means. No means no."

"Couldn't possibly say."

"Right, c'mon, are we playing or what? Money down. Hundred each?" ventured Simon.

"Fifty each," said Fiona, checking with Francesca for support.

"Not sure why you care," Francesca responded thornily, "but sure."

Fiona felt wounded but wondered if she was being oversensitive. She looked at Francesca for reassurance, a smile, but received nothing back.

"First round, I guess we can," said Simon, "one for the creative classes, the art students."

"Art is business. I'm not selling watercolours. It's a bourse for the ultras, they exchange and make taste," Francesca replied.

"It's all a performance. A sham. The fastest horse. The most accurate free kick taker. The superior Hamlet. Four hundred page works of fiction. The $200m painting."

Simon was getting into his stride.

"Ranking. Sorting the wheat from the chaff. As old as time. Who gets what. The rewards, the spoils, for being the quickest, fittest, smartest, boldest, ballsiest, the most talented, the most published. The first."

"The last Beatles song will be played. The last lines of Shakespeare read. The credits for Jaws will roll for the last time. The last remaining Picasso, used for firewood, post the apocalypse."

"Oh, you probably didn't expect me to foreshadow that. How can anyone see an alternative? Increasing numbers of countries armed to the teeth with nuclear weapons, the usual list of dictators and bad actors, happy to see the world end with them. But it's not here yet, so give me my fucking share. A bigger share."

More.

"Look at 'the' science. Scientific community have no consensus, it's all bullshit and ego like everything else. No endeavour to confirm if salt is bad, if low fat diets are effective, how to solve a problem like the pandemic. I'm weighing green energy, that's where the new money is at; the future, in futures. Not that it'll do mankind any good, but it's never been about that. The poor mugs in society, they can eat up all that stuff about rhinos, the oceans. Get down the cobalt mines, kids."

"My brothers are having a terrible time with farming in Italy," commented Francesca, in a cold manner, in between a tilt of wine and a puff of smoke, which suggested familial emotional distance.

"Change is getting serious. Let's see the next generations chain us up when they get power. Social credit scoring, climate lockdowns. Mandatory euthanasia."

As conversation took a nosedive into serious matters, so the atmosphere fell, the music sounded louder, and people took to organising themselves, their drinks, their cards and chips, monitoring phones. The typical rhythms of such a night.

Michael was the musician, since a boy. However, Carl was the master of the playlist. Every social group had its master of the music, the lead others deferred to.

"I can never find enough time to keep up with music," Carl carped, "what with the restaurants, and everything going on. I mean, don't get me wrong, we get to plenty of gigs, and things Michael comes across, but..."

Fiona cut him off, "Oh my god, you have no idea, you have it so easy," she implored, bloviating from the starter blow, "you 'get to plenty of gigs', wow, with your army of assistants, cleaners, managers, no children, no dependents. You don't even have a dog!"

"We're thinking about getting a cat," said Michael.

"Don't overcommit there," Fiona wailed with laughter, "they come and go as they please, like the two of you. You can get the cleaners to load up automatic feeding trays once a week and the cat need never see you."

"The cleaners come twice a week. Things get so messy here."

"Wow. You should see the lot of a mother."

"Go on, depress us," said Carl.

"Would that be the life of a poor mother or one with the money and help you have?" he added.

"Now now bitches," Michael commented.

Even though the playlist had switched up from jazz to hip hop, the minimalist interiors, which *needed* cleaning twice a week, meant the raucous caterwauling of the group became brutal on these old ears, and took the participants back to nights in their twenties, getting hammered in someone's kitchen.

"You need soft furnishings in here," Francesca pointed out, "get a bloody zebra skin rug or something."

"Ew," said Michael.

Fiona ran through a list of her tasks, which took the group quite aback. All the must-do's, tasks so routine and repeated in their daily automation, before adding some sample tasks from last week, things out of the ordinary, around a school trip or party. She then added, "that's a sample of what has to be done before eleven."

"Pfffffff," confirmed Carl, as they all felt tired from the experience.

"Imagine what it's like for a single inner city mother, doing three jobs, trying to raise three children," Francesca added, looking around as she did so.

Francesca awaited some agreement, some validation, a shake of the head, some empathy. All she heard was, from Simon, was, "Right, c'mon, wine, get some lines racked up, and give the music a boost."

And they were off again.

This proficient group of card players worked their way through round-after-round of Texas Hold'em. Popular when they started playing at the turn of the two thousands, and a group with no enthusiasm for variety. Life, for all, was complex enough. They kept two decks going, one for the dealer and the play itself, while another deck was shuffled ahead of time, during each round, for use in the subsequent round. Even addled with drink they kept pace with the movement, the dealer button, the blinds, the betting, the turning of cards, the shuffling, turning clockwise, all night. One persistent misstep was to burn the first card before any deal, but they etched it into their minds after some time.

Michael loved to watch the community cards turned over, mesmerised by the reds and blacks of the ace and the numbered cards, the blues and yellows and images of the Jack, the Queen, the King. As candles burned around him, and he focused in, his vision dimmed as if someone had turned down the lights. He sat unmoved, taking a moment, while others bantered, argued and joked around him. He felt content, surrounded by those he considered to be class acts. The end of a hand saw people get up, use the bathroom, pour, and a set of ten or so cards after the reveal lay in front of him in pairs, plus the five in the middle. He looked at the Jack of Diamonds, facing to the left, decorated, armed. He wondered about the riches that had been made by the turn of that card, the money lost, lives lost or devastated. Cash, possessions, luxuries, cars and homes even, passed on from that revelation. Next to the jack, a single red chip, separated from the stack. A matching crimson, edged with six white squares, the number one hundred in the centre. He thought red, and thought red wine, and after staring entranced at the candlelight, rose to select some bottles from the cellar.

Seasoned players made for an easy night. That number one killer of a poker night, the new player. Practice rounds, writing down the order of the hands with rudimentary explanations. The most frustrating thing they had to contend with now would be figuring out who had won a hand with several players still in at showdown, once they had made their way onto spirits.

As the evening proceeded, talk turned with each set of a dozen lines for the group, toward work, investments, businesses, art, markets, and Fiona found herself contributing less. She felt like her role was that of party girl, easy with the drink, ready to brighten up any occasion. Always handed the mirror to chop, as 'she made the most consistent lines.' Like the artist assistant who produced the best spot paintings.

She studied each of the others, one-by-one, clockwise, as with the progress of the dealer button. What she saw was an intricate exploration of the class system, defining and organising people, high and low, based on whatever criteria today's society set. Re-centering her thoughts to herself, she pondered the sharp comment made earlier by Francesca, her friend. Status which might need revisiting if she didn't give her a drink & drugs pass. Difficult at that age. Fiona wouldn't give up parenthood and *home-making* in a hurry for some independence and to remain *in the game*. Although she felt uneasy at others' perceptions, she also knew herself and the paranoia that came on a night like this.

One thing was apparent. As the wealthiest, best-educated, best-looking, most connected male, Simon was the pack leader in the room. And he was the bitterest, the most miserable.

Within the six, a majority of left-leaning elite intelligentsia, they dispatched with a general lambasting of current government initiatives, labelled in equal parts racist, classist, fascist. They added many *something-must-be-dones* relating to gangs, education, prisons and societal disorder, though *not* drugs. They talked the talk, but walking as liberals, they were pro-crime. Soft sentences, buyers of every sob story under the sun. As the powder was further absorbed, and nose hairs became tetchier, so the opinions loosened and the sneering began. Julian did his footballer impressions, "Airm... at the tarm... with everything what he went through," mandated for these occasions at the request of all. They all contributed with examples of fashion disasters they had encountered at work, with the family, on television, and as Carl pointed out about his sister, "her clothes are so old they've been through three five-year fashion cycles, and her wedges are back in again."

Returning to the action itself.

The dealer button came around, catching her off guard, yet Francesca riffled them through a shuffle with her half gone cigarette hung out of her mouth on one side, like a nineteen fifties labourer, one eye squinted shut as the smoke ascended into the curve of her skull, broken into her eyebrow. She dumped the cigarette into an ash tray and dealt the cards, managing the blinds, handling a round of bets before landing and revealing the three community cards.

Francesca slow played her hand with a restful face, except for when she met eyes with Fiona and relaxed a quick look at her, confident the others were looking elsewhere. Simon and Michael were drawn in, and Francesca completed the set she needed as the fourth card went down. At which point Simon and Michael, who had both caught hands, were committed to the end. Francesca twisted the knife with the betting, but not enough to remove them.

She clubbed them with a flush. A real zinger.

Simon was now well down, and had to swallow hard. The others might have guessed what he was thinking, and they would have been right.

"Maybe I shall put it into some young, upcoming artist's work."

She smiled.

"Another future wastrel, a nobody," declared Simon, addressing Francesca as if they hadn't come together, "why not invest in someone known, like that guy who chucks a pile of confectionery in the corner of a gallery and the patrons take one."

"Oh, seven figures, a magnificent work like that."

"See. Fucking racket," he sneered, "The leather jacket slung in the corner of the room, best part of a million dollars."

Fiona watched Francesca for a while, without shame, as she smoked, put her cigarette down and focused on tidying her growing pile of chips. Sticking it to the patriarchy. She was unaware of the attention, as Simon was of hers, and as Simon was of Carl's. Julian and Michael were straight shooters, who stared at their drinks and just wanted to play.

The group gossiped for a while about mutual acquaintances. They laughed and despaired in equal measures at the modern bullshit that surrounded each of them, in business, in the creative world, in education. And took the piss out of each other, something which was becoming difficult, even in small friendship groups. Society was moderating speech. For anyone in the public eye, the threat of a camera or microphone, hung over them, surveilling.

They went around the houses for a while.

"Remind me again about correlation not causation? Hold on, why the fuck were we talking about that?"

They lost their trains of thought, and had to re-group, going back a couple of stages to step through the amnesia, and to return.

A writer they knew was mentioned.

"Oh god," said Simon, "not 'as a writer...' himself."

"What?" Michael asked confused.

"I was at an event once where he spoke, and it's all *'as a writer'* this and *'as a writer'* that. Wallowing in hubris."

"Oh come on, like you've never said *'as a business leader'*..."

Simon thought about it.

"So I'm the cunt now?"

"Yes!" three of the group said in unison.

The night went on until they had topped up on intoxicants to a level beyond which they would all be in trouble the next day, and at a time which might afford them *some* night-time sleep. And most were prepared and ready, nodding in agreement when the first person suggested they called it. Synchronised groupthink. Power must coordinate.

As cars arrived, they said drunken goodbyes outside, where Simon fell over and heels spliced into gutters and cracks in the pavement.

Francesca said she wanted to wake up in her own bed in the morning, and instructed the driver on new destinations. This was a peremptory declaration, yet she was interested in his response, and his interest. Simon was sympathetic to this, but while he wasn't sure how he would feel when he got home, this might turn out to be a shame. The warm comfort of Francesca's body. He made contingency plans in his head, should he feel super horny. Becoming the third man an elite escort slept with that day. They ghosted through the dark quiet of Belgravia, and merged with the red lit hubbub of three-ayem London traffic as they swung around Hyde Park corner, past the dark park to the left, and the string of '*what the hell is going on in there right now*' hotels to the right, as they made their way to Francesca's.

As the car dropped Fiona and Julian off, they both struggled to heave themselves out of the car, but once steady, they made their way up the short gravel drive. Fiona checked her phone, waiting for Julian to pass her and unlock the door. The light splishing of piss on leaves alerted her to the fact that Julian was urinating against the flower beds, legs akimbo. A man free, living in the moment. One of independence and pure joy.

"Jesus," she said, on the rummage for her own keys, before she screamed as he grabbed her from behind, before they fell about, laughing.

The cycle of a couple, falling apart, yet boomeranging back to each other, that lock of marriage, despite the separations and distractions from their complex lives. Julian hadn't thought much of Iva.

It was good to be home.

They poured themselves large spirits, knowing that a solid slug of top up alcohol and its accompanying sedation might be the one chance they had of getting to sleep before sunrise. Julian knocked back a couple of large yields and Fiona forced it back, pinching her eyes and sucking the inside of her cheeks as she did so.

All over London, in the small hours, somewhere, couples, throuples and moreples screwed, made love. Young, middle-aged, senior. After drunken or drug-fuelled nights, or awakening in the night sober, next to a compatible partner. People were betraying, thinking about cheating, fantasising about another, exploring each other, pushing sensual boundaries and buttons, or sticking to a well-rehearsed magic formula, or giving it some missionary. Babies were tried for, engagements and marriages were celebrated, or horny people picked someone up or called someone. For those not getting any, these were either painful realisations, pragmatic acceptances, or something for which to be thankful.

Fiona and Julian got into bed, and were drawn together by the win-win of a chemical-induced quick fuck, for relief and pure pleasure, and to further induce sleep. It took a while for Julian. They passed out, and did not move until mid-morning.

10100
CHAPTER 20
Helen work life: Annual review: Annabel out of sorts: Coloured buns

While her colleagues went out to nearby delis, modern salad bars, for sushi or falafel, Helen padded down as she did most days to the nearest Tesco Express for a sad Tuna Mayonnaise sandwich, stale and lifeless; her life staring back at her. Plain crisps, a Wispa bar. Maybe an Aero. She wondered how long ago that sandwich was put together, where, and by whom, and in what conditions. It followed and crossed her mind that she should feel grateful for her life, for a moment. She threw in a lasagne and a dreary bagged salad for dinner, to save a trip. She nodded to the security man as she did every day on her way out, keeping them onside in case she ever screwed up the self-scan, distracted by any number of things.

She, too, would like to be mooching down to splash out on lunch, but that involved spending £10 (so £200 a month) and an extra 12 minutes (half a day a month) in distance and queuing, and having her bespoke needs met. Crushed under the pile of email, meeting after meeting shovelled in without pause. Every one lasting the exact length of the meeting, plus an awkward extra minute or two in which she would try to interject and extricate herself, yet come across as keen to be doing other things. Then onto the next meeting, late again, providing extra circumstantial evidence that she might wish to be doing other things. Stuck in a small meeting room or a booth, or at home on her own, on calls with agencies or partners. *Cameras on* meetings that sucked the life out of her. Seeing her own face would set her teeth on edge, and make her limbs ache with a faux depression. Being watched. Not *the good being watched*.

Now and then Annabel would thrust in whatever food freebies were going around. Éclair Mondays, Whatever Wednesdays. Give Me

Fucking Wine Fridays.

Her whack-a-mole normie life racked up the tasks, alerts, reminders and requests, while she was dog-whistled from meeting to call, from inbox to phone, from worry to event, always looking for ways to make a gain, relieve some pressure, give herself some head space. Each day its own race to get out at a reasonable hour so she didn't lose her evenings too. How she tried to stay calm at home, to park it at the door, but technology was there, pinging, prodding, poking her to offload on Phil. *You just need to get a new job, that's all.* Her brainpower used up solving the wrong types of problems. Unlike many, she felt her work could be worthwhile, when it culminated in real results. Or success stories, as Sam would bleat on about. Yet she needed new problems to solve, and not just the problem of how to get it all done and get home, and how to stop it all falling apart. She had worked at enough places to know that a move away, always tempting, would in all likelihood land her in the same place, after a few months' respite, and just amplified risk. The true nature of an unknown office surfaced after a week or two, a month or two, but it concealed itself in advance. And like her schoolgirl self, she didn't want to leave her friends. Career change, to what, other than less money? She couldn't fund a masters or take time to retrain, with what Phil brought home.

This was all doing laps in her head, as it was that time again.

The annual review.

Ticking, form-completing, bottom-drawer filing. Her manager, Sam, hot-housing her team's sessions to tick a box with her superior, not to develop Helen and her career, or address any major issues. Sam herself knew as well as anybody that completing these in full got her nowhere, but failing would block her. No one got promoted from going to work drinks, but you weren't getting on in absentia.

Helen brought up her forms, shared a week in advance at Sam's request, and now, being scoured by Sam for the first time in last minute preparation. Grasping for a few key phrases that could form a talk track to the inevitable praise sandwich and *some key developmental areas*. Helen had been doing the job for six years without being managed out, knew everybody and the business. So it came down to those old feedback staples: attitude, energy, proactivity, *going the extra mile*. Strike that last one, an eye-rolling metaphor. Sam scrambled down some comments, thoughts, and wove in the projects *she* wanted done to further *her* career.

But Helen was ready for her.

Sam was younger with vigour, and invested time and energy in how she looked, how she dressed and in her approach to politicking and getting on. In her presence, Helen felt drained and felt *less*. She looked as tired as her tote bag, felt unfit and strung out, and the feigned enthusiasm she had to ratchet up to match Sam's energy levels brought her down further inside. It felt like forever since any excitement was on the menu. She wasn't naïve enough to think Sam didn't have a lorry load of her own problems, not least the familial insecurities which drove her on, and which a colleague had told Helen about.

Helen had to make her way over to Sam's desk at a couple of minutes past the hour to get things started. Enough of a sign that this wasn't something that was top of Sam's agenda. Sam was on the phone but gestured for Helen to stay put and wait, and not toddle off and create further diversions. Helen listened in.

"Look, Marketing will capture feedback from individuals automatically so we will have good objective data *to be able to make the right decisions moving forward.* Key right now is to stay focused on the activities for the next month or two, so let's keep the open items list updated and progressing. It's going to evolve, it's going to change but just because something's on that list, does not mean we are committing to a timeline of when we are going to do it. It just means we are providing visibility so that we have a centralised record, so that we all stay aligned. I fully support you on this, but we have to stay focused on the things we are going to do in the next couple of months."

Helen's mind boggled at the emptiness and repetition. This continued to the point where it became awkward for Helen to remain there, recognising that someone with gravitas and important work to do would be away doing that important work and not being put on live-hold. Sam acknowledged this to Helen, but insisted she kept hanging around.

Things wrapped up and they made their way to a dingy meeting room with no natural light, of bashed cat-swinging radius, with a round white Formica table that wobbled, positioned against the back wall. A dark grey telephone which had seen better days, missing some broken plastic component, sat crookedly amidst a mess of pens and unattached cables. Bleak. It was twelve minutes past the hour.

Sam did a minimal tidy, Helen shifted a few things around, and looked at the whiteboard, upon which someone had drawn a pair of tulips, with petals of blue and orange, and with marker green stems.

Sam asked Helen: "How are things?"

Helen flipped through: exhausted, childless, unmarried, struggling to cope with family pressures and grievances, every day mired in joylessness, and settled on, "Yeah, fine."

She wasn't fond of the bottle or the needle, so that was something.

Things were not fine, and Sam chose not to dig, lest she excavate something grave or terminal. They cooperated in silence and left it there.

"Annual ticking and filling," Helen muttered starchily as Sam organised her forms, paper and online.

"It's important everyone has a plan for their year ahead."

"It's approaching summer."

"For the twelve months ahead."

"We put a plan together last year, and haven't reviewed it once."

"Let's do a better job this year then," offered Sam. Unconvincing.

They worked their way through a combined assessment of Helen relating to such topics as: job knowledge/productivity, communication skills, work/business relations. Helen wondered what differentiated work relations and business relations. Uneventful stuff at first. Sam threw out the odd 'can you give me an example of that?' to help eat up some of the forty-eight minutes allotted. Helen bristled as she felt some things were true, plain to see, and the absence of an example didn't mean they were *not so*.

Sam made furious notes on her laptop throughout the entire session, looking up at Helen when she was underlining a point, or attempting to show a little empathy and succeeding in putting forward a fake smile. She didn't want to take the note-taking away as something to complete after the session. She had important things backed up for after hours and the weekend. Things that might advance *her* agenda.

Sam began a sentence which on face value was good feedback, but which Helen knew after four words would turn into some *development area* or another. Some example of something someone felt she had managed well, but which might be even better run next time, providing Helen with *an opportunity for personal growth*. Helen started to make notes that she would never use, so she wouldn't be looking Sam in the eye when the downturn came.

"The Easter campaign was executed well," she started, before Helen interrupted, "Re-executed. It was the same as the previous year."

"Right," Sam was reaching, "but it still had to be delivered successfully, which you did a good job of..."

Well. Good. Successfully. Middle of the road performance adjectives. Other people would be getting the brilliantlies, fantasticallies, first-classes. Or not.

"... good feedback from participants, well-coordinated, participants up four per cent year-on-year..."

"I would ask you to give extra though to coordination between the live event and the digital content, some dislocation there. No major effort required, per se, a couple of stand-ups and emails should do it. Think about how to dovetail in with what the online guys are doing."

Helen had already counted Sam as having used 'per se' at least four times.

"They didn't do any dovetailing with me either. Will this be mentioned in their reviews?"

"Possibly."

"You'll be doing them."

Sam made some notes to deflect.

"More dovetailing," Helen said, hitting a note that Sam might think was genuine, but which Annabel would see through if present.

"Shaun at the agency is good at that sort of thing, watch how he, er..."

"Dovetails. Do you want me to also get drunk in the afternoon and create legal issues within our press releases, like he does?"

"I'm just highlighting things people do particularly well."

"Nobody's perfect, you mean."

"Exactly."

"Hold on, I'm going to write that down."

"Good energy levels too, Shaun."

"Can we get back to me now?"

"Something else to think about."

"If I'm low energy, it's because I've been doing this job for six years, that's six Easter campaigns, six 'Summer Cyclestice' campaigns, six of everything."

"Are you saying you'd like to consider a role change?"

"Maybe. What is there?"

"Well, nothing at the moment. Not within Marketing at least."

"I can hardly join IT or Finance, can I?"

"Let's see if something appears."

If a new and 'exciting' position came up, one of the *high energy* favourites would get it, and Helen would be saddled with making a poorer job of whatever they used to do.

"What should I be doing in the meantime, to help open something up?"

"Keep doing what you're doing."

"If I do that we'll be having the same discussion next year. Like we did last year."

"You do a good job with the campaigns."

"I've done them six times!" she exclaimed.

This was circular and they were against the clock.

Thoughts of Helen's life and where she was at, aside from work, interspersed the session, flashing here and there. And she swung between throwing up her hands and giving up, and concentrating and using the session as an opportunity for a reset. She tried not to piss Sam off too much. She knew that unless she had a route out and into another team, which didn't seem an option, she would need to toe the line, keep Sam onside. It angered her how one person could have so much control over another. She committed to herself to do a mini life review at the weekend, go for a walk and a coffee on her own. Leave Phil scratching his balls at home, which wasn't even a joke in her head.

They kicked around a section on competencies, after which Sam got around to attitude and living their *core values*. One of which was collaboration.

"I have some specific feedback in mind on this one."

"Finally."

"The meeting we had a couple of weeks back on the plans for next Easter," Sam went on.

Helen wondered if there was any explanation other than lazy management that she happened to pick a recent example.

"Jim was seeking someone to help him with the Bunny Funnies landing page, and someone said you could help, and you said you had too much on."

"I did have too much on. And Jim doesn't help anyone but himself."

"Well don't worry about what Jim is up to, you live the values yourself."

"I remember the previous planning meeting, you were there too, and I asked for his help on something, and he just said no. You then asked Pamela if she could support me. Jim's values don't seem core to our *mission*, if you ask me. I help people all the time. You know that."

Sam was feeling defeated and pushed for time, and wanted to end this and get on with other things. She scrambled down some objectives for the year ahead, which sounded like a list of things Helen had done the previous year, plus items which Sam wanted the overall team to do a better job of; things which her boss, Andrea, had asked her to improve upon.

They finished at four o'clock on the dot, as Sam had an important meeting to get to, which she 'can't be late for.'

Sam thanked her and tried the warm smile she had been working on, tilting her head like a dog as she did so.

Helen returned to her desk and was astonished to see her completed annual review form had been emailed to her, in full, with a short request for her to review, add her comments and return. She opened it up, and started to read the summary:

"Helen has had a solid year, with some good work on..."

She held in her left hand last year's review which she had taken in with her, and read the summary.

This started: "Helen has had a good year, with solid work on..."

Despondent at the lack of humanity and individual care shown by someone asked to manage her work life and development, given how paramount that foundation should be.

She checked a couple of high importance emails from panicking agencies, tried to access a shared document via a VPN, which failed, through no human error, and she hit a few keys in despair and declared, "Nothing works, ever."

She picked up her light jacket and bag, left her laptop at work, and returned home, to update her CV and start applying for new jobs.

Annabel was in the middle of a dream, in which she lived in a 21-degree world. She was outside in darkest Siberia, at night, with patio heaters stretching out in lines to the horizon. Then she was in south Italy in the peak of summer heat, with air conditioners cooling the outdoor air, chest freezers open, full of ice, plugged into the soil with giant coiled wires, viper thick. She was indoors, and turned the television to the global news channel, to catch the weather. A world map covered with the number twenty-one, with no deviation. She figured out this wasn't how the world was, and questioned how she had moved from Russia to Italy, and told herself she was dreaming. She pushed herself to wake up in case the dream took a nasty turn.

She opened her eyes and moved through a short paralysing phase, unable to wake in full or move her limbs, lift her head. She was pinned and fought to escape. Failing, she waited.

As things started to function again, she was reborn; the lord had given her a new day. But she was unsettled from the dream, from the wine the previous night, from other matters. One of those, or a combination thereof.

It was a Thursday morning, and she would be WFH, for which she was thankful. She made an instant coffee and returned to bed, where she zapped channel one, enduring the grating baby-voiced whine of the breakfast presenters, for short of three minutes. Appropriate once for Blue Peter's under-twelve audience of the nineties, now suitable for the infantilised general adult population. She scrolled through the day's new madness, before staring at the ceiling, and the rings of light cast by the shade.

She felt low from the dreams, a physical ache in her shoulders and upper arms, her gut tight and empty, her eyes staring into a fixed point. Her thoughts disjointed, of work, of current affairs. Which would once have been clear, a picture of the day or summer ahead, a bright oil or watercolour, now a cubist confusion of many angles and perspectives, of odd matters, in dark brooding colours. Losing her train of thought twice, on the same subject, lying there, her mind grasping, gasping, tracking back, entangled.

Tomorrow would be a day of protest, and a march through central London. Something which could enable her to narrow in on a singular purpose, a handful of messages, looped on repeat. An occasion where she could park the swirling details and debate and trade-offs. Which was less bad: newspapers or internet data server activity, disposable nappies versus real & washed, a new electric vehicle or making use of an old petrol car, the sunk costs of manufacture long gone. Fossil versus nuclear and the manifold risks *that* presented. The production externalities that went into turbine creation, solar panelling.

For every other protest she had prepared placards with friends, slogans, blue and yellow attire, yet she would take herself and her voice this time.

Annabel hadn't spent the time needed to understand cryptocurrencies or why they needed to be mined, but they appeared to be an additional and innovative threat. Always with the new ways and means of accelerating resource depletion, manufacturing and the rate of devastation. A growth rate of zero meant that destruction levels remained at the same level as the previous year. Yet it was spun to the public as low impact, not one hundred percent the same impact. New news, the fire tsunami. In some regards, she had to show respect, the environment was fighting back. With a ferocity unseen in the modern era. And it planned not to outfox, out manoeuvre, with smarts. Chaos ensured that this was brute force.

Her libido had evaporated, she thought, realising she hadn't masturbated in two or three days. Or had sex in four or five months. This wasn't healthy. Could a high energy man lift her up, get the blood flowing, inspire her back to life, get bloody active. She smiled at the recollection of an ex, all wild swimming, cooking three page recipes, hitting up every new movie, gallery show, music release. Trying to stop people padlocking love bridges in Paris. Mediterranean, vocal, brave, cool-headed while hot brained, and always on. His nicknames for her friends. Katie elbows. Climbing man Dan. Sophia tight ladders. Energy she sought at the time, but not now.

She continued to ponder if a female partner was what she needed now, someone delicate with soft beauty. That had been a while. Yet it was the pairing of opposites that created the spark. She brought the softness and beauty to the table, he would bring other things, and the meeting of these two seas made the waves.

Annabel had work to finish before Monday, left to the last minute. She worked best to a deadline; when it had to be done, it was done in an hour, when it didn't have to be done, she would pick at the scab all day. Last minute meant pure efficiency. She would start at three o'clock. A Thursday WFH day meant going for a run, shopping and cooking three salads for lunch. Clearing the decks of washing, linen changes, sparkle the kitchen, get some reading done, air the flat, so that Saturday morning, there were no tasks outstanding, save the good times. These days merely 'the times.'

Logging on, she let the mails thud down in batches, straining their way through. She set alarms for the meetings she had to attend, and made notes for what she needed to do in the gaps, coded, should someone be watching or sent tracking screenshots. She puffed in boredom at the dreaded recurring meetings, the monthly catch ups, one-to-ones that filled any typical Thursday. The pointless things she couldn't say no to, regardless of their efficacy. She felt in need already of a drink, and put the feelers out with a couple of her close friends, to set something up for that evening, before getting up, taking a shower and declining to foist a breakfast on her unwilling stomach.

She had to get the decks clear to have an uninterrupted free day for the protest. The city required a day off to be compressed into previous days. Don't like it? Work client-side in Buckinghamshire.

Beth was in town if Annabel could be bothered going in for drinks. They could get a plant burger. *Catch up.* That would do.

By four-thirty she had nailed her piece work, and lined up all the final emails ready to send in one batch, at five, followed by immediate shut down. Thereby preventing further questions coming back to her that day. And she would be free.

Running ahead, she had time to go to an old London bookshop en route, sacrificing range in return for independent credentials and no loyalty scheme. Wood panelling and spongey, old, patterned, grubby carpets, worn and torn from wear and tear. She overheard an old lady, in a cut glass, English accent, stuffed full of posh, enquiring from a young male assistant, whether they had anything on Nordic nineteenth century antiques and furniture.

Annabel puzzled at the unlikelihood of them stocking something so specific in a store of that size, despite the optimistic enquiries of a wealthy old lady, living in some seven figure mansion block round the corner. Until she began to ramble on, across a variety of topics, floundering the young man, cornered. It made sense. The mad lady, old money gathering or turned to dust. Annabel couldn't see her. Potential to be on the streets, seeking a few minutes of warmth and a friendly face. The immediacy and short termism of homelessness and poverty struck her. No long-term strategic plans, no ten-year vision for the shape of their lives. How to get the next cigarette, pound coin, find shelter to warm even just a little, for the next five minutes. All gains.

She meandered about. The *Smart Thinking* section. Twenty books parked flat in small stacks of half dozens. Three hundred pages apiece on what was wrong with the world. Oil, Ay Eye, Technology, New Economics, Green Issues, Addiction, Bad Science, and all the big name non-fiction giants, full of anecdote and observation, yet not one thing to take away and act upon.

History. All the terrible pain and death inflicted upon each other over the past hundred years, five hundred years, millennia. To Annabel, the most haunting. Each generation past, with identical genetics, move them in time, move them in geolocation, and god and law-fearing citizen turned to godless, lawless tyrant. Removing heads, gassing children. Writing the user manual for effective operation of the killing machine.

The calm and solitude was something that freed her. Bookshops retained an other-worldliness. As during the riots a decade previous, when bookshops went unlooted, so today, they remained set apart. Free from loudmouths, banter, bad energy. A purchase of questionable taste was handled with consideration. At least they were reading. Within, the introvert was accepted.

Annabel sought solace in Fiction, and selected a Mary Gaitskill, something feminine with backbone, to help her fragility. Short stories, to account for her twenty-twenties attention deficit. She slid it over to the young lady behind the desk, and wondered who she was. Mid-twenties, whitest skin. Her smile told Annabel that she was spirited, and the restrained environment within the sanctity of the bookshop held back what she imaged to be a wonderful energy once out in society. She imagined her dancing, arms up and around. Turning to replenish the pile of paper bags arranged in front of her, Annabel watched her floaty cream dress dotted with small flowers as it swung behind her hippy movements.

Annabel could curl up with her, something which mightn't be beyond the possible, given the look she offered Annabel as they finished the transaction. Something to probe further on her next visit.

Beth had given her pithy instructions – a time and a place to meet for a vegan burger at a joint in Fitzrovia. One central neighbourhood of London, for Annabel, lesser known to tourists, and established as the zone for locals and permanent residents. An area saturated by those from media, advertising, online advertising industries. While it over-indexed for white, middle-aged men who failed their A-Levels but had a lot of beery mates, Annabel fitted in. She liked the vibe, for central at least, if you found the right backwater pubs, and could handle drinking on the pavement among the elbow jostle.

Annabel didn't need to lead in the company of Beth, and could take a back seat, which was just what she needed. Despite the demands of the media agency and young children, Beth demonstrated rectitude; she never let Annabel down, never cancelled, and was prompt. She was the yardstick by which others were held. Late or cancelling with fewer demands on them. And for men who may go incommunicado, Annabel referenced Beth, who was always available, answering some petty text or other when in meetings with executives, business veeayepees.

Beth waited in a light, shoe length, pleated black skirt over boots, and a burgundy shirt under a black biker jacket. Smooth leather, minimal zips. Never to see a motorbike. She had shoulder length fine brown hair, and light make-up besides dark red lipstick. She possessed a large nose which on some might not go over, but against her confident aura and clear brown eyes, gave her a hot look beyond the sum of her parts.

Annabel arrived. All smiles as they went for a triple cheek kiss, right, left, right again, before embracing for a deep squeeze.

Arriving first gave Beth the wall pew of power, while Annabel took the subservient aisle stool. They settled down and Beth opened for an update on Annabel. Intuition was not required, Beth understood that Annabel needed support. Her own news would by-and-large be good. This would be offered piecemeal, rather than by setting out her gleaming stall and recent successes. A borderline obese man knocked their table as he tried to inch between the gap.

Despite her wry, deadpan humour, Beth was a person of positivity. An evening with her would be one of laughing things off, enjoying the absurdities of life and the idiosyncrasies and oddities of the human animal, as opposed to espousing any mocking or cruelty. Annabel had other friends who did that with distinction, and who were required at other times, in equal measure. Life had gone well for Beth. A steady and constant climb career-wise, a well-chosen husband, couple of healthy kids, nice home. Knowing her from school, Annabel saw the continuing thread of foundational success; that of a stable home unit and siblings who wanted the best for her. There was a straight-and-narrowing that this presented, which for many was non-existent. And it was a case of cards dealt, a lucky platform. Born on the top board.

And she liked to talk about her family. Although spread all around the home counties, they circled her. Annabel, on the other hand, compartmentalised them.

"I worry about mum," Annabel began, "you know dad. Overbearing, opinionated. All the middle-class competitiveness, the ancient views. Always moving on to the next thing they should be doing, bringing home what the golf club lot are up to. The neighbours. Who fucking cares."

"Man of his time, that's all. Or maybe a man of any time. What do you want for her?" she asked with a shrug, "get divorced, start dating new men?"

They both laughed at the notion, imagining a similar scenario of bringing a new man to dinner.

"Some old guy in a bomber and a classic car. Forget it Belle. She wouldn't be happy on her own, they've been together so long, she's always got things going on. She's busy, she's got friends, hobbies."

"Belle. Don't worry about her. What about you? It's not selfish to focus on yourself."

Beth looked at her, underlining her point.

"They've had children, done the holidays, the home-making, all that stuff. Led prime Boomer lives. Much better than their parents. It's your turn. When did you last go on a date?"

"Oh, fuck knows. Before Christmas?"

"I know it's awful, and you can't be arsed, but you need to. You can't give up. It'll happen."

"You know what. I *just don't care.*"

Their burgers happened.

One green bun. One purple bun. Lettuce, beansprouts, vegetarian patties, plant-based cheese slices. Edamame, savoury potatoes. Despite solid eco credentials, and no companion devouring a bloody steak, the colours clashed with her sorrowful and ornery state.

"Got my order wrong," confirmed Annabel, "this is fine though."

"You sure?"

"Yeah. Attack, attack!" she said, referring to a waiter on a holiday they took together in Asia in the distant past.

They tucked in.

Beth sensed trouble. And felt helpless that one couldn't just put effort, man power, hours, into helping someone find their way. It was too complex a multi-dimensional problem. And unlike others with problems, where supportive actions could help or ward away danger, with Annabel the things that were causing her regret and melancholy were things which either needed to be resolved by her, or benefit from a change in her perception or pragmatism. Beth resolved to see her soon, and to keep at her to push through it.

It was a mild evening as spring shifted to summer. As they parted, and as Annabel entered the tube hall before taking the lift down, she shivered through her shoulders and ribs. She closed her coat, and crossed her arms to draw her bones in, and walked with her head down along the platform. She chose to continue past the rear train carriage which would have been most convenient when disembarking. To keep moving.

Summer

10101
CHAPTER 21
Simon fights a protester

Flexing day-in-day-out, the temperature and wind spiking and troughing, the heat broke through that Friday, reaching up like a hockey stick after a chilled morning.

Simon had chosen a waistcoated suit for his meetings, and this had caught him off-guard. Now overdressed, he had been made to sweat under an accusatory line of questioning, involving lawyers and investors. Perspiration that was directed away from the face and into the pits, unless under extreme, prolonged heat. It was a bruising but necessary coming together.

The streets were heated, the tarmac hot from sun and friction, the air replete with the pungent London smell of desperate street piss from the night previous and the new day. The absence of any public toilets after a night of ale or pale, of pale ale, or Sidecars and a Rusty Nail, slow cooked and baked into the dark alleys from the mainstream main streets toward the more fashionable quarters.

The heat was held in place, exacerbated, the air flow stifled, by the sheer mass of people snaking their way in a square, travelling as water in straight lines, in protest. For what purpose, today, he did not know. The obvious candidates being inaction on the environment, extinction, social justice, on rotation after the extended *pandemic* counter-measures had been shuttered. Or to celebrate and promote anarchy or the need for *another way*. The drumbeats and cacophony from a dozen sound systems and their array of genres, pounding, rapping, dancing and hip-hopping their tunes, overwhelmed by periodic roars and cheers, as horns were sounded beside whistles. Flares drifted over in primary colours, red here, yellow there, held by youths stood on higher platforms, stairs leading up to the entrances of offices and municipal buildings set back from the street. Weed and flare smoked mingled, as cans of lager and cider were cracked open from a community pulled together from across the country to underline their point, make voices heard. A day among friends and the like-minded was never a waste. A walk in the park, with tinnies.

The rich had continued to get even richer. Surprise. They weren't going to conspire to allow their wealth to ebb away. To make a contribution to redistribution. The best fund managers, financiers, and all the rest, had all their skin in the game, beach houses to establish, rankings to improve upon. Yet Simon had grown up in a unique post-war time, and understood freedoms of his youth and expression. And when it came to protests, he saw their point, up to a point. However, he had to play the game in front of him. Don't hate the player, though they did. Despised. If they could savage him without retribution, given a free pass by the state, they would tear into him in the streets. Mount his head on a parking restriction post. These thoughts raised his energy levels, refreshed the primal drives in him for reciprocal evisceration, to sweep all away before him.

The globalist authoritarian elite's fourth industrial age of digitalisation, ran contrary to the beliefs available to him at university, yet it was the way the world was heading. Unidirectional, irreversible. And should this be the necessary way to get him to where he needed to be, always several levels up, so be it. When it would come time for him to leave this world, it mattered not what followed.

For he saw the world as one great map, unfurled across all time, from history on the left to the distant future on the right, charting the already laid out progression from caveman to extinction, and he was at one point on that spectrum, moving all the time. Be it climate, termination by AI, nuclear holocaust, a pandemic of true devastation, or any number of natural, accidental, or unplanned for threats, it was in the post. He was a speck, able to enjoy the trappings and pleasures of a better life, and the pride and privilege of winning in his time.

Simon was boiling over due to a business hold-up, some technicality. For until the business was exited, and the post-period years of tied-in handover were passed, and the last signature crossed, it was one difficult task after the last. A protracted and painful disagreement. A blocker that needed speedy resolution, or it would hold things up, have knock-on effects. It would set him back.

He was having to hurry things along to make his next meeting. The day's schedule and evolving needs meant he had to communicate with absolute clarity and precision of language and direction at all times. The clock ticked toward the window he needed to get across town to catch a contact before they left for a flight.

This was when the education, the upbringing, all the needless (on the surface of it) training and tasks, all through the years, culminated in lean action. Remove the academic qualifications and sporting accolades, the Oxbridge education, the years of combat with other brilliant types, and this was where one lost, were dominated, or made an inferior call. The rubber hit the road and the suitcase of money either stayed intact or flew out in a stream behind.

He ran through the myriad of ways in which a misstep might be avoided. A call, a conference call, papers to be sent by wire, yet it was on that borderline. That point where, in progressing a business relationship which had just begun, despite the fact that they had already met in person, needed physical presence. The shake of the hand, the look of an eye, for these hawkeyed spotters of deception. To show an investment in time and travel to get together was essential to keep things on the right foot. Without Simon, someone else stepped in. Always room.

He thought about losing the waistcoat, but it kept him sharp, and the Asian businessmen he had to deal with liked the quintessential English look. He grabbed his jacket, swung it on, hustled the arms through and straightened himself up in the bathroom mirror. Adjusted the blood red Windsor knotted tie, tidied the hair, checked chin, cheeks, shirt for specks of coffee or dust, but never crumbs.

He leapt onto the street, and forced those walking toward him to chicane their way through. Choices were made between each pair of walkers coming together on a busy city path. Like elephants ordering themselves at a watering hole, the dominance logic interplayed based on sex, class, wealth, race, privilege, health, strength, confidence and threat. This calculation went awry as both parties were walking too briskly, and Simon had to force the oncoming into the road.

Many walkers carried banners, dyed of hair, young and old, the greys overwhelming the protesting discourse. With their large properties, final salary pensions and retirement freedoms, through the luck of birth age. He gave way to one individual, a beautiful, delicate woman, dignified and sombre. Annabel Oakes looked at Simon, and they enjoyed each other's look, before passing. Simon dressed as he was, could have been Annabel's father twenty years' previous, though she made no such connection.

He was becoming heated and slowed himself. Better to be late than unkempt, and if he carried on at this pace he would have to duck into a cool coffee shop. He checked behind and crossed the road, so central to be devoid of traffic, save a couple of scooters for which he wasn't going to pause. He held out a palm and indicated the obsequiousness required of them, like an experienced central defender pointing a young right back into position. He skipped in maroon, bespoke crafted brogues, and turned into an alley which could expedite him across toward Fitzrovia.

Ahead, a handful of people walked away from him, one walked toward him in the distance, and one man in his twenties headed his way, closer, a straggler off to march. Long red hair, pony-tailed, with a scant orange beard, wearing well-worn grey jeans, patterned T-shirt, a chaos of white and black, as if to camouflage among an urban pack. Despite the hair.

The younger man didn't yield and they knocked shoulders and arms, sending each other off at 45 degree angles, and which was a shock and painful to both.

"Watch it fuck face."

"Corporate cunt!" the young man yelled, as he dropped his bag and threw a punch, hitting Simon on his upper cheek, in a glancing blow which was clumsy yet effective enough to cut skin not used to street fighting. Simon reeled and had to put his hand out as he went down onto his right knee and feel back. The man followed up with a kick and Simon knew enough to swarm him, to grab hold and take him down to the floor. It was messy and the two men handled each other with faces puce, full of hatred, teeth gritted, eyes screwed tight, as the detestation drained out of them. Yet Simon was heavier and muscular, and he forced himself on top where he was able to swing at the man's face, splintering his teeth at the front, knocking one halfway back into his grimacing mouth, leaving another angled inward. Blood formed on the gums and smeared across his teeth, and Simon forced himself further into a controlling position. He now had his left hand around the throat with his right hand planted on the man's forehead and grabbing his slick-back hair slammed his head into the pavement twice, to a twisted thwack of a sound. It stopped short of a crack.

He drew his right hand back, and with tens of thousands of years of predatory and defensive evolution urging him on to put his fist through him, with every cell of his body engaged and invested, he held tense and still, for he was at war with himself. His skull felt a swell, his spinal cord wanted to take the controls. Through his mind, the implications of such an immediate move, what could mean years of prison, or two years wasted through legal process, the pure waste in money or progress, the implications of a criminal record. How this would put him back. As it was, he had defended himself, and as he looked up to shouts, the distant witness was now there to help him.

He stopped himself, eased himself up and bent over and shouted, "You fucking prick!" as loud as he had in him, though it died from his exhausted state half way through. "Fucking vile," he reinforced.

"I saw him swing at you, take my number in case you need a witness."

They swapped numbers and they both went on their way after establishing the man on the ground was in a state to walk away before too long.

As he walked back toward the office, he could see ahead of him that disruption was taking hold. Blocking the roads, interrupting the flow of a stream of money. A scene of pure minimisation. Less.

He phoned the contact he was due to meet, and went with the truth. The background noise which was building could be heard down the line and backed up his brief synopsis. *Events, dear boy, were imposed on all people.*

10110
CHAPTER 22
Josie and a flood event: Steven and Josie

The Met Office issued stark weather warnings in southern and central England and Wales, and Josie had been in touch with her younger sister who lived at the family home to understand what they were anticipating. It didn't look good, so they were taking the usual precautions. Preparations that were once occasional now became regular. This brought with it the depressing recognition that once cleared up and passed, it was respite for a year or two before it swung round again. Each member of the house now had responsibilities; they had a checklist, a routine and sequencing. Moving things upstairs, sandbagging, packing for a stay, attention to the garden and out buildings, shutting everything down.

Flooding had hit the UK hard since the 2000s, with many unfortunate areas affected time and again, Scotland to London. *Or at least it felt that way.* Given a little research, and as the deniers would highlight, getting it right and wrong in equal measure, all was not how it was now made to seem. Something which could catch out any day-to-day social media contributor who hadn't done their fact-checking. While fortunate not to have to endure US-style catastrophes, it remained a trauma for families and the old. It left mental scars along with a watermark lined through living and dining room walls. Home trapping was now a risk, people unable to relocate without a massive financial hit, unable to sell. Insurance implications compounded the suffering.

As with any middle-class, secure professional family worth their Himalayan salt, they thought long term, and preparations had been made when the sun was shining. They had a place to go with friends in an unaffected area, somewhere they could take the dog. Josie offered to go down there to help with Steven, who raised eyebrows out of sight.

She checked her sister had money. *Let mum and dad know I can come to help.*

They disconnected after five goodbyes each, and Josie gave Steven the potted version. He asked a couple of questions to appear interested.

"What preparations are they making?" nodding with the occasional 'right,' or 'oh right,' or 'that's how they do it.'

"Sounds like they have things under control," he suggested.

"I can't help thinking we should go down and help, it's only an hour and a half."

"You don't want to risk getting stuck, they've said they're OK?"

"Yes, they might say that..."

He paused, let the silence speak for itself.

"It's my family," she said, verging on angry, "don't you care?"

"Of course, it just sounds like we wouldn't be helping."

She couldn't bring herself to fight. Not because she didn't want to, she needed it, but because she felt weak. There was a power imbalance. She wanted this more, and didn't want to concede that to be the truth, but instead to hope that it wasn't. That she was misconstruing his words and deeds, that if she gave him time and opportunity, he would *get into it*. She thought of Victoria, saw her face, heard her words, watched the shake of her head. 'Move on', she heard, 'it ain't happening'. What have you done for me lately? Not much.

Steven looked through some dating app chat, from someone who lived twenty minutes from London, in Surrey. One hour twenty minutes' door to door then, he mused. He caught himself, looking through without caution, while Josie was sat across from him. It shocked him how much he had switched off.

As Josie read through something online, he thought of the date he had planned for that evening. And something in particular in approach. Careful with the sense of humour. Being edgy with humour, a little outrageous, could get you so far, or further with the right woman. Yet for all the live laughs, in the background they might be asking themselves how a salty sense of humour might go down if released on their close friends, or relatives. Dating a time bomb.

He showed her something he saw online relating to Vietnam, where he knew Josie spent time travelling, years before. Feign some interest, and to help him get clear to leaving without a showdown. She read it out of duty, feeling unsettled.

"What's happening today?" he asked, to remove 'what shall we do today?' from the menu, adding that he had a few things to do, and needed to be getting on.

"Oh, I thought we would do something."

He didn't engage with this line of talk, and proposed that she had gained a day, free to do whatever she wanted.

"There's the flooding to worry about."

"Worrying isn't going to help."

"Is that how you see things? That's how you get through life?"

"I'm just thinking of you. Don't stress all day."

He went to suggest some things she could do, but stopped himself. He didn't want her out and about with the rarest chance of running into him, out with someone else. A day at home for her was his choice option.

"Weather won't be great here, anyway. Continual wind and rain."

"Suppose I'll do some bloody work then."

Steven was unwavering, amid silence. Didn't say too much. They lay about, separated, for another half an hour or so, then Steven stretched, asked if he could take a shower, agreed to coffee, orange juice and croissants, and progressed along the roadmap toward the exit.

Keep your eye on the ball.

They shared a brief kiss as Steven left, and then he was off, technology off and running, earphones in, podcast on. 'Gee-oh-graphical hatspots', he heard in Southern US drawl. Too much like work, he thought, switching to some music, something to time with his stroll.

Josie packed a weekend bag, got in her car, and left for her parents. As much as she could do to help, she felt the pull of loved ones.

For Steven, once again, *what was next*?

A pit stop in a European bakery at Notting Hill Gate, approaching home. He was surrounded on a weekend afternoon by affluent

Europeans and Middle Easterners, experiencing London in transit, five years here, eight years in New York. A stint in Asia, then back home for reproductive and imperial family purposes. Some enjoying the experience, others miserable and bereft at the things the world hadn't offered them on a plate yet. Things they would no doubt realise, but had to wait a little longer for. While others waited for clean drinking water or the death of an abusive relative.

Steven was them. He knew too the ups and downs, the fleeting times of victory, of progression interspersed with the drudgery of life's bread and butter.

His flat white arrived with a cheerful fern shaken onto it, a mini charcoal bread sandwich with salmon and avocado, and a sweet Georgian pastry. He exchanged smiles with the girl behind the counter, around twenty. Attractive up and down, she had a star quality, with a pair of thin, light pink lips, perennially wet, like a dog's nose. He regretted this unfortunate comparison.

This present moment a moment of the past in the future, back when a world star used to flip burgers. He wondered what she thought during this exchange, and what she would think of what was going through his mind. She wore a pair of black jeans well, and the cool, hippy saunter she used to swagger away left him a framed still image. He forgave her the egregious way she answered 'no' when he asked if he may have the items he chose. A pointless, humourless interaction, permitted by youth. No star quality after all.

Returning to the task at hand, there were any number of dating profile descriptions and desires which Steven dismissed with disdain. Kids who were someone's world, indicating no room for him. Looking for the one. A best friend whose pants are fancied off. Missing each other, looking into each other's eyes, greetings card schmaltz. God forbid, cuddles and snuggles. Seeking a lobster or a partner in crime. When you both don't want the date to end.

Steven swept real people away, one after the other.

Off putting, an exhaustive list of partner pre-requisites. Cycling garb. *Crazy* friends. *Funny* photos. Deep sarcasm. Forty-seven and seeking a perfect mate who ticked every box. Banging on about friends and family. Those undemanding. Those too outdoorsy, those who did nothing but party. Forty years old and still obsessed by travel. Taut faces from exercise addiction, ultra-running, yoga overkill.

Appealing qualities. Cabin crew. Rich bitch white shorts. Bikinid aboard boats. Long hair. Drinking in some mini pool in Ibiza, surrounded by flesh. Tattooed wildness, the badass. Middle-eastern women. Russians. Doctors. Princess.

Everyone had their lists, their buttons plump for pushing, their peccadillos, their untouched fantasies. Their deal breakers. Lists which could be flexed – tightened or loosened, depending on mood, depth and quality of pipeline, recent dating experiences, weeks since last action in the field. As with football managers, if it didn't work out with one type, one could lurch to the other extreme. Oscillating without end.

He broke from his perpetual imbibing of the female form, drunk on all the options out there, to perform one sickening task which was necessary, best performed from a mobile phone, to convey a casual nonchalance via a 'sent from mobile' footnote. A peer had been promoted, he had seen over the weekend, and although indifferent to her, he had to congratulate her on achieving a move he would have liked for himself. He knew it was false and envious, as would she. So he kept it short, snappy, positive with an exclamation point! He sent it and moved on. It could have been worse; she beat some 90th percentile arseholes to the prize. That email that had to written, could always be worse. Good for her.

He sipped his frothy coffee, and reverted to his primary non-work mission. Not fitness, nor family, nor charity work. He had to have answers to these approaches and lines of questioning, which came up on rotation. About siblings, where he grew up, all aimed at unpicking what he was about, his origins, and his *class*. Was there money kicking about, in the pipeline? Further resources at his disposal: holiday homes, a famous relative, connections to get him/them on. Anything concerning? No-one wanted to be landed with a problematic relative – an alcoholic mother-in-law, toxic sibling rivalry. At least without significant balancing perks. Alcoholic father? Oh dear, no. Mother worth millions, with one heir. Hold on. Everyone had a cross to bear, don't be hasty. Let's keep talking.

A product of his time. Given the educational resources to do well, enjoying a youth set in a short but sweet spot of economic growth, domestic positivity and political change. At least until nine/eleven and Afghanistan and Iraq had doused out the party in the noughties. Two thousand and one had set a tone for the new millennium, from the get-go. Yet the good times had revealed to him the path to getting on, enjoying the spoils. Clubbing, weekenders, country or boat parties. A few rued nights where double-dropping led to an all-encompassing blackout. Wasted, the memory wasted also.

He steered conversations in and out of his work successes and these activities of personality and lifestyle, dropping in wholesome experiences of times overseas, the one time he hosted and cooked for a dinner party, the one time he did some volunteering. And acted as if they were examples of many. Don't over-egg the pudding, no-one wanted a saint. Unless he was dating a female equivalent, a mirror, and then it was all-nighter war stories all the way.

The fight to get the kind of women *he aspired to* on the hook, while everyone was punching up or on a level. They in turn were looking above him, themselves aspirational. Rational. If they wanted him, if it were too easy, he could do better. It was a pit of madness, all hot and cold, in one minute, out the next. Girls driving him crazy, him driving others crazy. All in the game. Whenever he was let down though, he could step out of his shoes and into theirs, and observe himself exacting the same behaviour on someone else. However, the maddening rationality of fives dates where the one that wanted to see him again was the one he wasn't so keen on...

Cynicism was an emotion which he fought, to place kindling on hope. There were success stories among his friends. As far as he knew. For one *never knew* the goings on behind closed doors. The way he saw it, most relationships head down from a peak, a peak of varying height, and an incline of varying steepness. With a prevailing wind, one could hope it levels and declines at a slow rate, perhaps buoyed by new interests, successful parenting, or things they never knew and found out about each other. It could pull them together and increase the bond. Otherwise it could be a cliff dive, after the exhaustion and modern slog of raising a family, in which children were the centre. A far cry from the seventies where they were a bolt-on, an addendum, while the adults got on with life, and the children waited their turn.

Sat at a table of married forty-somethings for dinner, how many of the couples went home and fucked?

Turning his attention back to his surroundings, people came and went, ushering in buggies, dogs, shopping, laptops, business portfolios. A pair of men in their fifties could be discussing anything – how to open a second bakery, their childhoods, details pertaining to the looming assassination attempt, or the football. A wealthy-looking man dished out advice to a daughter in her twenties. This was advice she was expected to take. Her glossy black hair reached down her back in waves, as if trying to lift her wallet. Underneath, a cream blouse, and as she stood up and turned around to locate the bathroom, she revealed a muted purple, knee length leather pencil skirt. This signalled money and confidence. A walkover only to her father.

Steven was wary of the father's eyes, as he looked her up and down, noting the father had taken the bench seat, leaving his daughter in the aisle.

He wondered how she liked to make love. He guessed based on her gym-honed physique of strong athleticism, that it would be an energetic affair, vigorous, potential for yelping. Demanding of many positions. It could comprise a slow build-up of lingering touches with cold, bony fingers, as a piece of performance art, or it could be pure commerce, a thirty-minute full energy spin class. He sipped his coffee as he watched her walk away. He would be disappointed if it were to be that modern, porn-driven, American method of sex-making. A barrage of noise, piston-like pumping, rough rumpy-pumpy. War not peace.

He didn't picture her as the sensitive, yielding type, all tease and gentle appeasement. That might require a soft, slim-armed, English rose type, all pale skin and straight hair. Sex as seduction rather than as business, an alternative power structure and currencies of exchange. Nor did he suspect any obvious kinks, though again, one *never knew*.

While he would like the opportunity to find out, he couldn't be a serious dating proposition, it would be thumbs down for Steven from pa, with his cashmere jumpers and Italian lake summerhouse. It would take someone elite to discover, he accepted.

She returned and walked toward Steven on the way, to take her seat. Steven thought she was ignoring him, condescending toward him in her aloofness, her unavailability to him, but the truth was that he gave off no signalling vibes which might pull her attention, and she didn't notice he was there.

He had drinks planned for Monday with a redhead call Pippa. Somewhere central. They could run into one of Josie's friends, relatives. Yet he wasn't risking anything meaningful, other than the jeopardy of arguments and awkwardness. Something he could shrug off with a few double bourbons. He did want to meet *someone* and settle down, that was his preference, but in the meantime, it was a matter of relentless pursuit and consumption. The next girl, the next potential, the next next.

Josie's parents' desperate home situation had been tough for her to experience, and she felt helpless, as did they, at the limited things they could do to resist the weight and persistence of flood water. Always seeking its spiritual level, expanding through the doors to creep through an entire home.

However, it had been a reminder of kindness, generosity and warmth within a countryside community. Of people trying to raise each other's spirits, to levitate chins, to find some humour among the holiday dinghies and floating cars.

Within two hours of her return to London, she had been cut up and abused by a moped rider, seen someone flobbing in the street, and had to debate with herself if the three hooded youths dressed in black outside a townhouse were waiting for their friend to emerge, or were casing the joint. An internal war between her prejudices and trying to do the right thing. Acting in accordance with the times, she chose to leave them to it. They were kids on bikes, that was all. On balance.

She arrived home to a welcome of a Penalty Charge Notice for loitering in a box junction. Dead to rights, slap bang in the middle. She remembered it happening. Half price if paid right away, though. Thought that through, didn't they?

Her home, quiet, sat empty as her heart, as she rolled her case through the hall, and dropped her handbag onto the armchair. It had been an upsetting time, and although her relatives had relocated, her disconnect to them was exacerbated by the distance she felt to Steven. Her stomach curled, shrunken with anxiety, in need of food, but not wanting. She grabbed a couple of pans, and reached down for the pasta container and canned tomatoes. Set them on the side, and put her hands flat on the counter and leaned forward, her elbows locking out as her weight went forward and her head bowed. She stared at the can label, at the brand name, the image, the slogan. And stared, unblinking.

Refusing to sit at home in misery, she decided to force the issue, and if it broke, it broke, but she could not go on in limbo. She called Steven. She needed to call twice before he answered. She would come over; they would go out to eat. He couldn't think of a credible way he could put this off, and he had no plans, and wouldn't mind dinner and a sleepover.

In a failing relationship, on one side at least, there would be a moment when the first twinge is felt. Things had been going well up to that point. Maybe the sex was good, a shared enjoyment of the same styles of music, a game of tennis, getting hammered. Then a moment: caught them gnawing their fingernails for too long or wearing an unflattering item of clothing, or a waiter gets the treatment. One could give it time, but the slide has started. Before too long a balanced list would be drawn up in one's mind – the good versus the bad. Once the list had been outlined that first time, although it would be re-evaluated many, many times, it was done. How many reviews and revisions of the list, well that may vary, but the outcome, guaranteed.

They met at a local Italian restaurant on Kensington Park Road, and their arms clashed as they embraced. After they were seated, Steven griped about many things. The gloves were off, no positivity necessary as he and Josie were on the slide. Limited space between his male aisle seat, a lack of freedom of movement, and prime for the bashing of passing feet or a dropped plate of linguine down the back. Cutlery (featherweight), plates (square), menu (nothing original), room temperature (Baltic), cocktails (limited), children (proximity to).

Steven tried to pay attention to the words as Josie updated on her family situation, giving it the nodding dog, as if listening to a client with a small budget. He got through this with a couple of comments, playing back things she had said, giving some affirmative reinforcement on points made salient through body language.

"God, I need a break," she said, tossing the ball up for him to bat away for six. 'Let's go away next weekend,' was something he did not say. Instead, 'you work too hard.

As their starters arrived, she pushed on, "We should go away next weekend, even go Friday evening, back Sunday."

Steven loaded a large arancino into his mouth, providing some thinking time.

"Maybe. I'll have to let you know."

"Weekend after then," she shoved.

"Look. I'll have to let you know."

"Jesus," she said, reaching for her wine which she knocked yet recovered before it was lost. She almost shook.

He was taking liberties, but couldn't deal with the confrontation right now, so he smiled, said he was sorry, and that he needed to check on work and let her know midweek.

On the surface, this appeased her. Inside, she churned, spun, as lost as before she had met him. She saw Victoria, sat opposite her in Chelsea. She hoped she wouldn't run into her during the next week.

Over Steven's right shoulder, she watched a younger couple hold hands. The girl fiddled with her rings.

They finished the meal and the wine, and went back to Steven's for the night.

10111
CHAPTER 23

A London Sunday: Fiona home audit and stocks: Julian and Iva in Oslo

One week later and it was a Sunday morning. The slowest day, defined not by religion, nor by family, but by restricted shopping hours, compressing the day's activities with the traffic. The roads and public transport remained busy from overnight overspill. Those taking the first tube home after clubbing had plenty of company from those heading to clean other clubs or pick up shifts in retail, transport, healthcare. The arterial roads, the tunnels, the A roads out remained busy always, supplying airports and ferrying people home, delivering their goods.

Sundays felt different, in that undefinable way, to, say, a Wednesday, even with identical outside noise, traffic, passers-by. It felt like Sunday because you knew it was.

Annabel lay in bed after a fitful, sleep deprived night, after trying to sedate herself with drink at home. This interfered with her sleep patterns and had her awake, alert at five o'clock, doom scrolling on her phone, making matters worse. She tried to read but the words would not stick. Attention deficit for everyone. Short form was her sole option, which meant news, or an unbearable *Food!* section, comprising features titled *Paperback Raita* or *Pastor Bake*.

With a work trip imminent and therefore a horizon to aim for, Julian had had a week's respite from Iva management. She had busied herself catching up with her close European friends. And despite an evening in Mayfair of dinner and hotel bars, she was working in the late morning, post an hour run, a long shower, and a *keto* breakfast of spinach and eggs. A birdlike portion insufficient to fill a slimline stomach.

Julian was back in bed after the morning walk, his dog trousers and weathered T-shirt hung over the chair on his side of the bedroom. Florence Wyatt was getting homework done, while Fiona made preparations for lunch.

Francesca opened a window and sat with coffee at her desk, staring beyond the laptop and a jug of flowers, onto the garden beyond. She had slept in, and sat in a fine, linen gown, cupping a white china mug, the warmth seeping in, looking out, watching a squirrel safe in a tree. A cat peered up from the ground.

Once it reached eleven, Francesca sent out invitations for a garden party, via email, to a list of close friends and acquaintances, which she had prepared the evening before. Not to a long list of movers, shakers. Hoping for a soulful afternoon with good people to celebrate summer.

She made a second coffee and went back to bed to read, while elsewhere in London, Simon was enduring a punishing boxing class with his Personal Trainer, whereby a youthful, muscular, yet poor South African got to reverse the dominance hierarchy and beat down on Simon. For that sixty minutes he owned him.

Francesca's invitation led to some manoeuvrings. Annabel would try to persuade Barney to come along. Helen was figuring out if she could get away with going sans Phil. To enjoy a sophisticated afternoon without the threat of general idiocy, criticism of the playlist, uncouthness unravelling with the swig of label shorn bottles.

Helen's frustration extended further from his unwillingness to engage as she went discussion fishing, attempting to talk through some of her personal and familial worries, while she wasn't knackered as hell, and he had no band or drinking distractions. As they took the car to make errands, she was figuring out the order of topics she needed to talk to him about, and how to introduce and flow through them. He put the radio on, already set to loud, something they *did* agree on. And which got turned up further when a track he liked came on.

"Tune," was all she got from him, with an affirmative and continued nod of the head, as the door speakers and the glove compartment rattled with bass.

As indie made way for a switch up to new wave, they dusted off Orange Juice, and *Rip It Up and Start Again*. And Helen felt the divinest inspiration wash over her depressed state. And as Phil reached for the radio, she shouted, "Don't you dare," as she turned it up even further. Once a year, going against every incongruous song played counter to one's emotions, the right person was met at the right time by the right song, to deliver the right guidance. A song to sit alongside one's mood and carry one away. In this case, to inspire in her the need for change. Lyrics which touched and made sense of the moment and the months.

Rip it up. Cancellation. She turned over a conversation with a friend. How everyone had a right to move on, of a fresh start, to reject poison and personal trauma. The song played over in her mind as Phil returned from a sojourn in the convenience store to retrieve beer. It was noon.

Josie Porter had forced herself to the gym because it had been so long, where she followed a workout from her trainer which she had not run through in three weeks. Whereby she had to drop weight levels, repetitions, and take longer breaks. She showered and left unsatisfied, and checked it was late enough to text Steven, which felt wrong. She *should* be able to text whenever.

Steven was in bed with someone else, so she would have to wait for a response.

Annabel phoned Barney, who was walking Jess on Peckham Rye Common. It was a pleasant morning, and after a long week and an energetic walk on Saturday, he needed a low impact walk, albeit uphill from the parked car, to the colourful gardens at the top.

Jess was sniffing, competing, claiming, forming maps of the tracks of her peers. Seeking scraps. Stopping dead to scratch, and continuing to while getting going again. Annabel was trying to interest him in the get-together Francesca was planning.

"You should come. Her parties are fun, and timed for the best chance at good weather. Latest they are expecting it to be a decent summer."

"They said that last year, and it was lousy."

"Did they? I don't remember any more. Apart from twenty-eighteen, that was roasting."

Barney held firm that he didn't like to participate in big groups.

"They're not a cunty bunch, though," Annabel pressed.

"If you want to put it like that."

"You know many of them, they're all nice."
"It doesn't matter."
"OK, but let's organise a dinner for four after."
"Deal."

Back at Wyatt HQ in Wandsworth, Fiona had carved out twenty minutes or so to execute a consumer goods home audit, to ensure availability of stocks to cover ordinary normal use, plus, since the dreaded Brexit, *pandemic* and European war triple whammy, sufficient prepping for extraordinary economic crises. Not a task she felt comfortable outsourcing to the staff, as the complications of an unchallenged acceptance of an incorrect brand replacement or imperfect format or flavour edit would cause her to unravel, and she estimated, cost her more time, long term, than taking it on herself.

Toilet roll holding, held at a minimum of twenty-four rolls in garage storage, plus whatever was in the household itself (north of a dozen rolls) had been boosted to a sixty-four holding. Instructions for restricted use could further be deployed down and across the household hierarchy to make this a hundred worth in longevity and see them through any winter of discontent. Supported by a dozen strong batch of wet wipes.

Twenty-four kitchen rolls, 720 dishwasher tablets, 576 clothing wash pods. Twelves, sixes and multiples thereof of supplies for the cleaner(s); bleaches, lemon floor, surface spray and cream cleaners, polish and window sprays, cloths for assorted purposes, washing conditioners, toilet fresheners, washing up liquid. Bin liners. Half a dozen boxes of Miele hoover bags. Hand tissues, toothpastes, toothbrushes, heads for electric brushes, floss, interdental brushes, eye drops. Adult and child versions and formats where applicable. Ordered via online supermarket.

Onto hygiene and multiple websites from which she bolstered the domestic supply chain of luxury hand soaps, body washes, shampoos, bath oils and bubble bath, candles, plus shaving creams, deodorants and moisturisers for him.

Luxury child brands where necessary, providing a pang of guilt when considered against the national minimum wage, of which she guessed was around eight to fifteen pounds an hour or something.

In total, as float, over two thousand pounds of goods.

Her own personal health and beauty items would be handled when everyone was out and she had some head space. This would require a further thousand pounds to top up, and would be spread across online and in-store ordering for the pleasures offered by each. To give some mystery to the outgoings, some hidden by cash while it was still accepted, and which could offer some obscurity if questioned when under scrutiny.

Pastas: twelve bags of each of six major shapes – long (bocatini), tubular adult (paccheri), tubular child (penne), shaped varietals (fusilli, farfalle, gigli) plus some wildcards on rotation which included whole wheat, spelt and dyed types. Many, many varieties of rice yet never in sacks; risotto and paella rices, teas and coffees, hot chocolates, six types of fruit tea (four boxes of each). Piles of baking supplies. Pestos, four varieties, thirty-two total.

A bespoke list of things Julian asked always to be available, for example, tinned peppered mackerel and grapefruit segments, specific alcohol options. Further fresh items which he asked to be able to have at will, and which he might write his name on in marker in the fridge ('JULIAN ONLY'), to try to ensure he wouldn't return home like Tony Soprano, and there be no smoked salmon or chorizo slices remaining.

Frozen goods for the garage chest freezer. Starting with twelve bags of frozen king prawns, and going on from there.

For to run out of something necessary was unimaginable, requiring a sweat of stress and floundering hothousing. Come a major societal breakdown, a burgling raid of their supplies would represent a survival sortie of substantial gain. Something the burgling community would hit upon when they gain access to the garage, or the walk-in pantries, larders and utility rooms of Wandsworth, St. Johns Wood, Hampstead, West Dulwich, Kensington, Barnes, Kew, Richmond, Wimbledon. A bounty of looted booty to the good, some jewellery snatched in passing for old times' sake.

This activity took the best part of an hour, despite Fiona's searing pace.

After doing a final check through the list for environmental and ecological flashpoints with Florence, based on previous clashes on food miles and packaging concerns possessed by the young lady, she clicked through her various orders, emptying her digital baskets. She checked through the confirmation emails and added all delivery details to her whiteboard calendar, detailing every two weeks hence.

As she picked up a magazine and made an Organic Raspberry Leaf Infusion, global data centres whirred and purred, their cooling fans ablur, connectivity and activity lights pinging green, amber and red, organising the ones and zeroes from Fiona's hand, converting them to the re-sequenced binaries to be received by retailers back across the water in the UK.

Computers, servers, terminals, drawing on energy produced from coal, fired up in China or indeed the West. Warehouse robots took their orders from Fiona's order – have a zero, have a one. Chopin Potatoes ("light and fluffy, perfect for mashing"). More ones, some zeroes, extra ones, final zero. Corbarino Tomatoes, £2.40 per can. Eighteen of.

Orders organised by region, existing stock levels, vehicle journey plans, delivery times. Stages of manual loading by humans, requiring their own fuel, scratching their letterboxed boxered and briefed arses, exiting their methane, with discretion or otherwise, in loading bays country-wide. Supplanting the ceased gas emissions from the cows no more. Diced organic casserole beef, stored within the controlled air conditioned truck, gliding around the streets with a breeze and a hush, clattering its doors and stacking palettes on pavements in the small and the wee hours, and all in between. A quotidian dance between manual and automatic, as human tasks were eroded as the robots were upskilled by superior code, as the habitats of animal species and uncontacted tribes were encroached for palm oil and other *goodies*.

Fiona was about to leave the kitchen and realised an omission. Putting down her tea which spilled a smidgeon, causing her to despair, and waste manufactured kitchen roll rather than use a sink cloth. She made a final marker in her calendar, for after the delivery of the last of the four orders, of one final appendix order in which to complete a sweep up to capture omissions from the tragic missing items list.

Julian had a plan hatched, influencing a small but long-term client in Oslo to believe that they needed a face-to-face to hammer a few things out with him and Iva. He had to catch them before the whole business did their month-long European summer vacation vanishing act. Chosen from a timing point of view and the pressure Iva was putting him under, he was satisfied it was a masterstroke. Close to zero chance of running into anyone he knew in Oslo, whereas Paris...

"Oslo? What the fuck do you have to go there for?" challenged Fiona. She had absorbed enough over the years to know where the action was, and what was an unusual request or activity.

"Oslo?" plus frowns and puzzled looks from colleagues. Julian just had to front this one out. Long-term contact. Delicate conversation. Risk. Shakes of the head. "Rather you than me. In and out though I guess."

"Oh, we have to stay over with the flight times."

Looks of incredulity.

He could stomach all this. What he couldn't stomach was the puppy-ish enthusiasm of a Junior Analyst who had levered his way into the meeting with the client. Always wanted to go to Oslo. Now there were three of them going. Though this would give them some cover.

Julian and Iva coordinated to book a sociable mid-morning flight with British Airways from Heathrow, selected as he knew Junior Analyst lived with his mum near Gatwick, and shouldn't act as ballast on the flight. They could then go missing in the afternoon, get some lunch, have a look around, fuck.

Meeting at Heathrow Terminal 5, in that cavernous, familiar departures hall, with its whites and lights, and many shades of grey, brightened throughout by the sunny yellows of the lights indicating zones, gates, special assistance, baggage and the like. And whether one was indeed coming or going. In a place like this, the ongoing connection between air travel and terrorism, and the precedence for random attacks in unprotected vestibules the world over, gave him pause. He envisaged great streams of blood spilled and spattered across the shiny hall, connecting bodies, surrounded by the grim banality of rolling luggage and children's backpacks. Black figures and bodies, those of terrorist or police. Halls designed so that blood and brains were mopped away without resistance, and bullet-ridden walls had their dark grey panels replaced, slotted out and in within hours. A slight return to business-as-usual.

Spotting each other across the vestibule and meeting in the centre, they were distant enough from any other humans that Julian, with a quick lifesaver behind and a glance ahead over Iva's shoulders, acquiesced for a quick lip kiss and interlocking hands.

"There's no-one you know here," she commented, an easy statement to make for someone with nothing to lose.

Iva wore a fitted white Saint Lauren shirt, the best part of £500, that only the top nought point five percent without children can risk. Julian wore a casual shirt in soft fabric, dark and light checks, able to absorb pasta sauce, dog paw dirt, drooled coffee. Julian marvelled at Iva's form, and how she managed to elevate the casual elegance of the white shirt with blue jeans. That's youth for you, he thought. In her day, Fiona was the rose, with a sparkling personality to match. Eyes were led her way on looks and by her humour and laughter.

Very much the pack leader, Iva led them through the departure rigmarole. Julian, on the other hand, was focused on getting Iva to the destination, yet they had time, and progress was uncontrollable, so he strolled about, admiring the view. Security signs now in crimson. Settling the passenger now out of fashion. Deploy the fear.

Walking behind a pace or two, Julian played a canny game of putting his hand on her lower back or around her waist, when safe to do so within the setting, and dropping back when among the masses. He was present with her, apart. As they passed through, airlines fell over themselves to advertise their green credentials; savings on waste, fuel economy, efficient supply chains. And which amounted to relativism – *we're the least polluting bastard*.

They sat down for a salad and a glass of prosecco, and caught up, before Iva moved them on, for she had work to be doing. Nothing specific which had to be finished for the next day, just general tasks.

Julian read a newspaper and dicked about with his phone. Once boarded they sat in a typical Eurozone Business Class row, separated by the vacated middle seat unavailable for booking. Awkward design, like the horrendous high-backed vertical seats on trains. The flight was uneventful, which was all one could ask for. When in the air, no event was a good event. Two hours, the ubiquitous duration to anywhere worth going to in mainland Europe by air.

Arriving at the hotel desk, Julian wondered which type of reception greeting they would receive. Would it be a smile bomb, a garrulous informative briefing, or a flying business track for the busy people. An unsubtle male sensing the possibilities. They had a middle-aged man, who had seen it all before, who had executed the ancient, legacy booking forms thousands of times, who got them their keys sans fuss, and highlighted the passage to the lifts. Follow the corridor around, past the artwork, and to the left.

Julian snatched a few free local chocolates from a jar. Iva disapproved.

They checked into separate rooms. Higher end business-hotel standard. A bare walled echo chamber of light hard wood floors, air conditioned to the max.

He went to turn the television on, but the previous guest had stolen the batteries and housekeeping hadn't figured that out. Fucking two fifty a night, he thought. No great loss, he would save himself some tedious international news channel with weather maps of the Arabian Peninsula, or getting stuck on some hotel home page. Evenings of fumbling about for non-existent light switches awaited, figuring out how and where to charge various things. Lights configured to be ruled by one master that turned everything off and little interdependence with the endless other individual switches.

He received a photo from Fiona, which appeared to show that she had had a frozen eel delivered.

He cracked his case open and laid it on the steel tube and elastic doobry, and hung a few things up, set up his tech, plugged in a couple of things to charge, and then went to Iva's room for sex.

Julian knocked and Iva opened. As the door swung open, Julian imagined a negligee, stocking and suspenders. Iva stood there, unchanged. Her laptop, notepad, phone, speaker, all parallel to the edges of the desk. Cables, chargers, headphones sat organised. Luggage open, a few things laid out, folded, packing cubes stacked. As he walked in, and looked to his right, health & beauty products spaced out, grouped by category.

He put his arms around her and pulled her toward him, grabbing as she pulled back, increasing the difficulty level. He tried to turn a kiss into a tongue washing machine, but was met with pursed lips.

Iva touched him on the face, palm against his right cheek and looked him in the eyes. Beauty he coveted. However, Iva had not been to Oslo before and wanted to explore.

"I haven't been to Oslo either, but I've done Copenhagen, Stockholm. Been to one Scandi capital, been to them all."

Iva dismissed him as a cynic, an easy criticism to level at an older man. He protested that this was the truth, unrelated to his cynicism, which he held up his hands to.

"We're going out; you're not just going to fuck me. A walk, sightseeing. Dinner. After that, if you still have the energy..."

They wandered the city, breezed around the Munch Museum, dismissed by Iva as *average*, while rating the new architecture, reflecting a modern 2020s digital totalitarian brutalism. Julian thought it was *pretty good*. Critics nationwide felt the birth of a new tour de force.

They stopped for a glass of wine in a modern corporate globalist-inspired restaurant, situated on the waterfront, reached by the vast concrete approaches.

They could have been anywhere.

Glancing at a menu out of interest, it was the food, dill feathered across most menu options, that indicated where they were.

They walked the waterfront toward the Opera House as the sun fell, providing Julian with the opportunity for some public intimacy; the gloomy light, the sparse populace, as they walked from the shore to the top of the building, walking atop the angular roof designed for that purpose. They kissed and groped at the top, before they looked out over the water, Julian stood behind Iva with a semi on.

He looked up a restaurant he had made a note of, booked it for an hour and a half ahead, and they took a taxi to Frogner, an affluent yet residential area. They stopped for a glass of champagne at a large, dark bar-cum-restaurant, enjoying their spots in large leather racing green swivel chairs in front of a satisfying marble bar with a white and pink lit collection of bottles, and busy bar tenders. Iva swung her legs as she did as a child.

Settled in, drink brought with it laughter, intimacy, flirtation, and a lack of inhibition from the distance between them and anyone familiar.

They sunk a few drinks, leaving little time to make their restaurant booking, as they fell out onto the street.

The restaurant could go either way. It had a light interior, wooden tables and chairs, slate floors and bare walls. It yelled sustainability, *locally sourced* materials, foraging. It sobered them and brought them back to grown-up matters.

They ordered from a clean-cut, professional young man, who didn't delay in moving them through the steps, as he hoped to correct the bunching in the table schedule caused by their tardiness.

Iva ordered a beetroot carpaccio as she was wearing black, and halibut. Julian ordered a fish soup and cod. The starters were served up in no time at all, ahead of the Overton window of acceptable cooking times.

As Julian put down his soup spoon, from behind a tall blonde sashayed past in a short dress, and he looked right, and starting at the calves, worked his way. Back of knees, hamstrings, dress hem, arse, upper hips, waist, back (exposed), neck (covered, halter), hair, arms, jewellery, shoes.

"Already onto the next?" Iva asked.

"You should have seen how her bloke checked you out when you got up before. It's hardwired. You're better looking," he added, thinking that cheap relativism would be well received.

"I saw him; we always see you."

He returned to his creamy fish soup. Once again, a satisfying surfeit of dill fronds. He sat spooning away, between chunks of sourdough and butter with large salted flakes.

Julian let her in on the fact that Howard at work was being let go, any day now. "Poor bastard's wife just got over cancer."

"He'll be fine," she responded, "People come into jobs, they leave them, that's why the revolving door is so."

She slid across her cold hand and offered it to him.

"What's next?" Iva asked, her eyes meeting his, unblinking.

Julian understood this question could be aimed at a number of levels. Like *The Terminator*, he saw a number of potential responses, relating to what they were about to eat, to whether they would get a drink next, to when he was going leave his wife and children. This was the inevitable, ugly consequence of these liaisons, the inflection point, and power shifts, like plates, unpredictable, volatile, and oblique.

Until then, the direct power lay with Iva, as Julian wanted her body, a driving force. Iva had to wait it out, she couldn't start pressing for change right away. And the waiting meant she wasn't as fresh, not as new, and there was a power shift to Julian as her expendability increased, in line with her desire for commitment. Working across these dynamics the traditional power held by the third party – that of the dangerous big reveal with forces and consequences which cannot be known.

Julian fenced with a 'how do you mean?' while he thought through his answer. He had learned from Lucy a few years' back, and Vanessa before that, that the 'in good time' line waned in its credibility with these wily new generations. He chose instead to put forward a timeline himself, something which would have been laughable years ago. He parried with twelve months, expecting to want to move on before then. From Iva, that is.

This proposal was not met with a positive response, but he took the looks and sharp atmosphere as a boxer does glancing jabs. Part of the job. This was not acceptable and it was suggested he revise his expectations. He bought himself some time. Appeasement was a dangerous strategy.

Although unspoken between them, they were both happy to head back, each calculating that sex would take between twenty to sixty minutes, plus other admin ahead of the next business day.

Julian settled up, delighted that a mid-range dinner could be expensed and he didn't have to pull it up at somewhere fancy. After some of the home expenses in the last week.

They took a taxi.

Back at the hotel, the lobby bar was taken up by solo and pairs of business travellers, hunched over laptops and phones. The young collaborating, moving their billions of ones and zeroes from here to there. Whereas the older veterans plodded through the language of email, accompanied by their allotted expenseable couple of beers. Topped up with a few of their own, content to be away from exhausting home life for two nights a week.

To Julian, a depressing sight, reminiscent of too many nights and weekends lost to the slurry of business tasks, decks, corporatese. To Iva, it reinforced the work that had to be done. While she played, others were getting ahead.

They went back to Iva's room where they had sex for an hour. Julian enjoyed a slow hour of love-making, drawing out the pleasure rather than going for an immediate hit. Iva came twice, once from the toys she brought with her, and once from the sex itself. Julian observed that the high society girls tended to allow themselves easy climaxes. They didn't get stuck like some could. They took the pleasure that was on offer.

As Julian lay there, satisfied, one hundred percent done for the day, Iva went to remove her make-up, shower, floss, brush her teeth, gargle mouthwash, moisturise.

"You're not even going to brush your teeth?"

"I've got good teeth."

Iva considered where his tongue had been.

She put on thin pyjamas, said a clipped goodnight, put in ear plugs, and slipped on a silk sleep mask. All the routine, discipline, rigour, beyond what Fiona went through. We are subjects of our times, Julian pondered.

They slept a restless night. Iva too hot. Julian too cold. They never met in the middle.

Iva woke, not long before her alarm was due. She stretched and jumped into the shower, before dressing and going to use the hotel gym. Julian remained prone, his head slipped off the spongey pillow, an arm slack over the side of the bed.

He felt the ratchet of the new generation and their drive and energy at odds with where he came from. And although he swerved the 'slacker' aesthetic of his youth to study hard, he couldn't escape the overriding utterance of his day, which was to *chill out*.

He checked his phone. Nothing overnight from Fiona. He had mixed feelings about that. He started to scroll and swipe and began to wake up in full, his mind racing from the drumbeat of world events, work difficulties, and general notifications.

He figured Iva wouldn't be long at this hour, it would be a loosener of a session. He was wrong. He phoned down for some coffee to be sent to *his* room. He dressed without care, nothing tucked in, socks and shoes in hand, sufficient to shuffle the few doors down the corridor.

They met in the lobby an hour later, junior in tow, and took a cab to the client's office, quelle surprise, a ten-storey glass building in the city centre, with an automatic revolving door, and a spotless cream reception area, which gave Iva's high heels the acoustics and audience they deserved. Julian looked across and felt good about himself.

They were met by an underling and had to endure classic pre-meeting chat. Been to Oslo before. Whereabouts in London, I lived there for a few years. Time with the company. The Opera House, Munch Museum. Ate by the water. They were led through barriers, swiped doors, roomy mirrored elevators, a random flight of stairs which didn't feel right. Across the quiet floor where the workers laboured. Whatever tasks to enable a shaving of a percentage point advantage off a price. An advantage to four decimal places.

Julian straightened himself, standing tall as the organ grinders loomed in the goldfish bowl board room, navy or charcoal suits, an occasional stripe. Something they might consider *jazzy*.

Eighties handshake time. Seventies leering toward Iva. A look back to Julian, testing to see if they could sniff any relationship between the two of them.

The elder statesman began discussing his son and daughter, at or off to the best universities. Julian was relieved he had children, one had to in these situations. Single man, no kids, never trusted. No empire building, what else was there?

Julian gave them the fundamentals, elaborating on their schooldays, musical leanings, sports, enjoying their promotion and its positive reflection on him. Their high hopes. Iva winced at *their*, not *his*, and busied herself while this was going on, with computing and coffee.

They were on a break during the meeting, a couple of hours in. An opportunity for those present to double down on their email, which they'd all been checking all morning. Julian could see Iva was distressed. Not stressed as if a disaster was unfolding, but she was just *not there*. He reverted to a forensic scan of his inbox and there it was. Promotional announcements. One of Iva's peers had been bumped. Julian foresaw a tricky night ahead. It was all he needed. Timing, always the timing.

The Oslo hotel receptionist picked up the phone. A lady asked to speak with Iva Jovanovic. "Putting you straight through."
The phone rang once before it was cut.
"Little cunt," said Fiona, from her kitchen island.

After a long day of meetings and having wrapped up some things back at the hotel, they changed for the evening. Leaving her room, a few paces down the corridor, Iva asked if he had set the thermostat.
He turned back, "I'll double check."
"You mean check the first time," she challenged. Long day, long night.
The hotel systems would work away all evening, keeping the room the exact right temperature for no-one. Somewhere, pollution billowed.
They made limited excuses with junior, and left him to his own devices. No fucks given.
Iva vented over dinner, extolling her own qualities and accomplishments over her promoted peer, while picking the scallions out of her salad, something she had overlooked on the menu, not taking in the words, her head stress-scrambled.
"This is not in the plan."
"Her face fits. That's all it's about, assuming a certain level of ability. You'll be fine. Your face fits too."
"Oh, so I have a slower fitting face. I don't want to be fine, I want to get on. Now. I'm ready."
"So it takes you another six months, you're on track. Don't worry about it."
"Can you stop looking at your phone please?"
"Something's up at home."
"There's always something up at home. We don't have long here."
"They're my kids, Iva. Fuck."
Fiona was giving Theo, who was fine, a temperature, and suggesting he was staring into the distance.
"Theo's got a temperature."
"Oh god, is that all. Young boy has temperature."

Fiona embellished, knowing she could back out at any minute, and 'keep an eye on him.' She had him pinned. He couldn't dismiss her. And Fiona knew and he knew, that he would have to be *careful* in any story concocted. As any detective knew, it was about catching the first lie, and the loose thread could be pulled until it all unravelled.

Fiona turned the screw by calling five minutes later. He had to take it. Neither he nor Iva had any control.

And so their evening revolved around difficult and worst of all, dull conversations. Argumentative and destructive. Iva refrained from troped questions about leaving wives, but left it in no uncertain terms that she wanted to hear a plan. His plan for them. She complained about the wine and noisy children in the dining room. Julian hadn't taken much notice. They had no sex on the final night.

And so they returned home. Nothing resolved, no decisions, no forward movement. It had been a couple of days of escape, of some pleasure. Pure short-termism. A life lived in the moment with no recipe for development or contentment.

Julian returned to attempt to understand how his household came to receive a fresh eel.

11000
CHAPTER 24

Helen job hunting: Phil goes to a gig: Annabel and a Tate Modern protest

It was a Tuesday evening, reaching the high twenties in the day, but promising rain later. Helen had the windows open front and back, and a soft breeze broze through. A harder gust, a global warming gust, sufficient to catch the paper on her notepad and send her ballpoint off, skidding over the table, teetering on the edge. Helen scrambled which wasn't necessary and felt on edge as a result. She adjusted a few things to counter this, better angled the plantation shutters, and ensured there was nothing vulnerable placed near the windows.

The street gave the background soundtrack of rubber on road, vans piling through and hitting speed bumps, so that they could spend extra seconds stationary at the next junction or lights. From the twenty or so back gardens her flat overlooked, the sounds of children a few doors down, the odd cat fight, a tracking helicopter overhead but some distance away. Plates and cutlery were being set outside next door. So many lives piled on top of each other.

Helen had powered down her work laptop and moved to her desktop, which had remained running all day and allowed her to get plenty of non-work done in parallel. Not porn; Helen didn't watch porn, one of the last few standing.

It had been many years since Helen last had to find a new job, and things had moved on. She figured it remained true that for every ten kay in target salary, an additional month of search was needed. This was depressing and worrisome. If her employers were losing patience with her, as well as vice versa, she might need to build some bridges and play nice. At least until she had a bridge to a new company. She knew better than that at least, having seen friends leave in a blaze of glory and have problems with references and recommendations down the line.

She had given her CV a facelift, flexed a few versions for different roles and to highlight different areas of strength. And she'd begun to put the feelers out to her network. A solid start. A decade ago she would load her CV into a few sites and the phone calls would come.

Things required a proactive approach now, and the horror of online job posts. Plenty of benefits on offer she *didn't* enjoy at present. Health Insurance (immaterial with a free-to-use national health service, for the gamblers), pension plan (required by law), charity action days (for the virtue signallers who weren't prepared to do charity work in their own time), wellness allowance and *balance* days. How about resource the business, so we don't need mental health webinars, she thought? Learning and Training. That was a benefit now? 33 days' holiday allowance. Blimey, great. Including bank holidays. 25 days then. Helen couldn't believe what she was seeing. She didn't need organised fun. Nor team away days. Just to be treated with kindness and respect, with some support to get her projects done.

Roles at Big Corp Inc. A never-ending list of bullets magazined into sub-sections such as Role Purpose, Impact on the Business, Stakeholders, Leadership & Teamwork, Operational Effectiveness, Role Context & Dimensions and Observation of Internal Controls (go figure), Knowledge & Experience, Qualifications.

At the other end, the start-ups, where job descriptions included the words 'chaos' and 'fighting fires'.

She knew the sectors where she would fit in, the uncool ones, versus the ones which were out of bounds. Helen was pained, and sat staring at the screen with her left hand holding her temple. It was an unconscious action, but which she had caught herself doing during conference calls, and something she never saw other colleagues doing.

This felt overwhelming. The cycles and stages of the processes, the disappointments, the months of effort, for more of the same. *Meet the new boss, same as the old boss.* Layered into her mental trifle, her sister had called, where was Phil, and what were they even doing together?

She gave up, went to the fridge for wine, and poured a large glass.

Further south, in the denser, livelier and congested Camden,

London's liver, the warmth was felt and smelled, the flagstones absorbing and reflecting heat back. The roadside imbibers sweated and jostled in their pairs and packs, sucking the car fumes, cigarette and custard vape smoke into their exhausted lungs.

It wasn't too long before the band would be on, and Phil had taken a pill with a colleague, Stacey, as they approached the gig. With the predictable queue to get in, the messing about at the cloakroom for some colleagues (not him), the getting of drinks and maybe a couple of fags, depending on the untested chemical balance, he should come up as the music was getting started.

Once inside, given the reassurance of the sooty, sticky gig venue floor, Phil was playing at home. In his black soled trainers, he marvelled at his fellow audience members wearing white pumps. He wrapped the arms of his light jacket around his waist and tied them tight, enabling a quick getaway, to snaffle a last beer. The white soled crew, in turn, saw someone practical, with no desire for desirability. Where was the fun in that?

They got a round and found some seats on a higher level. They nattered about some up and coming acts signed and new releases. Their merits or otherwise. Phil picked away at the label of his beer bottle, stripping it smooth in places to reveal clear green plastic, while leaving soft, white paper trails elsewhere.

After some chat it was their vibe to join the throng, to embed themselves within the warm centre of the live music crowd, to face forward in expectation.

It was too full by anyone's standard, and these up and comers had attracted a mass of youth which brought with it a boisterousness and energy which surpassed that within the present Phil. He and his friends relented and let the mob pass through. After planting and holding steady, elbows out, wide stance, they were forced to drift back, as others advanced, as when olives and capers sink to the bottom of a salad.

The band got started and were LOUD. Phil pitied the audience at the wings who might be deaf on one side the next day due to the caustic speakers on the flanks. He eye-rolled at the first few tracks, a predictable set list of two full-bore hits, then dropping back on the third with a change of pace.

It was a good hour in, the pills were good, when Phil went to the bar for a few beers. He ordered and turned around to face the band, and pulled out his phone. A bevy of lights and notifications, green and red, flickering so fast that he couldn't get a lock on them, like a fighter pilot chasing wily prey. It took a while and a slow phase of flicker to register Helen's name. And then it was gone in a whirl, flashing and spinning, jittering in an un-trappable way. As Stacey came over to help he asked her to read what they said. A couple of rounds of 'what's?' and they moved to the hall to be able to communicate.

"Read this for me, would you? The one from Helen."

"She just wants to know when you'll be home."

"What?!"

They paused as a song ended and the applause died down. The band took some swigs.

"She just wants to know when you'll be home."

"Text her back 'elevenish' for me?"

"Eleven, yeah, funny," Stacey laughed, shouting, "you're better off being realistic and arriving vaguely on time."

"No, that'll piss her off now," figured Phil, any delay to grief welcome while he was trying to enjoy himself. Always happy to kick any can down the road.

Stacey texted 'See you elevenish.'

Helen pondered the full stop which Phil never included within his scruffy, rushed, haphazard communications.

He tanned a few extra beers at pace as the night continued, and put life behind him, cocooned by the music, the alcohol and stimulants. The nowness of it all.

Phil left the venue and bade farewell to a couple of his friends, a sensible couple, who went home. The others grabbed a last beer over the road. Phil neared the end of his pint, and knew it was time to head back. He felt pleasure chills running down his cool hamstrings and behind his knees, and didn't want to go underground. He would walk a little for the air, and jump on a bus. Although not what one could describe as hungry, rounding off the evening with food was habitual. Still unable to read and use his phone, he resorted to phoning through an order to his local high street pizza chain, which he could time for pick up and eat on the hoof before home. Ordering a delivery to arrive at home would set Helen off, and he had the texts to deal with as it was.

He phoned through a medium ham and pineapple stuffed crust, extra pineapple, and a chicken side with sour cream and chive dip. He remembered to pick up some refresher wipes, and then forgot at collection.

After collection, not for the first time, he found a low wall in a shadowy corner, a favourite spot a few streets from home. Dinner was passing without incident until a figure walking with bad energy began to cross toward Phil. Words were exchanged, of which Phil had no recollection later, and then a few blows. Phil was punched twice without great force, before getting one off himself and shouting nonsense. Two junkies on different junk from different worlds, confused.

Phil finished up his food and headed home to be met by Helen, once all the ingredients for a midnight argument were in place.

It was a Tuesday evening. Taking drugs. All he wanted was to drink beer and go to gigs. Laziness and lethargy. Wasted life. Directionless. Adult baby. Everyone else growing up, having families of their own. We're child free, we can do what we want. No responsibilities, shame. No responsibilities, great. Can't even text message. Bruised. Sauce down your clothes. Life is the same. I need something else. A different experience and challenge. Cliché? Meh, don't care.

Helen went fucking postal before going to bed, where she lay fuming, turning things over for hours.

Phil sat back in the armchair, in his post-prandial torpor and channel hopped, until he found some cricket. Except it flicked on an extra station to the speedway. Held down by the muscles he had built for laziness, he let it be.

In London Fields, Annabel walked around her flat, talking to herself more than usual, vocalising her thoughts on some despicable acts by charity employees in the third world, the trustworthiness of long term friends, celebrity virtue signalling, a local by-election, misguided fashion ideas of her neighbours and whether or not she should get a cat.

If novels cast and laid bare a thousand characters and people types, she felt that she herself had jumped from the original Annabel to play many others the last year, with her changing state of mind. She wondered where this might end. Despite the warmth, she had felt cold for days, so put on a latte sweater and classic American blue jeans; sneakers for the gallery and museum shuffle and trudge.

Distracted and rushed when leaving the flat, already running behind to meet Steven for a lunchtime drink, she secured the four locks across the two lockable doors and got fifty yards down the street when she felt for her headphones and found herself lacking.

"Shit," she exclaimed, realising the eight locks she would have to negotiate. She added in a quick toilet stop for extra comfort, and left again.

They had agreed to convene at Tate Modern before Annabel met another friend to see an exhibition, and before Steven had to attend to whatever he needed to in Bermondsey. She hadn't asked, assuming it to be relating to a woman, drink and/or drugs.

A typical London journey of a few kilometres as the crow flew, which could take the best part of an hour, and plural modes of travel. A walk to catch a bus to Whitechapel, where she changed onto the District Line heading west, which she took to Mansion House.

Exiting the tube, squared white tiled pillars topped with yellow and green striped cornicing, revealed by strip lighting. A strip flickered upon regular-shaped pillars, octagonal perhaps, pimpled with rivets, and a dirtier cream. A low ceiling, lacking any care to conceal pipes, ducts and cables. Ancient and lacking any maintenance, no industrial chic of the modern airport. Caution slippery floor. Emergency exits this way. The rail tracks carved in various directions. Onward, round mirrors improved pedestrian visibility of the lurk. Help points, fire extinguishers, maps and out-of-date *pandemic* cautionary instructions littered the way. For a weekend there was a surprising stream of people in carriages ahead and behind, and as she stepped toward the filthy steps to the surface, Annabel felt encased, surrounded.

At her stop she would, on any weekday, do the penguin shuffle up the stairs. The group plod, with everyone else. Today, she stepped aside before the stairs, waited twenty seconds or so to let others pass, and joined the back, giving the people in front a start of half a dozen steps. Up stairs and round, past illuminated advertising boards, through barriers, tighter for some than others, and onto hospital corridors, toward a vanishing point of the last way out indicators.

As she turned the final corner to daylight, she was met by a chain restaurant. She muddled her way through the streets and over the bridge, and along to the power station.

Although Annabel arrived late, Steven was even later, though he had apologised en route. She took a seat in the ground floor café, suffused with light from the large windows on this summer day, taking a seat toward the centre, hoping to stay fresh. On a table not adjacent to hers, but with loud enough occupants, what sounded like a first date. The girl in her twenties explaining how when she left university she wanted to work for Deloitte. A need her tone suggested she had satisfied. Annabel wondered how that could be a promising graduate's dream, but brushed it off, together with them. She got up and moved half a dozen tables away. She had to take a seat closer to the windows to compensate for her escape from the creeping corporation. She felt clammy, due to the greenhouse heat, her failure to cool from the stiff walk. The dirtiness of the conversation foisted upon her, and the sponsorships on the posters on display.

She ordered a double espresso, needing a boost but not a full, filling, hot coffee. The waitress forced a wan smile while radiating frostiness, both upon taking the order and leaving the small cup. She had problems of her own.

Gone in a few glugs and set aside, Annabel returned to check it was gone a minute or so later, and to tip it back for any last hit regardless. A pointless habit, rewarded with spotty dregs.

She saw Steven a hundred yards away, coming up the gentle incline from the street in the distance, by the west side entrance. And watched him amble up, moving through the automatic and manual doors, and over to where she was sat. Dressed in casual pants, a summer shirt and shades, he looked like someone making use of the weather, and not bothered about looking tooth-achingly cool, which he did not.

"All right?"

They settled down and Steven picked up the drinks menu and scanned for an acceptable white wine. Nothing of any quality, an unsurprising list of the fundamentals; Chardonnay, Sauvignon Blanc,

Pinot Grigio, Chenin Blanc. Wine salt and vinegar, cheese and onion, ready salted.

"What are you here for?" he asked, knowing that she would have to answer from a short list of around twenty artists for any sort of recognition.

"Nothing particular, just meeting Gaby to wander around The Tanks. Some video installations she wanted to see, plus whatever else is on. Welcome to join us," she asked out of reflex, before realising she'd rather be alone with her friend.

He didn't respond, just swung his head a little from side to side and pursed his lips as if he'd think about it and let her know.

"There's another art meet up you should come to; I'll get you an invite. Evening affair, *Francesca will be there*," she teased.

"How's the dating escapades?" she asked.

He was coy, but confirmed he was still seeing Josie. He neglected to mention he was going on a date with someone else after their drink. He deflected it back on her so she didn't dig further.

"How's *your* dating escapades? You better be getting out there."

Annabel ran out the old trope about wanting to meet someone *In Real Life*.

"Yeah, yeah, yeah. People say that, but if a bloke came up to you in the street, you'd be head down and out of there. You mean 'I wouldn't mind Gosling approaching me in the street,' and taking you out for cocktails. There's not many men like that about, and they don't need to approach girls in the street."

He ordered them both a glass of house white wine from Frosty, who forced out her three hundred times a day smile, which he returned with a warm smile and a wink, which turned her mouth sour. Something which Annabel found hilarious.

"Share a slice of carrot cake?" she asked.

He nodded.

"Put it away," she said after their order was taken, and called back to their previous conversation, "what's it with you and Ryan Gosling anyway?"

"Every woman should have a male coach. I've offered the male scoop before."

"Thanks," she acknowledged with sarcasm.

"If you want to get to the heart of men and male desire, look at what some gay men are up to. Take women out of the equation, and they are always horny, hooking up, bed hopping, threesomes, bored at home, thirty minutes later, in a stranger's bed. That's your average bloke, the average *bear*, let alone the hot ones. Heterosexual men have to be hot, charismatic, or have talent or fame bragging rights to be able to pull off that sort of behaviour. The underlying desire, same."

Wine and cake were dropped off, and Annabel executed the move burned into them by their parents when young. One cuts, the other chooses. Annabel cut them into equals.

Steven caught a colleague calling over to Joy, who turned around after putting the plates down. "Some anti-nominative determinism, right there."

"Don't be such a bitch," Annabel chided.

"Sorry."

"Don't apologise to me."

"Wow. What's been yanking your chain? Since when did you become agreeable?"

"The world is fucked up."

"Don't let it weigh on you. You're having a bad phase, perfectly normal."

"A phase that's getting longer."

"You'll turn into Aunt Lou, the po-faced cunt."

"God."

"Remember when we,"

"Yes, yes," she stopped him, mustering a smile, "stop, stop, I can't bear it. Cringe."

"What are your next phases? Charity do-gooder. Environmentalist. Protestor. Or are you going to revert to provincial nightclubber?"

Annabel laughed at the memories of their interwoven childhoods.

"A question I ask people. What was your provincial nightclub called? Moles. Bojangles. Destiny. Embassy Nights."

"Don't," she said, smiling despite herself.

"I think you'll find I was more of a metropolitan clubber."

"Eventually. Seriously though Belle, don't be such a Debbie Downer, you need to arrest that shit. Have some bloody fun. Come out with us, I'll let you know when there's something happening."

"Sure," she responded.

"It's in your power, it's how you see things."

"That's what Barney says."

"There you go. Good old Barneveld."

As they talked, an onlooker would guess they were relatives; comfortable and relaxed in a way that the years offered. The same years in a couple would have pulled all the conversation out of them, as would the familiarity of everyday life.

It wasn't too long before Steven had to leave and he got up, leaned down and kissed her on her soft, cold cheek, cupping it with the fleshy part of his left hand, below the thumb. And then he turned and was on his way.

Annabel's friend was running late. Half an hour plus late. Not city-late but beyond late. 'Be there in twenty'. Double it unless it was a large number, in which case add fifty percent. She couldn't sit on her own with another coffee or wine, so she went to have a look around the main building, for perhaps the fortieth time. While the permanent collection was limited, with little of note on the global art stage, save for a Dali of Narcissus, the exhibitions were noteworthy, if you could bare the crowd numbers.

She found some temporary exhibit and was scanned in, past a dubious corporate sponsorship or 'collaboration' sign, and entered one of the vast, wide white spaces. She milled about, looking at the people as much as the art. Watching the demographics and skews and biases, considering how these had changed, and noting some cultural shifts. Affluent-looking men who dressed like they were going to a football match, couples with young children, who were young and bored, ready for a tantrum. Men holding hands.

As she flowed about, steering clear of clusterings, there was a commotion, a primal sense that *something was wrong*, and as Annabel turned toward the entrance, there were young screams as red streaked the white walls. Her split instinct was blood and an attack, but thick black slashes joined then, tainting the clean walls, encroaching on the artworks. She saw the shooters, protestors firing paint, young men and women, in art school garb, not dressed in black. Her cream cashmere sweater from Chloé had caught spatter of both. Staff bustled in, and the crowd were privy to an untidy brawling melee, feet slipping into pools of paint, limbs aflail. Annabel ran past them and out the entry doors, while others stepped around the mess.

Light of foot, her Conversed feet ran and carried her toward the escalators. She ran down the first before turning back on herself and taking the next. She ran left at the shop and up the long, slow ramp of the Turbine Hall and out into sun. She carried on at a jog until she found a space on the grass among people, sat in small groups, touching grass. She fought her way from her ruined sweater. She wanted to cry but remained numb. As she looked out, the colour faded as her lights adjusted to the light and dimmed the view as if a cloud had passed. A noisy group of young tourists thirty feet or so away, men and women, laughed at the expense of one of their number. She lay on her back and looked up at the lightest blue sky, cut by a white streak from an aeroplane, and she tried to decompress. To decouple the sounds and to focus away from the buildings and trees above her. She felt cut through with a kind of light trauma. Not the heaviest kind. Which made her chastise herself. Mountains, molehills, first world problems. Yet she felt threatened, and aware of the danger society put her in. Terrorism. Or giant roided men, pumped up from porn, hardened and angry from rejection. She recollected a documentary of nineteen seventies prison life, all skinny convicts and larger prison wardens. Their control and menace. Contrasted today with society's failed attempts to control the modern stronger beasts, at protests or in the big house. The increasing level of threat to authorities, reciprocated, in a negative loop. Both sides dialling up their respective body armour.

Needing solitude, she phoned her friend to stop her in her tracks and she went home.

11001
CHAPTER 25

A funeral: Francesca and Simon end: Helen gets a push: Summer in London

The Bentley passenger door closed with a solid whump, as Simon squirmed for comfort in his black suit, catching a lift with an associate to the funeral of Marianne in the home counties. Of all fucking places. At least they could use the time to discuss business matters.

The air conditioning was a relief within seconds, as the weather had decided it would be a classic English summer day. Brilliant sky, unfettered sun, minimal clouds. A day to see someone off in a positive mood, a life well lived and all that. Contrasting this with a number of desperate, cold, winter funerals, all shiver, gloom and upset. Looking back, no chance of looking forward.

Forty minutes or so and they arrived, sweeping into a large, rectangular gravel car park, with old hip-height stone walls, rounded at the top, dotted with islands of brown, where fiery green winter moss had deceased.

There were numerous red Ferraris, one yellow, one black. Most under two years old. A pair of classics. A sea of wealth indicators. Set above the pool of lesser cars, the Range Rovers, the Bentleys, themselves in turn above the mainstream German family cars, the Ferraris then gave off their own *within brand* signals. Their own ranking, of pure price of course, but also of taste, elegance, scarcity. Matters of panache and flash.

The service inched along, as Simon moved his eyes around the room, identifying those he should speak with while he had the opportunity. He laughed inside as he thought of the savages picking over his cold remains one day at his last goodbye, getting on with the future without him.

At the wake, a never-ending string of moneyed associates networked their way through their social circle and beyond. Those that already knew each other commented little beyond variations of 'fitting send-off', before talking turkey, over a poultry wrap. New contacts were made, and after a few preliminaries, they probed how they might be useful to each other or others in their network, before details were exchanged.

Simon was cornered by an old acquaintance, forming a pair who might be useful to each other, but whom Simon couldn't stand. Still, it wouldn't do to rock the boat, keeping good words between them wouldn't harm any other future doings. He asked after Francesca and then began banging on about art, with the rapid-fire high articulacy for which he was known. Simon shifted into art-positive mode, rattled off a few modern names he had come across shadowing Francesca.

"Do you collect?"

"Oh yes," he confirmed, "I move things in and on," he confirmed before elaborating, making little sense to Simon who gave performative agreement. The gentleman placed his hand on his companion's upper arm, "must say hello to Sandra, good to speak with you," as he switched gear into sport mode, and headed for a financier, "don't be a stranger."

Tragedy though it was, it had been six weeks or so, after difficulties recovering the body, and Simon had been patching a gaping hole in his top team and advisory group. The matter of consistent access to Marianne's previous team took longer than was palatable to be agreed. And while he could resolve this elsewhere, his trust in their work was pure. Something he would prefer not to relinquish. After making nice with Stephanie, keeping it light, asking about her boys, he propelled himself on, to speak with Clarence. Simon's money remained sound money. He received a warm apology from Clarence that things hadn't been resolved sooner. It had amounted to unnecessary anguish. These words, spoken with ease, and which could have been said weeks prior, suggested there had been some discussions relating to Simon's character, or internal beef made tricky by imbalances of power.

The wake warmed. The volume now that of a pre wedding hubbub, and it wasn't long before the men were planning an evening of clubs. Simon on form would be at the heart of things, but he had to decline to partake in other matters. He gave a nod to his lift and said goodbye to the family, exchanged a few other handshakes and winks, and left, noted by a couple of admiring women, partners of less handsome men.

Despite the tragedy of the loss of such an accomplished woman, at a young age for the age, and despite a service with teared readers and eulogised evidence of a life well lived, Simon felt little. He was unmoved. At times like this he felt as if he were a fictional on-screen character, in a simulation people nowadays purported we might exist within. He struggled to think of the funeral he might attend where his own tears would be shed.

As he was driven back to London, thoughts moved to the next phases, the next steps. He had a list of people to call, and considered calling them now, but even he stopped himself, driven after all by a fellow service attendee. After they exchanged a few comments on the stories they had heard that day, the driver put on some classical music, as if to permit quiet thoughts on Marianna and her life. And they both went about formulating *what was next*.

Bury them and move on.

Returning from a business trip to New York, the dinners and drinks had caught up with Francesca. While she didn't feel too unhealthy during her stay, when she went to the bathroom on the plane, she had a direct comparison with herself from before the trip, on the flight over, and felt heavier, clothes tighter. As she would when at home in front of her home mirror.

She decided to eat light for a few days, do some exercise. And to end it with Simon, whatever it was. She always had his number, as she did as girl, watching men and boys. And the joke wasn't funny anymore. The extravagances, not just the lack of humanity. The simple pushing aside of the world outside of that which he inhabited. As she watched, she learned of the depths. And she couldn't bear the dinners out at the moment, the long boozy sessions. A short term consideration but it just gave her decision some reinforcements, as decisions needed now and then.

This wasn't a proactive call she would make; she would wait for him to call her. There was a slim chance he wouldn't after all. The dumper's daydream.

It took a couple of days coming. She got straight into it, and while she had a narrative to work from, she figured he didn't need reasons, he needed to hear 'no'.

It was a short call, an adult way of going about business. And when they ended the call both stood, their phones in front of them, disconnecting.

And that was that.

With no plans now that evening, Simon contacted a long-term female acquaintance, "I picked up, do you want to go out?"

A week later, Francesca met Helen for lunch, and after a few days of light eating, and having shaken the salt out of her system, Francesca was back, eyes wide at the menu. She booked a French outpost in Covent Garden, which didn't sound right to Helen. Not very Francesca. Of course, it was a good choice.

In good times, it would be all talk, later for the menu. Except the vibes were solemn, Helen was quiet and focused on looking at the options while reading little, eyes darting hither and thither, scanning.

Francesca watched, kept her head down to figure things out, then organised drinks and waters, circled back to the menu for a while, and once she had her plan of attack, launched in.

"Out with it."

"What?"

"Something's wrong."

She looked at Helen, and this in itself, a look of support, brought a tear to Helen's eye, which she wiped away from behind her spectacles.

"What's not wrong? Work. Family. Phil."

"OK, well, you decided last time you would look for a new job."

"Which I am."

"Good. Your family is a never-ending doom loop, so that's not going to change in a hurry. All you need to do there is compartmentalise, and get on with your own life. Do you want to hear about Phil? I mean honestly. Because I can tell you. But I don't have to."

Francesca stopped, gave a facial shrug. And waited.

Helen braced.

"It's like this. I can listen to you, and tell you everything will be fine, give you a few questions to ask him, things to think about. Like many of your English girlfriends might, but probably wouldn't. Or I can point out it's not working, it's not healthy, it doesn't move on, it's a dead end. And don't listen to your family with the relentless pressure of how they think you should be living your life."

"You and Simon never move on."

"Certainly not now, since I ended it last week."

"Oh, sorry."

"Nothing to be sorry about. Besides, it didn't matter if we move forward. It was a live in the moment thing. You want a family. For that, you need something that grows."

They sat in silence. Francesca shut up, for emphasis, to let it sink in. Another performance.

Francesca wanted to stretch an arm across the table, and put her cold palm on Helen's hand, which was in need of moisturiser after a tough day. But there wasn't a route through. So she leaned forward.

"I want you to get what you want, and look ahead to some light. If I upset you, or risk losing your friendship, so be it. I hear people's problems all day, and I nod and say it'll be fine. Because I don't give a shit."

A harsh finish so she put on a sympathy smile and leaned back.

"Can we get some water?" Helen asked, flagging down the waiter.

Helen felt the wine, dry in her throat, spinning her head among the noise and throng. She couldn't escape knowing that Francesca cared, and she either had to side with someone who wanted the best for her, or she would follow those happy to see her stuck, held where she was. The faces of the people who gave her positive vibes about sticking it out flickered in her thoughts. They purported to, but didn't want the best for her. Should she succeed at something, ever, it would be met with the gritted teeth and forced smile of resentment.

"If you ask me to never speak of this again, that's OK. We can meet, have a good time. Maybe that's not the best for us, though."

They were to be Francesca's final words on the subject.

"Let's eat. I have something that will amuse you."

The wine glasses were half empty which was enough. The place was busy and the glasses wouldn't be flying over. Francesca gave the waiter a look, gestured with a finger which hovered, switching above each glass in turn. He winked to a familiar customer he liked to accommodate.

The menu took some hefty blows from Francesca, after Helen commented that it all looked good. Too many options, they should keep it simple; four starters, five mains. And raise the care and quality attended to each. Strange price architecture, many dishes in the thirty to forty-pound range, several under twenty, too few in between. A little imagination in the wine list wouldn't go amiss, to accompany the pricey mains; this was the twenties. At other times, she might point some of these notes out to an experienced server who might see the feedback into the right ears. Once they had finished their meal of course. Yet the sweet young girl looking after them, who blushed when admitting it was her third day, via broken English learned via education and not yet bedded in by use in anger. Francesca worked through that they had a better common language and switched to French. She helped correct an error in the bill, smiled while doing so, and they left a good tip.

It was peak summer, and reaching thirty degrees during the day. Heat which imprinted the dirt and the filth into the paving slabs, no longer washed away by the rain. Which warmed the stenches and felt like it held the dry car pollution hanging in the air. Darker and visible as it left exhausts, no longer an innocent puffy water vapour floating away, but something caustic, threatening settling residue. A walk through central London and the tight streets surrounding Chinatown, dirtied with backed up with lorries and delivery trucks, all idling away at stopped traffic lights, created an insufferable spew for passers-by.

Street trees were green and thick, with squared holes carved out of them from the drip-drip of passing buses, shaking and fluttering from air movement and not from touch.

A time when dressing became easier. Don't wear much, and carry a light and well organised bag. Wear the whites and lights, and summer brights, and look out for flavoured oil threats and public transport grime. Take care not to brush things and don't lean. No threat of rain limited contingency plans, essential when twenty degrees in the sun and eleven degrees in the shade. For the young, street drinking in Soho, Fitzrovia, East London, spilling out across pavements, beer glasses piled up on pub window ledges, placed by feet, staff running loops outside, gathering empties. For the busier places, plastic, you drinking outside? To reduce breakages, *shrinkage* and glassings. White soles greying. Every beer garden worth its salt, full, with additional large outbuilding sheds with limited pumps. Just what you see here, mate.

Parks full, berugged with groups of drinkers and picnickers, with their staling, warming goods, clagging away and sticking to fingers. Rubbish left for others to clear, party balloons lodged in trees after tents and awnings have been packed away. A pink and silver number four stuck on a high limb. Sweet warming wafts of weed, each a tiny whodunnit.

The perfect time for mid lifers to spend indoors, in brighter, airier bars and lounging spaces. Windows and doors open, cold wines and fizz coming, served at table, giving life support. Plan and book ahead, the internet was all knowing.

For late lifers, the garden.

Most of this behaviour stretched out across the evenings, light until ten o'clock. Drunker citizens increased in sozzle. Gatherings morphed from the parks to the takeaways, to the queuing restaurants, while the street pubs of Soho remained flatline busy right through. The kebab houses, with their red neon-like isosceles trapeziums, selling their alcohol absorption solutions, their energy supplies to fuel young, grubby, grabby sex. Chicken cottages, the death row favourite and a nation's choice for theoretical last meals, deep frying their wings, breasts and thighs, shouldering them in their peppery, hot coats. Burger joints, fish and chips, and the high street hybrid: battered haddock and a lamb doner, under one roof.

In the suburban streets, brazen vixens and cool cats sat and lazed about wherever they pleased. Foxes hung out in the middle of the road, on car roofs, or wandering with sneak. Nose low, legs slowing and quickening in response to life and movement surrounding them, scurrying off to the fences, walls, and openings that gave them cover. Rough and scabby, a life lived harder than their bushier, brighter, country-based counterparts, but a life lived with less threat and panic.

Night terrorisers of rubbish bags left open and unshielded, of park litter bins, and park party detritus. Terrorisers of each other, with their savage night cries, communicating territory and strangling the celebration of the creation of life.

On steps, ledges, wide shelved bay windows, and under cars, local cats sat, away from walked dogs and the threat of those foxes. Clear from other warring cats, themselves with their planned escape routes over walks, through gates, via the flaps fitted within doors and windows.

Citizens celebrated these peak months, while for the homeless and animals, it was an easier outdoor life. Yet the heat came with a knowing itch. Heat was the enemy. Heat would become the end. The media capitalised. The moon and Mars were no alternative, despite the mad efforts of the rich. It was here or bust.

Elsewhere, floods in northeast India, Mongolia, southern Japan, southern Brazil, northeast Turkey, southern Italy, the Somalian coast. Landslides in Myanmar, Nepal, and southwest China. Heavy rain in Russia, the northern Vietnamese highlands. *Monsoon* rains in Bangladesh, Pakistan. Forest Fires in Ukraine, Greece. Tornados in the northern US, and wildfires in California. There's always been floods though, right?

11010
CHAPTER 26
Florence and Fiona and the environment: Steven & Josie ends

Fiona tried to steer Florence away from swiping tech, and toward reading something from their vast book collection.

"*You* never read them," she retorted, without malice, stating fact.

"I read a lot at your age," Fiona countered, with the natural dominance of adulthood, adding, "and when you're my age, you'll have a couple of full-time children feasting on any spare time you have. And making it to the end of the day intact will be your goal too."

She paused.

"You've got all this time and space for learning, exploring what you like and don't like. Make use of it."

Many would huff, but Florence took it in, and it registered. This fact alone told Fiona that Florence would be just fine, having seen her own siblings' less than delicate reactions to parental advice.

"Let's find a few books for you, something stretching. Sit down, read the first two pages of each. Maybe you'll get into one, and you can go from there."

"Remember, these books were written years ago, they did things differently there. The world changes, people change, so you're looking for ideas, themes. Then you can consider them against how the world is today."

Silence.

Florence had watched the tensions between Fiona and her grandmother. How they each saw the world. She knew Gran was young once, and that she would be the adult when Fiona was old. When Gran was dead. Bones. She would inherit a world shunted on from that which Fiona took over, a slow transition of power rather than baton passing. Watching Gran having to put up with the change about her, yet with power beyond previous generations. Boomer purse strings clinging to control, rather than stuck in the corner offering complaints. Florence understood the planetary inheritance she would receive from the Boomers and Generation X.

Motherhood was Fiona's core. The drive to find the right man, to build the beautiful home, that which give her the energy to get through everything the days slung at her. Once the fripperies and treats of youth were enjoyed and behind her, the career a mandated stepping stone only the super-rich could skip; to raise children was her goal. To show that the world could correct itself, that she could erase poor treatment and emotional distance from her own mother, and indeed both parents, and pass on love and affection. To nurture and set the world right again. It took a brave reset to undo many fault lines that run through families, and to avoid the line ending through despair.

Fiona saw a determination and singular focus in her daughter, through the façade of doubt and questioning. And whenever anger was directed at her, she sensed also an understanding of adult bullshit, lies, hypocrisy. The innocence of youth, growing into an enquiring mind of critical thought.

Fiona checked Theo was occupied, and gestured for Florence to move through to the living room with her. She prickled with a self-awareness of the focus she gave her eldest, but couldn't seem to shake it off despite her best efforts. Fiona pushed some hairs which were not in the way of her daughter's face to one side, tucking them behind her ears. She dropped her hand to her own lap. So that Florence sat apart from her.

"If you want a good life, a fun life, of achievements and pride, it's in your power. You're smart, you're intuitive. We're giving you the start everyone should have but few do. For those that lead an extraordinary life, they figure things out for themselves as well as take advice and guidance from parents, teachers. You will outgrow us. So, have a think, think about what your plan might be, and then I will help."

They hadn't quite been the words she had rehearsed, but they seldom were.

Fiona left her and went to see if Theo needed help with anything, since she had got on top of most of the day's must-dos. She reflected on some of her memories. Conversations with her own mother.

Florence pulled a few books down.

Pacing around his flat, Steven knew he couldn't delay any longer. Josie was pressing him as a serious option. And while it was convenient and pleasurable to have her on reserve for the odd dinner out, sex and company, it was becoming uncomfortable and stressful for him to continue, as the pressure built.

His inner monologue debated these viewpoints. Layer in his age and general loneliness and solitude from too many years living alone, and his alienation and distance from any form of deep love, and it created an (albeit flimsy) argument that at some point in life he had to commit to something. Yet while he felt he couldn't keep going on like this, where was the happiness or nobility to be found in settling. When younger, he imagined one reached a point in mid to late life where something changed and one had to reach acceptance. Yet the horizon never made this so. For to settle closed off all hope. Even at sixty-seven, that true love might be around the corner, and who could be bothered with the tedium of bad company.

He cycled through arguments and counter-arguments. Factuals and counterfactuals, both to work it through himself, and in figuring out how he would present this to Josie. How we would *do the telling*. For one had to hold back certain truths, yet it had to make credible sense with the redactions. He always had the evergreen fall back of 'we are just not right/the best fit for each other,' but this invited questions, further digging. Better to present something fuller, closed.

These unpleasant things which had to happen in the future, were both a mountain ahead, and a blip behind. The time ahead seemed vast, as it must for a hostage or someone in an emergency situation or dangerous incident. The next twenty-four hours to last forever, and then one day, two years ahead, it was all past, buried. No one cared anymore, all parties including the hurt had moved on.

The shock of the surprise end was something to be avoided. Although things had been rocky and spiralling down for a while now, he felt he had to zone out further, so that this became expected, a formality. To grind the system to a halt, so there was no way back. One had to take a run-up. It wasn't as extreme as a long-term relationship that has hit the rocks, where it would be so painful for all to terminate.

When one or both parties had to run it into the ground, to smash it to pieces, so there could be no rebuild. An affair that had to happen. A revenge act in return. As with many things, it was on a spectrum, and there was no future in this for one party. A unilateral fission.

He thought of the angles. He couldn't be *truthful*. One could be truthful if there were genuine irreconcilable differences – the desire for children, divergent world views, polarised libidos, questions on where to settle down long-term, or a fatal random or event-driven deal-breaker or revelation. Yet if it were a question of looks, intelligence, humour, sex, and all the rest of it, one must shield. He returned to old faithful – a lack of *fit*.

Although generic, a fit-for-all-purposes, Swiss army knife of an explanation, it would raise more questions than it answered. What did he mean? What did that even mean? Be specific. Is it the sex? Is she not fun enough for him? They have good sex don't they? They have fun don't they? Is there someone else? No, nothing like that. That could never be admitted to, if true or not. She knew they'd had a distant few weeks, but all couples go through ups and downs.

He worked it through and couldn't put it aside, as it circled through his mind over the next few days. He ate that up as his punishment. He would wait until the next time she called, make a plan to go to hers, and have the unexpected conversation.

It filled him with dread. It always did. Yet the world turned, and their lives needed this to be resolved.

All's fair and all that. She would move on. If they weren't right for each other, it was right for them. He hadn't wasted her time. Emotions evolve or they don't. It took a while to be sure. It wasn't personal or a judgment on her, they just weren't a match. He was certain of that. Christ, this was all a headache and painful for him. He wished he didn't have to go through the next day. He would get through it, and it would be history. It always was. Painful days played out for him two, five, fifteen, twenty years ago. And Christ, *he'd* been on the receiving end enough times.

Josie had wanted to meet out for breakfast somewhere in town, Marylebone perhaps. Steven was insistent that they started from her house and go from there. He'd come round. This didn't make a lot of sense, his keenness to travel her way was unusual. Nerves were raised, her body sending instinctive messages her brain was refusing to accept. Her hopes were that this was counter to her intuition and was in fact a good sign, he wanted to spend time at hers. Evidence of some effort, perhaps an improvement.

When he entered without a kiss and walked through, she knew what was coming. He sat down and began to spoke. The well-rehearsed lines of someone delivering a verdict, an execution. Not the best fit, best thing for us both. You're great, you know I like you. But, you know, different values and priorities. Think *you'll* be happier with someone you have more in common with.

"You will you mean."

"Both of us, Josie. Look, it's been fun."

Josie clutched at positives, highlighting some of the nights they had had, where *she believed* they'd had a great time, we have good sex don't we? Present tense.

"Of course," he confirmed, omitting that while it was agreeable, he was looking for something provocative, edgy.

Her head spun as the nervous energy that had built up since he phoned became heavier, with a thud, sinking down her arms and her torso until they felt weighty, dragging her down, in line with her mental state. The emptiness, the void of the future. Back to square one. The telling people. Carving out a narrative of mutuality to some, seeking solace and comfort with the truth in others.

As she highlighted positives, as she saw them, he kept words to a minimum as the finality of the outcome was made clear. Then the tears came, and with it the shame of further embarrassment. Inside she wanted to remain cool. Wasn't working out for me either. The toughs were able to muster a front of bad faith like that. The rest revealed how they felt. Some underlying human need that truth trump inauthenticity, no matter the vulnerability.

She recoiled and paced, unsure what to do with her hands. She knew, one hundred percent, that pride salvaging was all that was left. Yet she probed for an opening, to continue to talk. To prise open a desperate light of a possibility. Couples have ups and downs. The last few weeks with the flood had put her under stress, and what with work for the two of them.

His silence was unremitting.

This was advancing without pause, and her mind which processed ahead of everyone else in the room, was not staying apace, fogged by emotions. She needed to just stop the words, take stock, try and tie it down for a moment. Yet Steven was rolling it out, and he wasn't stopping.

He repeated how sorry he was. It was for the best. For each of them. This was hard for him too. You'll meet someone who is a great fit for you. You're beautiful, smart, fun.

No fool like a single, middle-aged fool, she thought.

"What's the fucking problem then?"

She seldom swore, an indication to him that she was accepting and going through the gears. And unpleasant as it was to go through in the moment, it showed him the road out of there, the way to the street. The walk, which step-by-step would take him to freedom and the future. And all that would remain might be an accidental bumping-into-her, a low probability event in London, even if they both remained in the city for forty years.

As he sat there in silence, staring at a plant, she filled a glass of water before standing and drinking it with a slight shake. Her spare arm wrapped around herself in a protective embrace. Body language she wanted to be rid of, alien to her in her professional guise.

She reviewed the things she had thought to herself over the last few weeks. The sex followed by quiet. The time he had things to be getting on with on a Sunday afternoon. Invites to join get-togethers which were passed up. Flooding. A lack of intimacy that she thought reflected the man. Once again she thought of her friends going through the lifestages. Hitting third gear at 35. And as she saw Steven sat down, while she paced, she remembered ditching her ex, both adopting similar positions in a different apartment. And the reflections of her message and the language *she* had taken advantage of, now *weaponised* against her. Swings, roundabouts. He had cried also.

She felt cross at Steven's callousness and gave one angry stab at the lack of care or support he had shown when her family needed help. Angry at herself for not ending it when that happened, given what had happened now. It mattered how a woman fell. It would be weeks in the rear mirror by now, and outside an agreeable window – a ratio of mourning time versus total relationship length.

Everything stopped, as he waited for her next move. And she further reviewed the awful behaviour. The invite to her friend's party which he couldn't make. When she had asked him whom he had told about her. Not many. And Victoria. Who saw this coming. One last humiliation to go.

She understood that this was final, and it wasn't something which could be negotiated or prevented. Her body felt separated, distant, from Steven, from it all.

"Enough," she said, pausing for a moment, then "just bloody go."

She turned her back on him, and put her hand to her mouth. Her eyes welled up with fury.

Stepping with care not to trip up on the edge of a rug, or create a clatter or anything that might shake the silent agreement, Steven left. The door lock closed. It echoed on the tiled floor.

Handed back her solo status, the world ordered that she resume her existence as a lone, atomised unit. Regardless of her connections, dependable friends, she once again faced the world on her own. To touch the physical world, to hang onto an armrest, steady oneself on a chair, or to move a mug to the edge of a table, were to connect with a new world. Changed in the support and protections it offered. And for days after, with the push of a shopping trolley, the hold of a bag, the lift of a pen or the nudge of a mouse. The feel of separation.

Her tightened stomach told her she would lose weight over the next month.

A feeling which is shocking in the moment and the direct aftermath, yet in the long term, trended to normality. Down the line, the solo artist went about their business alone and without a second thought, while elsewhere people were stuck in dull, habitual or even cruel, abusive relationships, dying on the vine. Awaiting their sentences. Go through this process once or twice, and come out the other side, positive about the next adventure, ready for *your time*. Go through it again, and the soloist hardened and accepted a new normal. Then the grief came from being with someone, beholden to their wants and needs, and their idiosyncrasies. The loss of independence, the horse-trading, the constant back-and-forth on plans, dependencies and commitments to a wider circle.

And what were we doing for food, *all the fucking time*.

Josie sat down and felt the numbness, the aching buzz in her shoulders and arms, the affliction of knowing these physical feelings were to be her short term future. Something which couldn't be shaken off at will, swerved via distraction or eroded through consumption. This would be with her for some time, and she would have to move through it.

Calculating how long they had dated, she figured she should get busy and get her act together. A sense of proportion.

For what purpose did the pain of heartbreak serve? Physical pain alerted on wellness, damage and threats. For the rejected, the searing depth and duration of the agony reinforced how terrifying it was to hand oneself over to the care of another. And to Josie, this seemed increasingly like a risk not worth taking, a fact which filled her with the dread of a void. A commitment of a life she might never make for fear of failure. That she would encircle herself with walls, and see others' pain from afar, and be grateful she had left that behind.

Unlike in youth, she could be grateful that this was a humiliation she could endure in private, if she could resist any public upset.

She thought through the routines which she would need to hook back onto. Increase reliance on the stability and trustworthiness of gym classes. Friends she could rely upon. Those that forgave the ups and downs of contact that came with a new relationship, or its ending. Some of the work events on rotation, regular dinners, which could pepper her diary, increase her general level of business, and get back to how she was before.

Returning to where she met Steven in the first place.

Getting out there again. Urgh.

She didn't know what to do with herself. Go to bed, to the gym, for a walk, phone someone? Looking around her she saw some things that needed to be done, and put herself into auto-pilot and moved about the place in between taking a break to stare at the wall. Whatever filled a typical Saturday at home, now also filled this one. When it moved from afternoon to evening, she poured herself many drinks.

Steven returned home and laid his keys, wallet, headphones down on the same table as ever. He sat down, relieved that was over and that he could move on, unencumbered by a painful future task, nagging away, one that was now behind him. Just like that. To be replaced by the pop-up reminders of the awfulness of his behaviour. He attempted to justify this by the bad behaviour he had himself suffered. It did not help. It served to underline that if he had suffered the indignity he had inflicted on Josie, he would be bitter. But what could one do?

A recruiter had been chasing him for thoughts on a potential role. He had delayed looking at it and getting back to him, a negative in itself. Not that they cared, as long as they could push him through their personal pipeline and workflow, from initial contact to discovery to validation. Through the interview stages to offer to negotiation to the deets, and through the three-month probationary period, onto the first anniversary. Everywhere he looked, humans as trafficked meat.

They had shared a video, which he played.

He leaned back, sinking into his sofa in a way which arched his back, and stared at the cornicing above the main window.

"One hundred percent automated... driving forces of... core of your business model... capability to integrate... huge range of data sources via our APIs... multiple touchpoints... evolving data layer... reducing operating costs... tailored customer-specific processes... out of the box... scale at own pace... non-technical users... scoring and rating... kick-start your digital programme..."

He kicked off his shoes, stretched his palms over his face, and pulled down before rubbing the corners of his eyes with his fingertips.

11011
CHAPTER 27
Garden Party: Annabel & Florence: Fiona & Harry

Luck had everything to do with it. Fortunate genetics, looks and smarts. Blessed to be born to balanced, successful parents. Given a fine education, socialised with other future successes from her formative years and beyond. The connections and opportunities to open doors in her first job, and a couple of moves thereafter. In timing. Born just on the right side of the property price surge in London. In the wrong relationship at the right time, sharing a home with a partner who was achieving much himself, and when they split on good terms, agreed good terms that meant she could take on the rest herself without moving. With an inheritance. This culminated in the small mews house Francesca owned in Marylebone, cobbled of street, with a patio and garden. A good size for London. Small to modest, anywhere else.

A Saturday afternoon and a classic English day transpired. One that belonged to another age. Bright, high, fiery sun against clear blue. Not a chemtrail in the sky. The occasional cloud drift, for the romance. Occasional light breeze, to serve as a refresher, to move the air around and cool a little.

The last time she hosted many of this group it was white exposed brick walls, awash with plants, an occasional sprinkling of artwork. Now challenging yet sombre colours, *elevated* drama in the art collection, classic pieces of furniture. Book shelves that contained a balance of classic paperbacks in black, green and white, coffee table art and photography tomes, history and *smart-thinking* non-fiction. Orange spines, not airport reads.

Sombre greys, dark turquoises, moody burgundies, contrasted with mustards, splashes of lime green. Photography, vases, the odd curiosity, little without a story. Oddities bought to be able to fit a minimalist setting, whenever time dictated the switch.

A hubbub was building as a critical mass had arrived. A gathering in the garden, and a few hanging out in the kitchen, making things happen.

Beyond the rear glass doors, large tiles to step out onto, which led away down the right side. To the left, two split squares of lawn, supporting two loungers and a large sun umbrella. To the right of the path, beds thick with shrubs, herbs, white roses. The border to the left, small trees and further plants. No plink plink of poppies, no flash of pansies, no iris fizz. The overarching colour of the garden one of the fifty hues of green on display, from the garden itself, and various trees belonging to neighbours. A monochrome in green. The density of central London meant the presence of high buildings in various directions, yet her place toward the end of terrace, with a short building backing on, created privacy and space which yielded to summer joy.

On good terms with her neighbours, a few of whom were invited to join, meant no aggravation with the happy, sun drenched vibes of noughties house. The type found on Thames boat parties on a Sunday afternoon, comprising pilled-up thirty and forty-somethings keeping on.

A large round outdoor dining table with half a dozen chairs, plus the loungers and some borrowed chairs were being filled. Italian snacks, cold meats, cheeses, and other deli staples were dotted about, already getting messy with the glasses, full and empty, purses and phones, and other party ephemera.

The rear of the garden which contained a number of dark shrubs, and which had potential to home a modest summerhouse-cum-office, had been designated the area for smoking. At least until attending parents and children had gone home. All planned and taken care of, a pair of ashtrays left on a short garden wall.

Francesca buzzed about, filling drinks, pushing the food, ensuring the kitchen was being cleared and recycled, keeping the whole machine oiled and moving. One thing she took care of was not to overfeed people, so they became sedentary messes, losing the will and fizz to enjoy themselves. To begin fantasising about bed and not each other. As she moved about, everyone took notice, the men, the women, children, of someone whose looks and personality were there to be enjoyed, by whomever was present.

Fiona and Julian had arrived with Florence, while Theo had been outsourced.

They sat as a three at the large table, Florence *fascinated* by the people and conversations happening around her. Fiona kept an ear out for some of the detail which was flowing through her ears, trying to establish if this needed managing via distraction or a new location. It seemed innocuous, for now, she thought, whereby Carl and Michael walked through the door, clutching bottles of spirits.

They greeted Fiona and Julian, and Florence was introduced.

"Take it easy, fellas," she warned, eye-shifting toward her young daughter.

"No fucking problem," said Michael, winking. Michael was one of those people who thought they could speak in hushed tones, but for which a whisper was impossible. They went to get a drink.

Could be a long day.

"Mum," Florence tugged at Fiona, "are they?"

"Yes."

"They must have a giant bed."

"Probably."

Fiona drank.

Julian had been approached by a spry old gentleman is his mid-sixties, a money-man from another time. Talking with lucidity about the past, once he had ascertained Julian knew of his world, or at least the objectives and outcomes.

Fiona knew Julian would be finding this interaction tiresome, which gave her a shot of antagonistic pleasure. She stayed well away.

Carl and Michael were talking with a young couple they'd met inside, when Michael turned up the volume as the third swig of alcohol hit his throat.

Florence looked at Fiona. Fiona drank.

The young couple chuckled and they clinked glasses, happy to be among fun.

"Man, the clubs we went to. So much outrage. Discretion advised, mind. Much easier for your generation, I bet. It's all out there, trumpeted on social media."

Michael went on.

"When someone came out, most of the time, it was a case of 'er, yeah, obviously'. You needed to know where you were on the pecking list. Whom have they already told? Whom are they telling next? Like the announcement of an engagement, it's an order of priority thing. Rank me, bitch!"

Fiona knew the day could either involve moving Florence around, steering her away from off-colour conversations, or her upping her drink intake so as to relax about the whole thing. She felt on good form, and the lack of a group of other upper to middle class mums relieved her of competitive duties. They knew what they were in for, it had been a conscious decision to let Florence in.

"Julian, get the music turned up a bit?" she asked, hoping for some cover.

A couple of other children lay about in the middle of one of the lawn squares, occupied by technology.

"Go and introduce yourself to those two."

"All right," and over she went. No wallflower.

Fiona had no idea what Carl was talking about, but the antics demanded she went on over to partake.

As the breeze flowed through, so it brought with it the distinct whiff of skunk. Fiona watched as Julian got up and sloped off to the end of the garden, as if going to check out the peat beds. God knows what they'll be doing upstairs, she thought.

She texted Julian: "Nothing harder than that today."

He turned around and gave her the thumbs up. An ambiguous response which meant nothing to her.

The doorbell shrilled. A guest moved to open the door, but Francesca appeared and ushered him away, "Go through, go through."

It was Helen, in a better mood, having received a job offer in the week.

"Voila," she said, thrusting forth a bag containing a couple of bottles of fizz she had picked up on the way. Something for Francesca to put away and never use, in all likelihood.

"Here, have a glass of this, let me introduce you to Michael & Carl," she said, leading her.

"So there we were, an old girlfriend and me, we'd been shagging all day, and the room service turned up with the trays, and came in, and oh my god, the room must have stunk."

Helen sipped her drink, wide-eyed.

"The poor people working in these hotels. Imagine bringing food up all day long to horny couples going at it, while slaving away. One after the next. Not just couples either, I can tell you that. Four dinners brought up at a time!"

"This is Carl. This is Michael."

"I'm Helen."

"It's party confession time, Helen," Carl reassured.

Helen knocked back some fizz which kicked her in the nose, right on the cocaine patch.

"The only time we ever had sex outdoors, in the woods, a family turned up on a walk. Phil fell in the nettles trying to hide. I covered up and ran."

"Oh, we like you Helen."

"I'm Fiona, these two are the living end."

"They're ace."

Fiona pointed out Florence, and Helen looked on, trying her best to put on an effortless *so-delightful-for-you* smile, while also wishing to communicate her personal sense of loss to Fiona, a problem shared. Fiona switched to the burdens, stresses and thanklessness of it all.

"Bloody exhausted all the time, keeping up with it all. I mean, I don't go in for all the competitive mum nonsense, I just try to let them be themselves."

Helen gave her the *yeah, right* look.

Francesca was having a good drink, slugging, and let everyone get on with it; they were adults, they could find their way around a kitchen.

Someone was being snobby about art concepts.

"Ah, fuck the rules," Francesca declared, "when I was at school, endless lessons about how you don't draw an outline. They don't exist. Alice Neel, just draws a bloody great blue outline around everything and goes from there."

An unexpected gust picked up and the edges of a tablecloth billowed and some napkins unfurled themselves, as those nearby placed something on top of them. It disappeared leaving stillness and a superb day remained intact.

Annabel felt a rare warmth. It was hot in the shade.

She took the time while not in conversation with anyone, to watch the feint ripple of a large deciduous tree a few houses down, a bristle of summer green. It took a few moments to confirm a distant and moving speck was a bird and not a drone. She questioned her general sense that things were becoming more surreal as the digital world took hold. The warmth and the chatter around her should have given her comfort. In years past, even with a hangover and a relationship going south, she would put the bad aside and liven herself up with the party.

The beauty of the surroundings and how privileged and charmed they were, brought home the people less fortunate, living in desperation.

"Pass the artichokes!" she overheard.

Her thoughts turned to the people of Hiroshima, who went to work on a similar morning, sunny, blue sky, and were obliterated by a flash and four-thousand-degree heat from something they didn't know existed. She wondered what may be in production now, that might yield such extraordinary instant devastation. An unknowable threat to the lay person. And of course, it was a day like this in New York, that extraordinary day.

Annabel felt bad for herself for feeling this way. The world throughout history was people enduring bad things while others prospered. Life on the beach in Israel didn't stop when bombs rained down on Palestine. If it did stop, life would cease everywhere. For brutal, damaging things happened at all times. Behind closed doors, in the city, in suburbia, in the country. Children, families, terrorised by parents or siblings, step-families. In nature, savage ends were meted out, the world over, each second.

In her head, she had a word with herself, to put things to one side, have a good drink, let herself go, and then she looked around, at the people, happy on the face of it. Yet what were the unseen stories and histories underlying these individuals on a prize day. For one walked among abusive relationships, addictions, domestic sexual savagery, and countdowns to suicide.

Francesca appeared. She sat down beside Annabel, and wanted to reach out, to put her hand on her arm, or her shoulders, but she looked too delicate, that she might flinch and the gesture create an awkward moment. A brittle soul sat before her.

Francesca took five out from shepherding people, and lit a cigarette.

"I heard you were caught up in the gallery protest. Were you OK? Are you OK?"

"I got a fright. I thought it was terrorism. There was nowhere to go, I'd have been fucked."

"Were you with anyone?"

"No."

"Don't go to one of those shows for a while. You may have some trauma. When you do, give me a call, I'll go with you. OK?"

"Thank you."

They talked small.

Francesca stubbed out the last two minutes of her cigarette, feeling things getting pulled out of kilter, from the kitchen outward. Dismissing her easy attitude, she reverted to being all hands on deck.

"Does your thirst needs slaking? Spritzer?"

"Sure, that'd be nice."

Fiona was helping Florence tidy her hair, when behind a small tree, a lady in her seventies declared that "men either come too quickly or take forever," and howled.

"What does that mean?" Florence asked, knowing what it meant.

Fiona ignored all of it and knocked back some wine, and went to get a refill.

"Do you want another Elderflower drink?"

"Yes please."

Francesca returned to Annabel.

"Have you met Florence?" Francesca asked, already beckoning Florence over as Annabel responded that she had not, hoping that the power of youthful exuberance would bridge and lift two kind souls.

"Florence, Annabel. Annabel, Florence."

"Hello," said Florence, first, thrusting out her hand.

Annabel was charmed and took it and shook it.

"How do you do?"

"How do you do?" Florence answered.

"You'll get on," said Francesca, and choosing her words with care, "you're both into nature, and this beautiful, tragic world."

Francesca departed, leaving Florence with the opportunity for an education, to see what she could learn from the well-informed. Someone had done the same for Francesca at such an age. It was a seared memory.

"Did you know frogs can't reproduce because of contraception ending up in rivers?"

Florence opened with, to Annabel's astonishment.

"Did you know the rubbish you dispose of is buried under hills, and they put grass back on top, so it looks like countryside again?"

"No?"

"Yup. And do you know what a fatberg is?"

"No?"

Florence's eyes widened. Here was a smart, elegant woman, talking her language with interest. Something she didn't get at home.

Annabel caught Fiona's eye as she looked around, and gave a nod, intended to indicate everything was fine, her daughter was in safe hands. The reveal of a genuine smile.

An environmental disaster-off ensued, as another child wandered over, around Florence's age, with little of the knowledge or nous. Helen joined them.

"My dad buys a new car every two years, but *it's a green car*," Annabel offered.

"Our car is massive," Florence added, "and we block the roads into school, and sit idling when mum's phone needs to charge."

Annabel looked up at a carefree Fiona, gregarious and free-spirited. Well-oiled and rolling back the years. She felt a pang, a twinge. To those that accepted the habits and nature of the world as it was, children, comfort, wealth, social standing, days like these were bestowed upon. As Annabel tortured herself with the cruelty of it all. The punchline, a joyous laugh from Fiona and the couple she was talking to. About what it wasn't obvious. Middle-class anxiety shaming, or other fripperies.

Florence caught her looking over as she heard her mum, and turned to look back.

"They've been *smoking* again," commented Florence, rolling her eyes.

"I'm sure they haven't been," she said, her eyes turning up at the ends as a sly grin drifted across her face, as the clouds did above.

As Florence turned back, Annabel watched as Fiona sniffed, and excused herself to go indoors.

"Tell me more. Something complex?" asked Florence, taking some effort to get her mouth around the last word.

Annabel thought for a second.

"Broken incentive structures?"

"What's that?"

"Yeah, what's that?" enquired Helen.

Annabel looked at Helen, then continued.

"The people in charge, making the laws and the rules," she said, seeking a nod from Florence, which she was given.

"Are they voting for things that are going to make themselves rich at others' expense? Are there incentives for them to vote that way?"

Florence digested.

"If your councillor votes to build a power station opposite your house, and he owns a Power Station Building Limited company."

"I get it. They're all in China, anyway," added Florence.

"He would vote that way, wouldn't he?"

The other child was puzzled, left behind.

"Water wars," declared Florence, above birdsong, as the music quietened between tracks.

"What do you know about them?" enquired Annabel.

"Where there's not much water," Florence went on.

"Where water is *scarce*," added Annabel.

"Scarce. Got it. Countries end up fighting over it."

"And what's causing this?"

"I didn't get that far. Sprinkling our lawn all the time."

Annabel laughed, "That probably doesn't help, but there's not much households and you and me can do to help."

She gave Florence a moment.

"Glad I'm leaving before the water campaign at work," Helen muttered to Annabel, "that has failure and stress written all over it."

"Dad's always going on about growth."

"Growth trashes the planet. So does no growth. Think about that."

"That's good. Ammunition. But he says everything we have is because of energy."

"That's the problem. Curl your brain around that one," challenged Annabel.

Florence stopped and they took a breather. It paused her, and she felt stuck.

Annabel interrupted an expanded silence, "Have you been on a protest?"

"No. When I'm older I guess."

"Go now. Make your mum take you. Make a banner, dress up, it's fun."

Annabel looked at Fiona.

"Is it supposed to be fun?"

"Sure, it's participating, sharing experiences with others."

Annabel opened her arms and looked skyward.

Florence mirrored her and then walked close and gave her a hug.

As they finished, Helen caught Annabel's face drop.

"Sorry," she said, shaking her head, as she walked inside.

"Oh no. She's upset."

"She's all right," Helen lied.

"You'd like our friend Barney's dog. Here, I'll show you some photos."

"No, I want to know she's OK," Florence said, staring at the doorway. As Jess would, thought Helen.

Annabel returned after tidying herself. And giving herself a talking to for being open about harsh topics with a child. Who had had enough to contend with in relation to their mental health these last few years.

She sat down.

Florence and Helen looked at her.

"Listen," said Annabel, taking Florence's hands, "people always think things are falling apart, always have done, always will."

"Maybe they finally are."

Annabel was conscious she was giving the talk Barney gave to her.

"Do your bit, stay informed, get involved with something if it interests you. Get people to help."

"I will do."

Annabel thought about what terrible horrors people around the world might be enduring right at that moment. It was a mercy that Florence didn't think in those terms, for now.

Fiona joined them as Annabel was starting to speak.

"Don't forget to read," Annabel said, tipsy, "veh important."

"Like what?"

Annabel rattled off some of the junior canon.

"Maybe not yet. Build up to them. Too old for her?" Annabel asked Fiona.

"Possibly. I'll have a look."

Fiona and Annabel got acquainted. Helen sloped off for resources. She would talk with Barney about Annabel.

Annabel complimented Fiona on her budding centrist.

Helen dropped off a glass of water with Annabel, indicated she should sink it, and went back for a large cold glass and snacks for herself, as the heat peaked.

Helen stayed small. Slipping in to join a few random guests, holding her plate, excusing herself from anything other than listening in for the foreseeable future. They were getting deep into something, slurring and baying, "Opinions are not truth or facts, merely the way one sees it. Whatever *it* is."

Philosophical stuff, Helen thought, chowing down a Danish open sandwich, with its sharp pickling and tickle of fennel.

"What are they?" one of the gentlemen asked.

"Herring."

"Urgh, minging," he declared.

"You can't say that, she's eating."

"What about those?"

"Crispy onions and rare roast beef," confirmed Helen.

"Call yourself a foodie?" one of the men bawled at the other.

Helen interjected.

"I was sat at a table with Phil in Suffolk, and there was a family across from us, and the gran, must have been seventy, give or take. She'd never seen a mussel before. Her daughter had a bowl. She asked if you ate the whole thing!"

Cue the kind of raucous laughter fuelled by drink, for something which said sober in the office would get little response. Booze, that which raises the tides for all jokes. Likewise, the worst stories told by celebrities on talk shows, bringing the house down. Helen was aware that Phil featured in her stories.

Francesca introduced Annabel to Harry Reaves and slipped off in a way which was obvious to them, as if a cartoon puff of air evaporated behind her. Between two people with fewer social skills, or on one side of a pair, there could have been awkwardness, but they were easy, good-looking types. Harry wore black jeans and a plain, well-cut, pure white T-shirt, and looked like he would wear a leather jacket were it not for the weather. Out of the light, he took his sunglasses off, no poseur happy to struggle with their vision to pull off cool, his soft blonde locks framing a pale boyish face, spoilt shabby with stubble.

Interesting, thought Annabel, while also reticent to engage in any optimistic romantic endeavour, or even daydream. Except behind Annabel, Fiona was looking over, and giving Harry the kind of unmistakeable, unequivocal look of attraction and invitation. The look that said yes, whatever the question.

An acquaintance of Francesca who knew Annabel came over to play gooseberry, and so Harry offered to get drinks for the three of them. As he approached the table holding drinks, and began to organise jugs, flick the cap off a beer, Fiona looked around, and ditched her white wine into a large plant pot to her left, and joined Harry at the table.

They exchanged a few words, and Harry helped pour her a wine. She didn't stick around, but looked him straight in the eye. "Find me on LinkedIn. Fiona Wyatt," and she stepped away, joining an older couple to the side who looked like they needed an injection of pace.

A turn up for the books, Harry thought. Not unprecedented, but a rare dish served up, no grift required.

11100
CHAPTER 28
Fiona and Harry have sex and hang out: Helen and Phil: A concerned Barney meets Annabel for lunch

Harry had to stretch to switch the radio off as the jazz was interrupted by adverts, which they both tried to ignore for twenty seconds or so before realising they couldn't. Mobile offers. Retail sales.

They went at it hard for a few minutes in silence, save the birds outside and a distant mower, until Fiona climaxed. High octane. Their first time together and they had found their way through the awkwardness. Should Harry get a condom (no need). Was it her *cunt* or *pussy* that felt good (whatever) – some found the former too coarse, some the latter too feline.

Fiona rolled off from straddling him and they fell on their backs, all arms and legs, a sweaty mess of expressed energy, their bodies exhilarated and spent, breathing life into them, carried away on the pleasure they had sought and realised. Lordy, did Fiona feel it in her hips and thighs, straightening away the stiffness as she moved her legs around on the duvet, hitched up in ridges beneath them.

Harry's place.

Fiona looked up at the low ceiling, with fine cracks forming in one corner, and in need of a lick of paint. No cornicing. The small white paper and wire lampshade, not out of place in student digs. Clothes hung over the end of his cast iron bed. Photography equipment on the table in the corner opposite, next to a scatter of man fragrances and jewellery sat on a lacquer tray, which was one thing to her taste. Two coffee cups next to the bed on his side. Little attention to interior design, much attention to having sufficient condoms and sex toys close to hand.

"Wowsers," was all she could muster as Harry's sweat clung to her thighs and stomach, cooling her as her breathing steadied. Neither of them spoke another word, staring at the ceiling, bathing in a pure physical pleasure celebration.

After a few minutes, Harry and his youth rolled to his side and sprung up, to further open some windows. Fiona watched him do this, eyes scanning from shoulders to buttocks and to the backs of his knees, which somehow looked sexy and arousing. As he turned to come back Fiona put a hand up, asking him to stop, so she could scan his front, taking in his lean chest and all the rest.

From the starting gun, it was obvious to both and therefore unspoken between them, that this wasn't to be *the great romance*. That Fiona wasn't to leave her marriage behind to pursue her new found one true love. Harry wasn't to be world's best stepdad. Fiona wouldn't be taking on the renovation of Harry. Yet their connexion was undeniable and needed to be lived through. They knew that although the runway might be of short order, it stretched in front of them.

The sun was away at the front of his flat, so the windows let in the warmth from the blazing day. Harry passed water to Fiona who took long, refuelling gulps, before gasping, as if underwater for too long. After Harry had drunk, he turned the radio back on.

Harry asked if she minded if he smoked. Not if she could have one, as she did on occasion at the bottom of her garden, unbeknownst to all except Florence, she who nothing got past. He grabbed the stacked silver cigarette case and Zippo, and offered Fiona a tab. He lit it for her. Fiona felt the last two decades ebb away, leaving her present in her twenties, carefree. Life seen and lived as tens of thousands of independent segments, compartmentalised, rather than of one whole.

Their mutual acceptance of what this was, gave an opening for sure-fire honesty and straightforwardness when they talked about sex, their preferences, their experiences. Fiona had had both flavours of threesomes at university. Harry had a thing for gingers, the occasional chubby lover, and had a side benefits situation with an ex; they called each other when they needed it (currently inactive). Fiona slept with an 'old man' when she was young and on holidays. Further details were not forthcoming, though she laughed to herself at the memory. They smoked and let it all flow. They were free.

"Are we leaving these butt plugs in for the time being?" she asked.

"Yeah, they're enough of a bitch to get in in the first place," Harry clarified.

Fiona clutched her head and mock wailed, before rolling over and kissing Harry while they laughed at themselves, "I'm forty-four Harry," she confirmed.

Harry blew a smoke ring, something Fiona had not seen done in years.

Never thinking this would be possible, she bathed in the sweat and the grime, the residual lube, the slept in sheets and the carefree filthiness of it all, conscious that after showering before leaving, and with a repeat at home, she would be her usual super clean self. Enjoying in private, over the next few days, the feeling of bitten nipples, a spanked arse and the working over she and Harry had given each other.

Fiona lay there, the salience of her large diamond engagement ring clear to both, as she toyed with it, as if at home. She felt no need to remove it, adding spice to the situation, the drama and the raunch of it all. And it existed as a reminder that this was temporary. Harry got off on it, ensuring as he spooned her to reach down along her arms to her fingers, so his fingers brushed her rings and they shifted on her fingers, as he moved into her. Peccadillos that existed within the parochial coming together of two individuals, and the secrecy of their time together. To be known to and enjoyed by them. Who didn't want or fantasise about a clandestine coming together of that nature? The essence of a life well lived, despite the somewhat lowbrow surroundings.

Harry showed her his photography. Fiona wondered how many times that portfolio had been opened and shut next to a new fuck. How many times he had uttered 'These were taken in Vienna.'

This was, however, helpful; it kept things boxed. It meant that she always had *'how many women have you done this with before, Harry?'* in reserve if her marriage ever came up as a barrier. She was annoyed with herself that these moves were already being imagined in her head, when she should be going with the flow. A great escape. A rest from her life, the children, the to-do lists. And satisfaction when she looked at Julian.

Harry lay there in utter quiet. No push to find the next words. She curled herself around his arm which lay down by his side. No clichéd arm around her, no nuzzling in for cuddles, yet two people connected. Fiona thought of the two track life she was enjoying in this moment, of a daughter, of a son, who had no idea where she was, what she was up to. An adjunct to a normal life. How was it allowed that adults could shoulder these betrayals, allowing the years of steadiness to reason their actions, while their young go on innocent of the whole thing? She smiled at the idea of her mother cheating on her father, in bed with a younger man while Fiona was at school. It seemed a laughable notion, but why not? Could she be sure? And what of Julian? Was this not what he enjoyed, an island escape? No. To her, this was a response, not an active doing. He pursued, enabled; Fiona responded, and not like-for-like. She wondered how it would feel to stab him, if provoked, with the knowledge that she had allowed someone else into her. And yes, she enjoyed it. What might come after a revelation like that. Perhaps a mutually assured construction of a balanced future, after she had weaponised his actions back on him, with the threat that, done once, could be repeated. Like falling off a log.

Feeling that she had turned bitter, she lightened the mood, and shook herself.

"What a wonderful, simple life you have," she stated after a while, "so... free."

"None of us are free. I've got plenty of commitments, and freelancing, the money doesn't flow in by itself."

Fiona paused for a moment.

"You look like you've found a niche."

"Yeah, nowadays," he answered, as his phone pinged.

Fiona couldn't help wonder whom that was. A girl, maybe. Yet he worked through his phone at an open angle, signalling he had nothing to hide. Then again, he might know that was harmless. She would note if the phone started being set aside face down, or put on silent, or kept trousered when indoors. For Fiona, this was a pure fling, and temporary pleasure, that was one hundred percent certain. Yet the learned behaviours of youth were streaked through her, never undone. The jealousies and reactions embedded at eighteen would surface at eighty.

"I've found some reliable guys to work with. There's a lot of flakes, promises. That's the trick. Don't let people down, find people the same."

He paused and they were quiet.

"Do you want a beer, glass of wine?"

Fiona calculated the backstory, booze breathe and whether she had to drive later that day. Lunch with one of the mums. Not that that was much of a thing now the children were older, but Julian wouldn't be interested into digging into that particular event.

"What are you having?"

"Just a beer, but I can open something. Have whatever you want."

Not the words. These were the words of any reasonable host. But the softness of the words, the sincerity and warmth. The battles of home felt distant.

"I'll have a beer and a cigarette," she declared, lying back and pulling him on top of her, "and then I'd like to do that again, before I have to go."

Harry disappeared and left Fiona in a ceiling trance, leaving her body to enjoy its moment of calm after expenditure.

He returned and left a beer on the side, which went untouched until halfway during sex when Fiona reached across and slugged back a deep glug by moving her neck to below the line of the bottle.

When they were done Harry listened as Fiona regaled a little about her life, where she came from and where she was at. If they were the same age they would be different and suited, but not a proposition.

Harry brought up the garden party which made them laugh and Fiona cringe, but it was a soft afternoon of humour and honesty.

Fiona showered and was grateful Harry had a cleaner. They kissed at the door and kept it loose. She would be in touch.

Phil never complained about food, except the time his pizza delivery was delivered to and accepted by the wrong address. Apoplectic at the thought of some thieving random chowing down on his bespoke creation, a set of toppings he alone could order. While he sat around for another half an hour waiting for a corrective order to be completed. He implored them to ensure this one reached him unscathed, but didn't give them too much abuse, as, well, they still had to prepare it. His capacity to overlook any number of issues in eateries: booking problems, blandness, cleanliness, atomic lighting, lazy cheffing, order cockups, was quite something. Issues with drinks, now that was a different matter. Wrong type of beer dropped off, elapsed time of drink preparation, other patrons cocktailing his simple drink order into the distance, being nickel and dimed over a splash of soda water. These received a proportionate response. To Helen this combination of approaches showed undemanding weakness on the food front, and alcoholism. The worst of both worlds.

Holding a beer in his left hand at a slight angle, which would be a spillage hazard if it were ever full for more than a moment, Phil swigged away, switching between short gulps and long pulls of his mainstream bottled lager. Nothing fancy. As he shook the bottle nearing empty, which was full six minutes ago, he remembered when he was a boy, his parents cradling a tiny glass of wine for a not insubstantial amount of time. Sipping. Now it was 250ml and back it went. He switched up the tunes and sat back, making the initial inroads into the label on his bottle, made easier from the confluence of the coolness of the fridge and the warm ambient temperature. The label eased back and creased like a heavy drape. He relaxed, thinking of nothing beyond the moment, and of which direction to take the playlist in. Life washed over him as the cool bitter liquid and its froth and fizz flowed over his tongue, hitting the sourest receptors at the back of his cheeks, which wrinkled.

Having thought she had carved out an evening at home, alone, where she could crack a few chapters of her book with a couple of glasses of wine, midweek, Helen found herself descended upon by her sister in urgent need of support, who phoned once while Helen was walking home (which could be ignored) and then again (which could not, by Helen at least). 'Fuck,' she thought to herself. And while she was pissed off, she felt backed into a corner, counter-intuitively, in a good way. Change wasn't just coming; it was being forced upon her. And this was what she needed. Her assertiveness went up in these situations, she found the inner strength and steel to dish it out, and her sisters would be getting it with both barrels too. Whatever load was going to be dumped on Helen, would need to be shared by others.

As she arrived at home, and upon seeing lights, her quiet night with a book had been ruined beyond any recognition, and would be parked for another evening. A better way forward than letting free-flowing bile to flow in one sole direction – toward Phil. She would shift her evening until the next day, and if need be she would vacate to a library, turn her phone off, and *fuck the world*. What was she delaying anyway? Mere leisure time. Which underscored the inaction she was complicit in, enabling her drift.

They greeted each other, with no move whatever from either toward a kiss or a hug. Helen surveyed an untidy kitchen, spying the plate and knife used to make a sandwich, the guilty drops of tomato seeds and nuts from granary bread scattered on the surface top, two sliced cheese wrappers discarded to the side. No ma'am, Columbo was not required at the scene of any long-term relationship, the automated patterns of behaviours, learned over half a decade or longer. Sexual attraction in moments like these were a world away. She made a passing remark relating to the mess, heard her own mother, and retreated to the bedroom.

"I've got a load of shit to deal with. Clean this up, please? Turn that down. Put your big headphones on. The ones you spent all that money on."

She had him there. He preferred the big audio experience, exhausting noise pollution into the airwaves.

"And with the drink again. Can't you go and play football or something?"

Phil plugged his large, wireless headphones in, which were fortunate to still contain some charge, and rejigged his playlist. Servers somewhere in the Americas flicked ones to zeroes and back again, as the music was reassembled and slung into his ears. Delivery systems expired the earth's resources, as the music accelerated his drinking and the rate he disposed of crafted green bottles, high quality packaging. Somewhere, a bird trapped in manmade refuse, cried.

Annabel woke from an uncomfortable, fitful dream. Half caught by paralysis, struggling to wake, she was glad to see the ceiling and shift her light legs, and push the duvet back. Her dream consisted of the wrong persons in the wrong roles. Reverted to childhood, her aunt now her mother, her father replaced by an older man she had met in real life, in recent days. She recalled disjointed sections to the dream, some words said, deeds done, but the overall arc was lost on her. Elements of her dream would run in parallel to her day, stepping in, leaving mood music in the background.

It was earlier than she would have liked. One of the great ironies of this depression, the longer waking hours she had to suffer.

Barney had insisted they did something, intimating he had something to discuss. Her intuition was that they would be talking about her, and not him. In case she was wrong, she committed. Challenge or commit.

The Bush Telegraph had ignited. Helen had spoken with Barney about comments made by Annabel at the garden party, and her general concern. Going environmental mental with a pre-teen. She clued him up that she would be leaving work herself and not on the best terms. Sharp exit. They had better get her a fucking gift. All the years, her donations toward leaving presents never seemed to rebalance when she left a job herself. A quirk of maths, perhaps. Barney disagreed. Someone, somewhere, was enjoying all the leaving gift spoils.

Barney had declared a rare want of lunch and a drink. Annabel found somewhere on Bermondsey Street. It would be noisy she told him; boisterous and hot, until the roast dinners had been devoured, the people sated. Upon which a new wave of young, all-day drinkers would in all likelihood descend, and fire the energy levels up. He agreed. He wanted to knock things about a bit, talk with the drink. Without the high drama of the silence of a walk or the hard-surfaced clatter of a modern restaurant. When he was fine with it being a good idea that Jess stayed at home, the alarm bells rang.

Annabel chose to walk the long, arched, brick tunnel, where she had clubbed in years gone by; it wasn't obvious from the closed black doorways if the venues remained open. Thick red 'don't even fucking think about parking here' lines traced her path. The cold air cellar-sharp, she emerged into the light, and warm architecture, small businesses and the eateries that serviced such areas in midweek. Over the street, having a look across at her, a young man with blonde-ginger hair and matching beard, decked in black with white pumps and a sling-across bag, carrying a white coffee cup. A couple lumbered trolleyed baggage from a car toward their destination, disappearing behind a delivery van, and a young man in red and black hurried up and down the street, into this doorway and that. A pub with traditional tiling, common throughout London, cracked and weathered. She peered inside, and it was beige and pine, flowers, an all seating dining venue. Over the road, their down-to-earth destination. A wooden door with frosted glass imprinted with clear lettering of the establishment name. A mix of leather booths and standard tables down one side for the diners, standing room for the drinkers at the bar opposite.

They met at their booking time, mid-afternoon, peak gravy, and Barney went to the bar and ordered lunch for them. Chicken and a Sweet Potato and Mushroom Wellington. A bottle of white wine. He returned with wine and glasses, and a numbered wooden spoon in a plant pot.

He didn't fuck around.

"I'm worried about you."

"*I'm worried about me*," was the honest response.

She let out a half smile, at his caring face and solemn tone. He almost looked rugged in his plaid shirt. He *would* be OK, she thought, seeing the glinting assertiveness. It needed time and some luck.

Her fragile eyes shook him from the peace he had felt that weekend, going about his business.

"Take a break, have a holiday."

"And go through all the testing shit? The risk of ending up in a quarantine hotel, eating gruel. Camps. Papers, please. No thanks."

He understood her concerns.

"Most of Europe has lost it. They have gone fucking insane. Police thugs batoning people in the streets, an emergency law change away by an authoritarian leader from going further. You know I love Paris?"

Barney nodded.

"Fuck Paris, Barney," she said with venom.

He glanced at the tables across from them, full of transitory Europeans.

A few of them looked across, which Annabel caught.

"Fuck Paris," she said, louder.

She drank and leaned on her elbows, forming prayer hands which met her mouth.

"They're being phased out, all the tests."

"How can we be sure?"

"Take a break at home. We'll go away with you for a week."

"Misery loves company. I'll drag you down."

"You need to distract yourself, spend less time scrolling, get back to what you love. Books, art, film, music, restaurants."

"I've given up trying to keep up with it all. That's the game, isn't it, keeping us all occupied, divided and fighting, preventing any proper thought and formation against the tyrants that be."

He paused, swirling his wine.

"May you live in interesting times," he quoted.

"And aren't they fucking interesting?" she responded, without missing a beat.

"Book the theatre, I'll go with you to something."

They both knew Barney hated the theatre, and this level of sacrifice underlined to Annabel his care and desperation.

"Thank you," she said, putting her hand on his sleeve, looking up to prevent any tears forming.

"Are you dwelling on the paint throwers?" he asked.

She shook her head and frowned.

"No. I mean, yes, a little. Among everything else."

Food was dumped down in front of them by an overworked student.

"Glad those days are behind me," Annabel commented as she disappeared, her black apron strings fallen down over her bottom. Barney didn't see Annabel catch Barney watching.

They started to eat, the first few minutes devoted to making inroads into their meal. Annabel stopped to liquidate the stodge in beige of Wellington, potatoes, Yorkshire pudding. Wine and water in turn. Barney had his head down, and she thought of the reliability and attention paid by some friends, versus others. The friend she met the other day, as positioned to have a grasp on where she was at, who after a few questions, segued into her own predictable problems. Brought on by herself. One who had children with the wrong man. Annabel was unsympathetic, and it was reciprocated.

"Strings are being pulled behind the paint throwers," he said, after some pause.

"Based," said Annabel, in the mocking tone of the slacker Generation X that preceded her.

Barney minded to look that up later. Modern flim-flam, no doubt.

As was his tendency, Barney bounced around in his line of questioning, something which Annabel had picked him up on before, suggesting he keep to a linear, connected set of topics. He would follow up a question on parents with a question on films, then onto geopolitics. Without meaning to be cruel, she found this antagonising and expected others did too. She was hoping to help.

After he asked whether she had been cooking much for herself, he began a discussion about the roles of big government and the individual relating to free speech. Then slipped back to the dog, then the environment.

"Can we talk about something else? You know what? I've been obsessing about this stuff for twenty years, and now, now our world governments, plural but maybe future singular, have all got their hands on the agenda, it's now about elites getting even richer, utter corruption, as if the *pandemic* Big Pharma tax-funded subscription scheme wasn't bad enough."

Forked morsel.

"The fight's now in the hands of the wrong people. Look at the way the state is encroaching on our lives now. On the surface, it's all green initiatives. Honestly? The elites *care about the environment now*. Sure. Even I go back and forth on this. Capitalist democracy has shown what humans will do if free, free to do what they choose. Maybe we all need control, to desist the depletion of nature's resources, the great extinction. It's hard to argue enough of the freedoms we enjoyed were put to good use. I'm never happy. We've got a few years until we're microchipped, surveilled, tracked to within an inch of our lives. Want to use the local swimming pool? Sorry, you have an unpaid parking ticket on your account. No flights for you, young lady. There's just no way this can be turned around and we can see a viable long-term future. So fuck the environment, this sucker's going down."

He said nothing.

Her eyes, in youth soulful, now doleful.

Her half eaten lunch sat in mourning, as she dumped her cutlery down with a clank which reverberated around a room of music and drunker chatter.

"Don't have children. Don't have pets. Kill yourself."

11101
CHAPTER 29

Steven and trouble at work: Steven and Francesca fuck: Iva worried and Julian appeasement

The sun pierced the gaps and corners in between his bedroom blinds with thin streaking beamlets, as Steven turned to establish if it was five forty-five ayem sunlight or eight-thirty sunlight. In his youth, his preference would be for the former. To wake in the night and discover the time was two o'clock would mean many hours of sleep ahead and the pleasurable drift into it. At middle age, the preference was to have put away eight hours' solid sleep, even if it meant rising.

It was seven o'clock, which combined with a level of alertness, committed him to getting up to make coffee, before retiring again to clear down the phone backlog, and whatever had accumulated overnight.

He surprised himself by bothering to make a real coffee with a French press, what with having to clean it out after. Yet he felt more energised and positive than on a usual weekday.

That didn't last long.

A long open-backed lorry reversed into the temporary reserved parking in front of his flat, guided by a filthy, light tracksuited young man, smoking. Seeing the piles of pipes, he knew he was in for three months of noise, as two men jumped out of the cabin and went next door. Before too long the ricochet pings of scaffolding joints began hitting the floor, as they took to their task with abandon. The extra-long scrapes of extra-long pipes. The process of putting things up, to take things down. And move on to repeat, like the supplier of summer reception marquees, or the roadie.

A month had elapsed since Steven and Josie split, and while Josie continued to chew the whole affair over, a constant ticking and tocking among her thoughts and work, Steven had dropped down through the gears week-on-week to the point he thought about her a couple of times a day. Even then it was a cursory review of what took place, wishing she was doing fine, relieved she hadn't been in touch. That sort of thing.

As he sat up against three pillows in bed, in boxers, drinking cooling coffee, his sense of dread was already well formed. It was mid Q3, and while colleagues across the business were fearing redundancies, as a salesman, he feared being fired. No matter the strain on the business in people costs, the ability to bring in $3m for a salary on target of $300k, meant you got to stick around. Yet the percentage probability estimates for conversion against the deal sizes meant he was in the position the salesman dreaded. The hope of closing deals. You're only as good as your last quarter. And as the weeks inched closer to the cut off, and the promises began to drag, and client positivity waned, or indeed remained, but *not before Q4,* the bravado to the leadership would be received with added frost. Tougher, spikier questions asked in each additional meeting. Pressure piled on from the top, sent down the chain. Desperate scrambles and fiery tactics were considered with clients. Even straightforward 'sign this now and we'll discount' was discussed, yet seldom offered, for here's the thing: *don't act desperate*.

He skimmed hard through his inbox looking for one or two key names, the names that could make the difference and get him over the line. He got ahead of himself in his concern, worried now that if he did get them over the line, next quarter would be *even fucking harder*. Things had turned over the last six months. It wasn't him of course; it was the product to sell and the team talent he had at his disposal to assist him. The names weren't there. He checked when he mailed them last and the exact content. Paranoia washed over him.

Even as his thoughts darkened, he saw a name from the US which brought a smile. Some client who was on a global call, including two vegans from Steven's company, was discussing the bachelor party he had come back from. A long weekend of gator shooting. Career laughs all round by the appalled agency team. Here was one person who told you who he was, to which people listened.

Steven scanned further and set it aside to shower and clear his head, which ran away with itself under hot water and steam. His inability to escape himself condemned him to an inadequate future if he didn't find a partner with whom he could set something in motion. In relation to his immediate problem, under the hot spray he considered *reaching out* to a few former bosses and contacts. Always have an escape route, run it in parallel. If you didn't need it, so be it. Very well, just so. He would put some calls in that afternoon. They would know why he was calling.

By mid-morning the scaffolders had gone, and now overhead, a helicopter rotored across, buzzing, yawing in oval patterns above Ladbroke Grove. Seeking a bad actor, dead to rights. It settled on a location, and whereby Steven expected it to be dead overhead, such was the noise, it was hidden as he leaned through the open window. The eye in the sky a prevailing reminder of how surveilled he was. The futuristic noise of an electric car passing at slow speed added to the uneasy sentiment that the future was coming. And a crushing one at that.

He dashed off a few emails, some of which required some nous and some horse-trading. A pragmatist, he accepted that in many or most matters in life, people refused to change their minds, and dug even further into their incorrigibility. Some of the finest business leaders he had come across were open to change, and indeed wanted to be challenged, valuing the spectrum of thought and the ideas that talking through a problem created. Few and far between. He compared this with the dictatorial approach, all brio and bombast.

He clamoured for the presence of his colleagues, hoping to take a positive temperature when being around, so he went into the office for the afternoon. Although he may sense something to drive up his paranoia, to know was to give him first mover advantage.

A job not working out, being let go or managed out, 'redundancy', or redundancy, were near the top of many people's worry list. Something tangible and close, with constant changes to the risk calculations. As a business evolved and with it its requirements, bosses moved on, new competitors joined an industry. Hero to zero, seldom the other way, though it was possible.

What were the worst things that could happen to an individual on any given day? A true list would comprise personal health diagnoses, accidents, or the same inflicted upon loved family and friends, the death of a pet, heavy criminal acts, an incident generating police or legal focus, a threatening news event. Work problems would feature low down.

Yet, ever present they were. While not fatal for the skilled, they could be a trajectory killer, enforcing a step-down, taking a suboptimal next job, and with it a lower salary. And all the while Steven worked for the man, this wouldn't go away. Still, no matter what the state of play was, for any individual, in any circumstance, it was a case of 'put one foot in front of the other' or kill oneself. The human condition, the commitment and grunt to keep on going, dragged the species further forward, on the promise, that one day, things might improve. Even wily fifty year olds who had not been happy since childhood, felt there was a light ahead. A reasonless standpoint, given their genes and experience had been causing the same actions and strategies, and therefore outcomes, year after year to no avail. And why should the next year or decade be any different?

Elsewhere, Josie struggled at home, depleted, focusing on work, weeks after the event, unable to find anything else to do that wasn't bathed in misery. Meanwhile, Steven joined Annabel for a private view at Francesca's work, after Helen got them on the list to keep her company while all the elites ignored her and her (perceived) ordinariness.

The spotless entranceway on one of London's marquee streets, with velvet soft mustard armchairs down one side, and impeccable reception staff down the other, who ushered guests through to the spaces for the evening. Steven was surprised at the restricted ceiling height, no grand halls, then it dawned that this suited the items on display.

Helen stood with a glass of free wine, talking to an older couple, trying to convey knowledge about and feign enthusiasm for art that she did not possess. Art in general, not even the art on display. She watched as Annabel arrived with Steven, walking through as glasses of champagne were eased into their hands. While Annabel searched for Helen which made her feel valued, Steven chatted to one of the staff helping with the bubbles and nibbles. Getting warmed up, Helen observed.

Annabel joined her.

"How are things?"

"Nothing works, ever."

"Nothing like leaving your troubles at home. Give me a hug."

Champagne flutes and handbags made for an awkward embrace.

"Drink's always good," Annabel suggested, smiling and turning her head to make a wink without doing so.

"Who were those two?"

"Oh, I dunno, he kept saying things were a pastiche, or discordant."

"Ah, yes, the old discordancy."

"You alright? You seem chipper."

"Setting aside civilisational decline, the dismantling of society, ever-constricting totalitarianism. All good."

"Discordant, then."

"Yup. That's about it. Hold on, I'll get us drinks. That's what us liggers are here for."

"Hold on. You don't know yet, I got a new job. I'm leaving soon."

"Are you pleased?"

"Hmm," she answered.

"OK, hold on."

Helen watched Annabel walk away and tried to form a picture of her state. Her walk, her couture, effort made, her looks, the brightness of her eyes. She tried to create Annabel from a year or two prior for comparison, picking a similar event she attended. The drink made this difficult, her thought track disrupted, losing hold and looping back on itself. Two people who cared for each other, with disparate lists of problems.

As Annabel returned, she spied a gentleman she had met before at one of these dos, memorable for the wrong reasons.

"Oh here we go," she whispered to Helen, without moving her lips. "Mansplaining missile, incoming."

As he got started, focused on Annabel, Helen took the opportunity for some sport, interjecting at every opportunity. So determined and bullish, that his cursory looks at her demanded to be turned into full-on attention. Satisfied this wasn't an opportunity to separate Annabel, the Rupert caught someone's eye and made his way.

"Looks like Francesca's gonna shag Steven," Helen stated.

It hadn't taken long for Steven and Francesca to coordinate moves around the room, drawn together magnetised, like a social shaking of the sand whereby the large rise the top. Societal manoeuvrings on display at any elite event, a wedding reception, even a training course replete with complete strangers. One didn't talk to the person situated nearest. As they talked, absorbed, Steven was relieved that the time of internal debate about Josie was behind him, and he was a guilt-free free agent. The weighing, the considering, the pros and cons, the benefits and concerns, swept away in the finality of an ended liaison. They weren't even seeing each other for that long, he thought. Enough, he thought to himself, as he slipped into negative thoughts. About the terrible person he was.

Francesca asked him what he thought of the show. He hesitated, thoughts elsewhere. He disliked the moment, she would have caught it.

Francesca caught it.

He swerved providing an arty, technical or philosophical answer of which he was incapable, by instead pointing out the works he preferred, and focused on the content, composition, colour. Trying to avoid the obvious and the cliché.

"I agree with you on that one," she concurred on one of the smaller, obscure works.

Steven moved them onto film. They shared a discussion on seventies directing, and a distaste for anything new. Franchise, the corporations, no risk-taking.

"We should catch something at the BFI," he ventured.

"Sure. Things are busy at the moment," she responded. In her tone, he saw it wasn't the brush off, just a statement of fact.

"Busy people are happy people."

"Right," she confirmed.

She went on, "Look, I have to spend time with people, but stick around."

OK then, he thought. An invitation.

Francesca had his number, and had heard enough about him over the years. But he was attractive, and why not? Too many stiffs around this gathering for her liking. Steven was punching above his weight, but she would allow it. This time. And since Simon hadn't been *love*, she felt no need to stew by herself for weeks on end. The upper echelons moved on without delay. For the A-listers, well, they bounced and flounced from one hot disaster to the next.

The next morning, Steven left Francesca's place after coffee. Walk of fame.

Greenwich. A microcosm of London. London. A microcosm of the world.

Depending on one's internal values, one's worldview, or which direction one was facing, a place of natural beauty, open, green, with satisfying architecture in symmetry. Yet looming behind, the encroachment of the ever-expanding city, driven by the shadowy technology corporates, and their office floor wars. For some, the mix of the old and the new, the demonstration of a technologically supported, advancing civilisation, dragging human experience through times of wealth and health. Increasing life expectancy and improving quality of life metrics, even trickling down and giving the poor a tickle.

For others, a continuation toward the end. The atomisation of humanity, the avatarisation of the lived human experience. Tap to pay. Scan for entry. Download the free pass. Register for the ticket. No need for print-outs, it's all on the hand-held device. The fear that hand-held will become *chipped*. No need to scan or tap. The painless and invisible insertion under the skin to do all the work. Never leave anything at home again. The digitisation of our lives, our medical records. That last bastion of privacy removed, the conversation between doctor and patient. The internet knew much about us already, and had your free speech tracked, analysed, assessed and flagged.

And as with Thatcher closing the mines, so this felt all too inevitable. The world was shifting, darting to a new paradigm, and to fight was to slow progress. To fight the industrial revolution, the internet, or the mass migrations of populations fleeing to a better place, was to punch drunk.

Walking around her apartment in workout gear, Iva Jovanovic switched on the pet monitor in the lounge ahead of the cleaner's visit so she could keep an eye on them. Ensure they had gone before she arrived home. She called out to her virtual assistant to select some music, to set a timer for thirty minutes and to nudge up the temperature to warm herself before she took a run. She flicked and swiped her phone, for updates to personal and work email accounts, chat apps, podcast downloads, share prices and other financials, news feeds, social media, and the general news. She synched photos and music across devices to ensure access to everything she needed, wherever she was. She made some financial transactions, transferred money to her sister, and ran a quick audit through her direct debit list, to check for any redundant accounts, payments that needed thinning. The various security steps required, with multi-device validation, pushed further via paranoia, meant she even reverted to some physical elements to passcodes. Written on paper and hidden. Things she searched and shopped for on one device, followed her on other devices. Quick phone calls to mainland Europeans cost her nothing, as would a one-hour call to her cousin and nephews in Australia. Her gas meter had flagged a low battery to her energy provider, and an automated email suggested she made an appointment. Work had 'requested' she download two apps, register, validate, in order to facilitate efficient expense claims and travel arrangements. There were various accounts codes, ID numbers and personal details to hand over, so this was best done at home.

The pure coordination between all the elements of her work, social life, opinions, consumption, access to essentials, conspired to hammer home that when all was just so, things were very well. Money coming in, money going out. It was, however, not lost on her the immediacy of demands, notifications, and harrying one would encounter from all departments, should a crisis of lack of funds manifest itself. At present, redundancy whispers at work continued, underlining the precariousness, the tentative hold she had on things. Let alone the risk of devastation that might befall someone at the bottom, living hand to mouth. Impacts of market slides, driven by lack of confidence, jitters, would filter down from C-Level bonuses to Analysts and other little big people. She wasn't going to starve, but risk was sub-optimal for personal mental wellness, and speed of progression. Every step back another step forward and a half to be taken, to regain lost ground. And the stipends back home might need to be suspended. Real pain for cared for people. Although she was never laissez-faire, anything but, her wish for progress with Julian was sharpened by this new uncertainty that hung onto her. Years ago it might have revealed itself in the re-energising of a declining interest in a sub-optimal mate, to stay with someone who might partner her through a predicament. Now she felt cast out alone. Despite his no doubt extensive outgoings, Julian could hunker down amid a work disaster, take some time to reorganise, and go again. Yet she had not the solid, liquid or bank assets to flail beyond the medium-term, and she had no desire to move down the potential mate league table, in a version of cling to nurse.

There had been enough ill feeling between them via phone calls and texts, that Julian had orchestrated a free evening, so that he could go and see Iva, and not risk her blowing up at work, or worse.

When he arrived she looked fresh, and she smelled of make-up, as he leaned forward for a kiss. She pulled on his lapels while he stood with his hands in his pockets. Body language she either didn't pick up on, or she did, but decided to pick her battles, off balance from concern.

As they went inside, Julian was unsteady, unsure of what was about to transpire. It was an open-ended spectrum. While travelling over, he had pondered what a successful outcome might be. *What good might look like*. Getting laid would be top of the list. Avoiding and mitigating a flare-up and full on argument, that was a short-term goal. Longer term would be the positioning via mutual understanding that this wasn't the future and didn't have legs. *She* would be better off if it drew to a close.

"I haven't seen you in ages," she drawled, kissing him and bringing him close. Her tactics for the night, for he was certain she also had them, seemed to involve getting into the sack.

He would have preferred to get comfortable in bed, but she demanded spontaneity and they fucked on the couch.

When they had finished she poured them a glass of wine and they lay around. Julian wondered why sofas were no longer comfortable. She brought up sex, asking him what else he wanted to do with her. He struggled to come up with anything convincing, happy as he was with what he was getting. Positions and all that nonsense was for kids, he thought. She gave him a hard time about being unadventurous, something that felt like a conversation about something else. Always the sideline, Iva was starting to apply pressure, not least to take some of the heat out of her internal combustion engine. She required relief, be it via progress or capitulation and acceptance of a failed affair.

"What's going on with our floor?" she probed, her stresses on multiple fronts accumulating.

To Julian, this was a gift.

"Oh, I see, you get me over, have sex, and now it's tapping me for work information?"

This had potential for fireworks, as he realised a split second later, from her physical reaction as much as the fire spat from her mouth.

"You've got to be fucking kidding me," she vipered.

She sucked air in.

Iva melted down as he stood there, speechless, stretching his intellectual acuity to conjure tactics he could use to either maintain her or move on from her, without disruptive consequences.

"You've got some nerve. Here I am, sat around waiting for something to happen with you and home. Redundancies in the post. And I let you bound over and fuck me for a couple of hours. And I get the company line. And accusations that *I'm* using *you*. You're the fucking living end."

Julian was impressed by her use of English colloquialisms, and thought how strange it was that he had thoughts like that at a moment like this.

"Jesus Christ," she bayed, "I speak four languages, I've already lived all over the world. Three passports, I've been to a hundred countries. Global citizen. You want to see me on skis. Look at the shape I'm in. This is as good as it gets for you," she challenged, in model pose, shaking her head on his behalf.

Julian listened to her list off her KPIs, and had to admit, no, he didn't want to have to give it up, but a line had to be drawn, and the way in which she was losing it, went to reinforce this as the right course of action. In return for her sex appeal, there was a price to pay.

"I get hit on at the gym and in bars all the time. You think I'm going to settle as a *Cinq a Sept.*"

"Of course not, Iva, that's not how I think of you."

"Actions, not words. It's how you behave toward me."

She began to cry. They were genuine tears, of stress and anger at her own culpability for landing in this situation. Julian was unsure if the tears were real, or played to perfect pitch, practiced over a lifetime. The perpetual cynicism he wielded had proven to shield him from much disappointment over the years.

"Look. I'm not on the inside-inside track on this, as you'd expect. They think maybe a fifth of the team will have to go, but bound to be a few of the older heavy hitters on the biggest bucks, and a few of the newer joiners. Obviously doing whatever I can to influence."

"That'd suit you, my being moved on."

He couldn't deny it, but had to feign a face of hurt, at such an accusation. A tough ask.

"Of course not, though if we were to be together, that would have to happen."

He heard himself say if, not when, as she did, and pre-empted, "If, just because it's bloody complicated Iva. And for you. You can get anyone, someone with a clean record. No dependants."

"Don't put words in my mouth," she drawled, through her pouty lips of dark smudged cherry, roused by fury.

'*Don't put verds in my mouth,*' Julian thought to himself, stifling a smile.

As he was gaming the risks and the outcomes of this discussion, so too was she. She could get someone with no complex history, just cast aside his children and all that bullshit. Start afresh.

Julian went to calm the situation, knowing things had moved on a notch.

"Let's have a drink and a laugh, we don't have long."

He embraced her, something she returned with commitment. Yet they faced different directions, and both wondered what was written over the other's face.

A couple of hours later, a couple of bottles of wine down, and an hour in the bedroom, he left, relieved that he had started a multi-stage process. As with that of grief, he hoped he could level Iva through the stages of a break-up without too much mess. The evening had not been unsuccessful. Not least in the way she looked when seeing him out the door. A white towel wrapped around her middle, post-sex hair framing her face, flicked out of the way, smoky make-up. It was one of those images of a woman that he would retain for the rest of his days.

11110
CHAPTER 30

Helen starts a new job: Fiona SUV jam: Helen & Francesca decide on Paris

Anxiety about the first day in a new job, plus an oily, salty evening takeaway and bottle of wine shared with Phil, kept Helen awake beyond midnight. Fox shrieks and the loud mumblings of local addicts and dealers, talking to crime partners or to themselves, kept her alert. She slept in fits, snatching half an hour here, an hour there. Each time having to focus to return to sleep, to organise herself in bed next to the still Phil, who slept without stall.

At five o'clock, aggressive female voices outside, which required thirty seconds of active listening to establish if anyone was in trouble or not. The girls broke into laughter and Helen was relieved. No shutter twitching, no police necessary. She estimated that she had called nine nine nine, ten times or so in ten years, something unthinkable in the suburbs where she grew up or in her university town.

An hour later, the rumbling and knocking of street sweepers, wheels and brooms, unfettered by the hour, safe that they would be forgiven, given the service they provided and the gusto with which they went about their work.

She got another half hour in and rose, leaving Phil in bed to go into work his customary forty-five minutes past. Leaving home, she reflected on how she felt in this position in her twenties. A new job, new people, a fresh start, her pleasant face with its cheery smile. Now gooseberry sour, having looked for a job, and found one.

She trudged to the station.

If she missed a tube or two, or was delayed, she wouldn't be bothered. Passing a shop which had changed hands again, from one café to another, with no doubt a new *take*, on coffee, she thought-muttered to herself that whoever leased that unit, never got it right. Every time. She thought-noted that she was being negative already, and she would have to get her smiley game face on. She put on a podcast on history to shift her mood to something educational, at least. And besides, having an earphone inserted was a get out in case she should broadcast her thoughts.

Arriving four minutes late, she was ahead of her new boss, who walked in behind her while she was signing in at reception, and collected her to take in with him.

She was shown to her desk, the worst positioned with the least privacy in her new team. On her desk, a bunch of branded swag. The catastrophe of the unwanted coffee thermos, water bottle, notepad, stickers. A balloon tied to her chair. And no laptop.

The atmosphere seemed light and things appeared in order. Manageable workloads perhaps. Yet as with the duck gliding across the water, there could be any level of filth going about its business over email. The people seemed nice, but *didn't they always*. It took a brazen arsehole to come over to a new starter and reveal themselves. Give it a day or two, Helen mused.

Her boss, CallmeGav, suggested they went out for lunch. She was concerned it would just be the two of them, but he added 'a couple of the team will come' to her relief, loud enough for a few of the team to hear, glancing up from their screens. Helen thought he might be all right, but had made that mistake every time before, so kept up her guard. Expect utter cuntishness and work backward.

Gav turned out to be a bad eater, which was a curious thing to behold in an adult. As there were no adults crawling around who never learned to walk, so there should be no adults who failed to learn how to eat property. Yet here was one, sucking on his fingers while putting away pitta slices, pawing and shredding away with a fork at a sliced chicken breast in his protein box. Welcome, Helen.

Helen feigned interest with her new colleagues, throwing in all the new starter questions, a mix of business and team and personal questions. Don't be uninterested in the business. Don't be too square.

Information she would like to glean related to working hours, weekend working frequency, backstabber identity, her predecessor's whereabouts, bonus payouts. She nodded away as the *right* questions she asked were answered, by Gav and his sallow face. Her thoughts moved on to pressures of her sick father's expanding breathing problems, how tight the finances were this month, and how in a few weeks' time there would be a pile of work pressures, front and centre.

The end of the day coincided with the Company Meeting, and sixty hours of company time frittered away, providing no useful information for the attending souls. It had to be done, here and everywhere, to help create a sense of interconnectedness.

A prize awarded for a company player of the month, who worked weekends to deliver a successful project to a customer. Loving that FREE LABOUR.

Helen left on time with a forced smile, and a wave to the team. A gloomy evening lay ahead.

She forced her way onto an already heaving tube, sweating together with the populace. To wait for further trains would mean less time at home, and greater risk of a signal failure, delayed trains, a person under the track, absent staff impacts or any other fuckage which might add to her misery. All on rotation with ancient signals the primary offender. Although conscious that the first day back after a holiday, or a new job always took a lot out of her, she felt herself sink into the weight of a depressive state.

It took her a while to notice the woman who was jammed in next to her was pregnant, unable to get a passage to a seat. They exchanged a look and the woman said, "Just one stop, it's OK."

She wore no wedding ring, and Helen wondered what her story was, while despairing on her behalf at the state of the transport system, and what people had to endure. It seemed to have become risky to have a child, the investment heavier than ever, which hardened the requirements of a partner and the bedrock of that partnership to set a child on its proper way. Housing stock and the affordability of raising children in the city out of reach for many but the high earners. Landing places at good schools.

The adverts above heads piped in messages, the banality of which contrasted with her swirling thoughts and her predicament. She couldn't see a way to children in what was a failing six-year relationship, with as chasmic an asymmetry in their life goals. Time was all she had.

As she arrived home and went to unlock the first lock and it was open, she realised Phil was home, for which she was thankful.

"Yeah mate, book those. Was it Thursday or Friday? Friday. Nice. We can go on after."

Helen sunk into an armchair in her coat and put her hand to her forehead.

"Nice. All right mate, talk soon. Ta-ta."

Phil walked over, "How was your first day?"

"Fine."

"It doesn't look like it was fine."

There was a huge pause, as if an unsaid discussion were taking place between them. They were careful where to take this conversation next, dancing around the obvious.

"I thought we could go to the cinema tonight," Phil suggested.

Helen balked at the idea, "Not tonight Phil, I can't face it."

"You're always nag..."

He paused.

"Saying we should do more together. There's a couple of things on we both might like."

She said nothing.

"I'll make us some dinner then I guess. What do you want?"

"Make whatever you like, I'll eat whatever."

For a morning in summer, it was a throwback to previous autumns. A hefty wind blew across the widths of parks, car parks, arterial roads and open spaces. Bluster hurried through narrow streets with no hard end, whereas within the walled canyons of buildings beyond three storeys in central London, all was chill.

Fiona walked to the end of the road, and rounded the corner to post a card to a relative. It raised her, to walk the wide streets close to home, with the clean walls a mix of cream, orange, ochre and umber, with weeping trees and plants, light to dark to yellow greens spilling over. All looked after, cared for. The hit of the red post box, accented by the red and pink roses of a neighbouring garden behind black railings. Although spiriting, it wasn't too long before a gale blew up litter, kicking it out of gutters, sending it spiralling through the air, further down the road. A depressing sight compared with the leaves of a past fallen autumn.

The unseasonal high winds had un-socketed a large tree limb which hung down in the Wyatt's garden. Fiona had been negotiating with Julian as to who would investigate local gardening businesses that could help with its removal and repair. Summer, some summer.

The day unfurled to hurl itself at Fiona, as if she were moving through a computer game, trying to collect assets, dodge bullets, racing against any number of peers, dependents, siblings and general ballast, like her husband. A nip outside for a cigarette once in the morning and twice in the afternoon her main break from the onslaught of admin, organisation, shopping, tasks the cleaners didn't do. Clearing the whiteboard. Re-drawing out the whiteboard for the week ahead. Looking back, then looking forward. She had masturbated once the house was empty, a slow, drawn out affair. She was thankful that wouldn't cut into the day and her libido wouldn't need attending to. In all likelihood.

Rushing about in the same jeans she had been wearing at home for the last week or so, she made a note to change things up. Comfort had primacy at their age, but she didn't want Julian to stop watching her arse as she crossed the room. And with a couple of social occasions on the horizon she would be taking the opportunity to stake her position as a beauty within their sphere. Make sure he knew that it would be a mistake to make any move against her.

These matters ran through her mind for periods of the day and then didn't, as she auto-piloted her way through school trips and equipment purchasing, party and social coordination for all members of the household, and getting the dog out for some fresh air. Matters of the children were paramount now, more than ever. Maximising their lives, opportunities and futures. Her marriage spluttering along in second gear while they were both indulging in extra-curriculars, could wait for a kick start. Moreover, conversations with a couple of friends in the last week, one of whom was deep into a multi-year affair, another close to falling into a casual fling, had turned her head to the fifteen year itches all around. Like a record producer sat before their desk of hundreds of dials, knobs, buttons, faders, so her thoughts would dial up the inputs of some and down the noises of others. Harry would never be dialled up beyond secondary background percussion, but it helped keep the beat.

While Julian was beginning to buckle under work pressures and the mental weight of keeping Iva on the rails and not causing him work and/or domestic issues, Fiona kept dealing, juggling, whirring away. Handling it all. She would not lose it, but he might, if she turned the screw.

She washed his jeans with a splash of rancour and self-congratulation, as it annoyed him when they were clean and tightened by a size for a few days. After he'd put on half a stone over spring and hadn't lost it deep into summer.

Also that day: pick up items left behind at Florence's friend's house. Book the boiler service. Order replacement kettle. Dry cleaning collection and drop-off. Always both on rotation. Speak with a contact about a consultancy project. Text Harry. Something funny, showing at least sixty seconds of effort. Replace tablet, the slowness of which was causing Florence and by extension Fiona, much consternation. Do shredding. Ready the paperwork for her upcoming hospital screen. Pay a parking fine. Check they were being charged the right amount by the gym. Check Julian's phone records. Contact Dad about a tax question. Put through a supermarket order online to ensure no gaps for the week ahead. Organise school comms and documentation that had piled up in online files. Diary refresh, across the board. Petrol. Pick up a book for Florence. And as she went about this busy ness, additional tasks were left at her door, phone pinging with needs to be met.

There was a limit to what any self-respecting upper-middle class Wandsworthian home-maker could achieve from home. An afternoon of further errands, tasks and distractions were to be navigated by car. Endless roadworks, street after street dug up to lay new cable, burst water mains and ragged streets, worn and torn, pot holed, manifold. Cycling lanes at war with the driver, buses and the blind. Fiona felt done over by the crushing conspiracy against the motorist. Abuse and aggro from angry men confined to their taxis, lorry cabs, hire and family cars. Largely men or large women.

The grind of hurtling and fighting with a competitor to get to the next set of red lights first. Slow movers at green lights costing those seven or eight cars back the opportunity to get through the lights, doling out an extra, redundant three minutes. Optimists expecting empty streets, rounding blind corners, having to rut with another. The rank and file of cars, vans, buses, lorries, and the final boss - the bin lorry. The huge council truck, full of hard men in orange, who didn't give a flying fuck if they took the side off an outmatched, old-fashioned people carrier, and took a few dents and collateral scratches. They were the gods of any London neighbourhood, and they were obeyed.

Fiona swung around the *Sports Utility Vehicle* this way and that. The full fat Range Rover, not their second car baby-SUV, the *Evoque*. Evocative of asthmatic children, reduced life expectancy and roadkill overkill. She swore the streets were getting narrower. As they upgraded their cars.

With Florence collected and now swallowed up by the passenger seat, Fiona drove her chariot on to pick up the spare from school. Observers from the pavement looking across would see a comedic profile of a woman, thin of face and thinner of arms, sat forward in this great vehicle, swinging around the junked trunk, transporting her engulfed child.

As she rounded the final streets toward the school, the stressful part. The pinch point. She had to wait several cars turn to get close to the final T-junction to turn into. Ahead of her, two Range Rovers and a BMW X7, a true beast of a machine. They had to wait the duration of the news on the hour on Radio 4, before they got to the dotted white lines.

Chaos.

Much horning and parping, the long, deep punches of the frustrated, affluent parent. Fiona was trying to figure out what was going on as she could see doors opening and closing and that killer depressant, the driver stood outside their vehicle, door open behind them.

She too got out, with a "wait here," toward Florence.

It was the perfect storm. Parked on either side of the road from each other, were two SUVs. Driving down the centre of the street, toward each other, two X7s. Four in a row. The occupants of the two centre vehicles now risked removing the wing mirrors of all four cars, or side-swiping doors. Which might lead to a number of angry households that evening, maybe a precursor to an affair or a last straw before a divorce. No contact had been made, but they couldn't get out, or get good enough visibility either side to communicate and coordinate their way to safety.

A car crash in slow motion.

Fiona walked off to pick up junior. Returning, she pulled off an eleven-point turn in front of raging road users queued up and desperate. She gave one bloke the finger. Something she hadn't done since before the children.

Florence seized her opportunity and she too gave his large, gammony face the bird. Mother and daughter high-fived and Florence found some R&B on the radio which she cranked. Fiona felt exhilarated, on speed, in a 20mph slow zone.

They returned and Fiona handed Florence a small paper bag with a thin paperback. "They didn't have what Annabel recommended," Fiona lied, having audited Annabel's suggestions as being too adult. She paused at the time, wondering if that was Annabel's point, to elevate, accelerate, but erred on the side of caution. "But I heard Annabel mention this book later," she lied again, having chosen something less edgy, and which she had enjoyed herself when young.

She doubled down, embellishing a little further for purposes of conviction, "When she was talking to the tall man."

"The one *smoking*, on the drugs?" Florence suggested, puffing on her two fingers, which she sent ahead of her into the distance. Special emphasis to poke at her mother and her habits.

Fiona ignored this, "Leave your tech here, go and sit somewhere comfortable and concentrate for half an hour. Then I'll make you a sandwich."

Florence half believed her mother, but had observed how convinced she had been in the past, before catching her mother in a lie.

Fiona had ambitions to reduce screen time. She counted the numerous tech pieces within sight, as Florence went to her room and left the noise of downstairs behind. She removed the thin, white and bright blue-green book from the paper bag, and placed it down on the bed. The seriousness of the image, in black and white, of young people in the frozen past made this feel like a significant moment. Therein lies ideas and knowledge, to take Florence on Annabel's path.

Opening the pages, taking care not to distress the cover or the spine, she delved into the first sentence, and went from there.

Fiona was about to shout up to Florence, who had been gone for half an hour, when she appeared in the kitchen.

"I read five pages," she confirmed, placing the book down on the island, wiping first to check for spotlessness. She touched the matt feel cover and smoothed it, as if it were wrinkled.

Fiona retrieved a postcard from the drawer that they had picked up at the British Museum.

"Here," she said, handing it to Florence, "bookmark."

"Thanks."

Fiona banked the smile as credit ahead of their next fallout.

"They are organising a protest as school. Can we go? They need volunteers."

Fiona envisioned being kettled by lumo bobbies, surrounded by flares and knotted dreads.

"In London? No. When you're older."

"Not in London. At school."

Fiona wondered what they were planning to protest. It couldn't be protesting cuts. *Kids just want to have funds*. Some initiative by a militant new teacher with *new ideas*, no doubt.

"It's about plastic."

"Let's discuss next week. DON'T commit us to anything. Under promise..."

"Over deliver."

"There you go."

Fiona was concerned with Florence absorbing too much from Annabel. Yet while she knew this fire burned, she wanted to slow it down, for now. Go the speed limit.

Florence stood on a chair that she had shifted across in front of the expansive bookshelves in one of the reception rooms, semi-segmented within the open plan, ground floor layout. She found something Fiona had read several years before, and now prehistoric. She snuck it under her top and went upstairs where she could digest it under the cover of her classic novel. On the first page she had to query something on the internet, and never returned to the book, as she spun around the internet's web absorbing all manner detail on the world's ecological problems. Presented to her as the inarguable mono-narrative of global body-approved *experts*.

Julian returned and after greeting the dog and one of his children, he shouted to acknowledge to the rest of the house that he was back. Fiona came down the stairs in gym wear, post home yoga, and gave him a short kiss. He watched her as she walked away.

"You have to go to a nine-year-old's party this Saturday. Don't worry, it's some event, not at someone's house," Fiona reassured. For they had both been at home-based parties rife with parents drunk in the afternoon, going into the bathroom in pairs for bumps.

"Fuck sake, I wanted to play golf."
"Be a good father."
"What are you two doing?"
"Shopping and lunch."
Three short words, which would cost £200 each.

Streams of backpacked twenty-somethings made their way along Mortimer Street in Fitzrovia with its mix of classic buildings and modern glass and white brick boxstrosities. A delivery truck hugged the kerb as workers harried and hurried stock inside. An indicator of the latest new food trends of years' prior, Hawaiian poke bowls, Indian street wraps, coming to a home counties town in five years' time. A pleasant lane cut perpendicular to the main street, with long-established independent sandwich shops and restaurants. A young man looked undecided, scanning which way to go, conscious to make a quick decision for his reputation. A girl in boyfriend jeans, a grey sweatshirt and sandals talked into her phone, leaning against a wall, so sloppily dressed as to suggest she came down from a flat upstairs for a private conversation, rather than to have left home like that. Many such cases.

On the corner, Helen sat next to Francesca in a Swedish bakery. The décor of tiled floors and walls, light grey benches and metal legs on small round tables, meant for a cold experience. Lack of comfort a tool for shepherding customers onward. Don't bring a book. Yet this summer warmth ushered in from the frequency of customers coming and going, and residual heat from the oven down a corner corridor, left Helen and Francesca covered with a warm film of heat.

Francesca allowed Helen to debrief, before interjecting.

"Let's go to Paris. I like to go in autumn," she suggested. Helen wasn't at the top of her list of choice Paris companions, but Francesca knew she needed it. She could tie this in with a few other matters, and *tuer some oiseaux*.

"I've never been to Paris. Always wanted to go. Phil always said we should."

Francesca looked dead ahead, resisting an involuntary eye-roll or shrug.

Helen saw the obstacles she had put up in front of herself, and compared herself with those who were barrierless. Who went about doing whatever they pleased. That wasn't an option for her, no matter what the self-helpers might declare. The boundaries demarcated around herself were impenetrable.

"I know, I know, it's like getting a train to Manchester," Helen added.

Francesca said nothing, unmoved, and let Helen try to unravel herself.

"Just go, just like that?"

Wait. Keep the silence.

Helen started calculating, and then she stopped.

"Fuck it. Let's."

"I'll bloody go without you anyway, and send you pictures for three days."

"Here's to horse, in squid ink."

They looked at a couple of date options that could work for them, and they touched on budget, before Francesca lied about being able to secure them a good deal at a hotel she liked to go back to. She figured her loyalty scheme points might be able to get them both Premium seating, though assumed she would end up in online terms and conditions hell. Seven iterations of selecting her requirements. This could cost her an hour. The money to prop up Helen could be absorbed, the sacrificed time and sanity from dealing with added modern nonsense, less so.

For each and every moment of enjoyment, an equal and opposite prerequisite moment of tangled anguish, at the hands of governments and technology.

Autumn

11111
CHAPTER 31
Steven dates Amanda: Overnight

At his request, Steven's taxi stopped short of his destination in Holland Park, giving him a short walk uphill along the main drag, to take in some cool air and top up on cash at the Express store. Always holding and folding, even in these tap dance times.

A unique tree-lined London boulevard, a wide carriageway, roomy pavements, a handful of pubs and a mix of shops. Always a few drunks, always a few homeless, but nevertheless safe, despite being nestled between the Bush and Notting Hill Gate, which could both get hectic. Steven recalled the genuine shock at seeing the blackened Grenfell Tower between rows of houses, eye ah el, while walking down this avenue in the evening after the fire. Things just didn't burn down like they did in the eighties, until that night.

Tonight had serious potential after a first date drinking at a hotel bar in Soho, which had Steven performing to his highest standards. He couldn't get a handle on whether this were sufficient. He'd layered in enough humble brags, selling points, signals as to his underlying calibre, and the better part of his character. But was it *enough*?

Amanda didn't care much for film, so *no more film chat*. They didn't go deep on the first date. The attraction was there and he sensed the sex would be good. In his experience, late thirties' first nights with new people don't tend to mean bad sex, unlike in one's twenties, so he was hopeful.

He turned into a side street and, as planned, arrived just before time at the restaurant – modern European with Michelin guide pretentions. Selected to be busy but not full, with good spacing between tables, delicate lighting and light music as soft as the magnolia marshmallow interior. All of which would allow for privacy, open conversation, intimacy. He sat on a stool on the bend of the deep, grey stone bar, and having checked that it was clear, pushed some prospects through the dating pipeline, glancing up every now and then to check the door. He ordered an Old Fashioned as a sharpener.

At six minutes past the hour, the door was opened for Amanda, who entered and thanked the staff with a well-practiced smile that got a good run out every day. Steven swivelled on the bar stool and she planted her lips on his, laughed and wiped a lipstick smudge from his face. After a blur of hat, raincoat and scarf removal, baggage handling, hair organising and phone securing, Amanda was *present and in the moment*.

Amanda Fish was textbook South-West London. Until she removed some layers it wasn't obvious that she was a treat of balance, strength, and weight distribution. Eye-catching, desirable, all divine proportions. She wore a cream and black dress with a high neckline, and which stopped just above the knee. Her feathered blonde hair sat just below her shoulders and she wore smoky eye make-up around her blue-grey eyes.

They ordered vodka martinis at the bar, and were shown through.

Steven worked his way through well-trodden patter, careful and conscious of what he discussed with her on the first date versus what he had discussed with other dates he had had in the meantime. Having to chuck in the occasional 'we talked about this last time / it might have been with a colleague' as a safety check.

He *loved* his job (he put up with his job), of course he wanted a family (undecided), he had nothing but warm things to say about his (with whom he seldom spoke) and was a happy-go-lucky kind of guy. He took care not to contradict anything shared before. Even if he did, depending on how much she liked him, he might be able to talk his way around it and she would find a way to let it go. He had got away with some astounding mistakes before, and other times, one small mistake and it was done. He suspected Amanda would give little leeway.

Steven recounted his last couple of days, and when he didn't ask Amanda any questions she had to interject. Her day had consisted of a litany of administrative tasks, body maintenance, wardrobe bolstering, home organisation, and three hours of work-work. A standard unrelenting Saturday. The lowlights were vacuum-packing her summer wardrobe, getting Brazillianed and organising her odd-job man to fit a new bathroom cabinet. Jim could pretty much do anything, but while she would trust him to complete a hundred varied jobs at £50 each, she wouldn't trust him to complete a five-grand bathroom to any sort of standard. Amanda had reduced the to do list that would never end, until it does. Steven formed his own list about what he had to do the next day.

They ordered. Wine was dropped.

Steven talked with confidence, yet inside he turmoiled about work, and the possibility of staffing cuts. This splintered his focus. Life was multi-multi-faceted, he reminded himself, and work was but one part. This was another.

He selected a new topic to shift gears.

"How do you feel about discrimination toward short men? A girl's profile I saw asked what you call a man under six foot?"

Amanda gave a little shoulder shrug and a head wobble. Her blonde hair shook.

"A friend."

This tickled Amanda and she felt a warmth in her cheeks. This served as a marker that she was hitting tipsy.

"See, hilarious. To any woman, every other discrimination, awful, except this one. Even the short girls, the shorter they are the bigger they like them."

Amanda laughed at this.

"A friend of mine is five foot and her taller sister tells her she should be taking the five foot six guys out of the pool. She refuses."

They both enjoyed this passage of play.

Not yet comfortable in silence, Amanda asked Steven what he thought to be a rather odd question. "So, are you a nice guy?"

"Ouch. That's a Morton's Fork if ever I heard one. I'm not answering that."

Timing was everything as their main courses were placed in front of them and the verbose waiter pointed to Amanda's plate, drew a long breath and began. "For you madam: the poached Baltic sea turbot with a fennel velouté, dill oil, crushed Vivaldi new potatoes with salted Brittany butter and Siberian garlic chives. Accompanied by sautéed hispi cabbage with pancetta and banana shallots." Steven exhaled in relief - halfway. Amanda was lapping this up. "And for you sir: the roasted venison loin with roasted chestnuts, a celeriac puree, wild mushrooms, braised radicchio, blackberries, and a balsamic reduction, topped with rosemary sprigs." Steven recalled a ten course tasting menu where each course was explained in great detail and they were asked if they enjoyed every dish after its collection, including the single quail egg. Painful.

Steven began to *socialise* his theories, which Amanda enjoyed. A hypothesis was date catnip. "On a date, any question asked may elicit the same question in return. So all questions are set up for bragging opportunities."

"Example?" Amanda enquired.

"Example. If I do no charity work, it's not a great idea to ask you if you do. You regale the Christmases you spent in soup kitchens and the weekend support you offer to local children's hospitals. You then ask me and I respond, 'Nah'."

"Go on..."

"However if I played the piano at an embassy concert and warm the saxophone at one of those, ahem, charity gigs, I may ask you if you play an instrument."

"So, have you had sex with anyone famous?" Amanda asks, turning her head to the right while looking straight at him. A sexy smile, a lift of the eyebrows as she pointed at him with her right hand. Steven was interested in her, and so felt threatened by this topic. He dreaded her response. This was a power play.

"Touché. The nurse from *Holby City*," he replied.

"I slept with him too."

The food tasted good on the way down, being over seasoned and doused and soused in oils. Once down, it would sit heavy into the afternoon the next day. That was why Steven loved Japanese food – so clean, so temporary.

He upended the last of the white into Amanda's glass first, then his. He sniffed at his glass, and, placing a forefinger on the fleshy part at the front of his left ear took a swig. He breathed in and then sighed. "Banana leaf, pipe smoke; a flutter of chicory."

"Right."

"Haven't a clue. I can sometimes get grapefruit or berries, which is more than your average bear. Pinot Noir is gettable for its distinct clarity. Shall we get a bottle of red?" Steven segued to red wine, despite Amanda's fish main, as it did raise the temperature.

Bloody, pious, reproductive red.

"Sure. Getting me drunk, eh?"

If a set of Steven's dates could be observed, one would see that his politeness, attentiveness, listening and conversational risk-taking varied depending on his *perception* of value. If he didn't feel he needed to impress too much, he just wouldn't try that hard. This was just the kind of toxicity that the smarter women picked up on and which if the others were attune to, would lead to less hurt. Too many let him take liberties. Steven could not believe what he got away with, unchallenged.

The Syrah was washing things down when Amanda ventured, "So, what do you like in bed?"

Steven took notice of this and started to get hard and reached out to initiate footsie. Amanda had signed him off and she had allowed the power to shift.

"No, we're not going there; I've made that mistake before."

"Oh, c'mon, what are we in for later?"

Fantastic, he thought. He could relax now. It would be back to his tonight.

"I've been asked that before, and after we discussed it at length, she announced we had different tastes, and that was that."

"What *were her* tastes?"

"Stop it, seriously." he laughed.

"Boring," she mocked, that ultimate criticism of the elites.

They were not *the* match but they were *a* match.

Before dessert arrived, Steven excused himself to the bathroom. As he made his way, light of head and heavy of leg, he wondered what toilet sign challenge awaited him – it wouldn't be animals or symbols in a place like this, but it could be letters or something that required translation. He was pleased to see good old *Ladies and Gentlemen*. One less mental task. No action required. Those three sweetest of words. As he stood to relieve himself, he suffered a splitter – two streams like a lizard's forked tongue, which each sprayed one of his shoes, and which both missed the bowl. It was a W that he hadn't chosen light suede shoes.

After he took his seat, dessert was whisked across. Forty words to describe chocolate mousse and lemon posset. Amanda dipped into her mousse. They took a moment to focus on polishing it off.

"Back to mine for a nightcap, it's not even ten?" Steven ventured.

"Oh, James..." she mimicked.

The protracted four stages of settling the bill had to be endured. Any time Steven had ever asked for a bill it was at that exact moment that he had become desperate to leave. The bill must be requested, the bill is then left, the staff must then be retrieved, the financial transaction then completed. Any of these steps could incur a significant delay, the most testing of which could be the second coming of staff. An emergence of some tap & go casual joints had given Steven some optimism for the future. Though the tyranny of a cashless society and pure government control weighed upon him. The bill was left and they had given desserts for free as they were a little tardy. Amanda did the *slow reach*. Steven had this covered, and she thanked him.

With the car ordered inside, they walked straight out, got straight in. A modest modern luxury. Steven wondered the same thing he always did at times like this. How did the drivers cope with carrying a succession of people on their way home for sex every night of the week? He guessed they played the long game – 'let's see how much sex you're having after three years.'

They held hands and both anticipated a good night.

As Steven opened a bottle of red in the kitchen, Amanda had a poke around the flat. Tidy, well organised, decent technology but not showy. No five grand speakers. Limited edition art and photographic prints, but no originals. Some travel photos which were his own. No photos of people. Dark wooden floors in the living areas, light grey carpeting in the two bedrooms. The modern classic, if trite interspersion of plants with their splashes of mid and deep green against the white walls. The yawn of the all too predictable coffee table books. This put him at the top end of the Higher rate tax bracket, but not into Additional rate territory. A smattering of trad media – Compact Discs, Digital Versatile Discs, and a couple of books shelves containing few classic novels, few female writers, and a surfeit of white middle-aged men and their seventies to noughties adventures in London, Los Angeles, Leith.

The final element to set the mood was jazz. Steven knew little of jazz except its effect on women already squiffy on red wine, and depended on some reliable radio stations from the coastal US.

They talked for a short while about some of the things on display, photos he had taken, Ladbroke Grove and some of the local places Amanda used to hang out at, years ago. They shared brief overviews of recent relationship histories and Steven was embarrassed as usual at his longest relationship. Eighteen months, and that dragged on for at least the second half. At his age, that was the *wrong answer*. The right answer at his age was four to five years. This would have garnered further exploration if the evening was just starting, and might have put things off course.

They kissed and Amanda was handsy from the off, so Steven didn't need to go slow. Heavy petting. They both went, in turn, to each other's necks. Amanda to breathe the faint mix of his shaving cream and cologne. Steven to nibble and suck (with care) on her ear lobes. The closest thing he had found to a key to all doors.

She stood up and led him to the bedroom. He brought the fuller of the two glasses of wine for them to share.

They half undressed each other, then stripped themselves down to underwear to be quick and to retain the mood. Getting into bed, they canoodled for a short while until Steven slipped her knickers down to her thighs and Amanda disposed of them with some reaching and leg-wriggling. Her feet helped out too. They gave each other oral sex, figuring each other's bodies out and how they liked it. Amanda was reminded of a similar previous lover, then she moved on and came without effort. From talking with girlfriends, she knew she was lucky to be blessed with that talent.

"Condoms?" he checked.

"Yes," she replied. Though she loathed them, this was the done thing first night.

Once on top of her, Steven wondered whether Amanda would roam her hands around his bottom all night or if it would be a finger straight to the arsehole. Oop, the latter.

It was obvious to both that Steven needed to focus a little what with the wine and the condom, and Amanda was patient. As they finished, he rolled off a little quicker than he would someone with whom he felt confident. However, Amanda wasn't the type for cuddles and they threw the duvet back and took turns topping themselves up on wine as they chatted before they both slept.

In the morning, once they had woken with light hangovers, Steven suggested they could go out for food round the corner. "I'm not a fan of brunch, eggs slopped out, no discernible creativity or skill on show. Buggies and screeching. But we can do if you like."

"You're a cheery soul of a Sunday morning." She laughed.

"I'd rather go out for lunch later, or I can cook scrambled eggs."

"You cook," she decided.

They had sex again, better sex, without the circulating alcohol. Post-orgasm blood coursed around their system as they sunk into their pillows.

"My friend wants to go for brunch. God, she'll say I've been eaten by *the new boyfriend monster*. Not that we're..."

"Organise to meet later, lunch, beer garden. I've got a load to do this afternoon."

"Smart thinking."

They caught up with what was going on in the world, until Amanda asked, "What do you look for most in a woman?"

Steven didn't reply with the honest physical answers and picked "It's all about connection. Girls always say *kindness* don't they?", at which point he howled with laughter. "I've always noticed it's the kindest guys that get all the girls. Not the rich loudmouths with big dicks."

"Maybe they are the wrong girls."

"Fair point. Not buying it though."

Steven rustled up breakfast in bed, they had sex again, and Amanda called herself a car.

100000
CHAPTER 32
Wyatt roast lunch: Finances: Iva start of the end: Ghosted

A mild Sunday in SW London. Before leaving Fiona checked the weather outside the bi-fold doors. It remained overcast. Within half an hour of leaving home, the skies had cleared and the September sun had boosted the *feels-like* temperature by six or seven degrees, and Fiona, Julian and the children were now clammy and overdressed.

As violent crime rates go up in summer, so too moments of irritation combust within otherwise peaceful moments, when a deep breath or two and a little self-distraction might bring calm.

They all trooped into the pub with the dog, "After dicking around parking the damn car," Julian summarised to Fiona's parents, before they organised themselves and bedded into the large table.

The get together of three generations. With its moments of adult conversation, its inclusive topics of childlike chatter, and its partitioned conversation within pairs of adults, divided by sex.

Julian and father-in-law had got into some tax complication being meted out on one of Fiona's cousins.

"Better check we're OK on that," said Fiona.

"Julian will have all that in place," her father splained.

"Leave it to the man," Fiona's mother confirmed, "they know all about that."

"Er, mother, you know that's not the modern world. You're just being provocative. And I'm trying to raise a daughter in control of her life."

"Give me the Bitcoin," Florence confirmed, rubbing her fingers and thumbs together with both hands, something Fiona might have done herself as a child.

Fiona felt a cold sweat, as she cornered herself with her own words.

The idea that she wasn't as close to the intangibles of *what they were worth*, beyond the obvious bricks and mortar assets. She had a hundred thousand squirrelled for emergencies, but the active money, out doing its thing. What was it doing?

The warm still air stifled the knackered floor workers, one puffing away in a mask, surfeited by a large cast iron radiator which hadn't got the memo. Pumping away as if in winter. As Julian went to mention it, the staff just cut him off, "Oh we know, someone is coming out to have a look. We don't have any other tables free. We'll bring you extra iced water."

"That'll do it," he muttered.

There was a clarion of gripes to be foisted upon the staff, puffed out from running about on Sunday after working whatever jobs and shifts they needed to keep their heads above water. Fiona felt the cauliflower cheese was over browned, Florence perceived her asparagus as past al dente, and to Fiona's father the broccoli was *barely cooked at all*.

Julian had an angry Iva flashing up on his phone which raised his hackles. Like energy itself, bad *energy* also flowed from one source to another without dissipating, as Julian passed it onto the staff, with his complaints about a rogue hair among his roast pork. The staff began with a Crackling Defence, but were made to yield once Fiona and her mother backed up their man, turning in unison, twenty-five years apart and not a cigarette paper between them.

The men went from bloviating about all manners of things to sitting in silence, resting and digesting, like constrictors who had done the hard work. The mothers discussed options for further time together, wider family events, and whether they might get together for a long weekend before the Christmas nonsense. They poked about among each other's accessories, pullovers, and their respective brands.

Iva texted Julian and received a lengthy delay, then a lame answer, which was worse than no response at all. While Fiona was orchestrating their extensive, rich lives, of friends, activities and of family, Iva was swinging in the wind, resentful with each turn. Twisting like a tightening cord toward its inevitable limit, after which it would yield and unravel. A timeless form of craze. The wait was the point.

His phone on silent, he didn't need to look as it buzzed. He choked down his dry crumble with gulps of still water.

Iva's stress levels were high due to the proximity of her paternal grandparents to summer wildfires in Serbia, which was ironic given the environmental problems the country faced due to deforestation. Out in the wilds, their children and grandchildren had been urging them for a decade to move into a town or city, close to amenities, healthcare and general help. They continued to do so, while knowing it would never happen. To justify to themselves that they tried, that when the worst happened, it didn't unfold through their silence.

Fiona refused to leave a tip. Her father palmed a twenty and handed it to the frazzled young lady, out of sight, as the others hurried and bashed out the door.

As they said their farewells and loaded the young into the car, if you could call it a car, as a smartphone was to a phone. When the doors were shut, Fiona stopped Julian.

"Once the children are in bed tonight, you're going to walk me through our finances, I want to know where it all is, and what it's all up to. Don't. This isn't up for discussion. Or we can talk about something else..."

She took the keys off him, got in, and started the engine.

Finances.

It was the finances *what did it*. Sat with Fiona, opening the kimono on the myriad of assets, their homes, a buy-to-let, pensions, index funds, shares, and *other investments*. Fiona was *good* surprised, that as well as the money hurtling out the door, the money that remained inside was feasting away on society, spawning. The outgoings when he laid them out were extensive. Bad surprised.

While Fiona winced at some of their expenditures, Julian messed about with spreadsheets while he gamed how things would evolve if they ever got divorced. With the house close to paid off, he wouldn't see that again for starters. What a kick in the guts that would be. Dividing and apportioning the rest, however the fuck that would work, gave him a headache. How to open the door and shovel millions of pounds out onto the street. The second home sold to allow him to buy a flat somewhere, with just enough room to have the children to visit with a room each. A downgrade in location. Dividing up the rest didn't feel too troubling, that would halve the assets and halve the people it served, although the threat of his children suffering any educational downgrades was unutterable. Yet these thoughts bled straight into the social, the logistical, the familial. Telling the children. Telling the families. Are you married? No, I'm divorced. Shock among friends. Household maintenance. A bevy of day-to-day administration that Fiona took care of. Sure, he'd have freedom, yet at what price. An empty apartment, devoid of action and problem-solving. The silence. A re-orientation of his social life. And Fiona remained the one he chose.

His thoughts moved on but reverted. Another man. A step-parent. His children's victories less about him and his fathercraft. Victories he may not even be told about, or maybe heard of from third parties. Another called dad. Slipping in and enjoying his money and his wife.

No.

Surrounded by a home with bespoke fittings, everything they needed, of the highest quality their level allowed. The branded goods, the odd super-luxuries, and all the names and bragging rights for their circle. Their circle. Extra disruption.

He realised as he opened everything up, that he had had it good, for too long. Had lived high on the hog, having it all. He cared for Iva but that was *unsustainable*. A watch word of the day, and one he made a note of for his dealings with Iva over the next week or so. Fiona had to jolt him out of his daydream as he scenario planned the conversation with the Serbian siren, thinking up lines, parallels, and most of all, a vision of the future *she could have*.

Instead, he felt a new charge, spurred on by the status of fatherhood, as winner of bread. A new exhilaration from the possibilities of taking their finances up further notches, to further solidify and ring-fence their freedoms, standing, and control. Keep the money flowing, for it flowed up. Meeting the challenge of the neighbours, who had been flaunting some lifestyle upgrades. A boat. A boat.

Pressured by Iva to meet up, Julian agreed for them to get lunch together, away from work. He would have preferred to discuss this over the phone, or text, or to never hear from her again, and for them both to ghost and slip into oblivion. She sounded shaken when they spoke, so much so that he had to ask.

"My grandparents and the fires. I bloody told you this."

Oh yes, he did remember. When prompted. Gun to his head, a million in prizemoney, *'What is Iva concerned about at the moment?'* would prompt nothing besides a guess. He backpedalled, running through some specific questions, agitating to move her to a steadier place.

He now had to step her through this. Through and down, level by level, week by week, until they reached an impasse. He had to talk his way *out of* her bed.

Iva benefitted in all circumstances by the obsequiousness shown to the good-looking. The higher bar that was set to challenge them in social and business settings. The look which questioned whether The Rules were going to be applied to the beauty stood opposite. Oh, I see, you're not *good enough* for me, so you're going to *punish me* for your shortcomings.

Their booking wasn't on the system. While Julian was ferreting about with his phone, *Iva* cut into proceedings, "You're half empty, can we just sit down already?" whereby she pointed at a two berth next to the window, indicated "we'll sit here," and walked over, taking the window seat. Julian was concerned with the proximity of the neighbours, but weighed it up. It could be worse, so he joined her.

Once the fuss around menus, waters, drinks was dealt with, Julian led with an enquiry into the grandparents. Iva answered without tears. Julian wasn't sure if this was unsentimental or a construct of her upbringing. It jarred with how unsettled she sounded over the phone. Alarm bells sounded manipulation. He tried to stay with the response, take in some details, listen for god's sake, he cared about Iva, didn't he? Yet the words found no landing, as he nodded, running through the lines he had to take to progress his liberating agenda.

Iva had problems with the portion size (lacking control), price (low), food temperature (too hot, raising suspicion of microwave use), atmosphere (dead, and why were they eating there?) and later, the length of the wait for the bill with the clock ticking.

It was a fractured time together, and neither of them seemed to be able to pull it together, to create a consistent thread in the conversation.

Julian crafted his usual language, moving away from talk of time, and talk of difficulties, problematic disruptions, how easy this wasn't. Tropes told and sold across ten generations. The welfare of children, how to desist might be beneficial to all. He laced in compliments, reassurances, they needed time to think and to keep talking, nothing was decided of course. Space, thought, discussion, adult agreement.

He wondered what was going through her mind. Was she also computing the options in front of her, to what extent was she bought into him. He just couldn't see how the end wouldn't also benefit her. Set her free to pursue something of her own, in all likelihood with someone with more potential than him, given the time. He watched her, trying to put the right face patterns together, the soft, considered words to match her reactions. With a diplomat's deft.

Iva appeared calm yet roiled beneath.

"I see," she began, tilting her head to one side, harshing her features as the strength was ushered through.

"The bullshit is all done with now? The fun is over. While I've been making plans."

He went through the calming measures in his head, the words that needed to be said to bring her back, as the bitterness curled from her rancorous lips.

Making plans with someone was something Steven hadn't given thought to in a while. When meeting girls on the casual, sure, dinners, drinks, a bit of culture, at a push a weekend away. To think further ahead, a longer weekend or a week or two away, somewhere intimate, to the US, Japan, the romance of Italy or the south of France. Skiing, diving. Money, planning, hassle, all worth it. Things they could do together, with his friends, her friends. He had that wedding invite on the horizon. These things came to him with the possibility of Amanda. A plus one he could accompany with pride. A chance to mature into something new. He mentioned her by name a couple of times when asked about dating life.

Steven had given Amanda some room, left it a couple of days. He hadn't heard from her. She was a busy person, and he didn't want to overplay his hand, as much as he was drawn to. Interest and keenness were the devil, for the man trying to slow-play a woman of interest into his long-term plans. He texted something breezy, couple of things he had been doing, how was she?

He got on with his day, as best he could when checking his phone every fifteen, ten, five, two minutes. As the elapse time increased, so did the frequency of the checks. For he was heading toward the oblivion zone.

Amanda got a sense from a couple of his evasive questions about family, that it was not all calm waters in Steven's life. Time spent in his home revealed him to be solitary, and at his age, she expected a better relationship track record. He wasn't as ahead in his life as her typical beaus. The sex was good, and it scratched an itch, but it would go no further. Able to read his message from the alert, without revealing she had read it, she turned her phone over and got on with her day.

He cursed himself. There was a narrow window between two people being good enough or insufficient for each other, on either side. And his enthusiasm had run away from him. He knew from experience that when he was into someone, it wouldn't be reciprocated. He wasn't enough for them. The sure fire indicators that he was punching above his weight, his desire to tell other people, to think ahead and make plans. The elusive match, two people appealing to each other in balance, and positive vibes, out of reach.

Though he knew it was gone before it even got started, the nagging doubt of everyone dumped, left alone, forgotten, the 'what if' something terrible has happened, or *they* think *he* is lukewarm and not that interested. The awful inevitability of 'one more' text or call or visit. Then the regret, the humiliation, the lowering of oneself to carry out that last act, when one could instead choose to retain some pride. The last fall mattered. Yet if the prize were high enough, even a five percent chance made it worth rolling the dice.

He didn't want to move on from this one. He thought they were a good match. She'd wasted his time, tired his emotions. Didn't she know at the beginning? He's not good enough for her. Not sure about that. She's just disappeared without word. Met someone better. It no longer felt *all in the game*.

He decided to leave it twenty-four hours, put through one phone call.

Keeping busy, he went to the gym, went shopping, went for drinks that evening, the phone a constant. Check, check, tap, tap, double-check. Checked for online status, read message confirmation. A hundred times plus.

The next day, voicemail, after too many rings. Amanda blocked him. And got on with her life.

100001
CHAPTER 33
Richmond Park: Annabel falls: Helen has her own problems

While the calendar had determined that autumn had begun, Richmond Park was still in summer splendour, thick with greens, trees full and low. Shrubs, grasses and ferns reached high so that they almost met. This created a dark snake of varying thickness which undulated over the lush carpeting, speared by the bobbing antlers of a stag going about its doings.

The ferns died out over winter, and left a flat mess of brown, deaden straw, but as they grew through spring and the start of summer, they filled and fanned out, and reached a peak of six or seven feet in great swathes. This gave good cover for the wildlife, both the inhabitants and the visitors, and the deer would strut through their own cut paths, and the odd rabbit or rodent would hide out within.

At its busiest, bushiest peak, open expanses of knee high wheat-coloured grasses merged into woodland, with streams, lakes, ponds, brooks. The vast centre rolled up and down, with a hundred routes with paved roads, sandy horse tracks, grassy causeways and well-trodden meanderings through the taller flora. Monoliths of large blackened trees stricken by lightning attacks. Trees fallen and upended in storms, now climbing frames for children and dogs. Dens and camps dotted about, built with logs and branches in the woods.

First-thing photographers were out in khaki, all the gear, shooting deer. Their long lenses with camouflaged barrels, their Canon cannons, signalling their level. Agitated by the potential disruption of the distant dog walkers and their random beasts. Fixing tripods, scanning for a suitable mob, twenty strong in parts, to get their iconic shots. The stag raising its head, covered in green and brown ferns, living and dead. The males settled in their rank. A crèche of fawns with protective females sauntering around, wondering how they'll get a moments peace with the visitors and their camera phones.

Fishermen, fisherpeople, setting up in the central lake, hopeful for a strong morning. Happy enough either way. Elsewhere, rugby union training reflected the local population and its demographics, as did the ballet school, the golf course, the LTA National Tennis Centre down the road. Its neighbour, The Priory, treating the upper echelons, suffering, having reached the uppermost echelons of the hierarchy of human needs.

Dog walkers had their mental map of locations to get coffee or to snack, the toilets. The unofficial toilet spot, a copse with a clearing which gave good cover, but which led nowhere. If you saw no one behind you, you weren't going to run into anyone.

From the high points, a clear view across London to the classic central landmarks and the city beyond a distant layer, sat atop the treeline, frosted behind a warm summer haze. The occasional lodge or what could be country homes, to puzzle over.

Despite the plentiful traffic and aeroplanes lining up at one minute intervals on their descent to Heathrow, it was so well looked after. A rare enclave that felt apart from the world's problems. Litter disposed of, or at least cleared up by the rangers. No drunken picnic fallout, common elsewhere at weekends. A peaceful home for the deer, until selected for culling in November or February. Population control, health and prosperity for the lucky ones.

Planes, tick, tick, tick, one minute after another, fifteen hundred a day. Regularity manmade, imposed on unplanned nature. Though the woodpeckers displayed their mechanical chops. Richmond, the final destination for the occasional stowaway, frozen and dropped from the sky as the doors hiding the wheels open on final descent. Potential for a nasty surprise, reading the papers on a sunny morning. Marmalade dropped, hitting the ground seconds after a rigid torso. Could spoil one's morning.

With its cultivated plantation, its education notices and natural toilets, and its quiet warnings against mushroom rustling or disturbing ground-nested birds, it was hard to imagine much bad happening here. To kite-flyers and school troops on rugs in their mini neon vests. But of course, all things happen everywhere, given sufficient time. The occasional started fire, a disagreement, fisticuffs or serious collision between warring cyclists and motorists. Cyclists bumped off before their bikes were stolen.

For the most part though, tranquillity, such that a swoop of parakeets would sound a whoosh before they flashed by.

Annabel and Barney had driven to meet in the central car park, away from the main circular road, and where they could get straight into it. Annabel was returning from staying with friends south of London.

Although too early for families and adults without dogs, the triangular road around the park was filling up with road cyclists, in blacks and whites, oranges, pinks, neons. And various exotic versions, three-wheelers driven by hand, and what could be described as road skiers, with wheeled boards on their feet and poles to shove themselves along. Every day the tension between these road users and drivers, trying to pass cyclists chatting two abreast. Barney sat behind them and took in easy, Annabel less so, looking for any opening to swing out into the path of distant oncoming traffic. Tens of thousands of decisions of this ilk made each day, where the consequence of bad timing might cost someone's freedom. A low probability, high impact event, to shave off a minute or two. Annabel carved off a few minutes, which would be absorbed within a couple of slow hours.

As the second to arrive drove in, they waved and then met at the picnic tables, in front of the kiosk with the noisy, choking generator. It was too soon for them to get into that so they both ignored it. Jess raced over to Annabel and jumped up, pawing at Annabel's old coat. An attempt to own something she never could. A feeling felt also by Annabel, who felt saddened by the transitory nature of her time with Jess, one moment there, the next gone. The adults shared a quick hug and a single cheek air kiss. Barney checked she too had a homemade coffee and they set off, Annabel carrying hers in a thirty-pound Kinto Travel Tumbler, Barney in something he picked up in Sainsbury's, six quid.

Terrier heaven, for identifying and tailing rabbits, fallow and red deer, squirrels, rodents, other life. Fresh horse poo for snacks, droppings for rolling and scent masking. Odours to track, legs to cock or bottoms to squat, markings to make. A time of the rut, and energetic, noisy stags, all bluster, strength, competition and signalling. Their antlers, nature's fastest growing tissue, a pointed threat to any dog or human straying too close.

Three aeroplanes in a line, large plane, small plane, large.

"Back to one per minute," Barney observed, reflecting on the walks they had done during the bad flu season when it was a non-existent or much reduced service. And the park was rammed at eight o'clock.

"Yeah," was all Annabel could muster, nodding to feign energy, keep Barney off the scent.

They found their way, led by Jess, who figured her way through the ferns and woods to the small Leg of Mutton pond, away from the large split lake of Pen Ponds, a beloved spot for dog swimming. Jess turned to Barney to prompt him to appear the ball and throw it in for collection. They went through the motions many, many times, and it would end when Barney chose. A few of the other dog walkers dissipated, with their shiny, wet black labs carrying large, thick oversized sticks, stopping to roll shake the water out of their coats. The humans knew to stay well clear. It was a good time to talk to Annabel, and Barney took the opportunity.

He threw the ball into the pond, toward the centre. Jess threw herself in, and, it being shallow enough, propelled herself forward with her feet before depth moved her into a thrashing swim, before a smooth flow with bobbing head.

"How have you been since last time?" he ventured.

Annabel welled up, something it was impossible to cover up, though she tried, as most people did. Just as Barney, and most people, pretend not to have seen.

"I'm all right," she attempted.

He tilted his head and raised an eyebrow. C'mon.

She decided dishonesty was the best option, and tried to inflate the stress of some matter at home.

She hoped to take Barney off on a tangent, distract, but he didn't buy it. He continued to throw the squeaky ball, watching the ripples move out in a wider circle until Jess cut through them. He would give it until they reached the next woods before having another go.

Great sections of the park were dense with great tall trees, dark from the high and leafy canopies. Home to what sounded, even to the least knowledgeable of listeners, a rangy ensemble of birds. Calling, shrilling, squawking and tutting, at different frequencies and cadences, competing for what could have been tropical or jungle air.

Jess dove into the tall ferns and was gone, leaving Barney and Annabel to follow the shaking, shuffling tops, as the dog cut its way through, following her nose, and the scents trailing hither and yon. This could be a precarious moment, as if her sensory receptors were over-stimulated, all other thoughts would clear away. She would pursue with a singular focus, and switch off the ears. Barney had lost her once here, as she tracked all over and round and about, before she was spotted by strangers who joined the dots of an independent dog and the dogged calls of a worried human.

They watched as the tallest ferns shivered, and then spotted movement further across, until the shakes met and a young deer sprung out of the side and belted off, with a slower Jess in full pace pursuit. They watched the chase, each clenching their fists or fingers, hoping the deer would get clear enough and Jess would return. Barney called. Jess had reached a section with a body of water, in a wide, muddy banked pit, and stopped. She drank from the clear edge. And then turned and headed back as they watched, as she tried to distract herself with new possibilities.

Annabel watched as Barney chased Jess to urge her away as she bent to scoff mouthfuls of horse dung, giving it the old college try, circling back in disobedience for a couple of cycles, before accepting she had stolen enough extras.

Barney floated the idea of getting food after, at a chain they were no strangers to. Annabel had no hunger, but didn't want to say that, and instead chose to impersonate the staff. Barney felt this was snide and unlike her.

"Here they come, yet again, for the same orders they always get, off our never-changing menu. Same drinks, same tip, same bathroom breaks."

They passed an old couple, who looked relaxed in that comfortable, privileged, Richmondian Boomer way. Just the health issues and death to fear now. Just. In that safest of environments. No miscreants were to be found in Richmond Park. Tripping over a ground hole or rough terrain the principal dangers. Their hound caught up with them.

"Morning," said the gentleman, full and clear. Someone who had spent his life being listened to.

"What model is the dog? Parson's?" the wife asked.

"Yes, that's right. Jess."

The two dogs mixed, executed a ying-yang and zoomies, chasing each other in great arcs, across uncertain ground, at speed.

"Jess," she repeated, "wonderful. Good day."

They all continued on, bracken summer-crunching under walking shoes.

"They're refreshing our company values," Barney mentioned, looking across.

"Number two. No sex worker abuse in third world countries," she advanced.

"Annabel."

"Sorry."

"First do no harm might be a good starter."

"Unfashionable."

"I'm trying to get on the group, try and push some greenery. It's a big organisation. If I can make a small difference in policy..."

"Sure. Sounds good."

That most uninterested modern response.

He pressed on, "Whether it's recycling, or travel policies, procurement of better products, thinking about tech sustainability, recycling of computers to the third world. There's so many ways we can be better."

"While humanity is choosing all the routes to be worse. Look at us," she said, "even us! We've both driven all this way, separately."

"We can partial car pool next time," he said, "you can trek down to mine and I'll drive," he joked, having a rare dig at her, "not that we'll be back here for the *sorefeeable* future. A Christmas walk, maybe."

"Car-pooling five miles. It's not enough. Who's working on the big things? China, coal, India, oceans filled with plastic."

"They are going to do what they are going to do; don't forget the poverty they've endured. It's their turn for all the stuff. We need to lead and hope they'll follow. Politics, Belle. There's people to be elected."

"Not in China."

"It'll be the cull again," she added, "after a summer of watching and enjoying the deer, it'll be shotgun time and night assassinations. Nation of animal lovers."

Annabel stared at Barney, who sensed emptiness and tried to lighten the mood.

"For years I though a shotgun wedding was one arranged at short notice. What are we going to do, campaign to change that too? The deer would have to go altogether."

He felt every conversational switch met a junction.

"Environmental collapse is like Alzheimer's, it's the long goodbye, happening slow, then happening fast."

She paused then continued, staring at him, "Heatwaves in India, water wars, acid oceans, mass extinction. Without even getting into the robots coming, an extinction of truth, the next hot cold war. And we're all complicit, we're all fucking hypocrites. In our nice warm homes, clicking away at the bait, deliveries turning up every other day, in our new season cashmere."

Annabel gasped, wailed and her legs buckled, wounded, as one of the surrounding deer might during a cull. Over her shoulder, a female deer looked at Barney, and he felt distracted before reverting back to Annabel's gaze as she looked away and fell.

He flailed at her, trying to get his arms under her armpits to help hold her but she was already on her knees, soaking up the autumn damp from the marshy ground, before falling sideways into a mermaid pose. He knelt down with her in sympathy, he also now wet of kneecaps. He thought she might pass out, then he felt her hands grip the top of his arms as he leaned down, and he heard her sobbing. It was an uncomfortable and awkward coming together, and he tried to move her to a dry area and sit her down.

Panic attack, a meltdown, a fallapart, or whatever this was, Barney imagined this playing out dozens a time a day on the streets of Haggerston. Young people, drunk, skunked, spiced, stressed and working through their childhood traumas. But for this to be happening in this setting was drama. His mind was scrambled, as her mental overheating and exhaustion manifested too in the physical. He could do little but check a few things, as if dealing with an emergency, sit with her while she calmed, gather and tether the dog. They moved under a tree for shade, and he waited as she tried to calm herself. They took their time, before walking back to the cars, where they took one of the picnic tables, sat down and drunk their hot drinks in silence. She agreed to drive back to his ahead of him, where she could recover and have something to eat, which she didn't want. He put Jess in with Annabel to keep her company, and they drove away.

At work the next day, Barney kept a low profile at his desk, pretending to be in the middle of something, scanning for Annabel's arrival. He had texted to make sure she was on her way in, and still alive. The message had been read so that was something. He phoned Helen from a meeting room.

Helen was standard-late reaching her workplace. Didn't leave early enough late. Missed call, Barney. She put her phone and bag down, took off her warming autumn accessories, logged on, and went to make a cup of tea. She was stopped by the CEO's Executive Assistant on the way. She (always a she, even now) was taking an order from her boss ahead of lunch, taking down some new rich-people allergies belonging to the attendees. She added to the ever-increasing list of anaphylactics, irritants, and pleasantries, the dos-and-don'ts she had to accommodate and navigate around.

Helen couldn't be bothered to wait and walked off to the kitchen. Passing by the ee ay on the way back and still on the phone, Helen mouthed and mimed her way through an office summary of "I'll come back later, it's OK."

Helen took her tea and her phone into a booth and called Barney, who spoke about Annabel. She steadied him before unloading the potted history of her own current woes. New job problems, *shit at home* (level of which was conveyed via tone rather than detail, which was not given). How she herself was just about managing, holding it together, keeping the balls in the air and the plates spinning. Tiredness of which she had never before experienced, she admitted, spilling over into her tired use of metaphor, which they both had to laugh at. As a general rule, Helen advised, if things were getting serious, he had to involve family. Friends were all well and good, but there was a limit to the support they could provide. Get in touch, or sit down with her and force contact that way, that was what he should do.

"Sorry, I can't be much help, beyond that," she added, pausing to have a look around outside her glass goldfish bowl of a room, see who was sitting outside listening, who was waiting to come in. "Sorry again, it's not the best time."

"If you want something done," he said.

"Give it to a busy person. I know."

They had had these conversations before.

"Call me if you need anything. Love."

Annabel walked in.

He had to give this some serious thought, but he had a lot to get done that day himself, and just had to park the whole thing until the evening, when he would be able to cogitate and formulate a plan. After all, the paycheck demanded that the machinery of commerce turned.

The annual visit to the optician, for Helen to learn how much poorer her eyesight had become. And an opportunity for her to take a few hours off when working from home for journey to and fro, and add in some shopping on the way back. An appointment which, for years, was attended to by the familiar Mr Jeffery, who she trusted to take honest care of her, despite being part of one of the large logos. Since it was *merged with* (acquired by) an even larger corporation, the humble Mr Jeffery had gone, replaced by an ever-changing cast of young, energetic replacements, bringing with them new methods, new technologies. The convincing cleanliness of new machines and a facelift of the stuffy interior.

Fancier ranges. Rangier fancies.

The straightforward Mr Jeffery, with his oodles of scruples, was no doubt out there, working, traceable. Yet the new technology, the new methods, comforted Helen in new ways. New-fangled trackers and tracers of fearsome and emerging conditions, diseases, syndromes, difficulties, had Helen locked in. The fear machine took and then it returned.

A visit, which, like many things in life, tended to bring the negative. There was little chance of upside, just the hope that one left stable. Unworsened. As was tradition she crossed her fingers as the escalator rose. Year after year, same month, same escalator, same ritual.

Greeted with politeness and dealt with in a smooth manner, worthy of a workshopped workflow. Occasional low-level smiles and an attempt at humour, she was offered a seat and invited to preview the stock, which she did. Then beckoned forward, with a wave of the arm, and up a couple of stairs to the examination section.

Then onto eye pressure, glaucoma, and peripheral vision checks with its peppering of lights. Machines so new you could smell them. And guided into a separate room for the test itself, and some *chat*. A thin, bright-eyed girl in her mid-twenties, with gold costume jewellery and a high necked jumper for the season, settled Helen in. Her dark brown eyes shone, set against her tanned, and, guessed Helen, middle eastern skin. Bright with elan, she moved and fussed about between paper and computer, between paper files and digital files, dealing with the physical equipment, the tools of the job.

Lifestyle questions, the usual; exercise, diet, recent issues. Work.

Helen wanted to say 'work with computers,' as if talking with nan. She muttered, "Marketing, charity."

"You don't sound so happy about that?" the youngster replied, wide-eyed.

"I'm thinking of doing something different," she confirmed, to explain her nonplussedness.

She regretted it, as she tightened for the next question.

"Oh, really. Like what?"

"I don't know. I'm trying to figure that out."

She boiled inside. The white prison cell of the twelve by six-foot room had her pinned under a dozen spotlights, firing down their headache inducing rays. Here, even here, she was quizzed, under the microscope. And she knew, that to have no answer could not go on. And no one was going to provide the answer, except herself.

100010
CHAPTER 34
Iva and Julian strains: Francesca and Helen leave for Paris: Pigalle bar

While Fiona was dealing with her daughter hurtling away from childhood, Julian was having intense sex with Iva. Although indifferent to blow jobs, Iva had a soft, wet, gentle mouth and she liked to give one to kick things off for them both. She would then kiss him with long wet French kisses, knowing he was tasting himself, one of those grubby little sex acts that went by unspoken. Once he was inside, spooning her, Julian thought about and got off on the notion of making Iva pregnant. A nightmare in real life, but for the short-term purposes of intensity of orgasm, a winner.

As they lay there spent, a fog of atmosphere hung in the air, waiting to be broken. As Iva got up, pulled on a robe and walked through to the kitchen to pour a glass of wine for them to share, it would not drift. Julian regretted coming over, that the hangover of a serious conversation wasn't worth the sex. Of course, it was easy to say that after the act itself.

As she walked back, wine in hand, she demanded to know what was happening with staffing. And don't give her any of that confidentiality bullshit. Straight to the point. No seven rounds of 'What's wrong? Nothing'.

He watched her walk across the room.

While handling her panic, his mind wandered on another track, like when told a relative had died and one noticed an ornament or remembered not to forget to pick something up later. Julian made a note of some fitness tech kit that had appeared.

"They're looking at who they can cut, that's no secret. Whether it's a case of taking out a team and re-structuring, or picking off some weak antelope."

"How is that fucking measured?" she said, stirred.

"You can't fucking say any of this, OK?" he fired back, raising his voice, underlining in red.

"Make sure I'm not on that list then, OK?" she said with menace.

It was the first time that he sensed she was feeling flighty, yet he remained sanguine. He envisaged seeing her erupt, touch paper would not require much, yet she was too driven beyond him to jeopardise her career track for a riotous exit. There would be no house-burning.

"Jesus. I don't even know if I'm all right yet," he wailed, "you'll be fine, you'll walk into anywhere."

He was about to say he could get her interviews, and stopped himself. It wasn't that he wouldn't, yet while it might reassure her, it just dug him deeper to offer without request. If she stressed more as a result, well, people stress all the time. Life in the twenty-first century. Life before that.

She sat down and slugged back some wine, and he sprawled out, running through his sector and the catatonic things happening at the moment. Fractured markets, bare contradictions in the laws of economics, all over the shop. Long-term system stasis, as the modern economic Ponzi scheme seemed to be grinding to a halt. Decade after decade of collapse followed by a new set of smoke and mirrors, allowing individuals the opportunities to ringfence great fortunes for themselves. Generation after generation. Energy, water, fossil fuels, all the green shit, as his boss was trying to train himself out of putting it. What the absolute cunting fuck was happening? Market, individuals, corporations, governments, all hawking about, trying to find answers. After the financial crisis of the noughties, when the markets went doolally, here it was, sectioned schizophrenia.

He kicked the can down the road with platitudes, people he would talk to, angles he would take on her behalf, while as the words tumbled out in smooth, educated tones, his mind turned over the numbers relating to his own home lifestyle, and the risk profile he put against Wyatt life.

Julian left Iva's place. It was dark, with the misty cream of streetlamps and the bobbing of cyclist headlamps propping things up.

A window of a ground floor flat was half lit from inside, and on the back wall, a neon sign, most of which was obscured. He thought it read 'betrayal' but it read 'portrayal'. He couldn't figure what the entire message might be.

Across the street, a couple of dope fiends, arms abuzz, all movement. Fly. Fiending their way to their next job. Creatives, working harder than anyone. Always thinking an hour and two moves ahead, and never beyond. They were no threat; he was sure of that.

He stopped and stared at a brazen fox, all agile, pausing before stepping up onto a car roof. Sat atop, watching Julian, as he watched back. Paw prints in mud dust led up the windscreen. A fox concerned with watching the streets, in need of food, sex, sleep and shelter. Both animals eyeing each other, seeking to understand.

Helen had been waiting at the café in the retail centre at London St. Pancras International for half an hour, removing risk, happy to be on her way from home. Misjudging the sugar in her milky latte, left her with a cloying coffee and a pastry swirl, glossy with glaze and sticky with raisins. The slow rate at which she picked away at these reflected their disappointment. Shame set in, with Francesca imminent, and she ditched the remains in a *clean it up yourself* bin.

That human instinct kicked in, whereby one preferred to see someone approach in the distance, rather than be pounced upon unawares, so Helen kept a roving eye out while selecting a podcast. It took her a few goes to find the right thing to listen to.

She assumed Francesca would come from one logical direction so kept watch there. The piano left in the large, white vestibule for the punters to use, was snared by a young lady. In the distance, she played in a skilled yet casual manner to match the location and state of the piano, and put something energetic together for the expectant travellers and shoppers. Shopping in the transport hub.

Francesca walked through on the horizon, and found Helen sat in the first place she looked. She passed the piano sounds, and strode through with rolling luggage, which had the hell battered into it.

"What happened to your case?" Helen exclaimed.

"It's pre-crashed. You buy it like this, then when it gets battered about, who cares?"

"Wow. Every day a new madness."

"Come here."

They embraced.

Francesca wore a black autumn coat – not too thick or thin. A long navy skirt, replete with pleats, and boots made for walking.

"Jeans get everywhere when I travel," she commented, looking at Helen in denim and a purple top.

"Purple is back, good choice."

Helen was messing about with her new headphones. Brushed black and copper and lights in lines of futuristic colour.

"Check me out."

Helen looked up and saw a couple, in their fifties, the woman taller than the man, who was wider. Bright pink roller luggage. Animal print, worn by him.

"Wow. How English are they?"

"The odd couple."

"Every pan has a lid," drolled Helen.

Francesca smiled, and disappeared for a cigarette. They had time, yet Helen puffed herself.

"Already?"

She girded her loins for phone sessions at tables in restaurants, on the half hour, watching a smouldering profile of Francesca behind glass.

They muddled their way through all the checks and bureaucracy, which reminded them of how the Europeans just *love* having their papers checked. Receiving their validation. Such a good citizen. Your papers all seem to be in order. Blush, pride.

Francesca thought of police across Europe attacking citizens attempting to enter places of worship, buy groceries, going about minding their own fucking business. Set upon, tackled and pinned down, harried like dogs, by dogs. To protect your health. She had no doubt whatever that given a gun and the legal authority, some would have dispatched these people and left them to die in a ditch. The savages of the past remained in our genes, walking among us today, waiting to reappear. Thoughts she would share with others, not with Helen, and not in keeping with the mood and objective of the trip.

Francesca let Helen take the window seat.

Once able to, she procured them wine from the trolley.

"Pour these," she said, handing the goods to Helen, "give me five minutes to sort a few things out," she said, applying herself to her network.

Helen pulled out a magazine for the next fifteen minutes or so.

"Right," said Francesca, "back in the room."

"Finally."

Francesca outlined the list of potential cultural and general daytime options for the trip. What *she* wanted to do. Helen was easy. Too easy. Francesca hoped to see some passion, some energy.

"Fran, I'm just happy to be here, you always choose good things. I'll go with the flow."

"OK then. A little less going with the flow may pay you dividends."

Francesca dug in a little, so that Helen knew they were going to have some conversations on this trip. It was not going to be pure leisure.

She outlined some of the cultural options, one-off shows, timeless stalwarts, parks, streets, districts they should call upon. Tying her plan into film, books. Helen recognised a few of the references and tried to keep up.

The ambient noise, and the clusters of chatty youth around them afforded them privacy, compared with, say, the morning train of suited bores.

Francesca gave her the lowdown on Simon, and some of his inner workings. Helen was rapt, fascinated by how others' live, not by any feeling that she was lacking, missing out on anything. It was obvious he would be chasing to the grave.

This moved on into reminisces of men past, some of which was caught by the man sat behind, who pretended to read for the benefit of those across the aisle. As Francesca dialled down to a whisper, Helen chuckled and he wondered what he had missed out on.

Helen revealed some things about one of her first boyfriends which should remain between her and Francesca. Francesca wound back through the years, thankful for the richness of her life. It was a lie that life was short. This continued until Francesca checked their mapped location and prepped Helen for the tunnel, in a motherly moment.

Maybe she wouldn't be a dreadful parent, as she assumed she would be. They drank wine and Helen felt a rush as they hurtled through the tunnel, with its flashes of strip lighting, free from signs of life.

They switched back to what they might do on the trip. Francesca shared a couple of restaurant bookings she made, for one lunch and one dinner.

As the air pressure change signalled their departure back into the light in Northern France, Helen watched, interested by the lack of drama from the transition, underscoring that they were lands separated by time. She felt sad at the fractures the two nations suffered, without end. This was shrugged off with a drink.

In youth, they would have garbled on the whole way, like the girls a few seats behind. For the final stretch Helen watched from the window, warm and smug in a wine fug. Alcohol rounded her system, and brought on the grogginess which would set in as they transferred. A cold wind and a snappy word from Francesca would be needed to wake her.

As the train slowed in that way trains do after a long journey, as they run out of puff and their last duty is to ensure safe passage, Francesca warned Helen that in the Gard du Nord, they would not be arriving at a terminus of great prestige and fanfare.

"Hold your nose for the next twenty minutes. Shut your eyes, I'll guide you."

They hustled their way through the tatty entrance hall and Francesca steered them to the two-hundred strong taxi queue, which alternated between moving in large batches and not moving at all.

"This isn't Paris," Francesca confirmed.

"I hope not."

"If you come on your own, get the Metro."

"Why aren't we getting the Metro?"

The taxi climbed the long straight incline of the Rue Des Martyrs, leaving a dragging blur of boutiques, patisseries, cafés; a drive-by of flowers, fruit and vegetables, and locals, which left Helen wishing it would slow down. Her head turned and scanned. Francesca reassured her that it was main street, they'd get to explore and know it well over the next few days.

As they stretched up the straight, to be sure, Francesca directed the driver to tuck into a street on the left, and they were at their boutique spa hotel. Getting out and taking the brief hit from the autumn cold, Helen looked at the black art deco styled front, black lines cutting into the window panes. She stared up at the towering light cream Parisian townhouse, dotted with black cast iron balconies and balustrades, under the clearest of blue, nine/eleven skies.

The driver worked at speed to remove their luggage as the narrow rue held a single lane for traffic, and one lane for parked cars. A lifetime of manners, the politeness that goes with not wishing to hold up others. Helen jumped across to hand over the Euros for the fare, after clarifying the total with Francesca.

"On the next street over is a hotel which used to be a whorehouse, walls adorned with photographed flesh," Francesca commented, "but this one's a bit of a treat."

"Shame. I like a brothel conversion."

"We can book the pool and wet area here for ourselves, with no hoi polloi perving at our supermodel physiques."

"I don't mind that," offered Helen.

"There's a place for everything, if that's your persuasion. As London, Paris is a playground for whatever smacks your taste. Sweet, unsavoury, tang."

They checked into their rooms, and Helen was delighted with the spotless room, white pressed linens, and the bedside fittings and conveniences. The patterned curtains opened to reveal bright greenery under that sky. Next door, Francesca was pleased enough. She would be comfortable, even if it were a little corporate and lacking pizazz.

Helen flopped backward onto the bed into a snow angel, and after thirty seconds or so got up and smoothed the bed over like the top of an iced cake she was glazing. She spent the next half an hour unpacking and organising before meeting Francesca as arranged.

"OK, are you ready?"

"Yup."

"Stroll and orientation?"

"Absolutely."

Leaving the hotel, Helen bid au revoir to the staff, and they turned right to walk the short fifty yards to the main street. Helen crossed over and stopped, spellbound, by what purported to be a whole patisserie dedicated to meringues, and which she scanned for confirmation. A flawless looking establishment, all whites and bright lights, ceiling lamps like floating saucers, downward light beams shafting down cream shadows onto the walls. The brights broken up by some small dark shades high to the ceiling, and the rich colours of preserve jars on the back wall, among bagged clusters of minis for those grabbing and going.

'This could be a long day,' thought Francesca, as she stopped next to Helen, peering in. After a few seconds she walked on, using her soft power to keep things moving.

They turned left to power up the hill, and came to the first of many florists which bloomed throughout the region. Helen was enchanted as they passed clothing boutiques, shoe shops, bistros, bakeries, and the practicalities seen anywhere – banks, mini markets, opticians. Francesca indicated a few things Helen should check out, including a bookshop at the top, with a small English-speaking section.

"You can explore tomorrow morning at your leisure," she indicated, "now, a drink to kick things off, let's head this way," and they strode off into the darker narrow streets off to the right, cast in shadow of the six-storey buildings.

They wandered until Helen insisted they stopped for a photograph of a florist, a burst of greens and colours, forced out by light, spilling onto the street, under a light grey awning with a white light strip slung over it like a rectangular white snake. Fifty shades of green. Oranges, pinks, purples, coloured pots, supporting tables and wooden boxes, bare branches climbing the white walls. Above, ramshackle, worn white shutters, some straight, others skew-whiff. One hiding most of the street sign. The final clincher, making it the perfect snap, two iconic dark blue tiles, the street number 59.

Francesca stood back and admired the shot, the setting, cool in the shadows, taking the opportunity now they were not puffing uphill, to light a smoke to puff on.

Helen took ten photos of the same view, which did not impress the shopkeeper, who looked on with disdain.

Francesca led them on to a casual bar she knew, the kind of rustic place to share a bottle of red, and a mixed board of cheeses and meats. From the street, the look of a wine shop, also selling vintage bric-a-brac. Inside, clusters of tables, a few tourist stumblers, regular after-workers, and friends of the establishment, on stools at the counter, enjoying the start of the latest session at the joint.

Helen loved the vintage signs, the endless bottles, and a feeling that she recognised this as Paris, as it had existed in her mind.

As they settled into their seats, the staff messed about with the drop lamps from the central switch, alternating them until they hit the right balance. Light enough for reading, yet not fierce. They chose to sit next to an iron bannister separating the main area from a staircase to the basement, the wall behind stacked with wine.

The room at the rear was awash with warm yellows and displays of interior items for sale. The main room comprised light grey slate tiles, a large wood bar, a mix of vintage arms chairs and bar stools, and dark teal canteen seating.

The server came over, and Francesca began discussing wine options with them in French. She chose something for them both. She ordered food, being specific about what she wanted.

"Would you like water?" she asked Helen.

"Tap's fine, please."

As any two friends might sit down together, an intake of breath, a pause, as a calculation takes place between the two of them. One that has a life of its own. A decision: what kind of conversation is this going to be? Or what are the gears of conversation that will be moved through, and where should they arrive? Is there an important matter at hand? Does one or both parties have an agenda? Intellectuals sharing ideas? Or a case of right, what are you having – let's drink. Maybe a regular playbook, through the key notes of life – progress updates on the usual. When did we last meet? Six weeks ago?

They circled back on the next day, and made a loose plan. Francesca suggested she picked them up coffees and pastries in the morning, which Helen could enjoy in bed, and that Helen take the morning to tool about, while Francesca met a couple of people she had to. Get that out of the way. Then they could meet for lunch and go to some galleries in the afternoon. Plan, Stan.

They chit-chatted until Francesca manoeuvred onto friends. Friends she had hung out with when she lived in the area, before opening up a line of conversation about those who had let her down over the years. She handed some vulnerability on a plate to Helen, who raised a friend from school who went on to be a gymnastics champion. Who moved on from her, as they hit their teens.

Francesca saw an opportunity, while circling the various issues at hand, and took it, knowing she could back out from the conversation if she didn't like the narrative arc which followed.

"You have to be selfish to reach a competitive peak. The most single-minded person I know is like that. Her partner is understanding but he's had a torrid time of it. A glass of champagne on Christmas day. A late dinner with friends. Any sub-optimal activity takes them a step away from their goal, another backward step a competitor is not taking."

They both paused in silence.

Francesca turned the stem of her glass, as the wine moved from side to side in waves, as the glass spun around it.

"Sometimes in life, ruthlessness. It is needed. Sadly."

"My optician had a pop at me for my lack of rudder."

"Oh, fuck them," Francesca declared, glass high in the air, "but, you know..."

"I know."

Francesca went for a cigarette and stood outside talking to the guy from behind the bar. Whereat Helen watched a passionate, earnest couple across from her. The young lady was het up about some matter or another, and the validation from the man and the coordinated interaction between them told Helen it was a matter of social, academic, philosophical importance, not some gripe. She wanted conversations like that, notwithstanding a lack of a man with mettle like that to contend with. They looked combative, seeking to carve out a higher truth between them. The flipside to the risk that they might fall out, that survival might elevate their partnership.

Red wine and its comfort wrapped around Helen as her body sank into the mini break, ensorcelled by her surroundings and the chatter and clatter of French and French ways around them. She kept a watch on the couple, expecting the young lady to erupt in a playful smile at some point, touch her man, laugh with joy, but it never came. These appeared to be grave, grandiose matters.

She was interrupted as a deli platter was delivered by an arm unfurling itself in front of Helen, who helped moved things around to create space. Appreciation via a smile was returned by someone who often had to figure that out for herself. She picked at some olives and a corner or two of cheese, and some meat slices while she waited for the No Smoking sign to ping on.

After Francesca re-joined, for the next twenty minutes or so at least, they ate, shot the breeze, and mixed their French wines. The people *were* classy, thought Helen. Then again, it would net out against an equivalent location in London. As the evening wore on, and a stopover turned into the night itself, the travel and drink caught up with them, writ larger by how the world seemed to have stopped. The relentless ebbing surge of London had left them.

Whatever topic they were discussing came to an end, timed against the background hubbub from conversations and consumption across half a dozen occupied tables. Distracted by what she had to fulfil in business over the next couple of days, Francesca caught and stopped herself from asking about Helen's parents. She kept it light and humorous, and they had a carefree laugh.

For a few hours, they were nothing but happy.

100011
CHAPTER 35
Pigalle: Walking & galleries: Shopping & dinners: Julian and Iva ends

Slinging on a pair of jeans and a black roll neck, Francesca emerged from the hotel foggy and thankful for air. A taxi stopped on the one-way street a few doors down, the driver helping remove luggage from the boot, holding up another driver with no room to pass. Francesca thought of the London neighbourhoods tightening their grips on the motorist. Over-engineering shared road space, low-traffic neighbourhoods, large planters creating new cul-de-sacs.

She lit a cigarette for a quick smoke, tense in case there should be any exchange of horns or words, but it seemed they were both calm area natives. Phone and cigarette working away, a younger man walked past. He afforded himself the luxury of a good look as she was distracted. She wasn't distracted and didn't need to look up to feel eyes boring into her.

Once finished, she walked the short distance to the Rue Des Martyrs and had a good look in both directions before heading down to find pastries and coffee. Traders busied themselves organising produce and flowers as the odd queue stuck out by a mere person or two from a couple of bakeries. She stopped at the first one that looked decent. As the queue moved forward her estimation of quality dropped. If it was just for her, she would have continued on, but having to return with the bounty the short distance to the hotel, she stuck with it. Before too long, she was dropping off coffee and morning goods to Helen, and returning to bed.

Returning to her room, Francesca saw there were things that needed attending to. She thought of swimming and returning to them, but they were already there, a ticking bomb in her head. One which would nag away as she tried to do laps in an undersized pool. Modernity and its bedfellow, bullshit, had her, as it reached through the phone and grabbed her by the throat. Firing off many emails in clear terms, which did not invite easy reply, she made a note of a couple of individuals who needed a personal call to smooth things. She would take the client call now to get that off her chest, and deal with the internal call after her swim. Once her emails had been digested. Bloody tactics required for everything, she complained. Technology gripped her, as it did everyone. Some business process, some bought software, requiring sign in she couldn't make on the go. She delegated this out to the IT guy (always the guy) who she kept on side with a smile. The IT smile.

She changed, catching a rare sight of herself due to the positioning of the mirror, something she didn't seek so much these days. She couldn't complain.

Later than planned, she strode through the boulevards and shaded streets with the pep of someone given a shot of energy from the people she had to deal with, the relationships and connexions forged. The whole damn business of handling and influencing people. Popularity brought with it pressures of its own, along with the rewards. Keeping all the balls in the air was her own version of modern relentlessness that kept her motoring in the absence of children. She thrived from the noise of the streets, getting things done, and the whole interpersonal struggle of wills. Desires, incentives, bargaining, coordination or otherwise. And victory or loss.

Her morning was planned to consist of a visit to a boutique gallery in Le Marais, where she had an off-the-books transaction to try to secure for a client. One who had a specific interest in seventies America photography, something a loose contact of hers was an expert in. One might expect this to require a masterclass of influence and negotiation, an approach of subtlety and nonchalance, a mere general enquiry. This wouldn't wash. She was walking into the office of a fellow expert, another twenty-year veteran of art world shenanigans, in the softest to the hardest of sells, all the way to straightforward fraud and blackmail. Someone who, upon seeing Francesca's warm smile and outstretched hand, wondered how far along the spectrum of lies, deceit and hard and low-balling today's transaction would stretch. Over from London?

Paying a special visit? WHY? Oh, yes, a light interest in that portfolio, oh that one shot looks interesting?

Francesca knew that she would have her number from the outset. She would send Helen in, but they wouldn't even sell to her.

This was what she did and it was never easy. As she entered, she reflected on Simon going postal about some petty inconvenience that might set him back half a day, or ten thousand pounds, or some problem with interior design.

The rhythm of the streets helped her run through her story, like that of a narrated movie. She would be straight, she had a client, this photograph was their bag. They don't know she was there, so she could move on. Her budget minus thirty percent was her declared budget, so they can tighter her up to her budget. If she couldn't negotiate to a close today, she'd leave them an offer for one week. While she wanted to seal it, her nonchalance was semi-real. It wouldn't matter, it was easy margin on the table for some side-hustle.

She had a few old industry friends she had to see while here, she could tick these off one per day. Grab a lunch once Helen had found her feet. Trouble with the older contacts was their perception of the elasticity of time, harking back to days of yore and talking as leisure. With millennials it was a purer form of transaction.

Modern mapping had freed up the traveller and their companions with no local knowledge, to declare a time and a place and leave it at that.

The heavy cloud cover that started the day was removed like a white duvet tugged from a bed, letting the sun in, opening up the powder blue sky of sheets underneath. Francesca gave Helen the Louvre as a landmark to head toward, indicating a few things she should catch on the way. Pointing out their mid-afternoon endpoint across the river, the Musée D'Orsay, she briefed that they would walk the river west to the Museum of Modern Art, cross a bridge, and return the other side. With stretches of the river taken in and ticked off, Francesca could focus them on Le Marais and the elegant areas of central Paris for the next couple of days, and cut the slog.

They walked a slow pace, taking in and snapping the collection of domes in stone, in a light racing green, in spearmint green, many topped with the national flag. Sage green rooves surrounded by ancient stone figures, matching obelisks, supported in their majesty by the tall trees full of autumn. The sights allowed them to switch off from anything but observational conversation, a necessary part of any mini-break, as Francesca helped secure the holiday snaps Helen wanted, and which she sent home.

As they faced the water in the same direction, Helen surprised Francesca.

"Dad said I should leave Phil."

Francesca nodded, which Helen caught to the side.

"He'll be OK you know. It will be a relief for you both."

Francesca paused, then went on.

"*Yeah but I love him*, needs to stop loving him."

Francesca spotted a point which offered a better view, and served to separate her from Helen. This was to be a slow-played hand, over the course of the trip. She remained quiet and looked beyond, toward the water, her eyes roving around in that way that they do on a trip, but seldom on familiar ground.

They walked on, toured the modern art museum, and whisked round the Palais de Tokyo opposite, which was more *out there*.

They crossed the Seine.

Helen couldn't quite get her head around how Francesca had continued to traverse Paris in boots, while she wore through her sensible shoe leather.

"They're magic; I've had them forever. Let's find you a pair."

"Can we?"

"Sure, as long as they are way over-budget."

Francesca was conscious of how she pushed Helen. She didn't want to have her elbow in between Helen's shoulder blades, prodding away. But it happened, against her better judgment. She failed to resist the urge and justified it on the basis that she was encouraging Helen onward, giving her a nudge. But she knew it was unfair and might cause a rift. She thought this to herself for the last two years, and here she was, still at it. It troubled her why she would not desist.

They passed a couple in their seventies, holding hands.

"I bet they're still having sex," Helen commented.

"The best many people can hope for, regular sex that declines slowly, until you make love for the last time in your seventies. That last time, requiring real shove and impetus. Like a dog who jumps on the bed for the final time, and thereafter requires a lift."

"That'll do me," Helen confirmed.

"Sex becomes more intimate with age, unless you have an understanding. When you're young, you fuck, put some music on, drink and smoke, fill your hours together with the distractions of youth. When you're old, once you've come and you're both lying there, that's all there is. Each other. And if people don't feel that connection with someone, it's just painful. The temporariness isn't worth it."

"That's why you don't have any arrangements," Helen commented, casting her eyes to one side.

"My advice, my wisdom, is for other people," Francesca confirmed.

Beyond the laughter, Helen was riddled with an immutable, pitted depression. Through her arms, down her core, settling around her hips and thighs. From a loss not yet real, but now a real danger. Self-inflicted it might be, yet the dumper to dumpee pain ratio varied, and in this case, could be close to parity. All she could do in these circumstances was try to shake it off, to enjoy the moment, the views, the gags. Fewer than five minutes later she was stuck in the same groove. Churning and turning.

They visited the Musee D'Orsay for classic art, and found their way to the top, planning to descend as they went through the collection. They went to gaze out on to the city from behind the clock face. Helen felt a wave of sadness pour over here, the awful self-evident hammering cliché of time and beauty stretched out as she sat turning over decisions on her future, and the painful end points. She took photos to distract herself, and Francesca spotted her turning away. She followed and they shuffled on, their weighty gallery legs taking hold within twenty minutes. Francesca gave Helen a personal audio tour of the impressionist period. Helen discovered Berthe Morisot and her plight, and had a new artistic heroine, gaining satisfaction from broadening her horizons. After an hour and a half, they left, Francesca pondering how she could have spent whole days at MoMA in New York in years gone by.

They called a car to return to Pigalle and stopped for a drink, before returning to the hotel. Helen needed a disco nap, before their evening plans.

"One of the best mid-budget restaurants in Paris. Sound menu, quality service, consistent."

'Dressy, not too dressy, and a bit of a walk,' was Francesca's peculiar brief for the evening. Helen took that to mean *don't do anything daft*, and put on a little black dress.

They left an hour ahead of their booking and walked fifteen minutes or so south, stopping halfway for a drink.

The restaurant had that air of a place run by people who knew what they were doing. They were happy with their lot, weren't looking for ever-rising accolades, nor an outpost in every global food destination, nor even a takeover of Paris. They owned a few places, made good money, took pride in the plaudits they received, and left it at that.

A classic long bar on the left as they walked in, large mirrors framed by wood, a spirit collection, a mix of labels and tones that signalled quality without further inspection. Stools for half a dozen patrons, and a little standing room, but the bar was there to serve the diners. As they were shown in, Helen watched the bar tenders whipping clean glasses into their place, at home with their families.

The restaurant was weighted to the left side, a long banked line of twos, fours and sixes, no tables for twelve. On the right, a few small round tables, spaced to enable room for ducking and moving. A large case of wines at the end, and bottles and art lined up on shelving, paintings leaning to the walls, light beams taking over the bulk of the wall space.

They settled in, ordered cocktails.

"I want to say sorry," Francesca began.

"What for?"

"I'm pushy with you. I'm sorry. I know I'm doing it. I see your potential, that's all. That's how I justify it to myself, when being mean."

Helen made no attempt to appease or nullify Francesca's words.

"We are all flawed," she said, gazing back in a penetrating, flinty manner which Francesca was not used to from her.

"All right then," was all she could say as she shook the menu, reminded that friends were just that. They came, they went, they always let you down on a long enough time horizon.

Helen couldn't be the woman who breezed through life unaffected by the opinions of others. She wasn't given the tools. But she could put her foot down and garner some of Francesca's respect.

They fussed about the menu options, agreeing to share some things, giving and taking on various options, finding middle ground, to blow the leaves scattered from the previous comments back into a neat pile.

Wine was delivered.

Voice activated alcohol delivery. That most precious of modern conveniences.

"How's the family?"

"I don't even want to talk about them at the moment, especially not now."

"OK, sure. They're still your family, though, you should try to hold it together."

"Stuff them," Helen asserted, "drink!"

They self-sozzled their way through the starters, as Francesca regaled Helen with intimate details of men she had dated in her youth and beyond, 'into my mature years'. She demonstrated an inversely related age profile, much older men in her youth, and some younger men in recent years. Dotted among the age-appropriate. Helen shocked Francesca with an admission from her own university days, which loosened things up a bit, and they then got into nitty gritty, full of details.

As lips loosened and the atmosphere dimmed after they ordered desserts, Francesca plunged in, and risked all.

"I've seen a lot of relationships, a majority even. They roll on. Tumbleweeds. And honestly, if I have another conversation with a girlfriend who wasted five, ten years on a dead end, I'll scream. One friend, twenty years in a sexless marriage, and she only left him after they were put in financial strife."

Helen appeared unappreciative of the lecture.

"And they all say the same thing. They whine over their wine, and it's 'why didn't you say something Francesca?' and sure, at least the friendship remained intact."

Intake of breath as she formulated the next few sentences.

"I'm not doing that with you. It breaks our friendship, and I don't see you again. For me, that will bring sadness. But I'll get over it. So here it is, I'm giving you what you'll ask me for in the future, for free now. If there's no plan for a future, there's no future. You're both, and that does mean both of you by the way, casting aside the freedom and joy offered to you with a life. And if you don't move on or at least test it with the jeopardy of a break-up, that's neglect and failure."

"Are you finished?"

Francesca got the attention of the waiter who would be along in a moment.

"I'm getting another drink. Do you want one or are you going to leave?"

Helen thought about it.

"And before you ask me to look at myself, I do, believe me. I'm not going to have children, that's the difference. The most important between the sexes, and perhaps the most crucial single driver on the direction of a life. I can waste my time with idiots like Simon as much as I want."

"You must want more?"

Francesca felt relief. She had said her piece, there had been no *scene*, and it had moved onto her. She could concede ground, bat away whatever she felt like now.

"We all want more, always. In everything. That's humanity."

"You know what I mean, don't be annoying."

"Falling in love? It's not me. To hand someone else the power to turn your lights out?"

Francesca ordered two after dinner drinks.

"Do you want a coffee?"

"Nice to be asked."

"Two double espressos, please."

They left and Helen asked to go somewhere like they went the first night. They found somewhere, and drunk the hangovers into them, and talked to the staff and some local men. Helen lived in the moment, as best she could after Francesca's risky, sacrificial words.

The next day was cool and overcast, so they agreed to walk the Jardin Du Luxembourg, plus some of the streets worthy of French painters and tourists south of the river, picking up the Rue Mouffetard to head north for lunch before heading shopping. They stopped for lobster rolls and a beer, 'not very Paris', 'fuck it who cares.'

They walked behind a young lady, mid-twenties, who wore a light beige raincoat, cut short, and black seamed stockings and stiletto heels underneath. Helen marvelled at this dedication to style, a look she had seen a few times since they arrived. And a look that would attract nothing but abuse and hassle in London. It took a certain ballsiness to follow through with. The attitude, Helen thought, before considering how many times in life she had identified something she would like to add to herself and her bearing, and tried, and reverted. It took determination to get hold of a look, an action, a phraseology and internalise it. She was beyond mimicking this look, though she recognised the moment as a visual prompt which would lodge and remain, as with the time in general she spent with Francesca. Surrounding oneself with inspirational people inspired. It created internal competition and drive, which one lacked with lacklustre acquaintances.

They reached their destination and their predatory drive for consumption took hold. *Some* culture and learning had been ticked off, and here was their reward.

Francesca mapped out a plan based on the fashion categories they were looking to attack, costume jewellery and dark clothes ahead of a winter London. Said boots.

Helen waited while Francesca tried something on. She looked awkward, and a nearby assistant made some excruciating small talk, in an American accent so prevalent among the international school types. Fakery of the highest order. Francesca flung the curtain back and addressed Helen, at which point the assistant paid attention. Helen tried a few things on and they bought something each and left.

They walked around, picked up coffees, dropped into boutiques Francesca knew, some she didn't. And they stopped off in a small photography gallery owned by a friend. Helen appreciated feeling part of an inner circle.

They carried on to reach their goal, to not have to shop on the next day.

"Looking good, huh?" Francesca stated, in an all-purpose blue and white floral dress.

"Big doings," she confirmed.

"Self-praise is no recommendation," she added.

Helen had picked a few things to try but wanted Francesca's opinion so she waited.

"If you need to rearrange it when you put it on, don't buy it. If you pick three things you want, put one of them back."

As it approached four o'clock, Francesca said she had someone to catch up with, and wrote down the names of a few labels Helen should check out in the area in case she wanted to continue.

Francesca realised when she left that her vagueness would prompt some questions, compared with the explanation given the last time. Helen wondered who he was, and what they would be getting up to in half an hour.

"I'll be back at the hotel at seven, and we can go out at eight."

With Francesca gone, the puff went out of her. She thought of the ballsy girl strutting about in determined fashion, getting after whatever she was getting after that day, and Helen wanted to persevere. Her back hurt and tiredness from the previous night's drinking left her wanting to lie down with a book. Once back, she read half a page, put it down, and tried to sleep. She was too tired and beyond sleep.

She went through a couple of cycles of picking up the book, trying to sleep, interrupted by the truth, that she and Phil were short on promise. All that bullshit schmaltz about today being the first day of the rest of your life, she thought. It's all true. Starting tomorrow, at least.

She gave up and went for a walk before showering and meeting Francesca. They strolled about until settling on a gyoza restaurant for supper. Simple menu, good food, clean, which they ate with beers, a rest after all the wine.

The pressure was off, Francesca had cleared her desk, and had not a care. Her mind free of all except what was in front of her, and her face revealing as much as Helen looked across, at a woman at ease.

An opening came in conversation, relating to something Helen had exhausted herself over and over. The direction of societal travel, digitisation and atomisation. Conversations she had had with herself time and time again. This conversation rehearsal now had an airing.

"I fear for where we are going," said Helen.

"It's a one-way street, if it can happen, it will. You may as well campaign to re-establish the steel mills and coal mines. Those ships have sailed."

"How does that not scare you?"

"It's like the environment. Scary, right? And the constraints they are putting on us, awful, right? But look at what we have done when we had pure freedom. As much as I hate it, what's the alternative?"

The evening took an agreeable turn, a needed change of pace, and they talked in a way that hadn't tended to in all the years.

"Much of class and standing in society is around how short or long-term one is able to think. The homeless person may be unable to think beyond a few minutes ahead, whereas the billionaire is planning a strategy a decade into the future," Francesca theorised.

Helen took a pull on her bottled beer, imbibing views and booze. It was a calm atmosphere as the staff, in utter control, looked after the half-full establishment. Helen wondered why restaurants bothered with huge menus at all. In a quiet moment, when the later diners had despatched their main courses, and before new tracks of discussion had been taken up, Helen said, "I'll do it you know."

Francesca nodded.

It was time to leave Pigalle behind. The eternal struggle that for every coming together and time well spent, so followed the separation and holing to memory. One could never grasp and seize the slippery present. The flipside of this quandary, the asset to its liability, was that bad times were moved through, and grief subsided. At varying trajectories, at least.

These thoughts troubled away within Helen as she showered and packed, plodding her way through the management of washbags, make-up, cupboards, bedside ephemera, cables, chargers and packing cubes. She clutched at how much fun she had had, or tried to have, and regretful of what would manifest on her return. The uneasiness felt through her arms and down to her clenched gut. Loss, present and future.

Hotel departure administration complete, with car ordered, Helen felt bothered that she had forgotten something, despite two full sweeps of her room. It lodged in her head, as if a spatial marker had been left upstairs pulling her back. She thought harder. Black scarf. Hanging behind the door. She reclaimed a key and raced back.

They were driven up the steep street in silence, the calm trip home the antithesis to the chatty, excitable out journey, full of anticipatory energy and zeal, now realised, expended, sunk.

The rigmarole of modern travel released into the speeding, still train journey through the green expanses of northern France, empty and bland, dotted with the odd curiosity of a windmill or large unmarked distribution centre.

They remained quiet as they sunk below into the burst of dimly lit tunnel, before the re-emergence from English soil, below to above. Onto the final weave into the capital and the odd coat hanger bend, travelling from the south into the north-facing station.

They remained seated and waited for the standing crush of coat grabbers and case pullers to fill the vacated seats and aisles with their piles, until the last few organised themselves and gave them room to manoeuvre. They joined the rear of a queue, whereby they were travellatored and swept through the shiny vestibules and around corners, through a vacant customs channel, until they departed into the main station and found their way to a spot where they could collect a car each.

As Francesca's car emerged first, they hugged and thanked each other, and Francesca said something that made Helen smile first, and then cry. And then she was hooking a booted leg into the back of the Mercedes, and with a wave of a hand, and the whoof of the closing door, which felt like it sucked the air from Helen, Francesca was gone.

Back in South-West London, Julian had readied himself for a showdown, for *words*, home truths, a lashing of revenge served hot. Yet in the end, despite his preparedness, it was Iva that gave up, who recognised the futility of it all. She weighed it up and saw something better for herself. In her balance sheet of life, if she were going to put up with a bunch of noise from another person's past, she was going to want higher compensation for it.

After a lull in conversation, days without communication back and forth, she told Julian she wanted to see him at lunchtime. They walked a distance from work and she laid it out. She stuck it to him on a few things, said her piece. And as Julian kept an eye out on the horizon, she said what she had to say, pulled him close to her, left her scent clouding his nose, and kissed him on the lips.

"Goodbye Julian. I'll see you around work."

She turned and walked away. Iva had never looked so magnificent, and Julian had never wanted her so much. He considered if she had already found someone else, if they were enjoying the goods.

It ached.

As Julian got the train home, a short journey and penultimate leg, before a short walk, he sat wedged into the corner of a group of six. He checked his neighbours and over his shoulder, while he ran through a routine of self-surveillance. Messages from Iva cleared down, personal mute settings on. Notifications as he wanted them. Check of personal inbox and an occasional clear down of browser cache. He had no doubt that should she wish, Fiona could spot his passcode from the hundreds of executions a day at weekends, and seek truth.

Of course, she had done. Many times.

100100
CHAPTER 36

Halloween: Annabel and double standards: Helen and Phil relationship talks

London was in the grip of Halloween and fireworks. In turn, those American and English of celebrations, or times of great annoyance. Depending on *how one saw it*.

Supermarkets took a great run up at Halloween from September, aisles festooned with orange and black, further temptations and excuses to load up on sugar, carbed snacks and junk before the big one. The biggest blowout of all.

More plastic, single and multi-use crap, created to amuse children for another 24-hour cycle, before being consigned to the attic, shed, cupboard, or discarded, binned, broken, and off to landfill.

In its slipstream the annual roistering of Guy Fawkes Night, Good For Nothing, save to mine the planet of precious, expendable, finite resources, package them up and explode them into smithereens. Bang, whoosh, oooh, ahhhh, go the people, who have seen it all before, scores of times. Pets cower and the seniors feel the frighteners, for a few weeks. Beyond the everyday fear of a knock on the door by a prospective tradesman, people claiming to be the police, or a phone call from their bank.

For Annabel, at a time of fragility, a thousand bangs to startle and disturb, a time which seemed to provoke local ne-er-do-wells into random acts of danger and chaos. Fireworks shot off at ground level.

A time of fear and trouble for Jess and therefore Barney. And reasons to fret endless world resource depletion.

Annabel stood in the supermarket and watched a young mother deposit a packet of Halloween sweets and chocolates into her basket. She herself turned a corner, and picked up some white chocolate and some mints, and some cream napkins, to replace those used with her last dinner guest.

And stood next to Annabel at the self-checkout, that mother scanned the orange and black napkins she had picked up and placed into her bag for the next few weeks.

At the bus stop, people crammed under the shelter, bunched up to avoid the light rain. The poor overspill hunched over themselves to the side and behind the shelter, in a lacklustre attempt to keep some of themselves dry. One bus went past which was so full it refused to let anyone on, despite people getting off the back. Someone banged on the front door to have the bus driver open up, and when he shook his head, standing firm, he raced to the back door with his rage, and forced himself onto the back. This fight he won, as the bus pulled away with one new passenger.

Annabel resented having to endure a crush and turned, heading to the corner of the street with a large, stone doorway for cover. She called a car, created pollution externalities somewhere in China, and cursed herself. And sat in the back, scrolling to infinity. Somewhere, hundreds of millions of switch changes, to generate the filler to her life. Bridging her from one thing to another. Politicians and local councillors praised the reinstatement of the city fireworks displays, called out on the previous times they had called for its cancellation. Royals called for individual responsibility on climate change, after being dropped off by helicopter. The self-styled family man, having it away. *We were all in this together*, as the former PM took up Non-Executive Directorships. Journalists applied one set of standards for one candidate for high office, and another for another. Religious leaders called for funding for action on child suffering, while continuing to harbour and shield known abusers. Stink after stink of double standards, that went right to the top. 'This you Charlie, yeah?' as a screenshot of a previous comment, counter their current position, was dug up from months before. Charity workers and their overseas indulgences with poor sex workers, on their missionary missions. It was apposite to reposition when the facts changed, not so when they hadn't.

When she arrived home, she placed her Peruvian avocados and

Chilean kiwi fruit in the bowl and into the freezer went her Burst Shrew Chenin Blanc from Stellenbosch, for she needed a cold glass without a wait. She cracked ice cubes, which had been kept frozen for four months into her *Zwiesel Simplify* white wine glasses, which had replaced her old John Lewis ones, for their design, their beauty. After rinsing a pan and some plates in the sink she placed into the dishwasher, and adjusted the thermostat up a notch, to settle in for an evening of dirty streaming. Tears welled in her eyes, and though she tried to reabsorb them, they broke, and streaked her face with shame.

The streets of Kensington thronged with wealthy Europeans, and Steven passed the weaponised red police vans on the corner, close by for royal and political protection, to walk up Kensington Church Street. The large black and gold dustbins dotted along the long, kinked road, and ahead of him a pair paced at quite a clip. An odd couple, a short ragged man, and from behind at least, a blonde dressed in the wrong type of leisurewear. The two of them separated by six feet or so as they walked, each executing their own swerving meander, yet connected. The woman stopped at one of the large bins, and where they had a cigarette grill at the top for depositing, stubbing and end-dropping, she reached inside the bin and under the lid, and pulled out a great mass of dog-ends. She then filtered through them, dispersing the most dogged, and retaining those stubbed early and retaining a little burn. A cycle throughout the nabe. They thundered on, whereby she repeated the trick at two further bins as Steven followed, trying not to gag. He listened as the man complained about a mutual acquaintance, as the lady shifted and whipped her head around, always surveying, unresponsive to his comments. Something which didn't diminish his enthusiasm for following through his disjointed, angry thought train. She appeased him, implying they would find him later.

It had been a couple of weeks since Amanda's ghost and it nagged away, pulling his thoughts back as if he were owned by them. With rejection, realisation. That he didn't shape up enough for what he wanted, and that there could be no compromise. In youth, he assumed as one aged, one relaxed requirements, and this had not turned out to be true. Even in later life, from what he observed in friends and neighbours.

Amanda swirled his mind, and while she had not appeared in his dreams, as far as he could remember, he woke each morning, vivid in the imprints of lost teeth, punches unable to be thrown with leaden arms; a memory of youth played out in an adult body. Then Amanda waited for him. What were the signals which she had taken as means to dismiss him and move on? He couldn't pinpoint an obvious area of egregiousness. She seemed into it at the start. If it were looks she wouldn't have slept with him at all. They got on. Her orgasms seemed genuine. It was, in likelihood, a cluster of small shortcomings. A wrong word here, an off joke there, a few years away from the required ladder rung, some country pursuit he had no experience in.

Dazed, he returned to the source. Looking for 'someone who makes me laugh.' I'm an entertainer now, he snorted, and stopped, despondent. Not for too long, the only way out was through, so he punched back in and picked up again. Continuing, he looked up and was startled and a worryshock went through him, as he thought Josie was walking straight toward him. It wasn't. It gave him fright.

In East London, Josie was out with a group of friends for a birthday lunch. The setting, a relaxed wood-panelled dining room with little natural light. A busy and relaxed vibe for a hotel eatery, full of young energy and personality. An attractive guy sat a couple of places away kept his eyes on her, listening to what she had to say while trying to converse with his neighbours, trying to tune into two conversations at once. Her friend asked her about dating, and if she had been getting out there again. She said she went on a first date the day before.

"Have you heard from him?"

"Yes, there's been a bit of chat this morning."

"Excellent, cheers," and prosecco flutes were raised.

Table guy was disappointed in this information, but was patient. He would chat to her, and could circle back later. The chances she had just met THE ONE, were small, of course.

Unbeknownst to him, Josie had a couple of options. But if you didn't know which one was your Derby horse, you didn't have one.

By midweek, elsewhere in the capital, the next tranche of misery was waiting, coiled, in the grass.

Helen had become embroiled in her work's social committee, for no other reason than she was offered as a relative new joiner, and something which would be bad form to say no to. A rhetorical question to which the answer was 'yes'. They had tasked themselves at the behest of HR with carrying out a review of the next year's planned events to ensure they *align* with their updated company values. She had no idea how they would go about that task and thought it was daft.

Bowling, a rooftop barbecue...

Yet it took her minutes to consider the heaviness of the bowling ball, and some of the petit/petite members of staff, or the vegetarians/vegans, to realise fun was now an occupational hazard. Exclusion. She concurred this needed to be looked at. This was just the sort of thing she could do without, while starting off the process of ending the longest relationship of her life. She fumed. The time thieves were dipping their hands into her pockets again.

Behind the curve, never ahead, Helen arrived home dishevelled, laden with bags. For what was about to happen, she needed to get herself in order, set herself straight, regain whatever little composure she had. An alert popped up from her bank. Something needed attending to. That would have to wait until the next day. She tidied things away, got changed. Talked to herself. A validation of what was about to unfold. To delay was just to delay. This had to happen. There couldn't be a way around it.

The outer door slammed shut. Half a dozen steps. A large bunch of keys jangled. In the lock. Phil opened the door. They exchanged a 'Hi' and Phil put down his cross-body bag, removed his light jacket and shoes, and went straight to the bathroom.

As he came out, Helen was sat on the armchair, leaning forward, her hands in her lap. She tried to choose original words, there must be various ways of starting, but there weren't, and before her brain caught up, out had tumbled the desperate words.

"Sit down, we need to talk."

This registered with Phil as trouble. And while he sat down on the sofa opposite, he waited to understand how much trouble. The next words from her mouth would indicate if their relationship was a shipwreck, or if she had a surprise in store worthy of discussion, a job offer abroad, that sort of thing. Or if it was a warning shot across the bows.

"Things aren't working, are they?"

She left it there, ready to go on, but wishing to check his reaction, to get a handle on where they were at. The easy answer was 'no', yet she knew to hear 'no' would be heartache for her and a terrible stab. That it confirmed the cavernous opening up of their worlds and lives, the security that came with a life shared, dismantled.

"What do you mean?" was the gormless response he gave, as his face screwed in puzzlement. A softer landing for Helen.

Inside, she urged herself on. Toward agreement. Or maybe not. Maybe the cries of change, of difference, of renewal, at which point she had a fork in the road. Change must happen, she thought to herself, holding those words in her head on repeat for the evening.

As she gathered her thoughts, he jumped in. "It's been a bumpy few months for you, I know that," he said.

She resisted the urge to critique this comment, and stuck to the plan. They didn't have sex much ("we *do have sex*"). They didn't do enough together ("we went out *the other night* for dinner, we had a laugh"). They hadn't made any plans for getting married, or children ("there's more to life than getting married, Helen, look how miserable some of our married friends are.")

"That doesn't mean *we'd* be miserable," she retorted, anger building. He regretted giving her that easy opening.

He got up and went to the fridge.

"No beer," she said, as the top door swung open.

This tested his defiance, and would signal to her his intentions.

"Sounds like I can do what I want now," he said, and she caught true sorrow in his voice. The boy underneath.

While Phil popped off the bottle top, Helen composed herself, and ran through a few of the thoughts rehearsed countless times over the last few weeks. They came, and left, her mind blank, like a child forgetting everything before an exam.

As he sat down, she opened it up to him, for she wanted to learn. She took care with her tenses.

"How do you think things have been going? What did you see for our future?"

He wasn't prepared for this line of questioning, having had no preparation, and as it did not feature in his day-to-day thoughts. He slugged back the green bottled continental lager which was his current flavour of the month.

He shook his head in a confused manner, "I don't know."

"Getting married? Children? I don't know isn't good enough. Do you want these things? Do you want them with me?"

"Of course," he muttered, contradicting himself.

"Of course. Well they don't happen by themselves."

She was straight, concise and firm, and for once her eyes did not dart about the room, looking away, seeking comfort in a light switch, a photo print, a mirror. They were eye to eye. Her unwavering eyeline and the gravitas of Helen's determined words underlined to Phil the gravity of the situation. His head scrambled, he scrambled. The end of a relationship inflicted, elicited pure and undoubtable feelings of devotion.

"Look," he said, trying to steady them, trying to slow things down before attempting a rewind.

"Let's just pause, talk things through, this week. I know I," he had to stop as Helen cut across, "Phil, no, this isn't what this is about. This isn't working. For either of us. And I've spent enough time waiting for things to change, and you can't start telling me now we can have a different future; I can't keep waiting."

"But Hel."

He hadn't called her that in a long time. This time she paused, for silent emphasis.

They both felt sick. No longer were they two cossetted, cosy halves. They might become solo individuals, and have to toughen the hell up to a harsh world full of risk and pitfalls. And no safety net, beyond that negotiated with others, with their conditions.

"Is there someone else?" he asked. He hadn't wanted to, but it was mandatory.

Helen laughed, a generous, honest laugh.

"No. C'mon, you've got to be fucking kidding. That's the last thing I need at the moment, someone else to deal with."

Phil laughed too, relieved. One fewer barrier to overcome. Should he want to overcome it. They smiled at each other, connected. While Helen took leave to use the bathroom, Phil mapped out in his mind how a post-Helen life might unfold. An obvious positive was that he could sleep with someone new. A benefit of any potential break-up, if things had turned stale. Yet the enormity of the new challenge dawned, going out of dates, something he was never good at. He got together with Helen because they were both drunk and he got lucky, when he made her laugh. Urgh, he thought, the flat. Boxed living in a studio flat, or moving to Zone 3. This all felt like a bad move.

Helen sat on the loo, tissue in hand, and when she was finished, remained seated, thinking through what had happened, what was next. She found herself taking her phone out, from habit and caught herself on. She couldn't help checking before re-pocketing it, wiping herself, and pulling her jeans on.

She looked at herself in the mirror as she washed her hands. Those same eyes.

As she came back in and settled, Phil was staring at a coaster on the dining table. Next to the coaster, a few magazines and papers. He hadn't got to reading them since the previous weekend. Atop, some CDs, and a greeting card. It had no slogan and he wasn't sure what it was for.

"Phil."

"Yeah."

"Say something. What do you think?"

"What do I think about what?"

Helen looked cross.

"What do you think? About all this. Anything I've said."

"I don't know."

"You don't know."

"No," he paused, "I don't want us to split up."

"Well you better bloody well start talking then."

Phil felt queasy and his mouth dried. He began to cry. For himself. At the situation, and the sheer unsteadiness of it. His face creased and his chin crinkled as his muscles tightened. A well built by the duct, until it brimmed over and a thin stream bent its way down his left cheek.

Helen reciprocated out of reflex. Tears were warranted in this situation, they both thought.

"Hey," she calmed, eyes of warmth and love, whatever was happening.

She pivoted from tough to pliable.

"Look. I know you find it hard to talk. Take a few days. I'm going to stay with Fran. I'll come back over the weekend and we can talk. OK?"

Phil winced at the planning. It wasn't a reaction, the letting off of steam. It felt like an assassination, and he had to stomach it.

She looked him dead straight. "Whatever happens, it's all going to be OK. For you and me."

He nodded, and pursed his lips. They both wanted to pull each in, for the last two years to have been better. To not be painted into this corner.

Helen repeated herself.

"It's all going to be OK."

It wasn't the hellfire, *it's over and that's it* ending. And it was better done in two parts. The initial realisation, space with hope, and then either a full end, or reparations and reconciliation and a chance at renewal. She was throwing him the ball. Their time together deserved that much. And besides if two weeks before, he'd proposed, all would be good. So it made no sense that this was final.

She took five minutes to put a backpack and a small weekend bag together and she touched him on the shoulder before leaving to walk down the road and catch a bus.

100101
CHAPTER 37
Annabel suffers and visits the IWM: Helen & Phil crisis talks: Moving on

The difficulties and troubles in the country and beyond had accumulated since the start of the twenty-tens, and had plumbed ever further lows, as successive governments lurched from one crisis to another. They seemed unable to resolve and move on from any specific single event unless the media spotlight went in search somewhere else. No tangible improvement in prisoner welfare or child protection powers. They remained stuck in urgent need of major reform, things declining even further still, while the attention moved onto shinier new things. The public bored themselves of whatever was current; hundreds of deaths in the Middle East, a failing social care system, human rights and freedoms. A bottle of wine, a takeout and Gogglebox at the end of the week. The new bread and circuses. Passports, permission slips, validation, scan your code here, your email is your ticket, as long as they could scan and *be validated*, to hell with being free, or whatever nebulous philosophical concept were torched and expunged. Tell me what to do and how I can be validated, and I will be happy.

Annabel had felt the blob of problems mounting since she had become an adult, having to concern herself with how the world worked as she had to wrestle with her independence and autonomy. Years ago, to feel relief, it was a case of getting drunk or having a long bath with a book. Giving up the booze for a couple of weeks. Booking a holiday. Now it was laughable to consider these pitiful actions a remedy, treating the symptom not the cause. Book a mindfulness session to de-stress from overwhelming employee workloads.

To leave home was to be stabbed by the glass daggers of

rebarbative contemporary architecture, a reminder of where power lied to scar the everyday citizen. To create separation and alienation from the individual toward their environment.

The reminder via chain restaurants and stores of the squeezing out of independent families from making a living, leaving the *consumer* with consistent mediocrity and no surprises. Served by poor workers given their centralised rules, processes, temperatures, timings. Cash almost removed from society due to '*pandemic* safety', and never returned. *Never let an emergency go to waste.*

Give in to a life indoors, lived through a screen; a scroll on Social Media, oh a well-known figure has died, scroll, nice recipe, a comedy video, but that person just died. Switch to dating app, swipe, swipe, left, left, right. But that person just died. People now separated, kept apart by the technology that promised contact, touchpoints, sharing, more involvement. Dating now a sequence of typed chats and audio calls, without progressing any further. Carrier bags dumped on doorsteps, empty bags removed. She felt so sick with the reality of how the world was changing, panicked by the prospect of the future. So much so that environmental concern was ebbing, something she couldn't believe when she admitted it to herself. She saw the timeline of the world as she knew it, humanity, earth and its beauty, collapsing under the weight of the threats of AI, surveillance, and the expansion of totalitarian rule, something she never considered for a moment would need to be a concern of hers in this lifetime. Her future appeared to be defined now as five to ten years. Squeeze any enjoyment. Bucket list item – go now. And still the boiling frogs went about their business, working, shopping, watching telly, heating meals, exercise, drinking. Did you see the football at the weekend? Good new crime drama on ITV. Sharing a good pod episode. Got my eleventh booster.

The kind girl, who loved her gymnastics. Who grew into her humble beauty. Who shared her sweets. Who loved history and geography. Who wrote when she didn't need to. Bookish, English, Annabel of peace. Who now felt life close in on her, as when one walked down the length of a plane, and the sections became tighter.

As a marriage was its own entity, separate and unknowable in full to both its participants, so Annabel's own life was a mystery to her. The words of her mother when young rang in her ears, dismissed at the time as fortune cookie wisdom. *Use your time wisely*.

Annabel knew. She knew this was not where she should be going. She knew this would not help. This would make her feel worse. Yet she refused to turn away. She invited the distress upon herself with defiance.

She took an Overground train to Liverpool St, switched on foot for a ten-minute walk, whereby she took a Northern Line train to Elephant & Castle. The Elephant, now undergoing colossal regeneration, its personality and quirks being stripped away by the modern developing beast, bringing in towers, extensive glassware, and *cleaner spaces*. New jobs. To replace the old jobs. Diverting people from jobs they had elsewhere. No *incremental* societal jobs. No halo effect. A hollowing out of the middle.

She closed her eyes for seconds at a time as she walked the streets, overcome by the emptiness of it all. It made her want to leave London, to flee, but where to? She picked up a coffee for a boost as she approached afternoon. And to occupy her during the walk.

The Imperial War Museum, one of London's top cultural centres, sat in a grass irregular pentagon, a ten-minute walk from the river, beyond which one reached the recognisable postcard sights of London.

The classical pillared portico and spearmint green domed roof, guarded by two imposing naval guns, a reality check among the tales of history. *Their versions* of history.

When she arrived, she wrestled with the railings and hedgerows and how to get into the damn place, and once she found an opening, navigated a curious sundial and oncoming people with children. She felt an exhilaration and then a shudder from the colossal guns, as she stood in their shadow for a few moments before entering. Her bag was checked and she entered and sought the floor menu, before taking the lift to the second floor for the Holocaust Galleries.

A large screen with modern video of peaceful European locations, leaves, tracks, wind. Indicators of the many camp locations where filming took place. As Annabel moved through, a list of the tactics and small restrictions inflicted on the population in increments, for they didn't build shower blocks and start pushing people in. First, the othering. Creating the public mood for the build of hatred. The places they were not allowed to enter. Or where they could partake, but apart. Onto punitive measures, fines. Annabel considered how this aligned with the *pandemic* plans put in place for a fractured populace, country-by-country.

She was ready now, to be broken, for the breakdown to overwhelm, as if the only way she could ascend, to re-build herself, was to submit and bottom out.

The large photographic images of smiling, carefree faces. Families, friends. Set in their time, aged by their clothes and the settings, the items surrounding them. Yet the same faces, of impish youth, of tomfoolery, of shy innocence. Or the solid parent, wearing with pride their responsibilities, carrying their years with stoicism. Innocent of what was coming next. The poor young boy, under five years old, all smiles of pride in his playful outfit.

A young, well-informed American or Canadian mother, a teacher or professor perhaps, walked her two boys around the exhibition. They all wore masks. The mother whispered the historical story, as Annabel came to the photos. Small photos. Of girls, of women, of men. Undressing, staring, waiting on the beach. Photographed. Reserved, in their meekness, before being lined up, some huddling into each other. Before shots to the head. She ached, one hand over her mouth, the other wrapped around, attempting to hold herself.

The colour video recording, taken after the liberation of a camp, switching without commentary from the arrival of wagons of bread for the starving who made it, the luckiest alive, to the pile of scores of yellow-pink corpses. Men, eyes and mouths wide, staring in death's agony, their bodies gone, withered to ribbed remains. Stomachs caved in on themselves, an empty nothing before the skin stretched and returned over a pelvis. Annabel wretched but would not turn away, holding a handkerchief over her mouth as she gagged and her mouth watered.

One of the young boys had left his overbearing mother, and stood next to Annabel and looked at her, and she didn't meet his gaze. She turned away and left.

A gentleman struggled down the stairs between floors with a crutch, taking one step at a time. Annabel could see the lifts a short distance and pointed these out to him, as she leaned down, checking he was OK.

"I'm fine. I'm just stubborn, that's all."

She managed a thin smile at the human struggle and the power of pride. And reflected on her dying uncle shaving in his last days, keeping up appearances, looking the best he could. The photographs of the executed girls, stood with dignity as they were terminated, rang through her, as she left the old man, left the museum, found a bench, and doubled over.

The following day was a middling autumn one, neither here nor there. It was cool through bluster, and to wrap up too much meant a sticky meander through the streets. It was cloudy yet didn't threaten rain.

The weather was ideal for such an occasion, our happiness and optimism driven as they are by the prevailing conditions. A sunny or dreary day may tip the balance in one direction or another. Something which may become apparent the next day, with a change in outlook.

Phil Sheffield rose earlier than normal. He had *a few beers* the previous night (six) so could be described as fresh. He made a cup of tea, and while his stomach was tight with anxiety, made some crumpets from the freezer with salted butter for breakfast. He sat and checked some online information on music and the football, yet he didn't take it in. He checked the time and had too much of it. Helen was coming around, and it had been a long wait. One wished these moments of drama and impact could be brought forward. That one could reach into the future and draw them along like a rug.

After a second then a third cup of tea and a good belch, a rare morning shower. This change of routine was made necessary to lessen the routes of disappointment Helen might be able to take. *You haven't even showered.* He hoped it wasn't too obvious, knowing that she knew he was on an every-other-day shower rota, and weekends were even laxer.

He organised the shower screen, blasted it on at a high temperature to get the bloody water going, and checked himself in the mirror. He needed a shave, but it was just a couple of days, and he didn't want to appear to have tried too hard, like a tearaway child dressed up for church in the eighties.

He brushed his teeth while the water warmed, and looked at himself doing so. That same face, staring back, underlined that what unfolded today would have ramifications for the future face staring back at him.

He spat out the warm thick dregs of paste into the bowl and helped it down the plug hole with a burst of water worked with his fingers. He pulled a bottle of mouthwash from on top of the cabinet, thick with dust, and took a slug. The sting pained his gums as it sloshed and swished around his mouth, fizzing between his teeth and gums, before setting alight a burgeoning mouth ulcer, reflecting his rather cursory and sparse dental hygiene routine.

As he ejected the mouthwash, a further wince of cleansing pain.

He focused on the shower and adjusted to an accommodating temperature. A haphazard routine, which took him from head to legs, to arms, torso and armpits, and to feet and then groin and arse. He washed the suds off until he was his bare, wet self, and decided to go over a second time.

After drying and dressing, Phil sat on the sofa, and surfed away the planet's fossil fuels. How the hell did the Tory party end up the party of high tax? Labour, the party of the poor, backing Tory policies, pushing government legislation through?

He pondered, as if it had just happened. Everything got past Phil.

Time inched on for the next couple of hours.

Helen rang her own doorbell.

It was an odd thing to do, and this an odd thing to be doing. Returning home for crisis talk, and to make some decisions on their future lives. A private conversation held indoors while the quiet street went about its business, unknowing. Men with ladders, cyclists cycling their dogs, postal and delivery workers, trundling cars, cars under-swiping speed bumps.

Phil opened the door and gestured for her to come in. It was a reflex action which they both felt awkward about. Helen resisted some mocking remark, accepting it was unintentional. He smelled clean, citrus notes.

He offered her a cup of tea. She would be staying long and accepted. He flicked the kettle on without care, which grated on Helen now as it ever did. There was no point getting started with a five-minute tea-making breakwater, so they made small talk about their weeks, Helen used the bathroom, and picked up a couple of things she needed. The place looked ordered, though in an unnatural way, but nothing indicative of untoward behaviour. For all his faults, he was consistent and transparent. Even so it was human instinct for Helen to poke her eyeballs about a bit.

They sat down at opposite corners of the sofa, taking their usual sides, but sitting side on, backed into the corners, like boxers. They faced, with a knee each pointing toward each other, and their legs in mermaid pose. The hands of both rested on their laps. They took reticent sips from tea too hot to drink. The rules of engagement were agreed, unspoken. Helen did the talking last time, she hoped Phil was bringing some of his thoughts to the table, and wanted to hear them. If the dog ate his homework, then they were done, before they started.

He began to talk, and Helen cut into him to let him know she knew he didn't find talking easy, and to encourage him. Then chastised herself for disrupting his flow from the get-go.

If he told and convinced Helen that he knew it was time for change, that children *was* something he wanted, even at *some point*, whereby he could say that that point needed to be now, as it couldn't be shelved any longer, Helen would accept this. They could move forward. For the first time in years, since they moved in together.

The truth was, and they both knew it, that Phil was content with his routines, his modest lot. He didn't seek a rangy list of outcomes across a span of hobbies, sports, social and familial networks. Music was the food of his love, and while for most the background soundtrack to the lives, it was his forefront.

He didn't see himself holding the baby.

He tried to figure his way through this discussion without tripping himself up, yet he lacked clarity of thought. And although it went unsaid by him, he conceded as it was said for him, that the energy for commitment could not be summoned.

Which left them poles apart.

"I hoped you might find it within you to fight for us. None of us live forever, we all grow old. I thought you might like children and," at which point her voice broke, her face creased and her lip went, before she cried out, "you'd enjoy playing music and dancing with them."

As tears flowed they embraced. They felt so warm to each other, their bodies anticipating the departing of the familiar.

They took their time to recover.

"I'm gonna go," Helen stated, "We can't take a break or anything like that. I'll take some things, and we should give each other the space to start to figure things out on our own. We can talk about the flat and everything another time."

He nodded through tears, and caved with craven acceptance.

Fiona received a text from Harry. Harry, wonderful Harry, she thought to herself. She phoned him and he answered.

"Hey," she started, before taking a breath. He caught the pause and knew.

"We can't see each other any longer."

Silence.

She was about to continue, when he stopped her.

"It's OK, I get it. It's cool."

"You know I love you. A little bit."

"Course. Me too. I'll miss you."

Another pause.

"Life's about moments, and *the* moment. It's all good, don't worry."

"All right," she replied, relaxing. She hadn't the laissez-faire perspective of millennial arrangements.

"If you ever want to meet up, for a drink or dinner or whatever."

"Yeah, right. And a session in the sack. As if we could resist."

"Hey, you said it. Sure."

"I might take you up on that. I'll try not to."

"So it's au revoir, then."

"Yes. Au revoir. Maybe."

She paused. "Bye Harry."

Harry heard her voice go, he said 'bye', and the phone disconnected.

It wasn't so much a case of setting him free, than setting him free to get on with whatever he got up to when she wasn't around, which was all the time. And hoping he figured out a life for himself.

It hurt Fiona.

It hurt so that she couldn't be sure she wouldn't be in touch again. Although that would invite the agony of his response. He might have to tell her that he was committed elsewhere.

Fiona got on with the day in the manner which felt natural. To get some bloody things done. The mothers she was still in touch with were dwindling as her children were going through the gears of the years, and for the most part it was cursory greetings from the SUV window or at the odd sporting occasion. Yet Fiona remained knotted into chat and online groups which needed attending to. And none of these damned people stood still for a second. Developing their interests, charitable engagements, pushing their children and by extension the circles of their children, on to the next new things. A level of sharp elbow wrestling and natural competition which Fiona could not put aside or rise above. Her position within these circles, and by extension her children, were at stake. And she could not see Florence or Theo ostracised from mixing with the *right people*, to get used to mixing with the wrong people. That would have longer term implications in whom they were easy around, with whom they were comfortable competing, and the extent to their ambitions. She had an afternoon to address these needs, and to the branded clothes Florence needed for an upcoming party.

As she did so, in Julian's world, the round of redundancies had been dealt with, people had been paid off, well or otherwise. Cardboard boxes distributed, lanyards relieved. Save for the odd moment of gallows banter, the remainers fell into a subdued period of quiet calm. A time for keeping one's head down, lest HR figure they may as well clear some bad apples out as well as some at the bottom of the league tables.

Awkward farewells between those who got to just keep carrying on with their lives undisturbed, and those who were now at the mercy of the markets, financial and job.

Julian took the time to reduce the midnight oil, spend time at home. Settle into a routine, having relinquished a period of volatility with Iva. A time of order, before he would go looking for some chaos.

This was important time to steady the ship before party season got started, and all kinds of unavoidables were foisted upon him.

He and Iva were on speaking terms, lift and floor greetings and *how are you yeah I'm fine and you yes I'm well thanks* talk. He saw her in a meeting room with one of the young bucks pinched from a domain competitor. Tall, strong, young alpha lad. She was giving him some eyes, using the hair, the skirted arse lifted above her knees as she sat on the edge of a table.

Stood at dusk, leaning on one of the high glass panels, four floors up, as Iva skipped out of the building. Her hips swayed as her legs whirred her across the concrete concourse. She avoided the cobbled strips, sticking with the flat slabbed sections, followed by a rolling case. She stopped to sweep her hair round the back of her head, and dropped the case handle halfway down, before being interrupted. The case was taken from her and the door held open as she entered the rear of the waiting car. Long and sleek, burgundy, dark as blood. Julian imagined a suited arm reach out, a gold and steel watch, no wedding ring, as she took his hand to steady herself in, sliding into the oyster white leather. There was no arm; there didn't need to be.

He thought about Iva, how she looked then, how she looked on some of the occasions he had the pleasure, how she looked in photos she had sent him. He couldn't say he didn't envy the next guy. He thought about another man making her pregnant, and a streak of hurt flashed through him from his balls to his throat. He had made his choice. For Iva, a learning moment in earlymidulthood. The difficulty in shaking a man free of a high value wife who isn't difficult beyond belief or crushing his masculinity.

He swigged back the remains of a Coke Zero, before squeezing the middle and chucking it into an empty bin. "Onward and upward," he muttered to himself.

100110
CHAPTER 38
Helen moves in with Francesca: Barney and Annabel suicide risk: Julian eases off

Depending on family was the default after a tragedy, a break-up or other crises, yet Helen could not face the defeat, the criticism and the sheer experience of time with hers. Helen would stay longer with Francesca, the unspoken tone clear that after everything she had done to influence Helen's direction of travel, it would be unacceptable to refuse. She had the space, and she was always out out. Knowing from personal experience the grind of having people to stay, even for a week, she stated when she would leave, and went about organising a reserve stretch somewhere else.

Her friend Lou, down in St. Leonards-on-Sea, had always asked her to stay for a holiday, so Helen called, apologised that it taken a while, and stomached the awkward moment she had to ask a big favour. Yet Lou was gracious, delighted to have the company, and to help her friend during a tough period. Helen figured she would be all right there for a month, so she now had a six-week window.

She approached her manager about remote working for a month, kept the reasons vague, and went with the assumptive close. This is what she was doing and they would support her. It wasn't a request, and there were enough precedents set that a debate would be quick to close down. After getting through a round of conversations with the people she had to let know, or at least the super-connectors who could spread word for her, she sat at Francesca's admiring the décor, drinking wine and contemplating her own personal great reset.

These first steps, initial forays toward a potential new life gave her the jitters, yet it did feel like she was being winched out of a walled existence, and while she had no idea where she would land, the courage felt at least deserving of reward. Although it was human nature to think the worst, was it realistic to think she might descend into jobless, homeless destitution? No. She had skills and experience and the market would ensure these were met, within a range of salary and job satisfaction outcomes. And as with any business, as long as the cash flow held.

The nerves in her gut came from a conflation of a relationship in termination, work disruption, an abandoned home. The *what's next* of it all.

Her swirling mind tracked all over the place, compounded by a bad memory under normal circumstances, let alone under the stress of this uprooted life. A memory which seemed to retain the worst of circumstances, situations, things said, which she would like to see forgotten forever. She comforted herself that everyone carried these around with them, and some of the most successful were those with the heaviest baggage of all. The dire nights of bad decisions taken, caught by the law, captured, existing forever on an internet that never forgot.

Francesca tried to make herself scarce while being supportive when around, taking Helen out for long walks round the great parks, a new habit for them. The Italian didn't have the experiences of long-established and failed relationships to find the words. So fell back on the experiences of others, and generalist words of encouragement. Which was good enough. Words were powerless to repeal anguish and suffering; a matter for time to settle.

When alone, and indeed when Francesca was around, Helen reviewed and turned over recent events, the conversations with Phil, crafting them into a narrative which she replayed in private moments, organising how any next conversations with Phil might unfurl.

Misrepresentations and anachronisms within her timeline shone a light on the fallibility of human recollection. Thoughts which wandered off into the realms of criminality and witnesses and miscarriages of justice. She caught herself overthinking, and went for a swim, where she would also churn. However, the repetition and movement would iron her wrinkled thoughts out, like a massage freed the knots. It wasn't lost on her that exercise was positive, not least because she was now available, something she hadn't even been able to think about yet. The prospect of dating filled her with no urge, just urgh.

The impossibility of a carefree single life to someone in a relationship, unless an unhappy one without hope, in which one yearned for freedom. Starting each day and making each decision by oneself; assuming all the risk, no hedges from sharing the downside, even if one took on others' risk also. Should a long-tail catastrophe occur, a serious illness or disability, well then the singleton had a major problem. Yet for most, that was improbable, and not worth mitigating against in the organisation of a life. As the clamour to *keep us safe* should not drive all public health outcomes. A life lived in fear could not amount to much.

Helen walked to a swimming bath she had found to reset her sanity. As she walked down the middle of the wide paths of Marylebone, she felt isolated and alone, yet a sense of pride and bravery that she had opened up the abdomen of her unsatisfactory and dysfunctional life. Although untrained in how to operate, she would have to dive in, shift some organs about, get her hands dirty, and start plumbing.

Annabel was off work and Barney hadn't had a response within a day, and she didn't pick up when he called either. Her last time online that morning implied nothing untoward had happened, he hoped, yet also reinforced the fact that he was being ignored.

He left Jess with a neighbour and drove. It took over an hour. A surprised Annabel let him in.

It was the first time she had ever looked displeased to see him. The precariousness of interpersonal relationships unbound by lack of familial ties was underscored. Under usual circumstances this represented a positive – they were here because they wanted to be, but now he felt powerless to request anything, to lay down any law.

They said nothing as Barney walked through and they both sat down.

"What's happening?" he asked, his vague question accurate in conveying that it wasn't obvious what the problem was, but there was a big one.

"You're not ill," he said.

She got up, turned the kettle on, and poured them each a tumbler of tap water, handed one to Barney and sat down again.

"I just can't face it," she answered after giving it pause.

"It. What it?" he responded, confused.

"Any of it."

The kettle was already hot and didn't need long. As vapour billowed out, stuck under a long cupboard in a flat cloud, she got up and made them drinks.

Barney felt bad for eyeing her up for criticism, dressed as she was in pyjama bottoms and a T-shirt, and looking pale, tired, expired. Although he never saw her dressed like this before, the clothes hung off her in an unexpected way, her shoulders were bony, her hips jutted out at the top of her waist.

They sat in silence, apart on the sofa. Next to each of them the soft whispers of warmth spiralled from mugs of hot drinks. Everything in the material world operated as normal.

Barney wished he had a clue how to handle someone suffering in this way, how to offer consolation in the confident, close way he saw others that were good at it. With the warmest of words and biggest of hugs, from people who were naturals, as others were naturals at nefarious activities.

He drank a hot slurp and could, at best, reason that time spent in the company of someone that cared, albeit in silence, would help.

While they each fixed stares at a smudge on the wall or a photo hung on the wall, or read the spines of a pile of books on the floor, over and over, Annabel plotted the acting performance required to get Barney to leave. To convince that while she might be depressed, she wasn't a danger to herself. And as any air crash investigator could tell, a disaster required multiple, simultaneous points of failure for tragedy to unfold. Annabel needed to remove Barney, convince so that he stayed gone, and then she might be left to take the longest sleep. At her own convenience.

She thought her best route was to get things out in the open, appear engaged. To brush everything off, *everything's just fine* would be too obvious and convenient. So she talked it out, rehashing old tropes and arguments she had been over countless times with him, keeping an eye on the clock on the wall, setting herself a time limit, how long she had to run through things with him. She weaved in some uncertainties, not sure about this, hadn't much faith in that. Unclear how certain aspects might have any chance of resolving themselves. It was a master class in obfuscation and misdirection, sleight of mouth.

She was going to write some things down that day, commit her thoughts to paper. This detail and imagery pleased her, deception worthy of a classic from the eighteen hundreds. She suggested they met the next day once this was done and could discuss things in a better frame of mind. Offering him a slice of cake which she cut for them both. Cunning. She *was* eating, after all.

As Barney went to leave, Annabel underlined the timings for the following day, which he mirrored to show he had committed to memory.

Returning to his car, which was parked out of sight, he sat for a while, for some focused thought. He was concerned, yet there was always a balance between acting on known past events and potential future ones. And individuals had to judge the lines of where potential unlikely morphed into possible and onto likely. He was stuck, and the other line he had to draw was when to bring others into the know. Get that wrong and that jeopardised one of the things he held dearest. She was eating, he had thought, watching her fork the carrot cake. And thinking things through in a considered manner.

After they had said goodbye and the door closed, Annabel sunk onto the carpet on her knees.

Thoughts circled his head on rotation, as he tried to focus on the road, and the potential dangers of low speed high acceleration London traffic. Every junction a potential point of conflict. Mopeds, scooters, cyclist swarms. Chaotic local road planning. He was thirsty from the dry cake, and it nagged at him.

She had been distracting him and he wasn't buying it.

He turned back and hurried to her home. Someone pulled out in front of him, and he horned them and waved for them to get out of his way. He imagined an ambulance crew, energetic and exhausted, running with vigour, going to Annabel's aid, finding her with cut wrists in the bath. He received the finger for his troubles.

Arriving, he rang the bell and banged on the door.

Annabel opened, surprised and relieved to see him. The loneliness in her cried out.

"Let me in," he said, pushing the door.

He sat down.

"What do you think you're playing at? Have you taken anything?"

He looked around for any sign of packaging.

She shook her head.

"Promise me?"

"I promise."

"You're thinking about it though."

Annabel said nothing.

Barney's thoughts were a mashed mix, unable to be formed into lines. He was out of his depth, and this was way outside his human experience. He tried to remember anything from his thirty years, things he had read, watched, experiences retold by others. He had to understand how credible this was, and he didn't know what to do but ask, and try to decode the answer to reach the closest thing to a truth.

"How bad is it, is this all-consuming?"

"I don't care anymore. I've been banging on about the environment since I was a teenager, and finally the acceptance and recognition is out there, in the mainstream. And now it's been taken over by the elite tyrants. It's agenda time. Keeping the planet in good shape for future generations was my hope. Now we are left with a dystopian future, run for us by those evil motherfuckers. They don't give a shit about the planet, it's about power and control. Communists! I'd rather we let it all go to shit, have another thirty years, and accept out fate. I've got nothing left."

Barney was unsure if she would go on, but gave her the space to do so.

"I haven't got any fight in me, look, I'm exhausted by it all. Work isn't even that stressful, and I've got no relationship failing away, yet I'm mentally done. Don't tell me I need a holiday."

She glared at him.

"Maybe you need a holiday."

They both cracked reluctant half-smiles.

"I can't remember the last time I had something to look forward to. And I don't mean a day out, something substantive."

He thought this was low level in the context of what they were discussing, and said as much.

"That's life though isn't it, past thirty-five. Don't most people feel like that?"

"You asked me to explain. I'm painting a broader picture. The core of it is, there is no hope."

"You need support, beyond what I can give. I'm useless. And I can't keep this to myself. You need to speak to your family. They need to know."

He couldn't believe this was happening, and wished that is wasn't so.

The next few hours contained great swathes of silence, interspersed with honesty and comment. It was about two people being present, and a reminder for Annabel that she wasn't alone. He would have to go at some point, and while reticent to leave her, she convinced him she was balanced enough, and that they should stick with the plan for the next day.

"I'm not going until you've called one of your sisters."

She raised her eyes.

"Tell them you're having a hard time and can they come round this evening. Do it now."

Annabel did as she was told, while he checked his phone.

He looked at her, dead straight.

"If you do anything to *yourself*, I'll never forgive *myself*. And other people will never forgive me."

Unblinking, he looked right through her, and let the words sink in.

A dirty streak of manipulation, unworthy of him. One could never know people, she thought, showing him admiration.

"She'll be half an hour."

Tears formed at the thought of wronging him. And this was enough for him to accept her word. He waited a while then left, not wanting to have to carry out an excruciating handover.

Late that evening, Barney spoke to himself and to God. He did that. He couldn't tell others that of course, that was a private matter. For the curious thing about religion was that while people might respect and admire those with religious conviction, if you claimed to speak with God, and *especially* if he spoke back, madness was proclaimed.

The dark nights and the deterioration in the weather and daylight hours and sunshine were anything but helpful at that juncture. And months of waste lay ahead, before the hopes of spring.

Annabel lay in the gloom, her curtains half-closed, and the light from a streetlamp cast over her sofa, and got into her eyes, until she moved. She lay riven with confusion, trying to turn her mind off by coaching herself to think of nothing, to stare, to wonder what it would be like to finish.

Another midweek work trip complete, an uneventful one spent alone, and time for Julian to take stock. The aching, chilled loneliness of a dark evening in a European departure lounge, with the sinister comings and goings of vehicles and great planes over tarmac plains.

A flight full of turbulence, so continual, disruptive and jarring that he swore to himself. They could fucking well fly around it. It seemed they were determined to take the direct route home, and chose to go hell for leather. For two hours. As the plane broke the clouds on its descent and rounded the black of the south-east coastal seas, things calmed, and Julian traced the lines of light around the Kent and Essex coastlines and their various inlets, rivers and structures of industry, power, defence. The travel emitted the best part of half a ton of carbon dioxide on his behalf alone. Bricks, feathers, carbon dioxide, a ton was a ton.

They crossed the mamba of a midnight Thames, the dome a pang of all the years London had been his generation's playground. The darkness and street lighting an appropriate callback to the nights, for it was the nights which drew the story of a London life together. The pubs, clubs, evenings out, pleasure and work, the all-day sessions which burst into nights and hangovers of morning. And flashes of reminders of the things one got away with, the scrapes and dangers and close encounters with those capable of great harm. The route and its descent took him from East London nights, to awards evenings in Mayfair, to the Soho nights, and over to the days out with children in Kensington and the comfortable pubbing in Battersea of Putney. Before the final return over distant West London, with its towers and logistics infrastructure, and beyond the airport, its reservoirs and relief into countryside. Stretching onto a darker place, second in its menace to the rougher of Britain's seaside towns.

Thoughts of the night reminded him of the warmth and comfort of his home life waiting for him. The strains of living high on the hog this last year or so had left him resolved to take a period to settle. Time with the children, all that. Time off from any side action.

The tumult of a turbulent year felt behind him. Things had calmed down for Julian at work, confidence had returned after some decent forecasts for end of year. Although it was never discussed between them and no collusion took place, both Julian and Iva had engineered her move out of the team, and to a higher position in another department. A bump for her. The only bump, a relief to him. He had a few things to help the team close down in the last six weeks of the year, and while it was never done till it was done, he felt able to nudge and push, and move through the end of the quarter.

The next day, the order which had been restored was reflected in the relaxed, reclined position he adopted in his fifteen-hundred-pound office chair, as opposed to the stiff posture he had suffered over summer, when a colleague slapping him on the shoulders would give him a start.

His boss sauntered through, also representative of year-end targets in sight, and as he passed Julian, mentioned, "might have solved the replacement for Iva, will send you an email later."

He returned to his screen and a message popped up, from a Claudia, asking to meet for a chat, and not one to hang about for due process. He leaned into the screen to get a better look at her photo, of her in a blue suit, arms folded, against the skyline of London. Blonde hair and a full, broad smile. *Interesting*, he thought.

One of the leaders on the floor passed in Julian's view, and he kept eyes focused on the screen in front of him. He was owed a short paper on the prospects of a business, that Julian knew this guy had a vested interest in, via a long-standing friend. Prospects which after a cursory glance at some of the key variables looked in the balance, to say the least. The world demanded, for his several hundred kay a year, that on occasion he write up a few hundred words, placing his opinion in a camp a distance from reality and the truth, as best as he could. The game. Some report, buried, skimmed over perhaps by half a dozen people. Thousands of similar pieces flung out there each year by him and his colleagues, all claiming to share some *insight*. Ask three different people, get one positive, one negative, and one middling viewpoint.

His technique in these situations was to write the report in an honest manner, as he saw it, including the important metrics. And then go to work dialling adjectives up or down, applying caveating adverbs, to the point where he considered his piece to be able to ride the storms of a crashing outcome without discrediting him. Give himself a couple of outs. Prevailing market conditions, potential government edicts. Unknown unknowns. If he were to take the piss, he would take a couple of inversely correlated variables, and highlight the outcome of each of them increasing, thereby building in a hedge.

He yearned for an impasse, and reached the one he could think of, which was to park it. Do it tomorrow.

A meeting ended. Colleagues gathered laptops and tech, while Julian watched a few stragglers looking to politick some post-alignment. He was unable to escape a reminder of his outstanding task as he felt a lurker behind and swivelled to meet his gaze.

"Had time to look at that matter for me, Julian?"

Matter, classic vague term in front of the hoi polloi of the open plan office.

Starting on it today, will have it landed tomorrow.

"Good, good."

He went on to ask after Julian's children, before segueing into the accomplishments of his own offspring, oozing maxed out levels of smarm, which Julian loathed him for, hating in others that which he hated in himself.

The day ended for some and not others. People departed in pairs and solo until he was one of the few remaining. He collected himself, and went to leave until a member of his team door-stepped him, to lobby for his views and influence on some team-building event in the pipeline.

"You know me, right? We've worked together for a while now, right?"

She looked at him, shrugging, "Yeah?"

"I just. Don't. Care."

He laughed and walked away.

Returning home that evening, every single light was on, inside and out, the gravel drive surrounding their car illuminated, with an extra light flicking on as he approached the front door. Energy crisis indeed. One hitting him in the wallet.

Theo greeted him as he walked down the stairs in the middle of something, staring at technology, before walking off into the overheated lounge. Julian dumped things down and removed coat and scarf, trying to beat the sweat that was about to take hold after a spirited walk. Before going to change, the true breakwater between a day of work and evening of leisure, he walked into the kitchen. It didn't go unnoticed by Fiona that he had been back at a reasonable hour for the third day in a row, and she sensed that someone may have been cast off, or moved herself onward. For this good deed, she walked over and gave him a kiss, and called him darling.

"Homework's done," Fiona confirmed, nodding at Florence, busy drafting up placards.

"I don't want to know," he muttered to himself. He checked through a few things Fiona had sorted for him, left in the same place as ever, before turning to go upstairs, and calling back.

"As long as we're not getting tutors on top of the ones we already have."

100111
CHAPTER 39
Helen in Hastings: Barney helps Annabel: Fiona and Florence discuss Annabel

Helen woke in the darkness, something which had become habit since the move. The clock teetered toward seven o'clock, and after kidding herself that she might return to sleep for ten minutes or so, she faced facts and rose. She put the kettle on, after checking it was at least half full from the previous day, grabbed a mug from its tree, and retrieved milk and a spoon and laid them out in a line on the counter. Stood in her thick dressing gown, she yawned hard, and stretched her arms high, stopping when her head felt spaced. The belt of her gown unravelled, and she gathered it up as the cold flashed in. She crossed her arms and hugged herself as the water toiled its noise to reach a roiling boil.

Her neighbour insisted several times that she go out at daybreak, despite the hour and lack of comfort, and Helen decided this would be the day, so she could say she had done it, and move their chatter onto other matters.

She put the mug away, and instead put together a flask of piping hot, milky, sweet coffee, and dressed into her loafing gear, a thick waterproof and a beanie hat. She pulled the door to, and gave it a check.

She walked with heavy legs and followed the path of a small street cleaning vehicle, with its rotating brushes digging out the gutters and keeping Britain tidy, for a few hours at least.

She panicked that she had left her phone at home, flicking through whether that was OK (take time out) or not (no photos) yet as she patted herself down, it wasn't a problem after all. She reached the metal posts and guardrails, and found the split, taking the stairs down to the stony beach. She passed the beach huts to head east into the sun and to walk past the groynes.

The sun was so soft she could walk into it, wide eyed. While stones weren't as pretty, they suited her as she was irritated by sand, a relic from childhood and queuing for ice creams by the beach in a café with a tiled floor. An irritant that she could still replay in her feet if she paused to recall. And stones kept the visitor numbers down.

There were better beach views. Elsewhere, golden sands, brighter, colourful skies, without the background beeps of a vehicle reversing. Yet she felt peace among the nerves. And an inner sense that a change was needed. Even if it didn't work out, it might be the shake needed to settle somewhere better.

Exhausted in the dismay of a job, she was afforded an excuse to reject the risk of taking a new path. Freed, the creative space had lifted her mood, and she began to notice new thoughts, possibilities, opportunities and permission to fail. The world, after all, was going to let her keep doing what she was doing, as long as she was competent at it. Those around her who got on, made their way into new industries or carved business ideas into reality, did it through their own volition. They got what they got, by refusing to do what they always did. Slowly and then all at once, she found herself digging herself out of her hole, and she felt on the cusp of making things happen on her terms.

She missed Phil.

That month had been so different to those previous, and she hadn't been able to say that for some time. Most of all there had been a change in tempo, a change in pace. The relentless waves of London energy, required to keep one's head above water, had relinquished. Having enjoyed staying with her friend by the coast, she felt it needed longer, and rented a cosy flat further along in Hastings. She had landed an interim role as a Memberships Director at the National Trust, with added responsibility and stretch, and while her pay had dropped, she cared not a jot. The team was lifted by what she brought to the table. They were good people.

She walked on and the usual suspects ran through her mind but didn't tighten her thoughts. They drifted in, then out, like markers, milestones of thought, like each bend or straight of a running track on which she was completing laps. This felt like a symptom of age, the youthful head clear of family or worries, swimming with the indulgence of the pursuit of laughter and joy, of sex and new experiences. Age laden her with the burden. She thought of the older people, here to retire, to watch out their last years, and also the revitalisation that the new youth and ex-Londoners had brought, with new ideas and ventures. It mattered not whether this were a long term move, or temporary patch fix.

She watched and listened to sea birds, some violent types, a robbery of gulls, perhaps, and tried to create a narrative of her experience, so she could relay back to her neighbour in some detail. After twenty minutes or so, when the coffee ran out, she picked herself up, and walked up to the promenade and sought some croissants to get her started. When home, she warmed them, added butter, and sat on the table by the window with coffee looking out onto the street.

The dull ache in her stomach had turned the volume down, but remained. The independence of making her own decisions, and the removal of frustrations and reminders of things not working, couldn't yet nix the loss of a shared life.

And as the sunny warmth and potential of a hot croissant turned to an empty plate and a singular knife, her response was to go for one more walk, as she sought company in activity. Keep on moving.

Global and local current affairs were going through a phase of accelerationism and Francesca chose to avoid them for the most part. A never-ending pile of things to concern oneself with, to elevate anxiety. Many people chose to occupy their minds with only that which affected them. Should Francesca concern herself with education? Of course, a well-educated population affected everyone. Moreover, should one ignore cries for help on topics one was not invested in, one was painted into a corner in summoning help when something relevant did impose itself. She resolved to give herself the weekend off from such matters, and decompress from warmongering, supplies of lethal aid, continued *pandemic* wars, and totalitarian technocrat strategies. Events and discussion involving money, corruption, and globalism, reminded her of Simon, the direction of material progress made flesh.

Francesca phoned Helen to see how she was getting on.

Helen sounded well insofar as life had been injected with a shot of change – views, new people, and alternative routines. It was obvious she was being reticent about something, and Francesca wasn't surprised when Helen felt compelled to get off her chest that she had been talking with Phil. Francesca let her say what she had to say and changed the subject. The horse had been taken to water, and Francesca would be wasting no words now on the matter. There was enough recognition in Helen's voice that things had moved on, that any re-emergence would be on new terms, and Francesca recognised that. She had reminded her that the move wouldn't be a move if she took London and her old life with her. Francesca was satisfied it wasn't working out like that, as she listened to the simple pleasures Helen had enjoyed in recent weeks.

There was a lightness in Helen's voice, one that came from a physical relaxation, from lungs and a circulatory system allowed to find their natural rhythms. A core responding to a brain not running hot. Francesca told her so, yet it didn't need to be said. Without the weight of Helen's old plight, they wrapped up the call. London wasn't Helen's place, and while it could be anyone's place in their twenties, it wasn't for her into middle-age and beyond.

Francesca's day was open and undecided. She touted herself about until she found someone available for the evening, and organised to see some live music in Chelsea. Old world but dependable. That would give her the day to do nothing, which was what she wanted.

Light dawned on Barney after the nth day in a row he'd fallen into bad food habits, and felt lousy as a result. Bread, packaged sandwiches, impulse foods, food on the hoof. If one was what one ate, Barney was a lumpen bag of carbs. As he strolled to the shop, he saw a chubby boy sat with a large bag of snacks, chowing down. Crunching under hypnosis, unable to focus on anything else but the slow grind to the bottom of the bag, hands aflame with orange dust. He saw an overweight future, burdened always, lacking in energy, drive, and no energy wasted on pursuing any dream or ambition. He had to walk on. There was no intervention or conversation which could be framed to ease the future for the poor mite.

Barney was made to realise that his lifetime of complaisance was not what was required in this situation. He had lectured Annabel about her diet, exercise, sunlight, walking, and all the other keys to wellness. Helping others. He made inroads into finding some charitable work she could do close to home. He paused after intending to send her a few ideas, helping the local elderly, food banks. Maybe depressing.

He spoke with Helen so they could organise drinks whenever she next came back to London.

When alone he felt the fear from not knowing that Annabel was safe. And after a phase of parking his own mortality for several years, it all turned itself on him. The simplicity of a domestic suicide. One could end it all in minutes should one choose. And while every hour and day that went by without any bad news relieved the pressure, to put too much faith in Annabel might damn Barney to an insufferable lifetime.

At home in the evenings, as he surveyed his life, he eyed his phone, dreading a moment that might change everything. Having to delve for meaning in the everyday, it felt like a form of grief, as with the end of a relationship, of which he had limited experience, or the death of a relative a step or two removed. He could check that Annabel was turning up at work, and each time they met, look for the signals. He would reinforce the language and emotional blackmail he had employed to good effect already. He could see her warming again, yet it was noticeable the topics of conversation she avoided, having cleared out whole areas of stress from her concern.

He switched off lights, monitored heating levels and the timer, prepared his recycling using techniques stipulated within the latest advice. Odd dishes would be concocted as things went on the turn toward the end of the week, and he decommissioned the freezer altogether. He put together a work event to raise money for some lesser known organisation. An event which his colleagues thought was one fundraiser too many with all the events they had to run, support and participate in. They found the recipient too random and would rather give it a miss, but they supported him nonetheless. He became embroiled in a neighbour's dispute with the council. A true nightmare of legal and bureaucratic wranglings, and a testament to the over-complexity of modern life. He participated in the odd protest which he kept quiet about, and that was the long and the short of what he felt able to do, albeit with an overarching sense of helplessness and loss.

Autumn was in full swing and in Wandsworth gardens were filling up with the deposits from large, ancient trees, sited in long gardens. Up and down the country, men were preparing to spend a Sunday tidying, collecting, composting piles of leaves. Fiona made a note to call the gardener, as she circuited the island, leaving Julian undisturbed, pawing at some documents.

"Oh, remember that girl from the garden party?" Fiona asked.

"Which one?"

"Francesca's."

"No, which girl."

"Oh. Annabel, short hair, pretty."

"We didn't really speak, the one talking with Florence?"

Florence walked in.

"They've got her on bloody suicide watch. Isn't that awful?"

"Annabel? What happened?" Florence asked, alarmed.

Fiona and Julian looked at each other, conferring in silence on what to do next. What flashed through Julian's mind was 'you don't know her, you met her once,' but kept his mouth shut, and deferred to Fiona, while brow-signalling that she should reveal or explain little.

A moment of realisation that the bad things out there didn't just happen to the nameless on the news.

Julian knew his worldview differed from Fiona's, and chose to extricate himself from these matters. He'd been behaving as an adequate husband, and why spoil it. Pick your battles.

"I'm gonna walk the dog. I'll take Theo."

A lead was clipped on, a couple of coats and shoes were shrugged and pulled on, and the door slammed.

This had given Fiona some thinking time, to calculate approach, what to reveal, how to provide reassurance. Her recall of similar conversations when young, at times of bereavement or a local crime, were foggy at best.

"I don't know a lot about it. From what I hear, she's become depressed recently."

"What happened?"

"Nothing *happened*. They thought she might try to. Do something,"

Fiona responded, with a most pathetic, veiled description, "but she didn't."

"They are keeping an eye on her, and trying to help. She's OK, it's OK."

Fiona kept it to bland, general basics, knowing that digging and questioning would take it to further layers, and wanting to start from a low base. She accepted that this was a time for honesty and letting some of life's darkness into one shielded by high walls.

Florence said nothing, but stared and shook her head a few times, to indicate with the most minimal of effort that that would not be sufficient.

"She takes a lot on herself, to heart. Lets the world get on top of her. From what I understand."

"Yes I know, we talked about that."

"What did she say?" Fiona enquired, getting on the front foot with a question, something Florence hadn't identified as a tactic yet, but would before too long.

"We exchanged facts, about nature. Fatbergs."

"Fatbergs."

Fiona laughed, "Did she say anything odd?"

Florence looked up, when other children might look down.

"No."

She paused a moment, and caught Fiona off guard with words beyond her years.

"There was a sadness there."

Perhaps her education was worth the money.

"She's too beautiful and nice to kill herself. Not that ugly or bad people should."

Fiona's instinct would be to pull her in close to hug her daughter, but she touched her on the shoulder, and let her absorb things alone, as she would have to begin to do.

"Annabel said I should go on a march," said Florence, as Fiona walked off to get something from a drawer, "we're going on that march."

Florence stared toward the window, toward the light, computing. Fiona watched her eyes, showing her workings.

"Love. It's all gonna be OK."

Jess questioned why Barney had brought her to one of the least dog-friendly parks, with a plethora of rules and regulations, uptight dog owners and critical passers-by. Leads were administered as they went through different zones. Off-lead here, on-lead there, on-off, on-off. Dog-themed modern nonsense of the highest order. Barney was stressed by the watchful eye he had to keep Jess under the whole time as she strayed too near the pond (banned, bird life) or tried to sneak a discreet ghost poo away from critical eyes. She approached a large lady, who backed away, asking Barney if it was his dog. He didn't understand the context until she kept backing away and he realised she was in tears and in distress.

"It's OK, she's friendly," he tried to convey to appease while rushing to get a lead onto Jess so the poor woman would stop panicking and calm an oppressive phobia. He secured her, but the woman had run off and Barney felt awful, but fearing a report to the park authorities, strode away with Jess. He aimed to call it a day, regroup, and go again elsewhere. Jess was on board with this. They were clear of the hazard so he let her go.

From behind a distant tree appeared a dog of the same breed as Jess, and they bowled over toward each other. It didn't always happen that way. Like anything else in the natural world, there were commonalities via genetics, and then huge variations in temperament, motivations and how they went about their business. These two gelled, and followed each other around, displaying a similar gait, sniffing in turn all the good stuff, akin, with shared priorities.

He led her off for a strident twenty-minute walk to another place, with extra space, and a view. Street-walking with a terrier, wishing to sniff all the tree trunks, each wall, any discard item on the pavement, every scrag of weeds sprouted between wall and pavement, sounding off their messages to other neighbourhood dogs.

He tried to be firm. Kidding no-one, least of all the mass of terrier and its sensitivities to weakness. They made it to the park, and Jess was so revved up from the stimulation of new dogs down seldom trodden streets, that she launched at a dog that came over to Barney for a polite greeting and a stroke. Possession. The monster.

Barney shouted at Jess, dismayed that the poor young pup had been schooled. The owners were old hands. As Barney put a lead on Jess, the couple shrugged. Dogs. He nodded his appreciation to them.

They called it before too long and spent the rest of the day doing fuck all.

Jess dozed. Barney slept also. Jess attempted to find some interest in balls and chew toys. Barney tried to read, to get into a film. The day just strung itself out without offering up any obvious method of achieving much. Barney ended up clock watching, willing the time away until they could turn in for the night.

As Barney called for the night walk, to empty the tanks and affording Jess a comfortable night, she resisted, as she had every night with Barney. She wanted that one night where she broke him. So that she could make these decisions in the future. For a dog was beholden on their owner's schedule and whims, unlike a cat.

On the essentials of maintenance, Barney was unshakeable, and he put the collar on her and led her out the door to lap the block. As they left the main building, Jess strained hard, and yelped, a long wail that increased to a half howl, as the scent of foxes flooded her senses like cheap cologne filled a pub. As they passed the gate, three foxes scattered, keeping their shoulders and profile low, padding off at pace, disappearing to their manifold escape routes mapped out in different directions.

Sleep-refreshed Jess was now on high alert, pulling hard to the point where her light collar cut into her, and she choked herself from her own determination. One hundred percent ready for the hunt. Barney wasted his voice, attempting to calm and redirect. Their relationship, like many close relatives or friends, was elastic, held to a point, and then failed. For Jess, it was back on; the pursuit, for more, for something.

101000
CHAPTER 40
Helen speaks with Phil: Annabel languishes

A mid-afternoon walk along a stretch of promenade and onto the stone beach allowed Helen to clear her head, having a few final work tasks remaining before being able to power down. The dark nights were upon her a few weeks after the adjustment of the clocks, and she wondered how a winter on the coast would suit her. It was a trudge through the deeper sections of beach, where her wellied feet sunk into wet stone troughs before she was able to reach a finer mix, close to sand, as she reached the water's edge. Wind and waves were curling, working together to thrust over her the smell of salt. Air so cold and clean that global warming felt as unimaginable as when one crossed the country by aeroplane and saw the country for what it was – vast and green, despite the lies buried in the hills.

A message came through from Phil which read: "Hope everything is going well in Hastings, how is it? Phil x"

Helen felt teary but didn't tear, that dry tightness of anxiety, as her nerves rattled. She began to respond, and then chose to phone him when she got home, as the wind was high. It put a smile on her face, and gave her a feeling that while she stood alone, a hundred yards from the nearest person, she was connected, a mere day away from Phil and others.

When she returned, she called and talked about her new set-up, the change it had brought in her, and about the many positives she had found beyond the downsides. She bemoaned a few things which were difficult away from the capital, and Phil conveyed that for him it was a jaunty case of *same old same old*. Everything was OK at the flat for the time being.

"There's a big music scene here."

"I heard that from Gaz who moved there last year."

It was a call that took a while to come to an end. There was a pregnant pause at the end, and they both began to speak at the same time, after which followed a round of *you go, no yous*.

Helen followed the call with a pile of photographs.

"Looks great! I miss you x"

"I miss you x"

Later that evening Phil went to join friends at a pub, a gathering for no particular reason other than the place served drinks to be drunk. It was a boisterous place, music to suit a well-informed crowd, a menu of beige goods – all filler, and the kind of place to which one shouldn't wear white.

The girl who served him was young, bright eyed, with a brash confidence beyond her looks, which were not insubstantial. She swayed across his beer, extracted his electronic funds with minimal pallaver, and then fussed about after others, going typewriter style from one side of the bar to the other, then sweeping back to the starting line, dispensing her attention with fairness.

Catching her soft Welsh lilt, to Phil at least, and to many better men, she was 'marry tomorrow' material. No matter the male eyes that feasted on her day-in-day-out, she was enjoying a female phase, picking off the customers she chose who returned the right looks.

Lazy he might be, yet he was a realist. He knew that when he and Helen got together they were a good match. And it hadn't been a case of personal development or quality drift. Where one of a twosome begins to accomplish things, improve themselves out of the other's reach. Nor the case that one had gone to seed or picked up an addiction, or a nasty affliction. It sat with him, and his unwillingness to offer their relationship anything new. Staying the same sent one backward.

He joined the others and the drinks started to go down. He tried to join in the laughs, the japes and capers, yet was quieter than normal.

After a couple of rounds, a friend of a friend whom Phil had not met before announced he was leaving.

"Look, I've got to get back, young daughter. But wanted to catch up, it's been a while," he directed to his friend.

"No bother," he said, and they shook hands.

Phil watched him leave, and while they didn't get to talk, he just sensed - good bloke.

Insisting he got the next round, and hoping to cover him for also leaving before they got into the serious drinking, Phil got them in, finished his last pint, and left.

Helen felt a twinge of dread at the thought of having to tell Francesca that Phil was back in her life, if it came to that, and she attempted to decode this emotion. If it were an admission that things were back the way they were, that would be one thing. However, Helen had wrestled control, and reverting to type would be off the table. She would make clear the conditions for a second coming together. This would be her pitch. A pitch made to Francesca, but it would satisfy herself that she was doing the right thing.

She saw Francesca putting her hand up to stop her, either because she understood it was rational, or to mutter 'you don't need to convince *me*...'

Stuck in an echo chamber of cynicism, either rejecting or being rejected, Steven Axford's soul hardened further. Amanda represented hope. Someone who could have pulled him out of the cycle, to raise him from temporary, narrow relationships and short-termism. He saw her on dating apps, looking optimistic and accomplished. Her main profile photo had been changed to the one he said was his favourite.

He hoped at least that dating was, for her too, an abject failure. He could say, 'I hope she finds happiness,' but they would be empty, dishonest words. He was stuck, with no options in the corridor of mutual attraction, esteem, and respect. That he would forever chase those out of reach, dismissing those that wanted him. Forever seeking the right partner that would accept him as a partner.

He had the bruising from Amanda coming. It had come around. How he responded might define his path and chance for future success. He could be thankful it happened early, as he reflected on the wounds he had inflicted much later, upon others. When the harm was real. Damage to the heart, not just the ego, or the inability to have what one wanted. Another reason to decline to open himself up, to make himself vulnerable to a future Amanda, wielding the end.

All he could do was continue. One foot in front of the other. Try to swipe and date his way out of this hole via work and sheer numbers. Yet he felt the hollowness of modern technological separation, the packaging of individuals as goods with attributes and specs, rated, displaying their benefits. A march to a future set apart from the past he emerged from, with its freedoms and shared experiences.

A fatalist, he saw the future already written. And the world wasn't going to spin in the other direction. He forced himself to emerge from the dread through exercise, hard work, and taking a month off from drinking, which helped. He had been here before and come out of it. A couple of positive moves, random or planned, could lift. He swiped, set up some walks and coffees. Put some energy into his real world conversations and connections. Increased the chit chat. Spanish Veronica appealed. Tessa in Finance had credentials, and looked the siren. Sarah from Brixton looked a laugh. One never knew.

As Steven met Nicola in Marketing from Peckham for drinks in Soho, a mere four hundred yards away as the crow flew, Josie was getting dinner with Victoria. A friend who had proven herself worthy, who had been a comfort over the summer, had made herself available to meet up whenever, and who was humble and sensitive enough to open the books on her own relationship failings and vulnerabilities when Josie had to front up her own. Steven continued to rattle around her thoughts over dinner. Josie knew this had gone on too long, and didn't need Victoria to tell her to put it behind her.

"Don't give up though. Never give up."

"Work is going well; the casework is heavy but satisfying," she responded as they talked on different tracks.

"For every fifty shits you meet, there's a good one."

"Just the one?"

"Pretty much."

"Better than nothing."

Victoria looked at someone who was becoming a closer friend. Who looked more invigorated. And she gave thought to the ups and downs happening all around them. For tonight, somewhere nearby, someone was being torn by despair, wounded by unreturned love.

Nicola in Marketing from Peckham had Steven's attention, and was being furnished with all his standard stories and patter. He critiqued the cocktail list, mocking it here, praising it there.

"Their bespoke creations look overly sweet, cloying, but the classics appeal. They've helped themselves with a well written ingredient list, signposting the picks. Good font, paper."

"Yes."

It was the first of half a dozen or so dates, before they moved on.

Annabel pottered about in her lounge ordering things, setting things straight, switching her mind onto practical matters to distract from her mental toilings.

Some business matter with such serious implications that it warranted being covered over a weekend, was evolving on television.

A CEO who had been brought in to sort out her predecessor's messes, implored that things were being controlled, with words which themselves could be indicative of any number of underlying health problems.

"Our balance sheet remains robust, our supply chain is in good order, and we are in an excellent position to meet the needs of our customers, so we can help them through what may be some challenging times ahead."

She knew how dedicated and relentless these powerhouses had to be to muscle their way to the top. How they had to be on top of everything, across every brief, not always out of a need to micro-manage, or a lack of delegation skills, but because any gaps in performance gave their enemies a wedge to open them up and drive them out. To send the opportunity the way of *a man*. While applauding the accomplishments and sheer energetic drive to meet the threats of the competition, it drove a wedge between how she saw the world for herself, what she was capable of, and what was out there in the world for her. Not that.

The business-ese rang in her ears. Robust. Needs. Challenging. It reminded her she had a work task to do for Monday. Ten-minute job. She opened her inbox, and scanned through her emails. She was mauled by the words. Execute. Under separate cover. Please find attached. Kind Regards. Catch-up. Check-in. Regular one2one. Lunch

& learn. Pre-align. Touch base. Skills matrix. Online learning. Shared location. New portal. Urgh. Technology at work which, on the face of it, made things easier, enabled productivity, freed up time. Yet it slaved her to the adoption of new methods for processing old shit. Employees trapped delivering against their KPIs, forgetting the human or creative elements. False productivity, as shown when a business was able to ride out a major storm: a hack, a *pandemic*, a bricks and mortar disaster. Management looking back at the lack of any catastrophic fall in output, left wondering what all the work done before was contributing. Mass layoffs and no move of the needle.

If the internet cables were cut, *nothing would work*.

Technology's reach into her personal life and wider societal behaviours had been every bit as pernicious. Every opportunity to shunt activity into new tech created a slew of millionaire slots, handing out second homes and lifestyle upgrades for the lucky victors, regardless of what actual innovation or improvements they offered real people. The gig economy removed the need for vocational training to gain knowledge and skills. Rented clothes were now a thing, as elites attempted to steer humanity away from ownership to nothingship. Save on new item purchase cost and environmental impact; raw materials, production processes, transport fuel. Replace instead with local carbon output as pieces are collected and scootered around the capital and beyond at a whim, and once looking a tad raggedy, commit to a Northumbrian hillside. Whence the demand for new items manifests, which was the point in the first place. All in the name of levelling up, ramping up, ratcheting, leverage. Openly, honestly, transparently. Way, shape or form. When two will do, roll out the trinities.

She checked her personal email.

Aeons of spam. $15,382 added to your account, returns of 30%+. Congratulations, you have a money confirmation. Hot Grandma for everything you want. Fuck Buddy [mwah lips] I want to sleep with you tonight [tongue].

She shut the laptop down, paused until it had expired, snapped it shut and tossed it next to her. She rubbed her eyes and dragged across the morning's lifestyle supplements, which in her twenties were the source of something else. She was not able to discern if it was the lack of the new or whether something had shifted, in the cynicism of modern journalism, or the production process of news, views and shoes onto the page. It's all politics now.

Doomscrolling. Busywork. Gone floppy. Woke fishing. Spear phishing. Bants. Jumbomoji rants. Swipe surge. Sportswashing. Cyber-flashing. Virtue-signalling. Gaslighting. Heterodox. Bin juice. Zoom shirt. Muffin tops. Laying pipe. Trans amorous. Seduction community. Sugar baby lifestyle. Borrow the doggy. Firenados. Deepfakes. MainStreamMedia. Pan-seared. Boiled, grilled and broiled. Synching. Idling. D/S. Top. Bottom. GGG. Switchy. Aftercare. QT/RT. Alt centrists. Cancelled. De-platformed. Garfield phone containers. Chin warmers. Covidiots. Branch Covidians. Insta. So extra.

Feed my narrative.

In silence, her head tight as her thoughts swung about, trying to find a groove, the needle scratching across a spinning disc, searching for some grip, some rough moral fibre to cling to.

As she looked over the newspapers in front of her, they revealed something to her which had developed over the last decade, which she hadn't noticed on the way, but now was clear. Each political, religious, community or service leader. Each business executive, actor, model, journalist, commentator. In common, the same single-minded, hard-driven stare. Gone, the warmth, the wrinkles of generosity, the unkempt hair of compassion. Now a cabal of sterilised, featureless, masked agents of more. More wealth, more ownership, more followers, more investment, more publicity. More for them, less for the rest. And the arc which followed the successful, drilled, organised, marketed, gold-ridden London Olympics, hardened its outlook during the European Union wars of the 2010s, through to the *pandemic*, whereby it looked like the corporations would be stunted. Yet it played out as yet another shift in wealth in their direction, as the ill-thought through and egregious totalitarian restrictions came in, cheered on by communists. This, coupled with the ensuing narrative control of environmental collapse, left an exhausted, cynical or unquestioning public surrounded, kettled by elites and leaders. The myth of corporate competition where the majority shareholders of competing brands are the same companies. Humanity dissipated from professions in health and social care, policing, education. Careers which *should* offer the reward of seeing another prosper, recovered, protected. Now vehicles for sadism, control, and exerting ideology. Riot police were going to do whatever their paymasters ordered. A far cry from policing by consent. Uniparties and the sham of democracy the world over, citizens with little choice at the polling booth, blatant voting fraud from third to first world. The powerful crushing the powerless. Every day a new insanity. The dismantling of everything natural, replaced by the artificial.

Annabel could not tell if these thoughts made her feel ill because her gut was making it so and should be trusted as per usual, or whether she was in transition to solid centre middle age, as her in-group was melting into the hedge of periphery and irrelevance. Her generation now a sideshow for whatever came next, despite the ageing overall power base. A finite world the two preceding generations and in turn, hers also, had continued to overwhelm. It mattered not whether it should be less or fewer. It had to be both. Less, fewer, less, fewer, less. Fewer. Less. Fewer, less, less. Fewer. Less.

Annabel looked across at her bedside drawer and she paused, raw. The pills she stored in sufficient quantities, right there. A route out whenever she needed it.

As she shuffled papers and supplements, more waste.

On a day of heavy rain she would have felt differently, yet a large slanted square of light had landed on the corner of the white sheets as she looked away from the window. She drew back the weighty covers and swung over her heavy legs of light strength. She thought of her sisters.

This day wouldn't be that day.

Dope.

She noped the fuck out of it.

THE START